BECOMING
Marie Antoinette

BECOMING
Marie Antoinette

 A NOVEL

JULIET GREY

BALLANTINE BOOKS TRADE PAPERBACKS
NEW YORK

A Ballantine Books Trade Paperback Original

Copyright © 2011 by Leslie Carroll
Reading group guide copyright © 2011 by Random House, Inc.
Excerpt from *Days of Splendor, Days of Sorrow* by Juliet Grey copyright © 2011 by Leslie Carroll

Published in the United States by Ballantine Books, an imprint of The Random House Publishing Group, a division of Random House, Inc., New York.

BALLANTINE BOOKS and colophon are registered trademarks of Random House, Inc.
RANDOM HOUSE READER'S CIRCLE & Design is a trademark of Random House, Inc.

This book contains an excerpt from the forthcoming novel *Days of Splendor, Days of Sorrow* by Juliet Grey.
This excerpt has been set for this edition only and may not reflect the final content of the forthcoming edition.

Library of Congress Cataloging-in-Publication Data
Grey, Juliet.
Becoming Marie Antoinette : a novel / Juliet Grey.
p. cm.
Includes bibliographical references.
ISBN 978-0-345-52386-0
eBook ISBN 978-0-345-52387-7
1. Marie Antoinette Queen, consort of Louis XVI, King of France, 1755–1793—
Fiction. 2. France—History—Louis XVI, 1774–1793—Fiction. 3. Queens—
France—Fiction. I. Title.
PS3607.R4993B43 2011
813'.6—dc22   2011010024

Printed in the United States of America

www.randomhousereaderscircle.com

2 4 6 8 9 7 5 3 1

Book design by Casey Hampton

For Nell

Bella gerant alii; tu, felix Austria, nube.

Others wage wars; you, happy Austria, marry.

— MOTTO OF THE HAPSBURG DYNASTY

BECOMING
Marie Antoinette

ONE

Is This the End of Childhood?

❧ SCHÖNBRUNN, MAY 1766 ❧

My mother liked to boast that her numerous daughters were "sacrifices to politics." I never dared admit to Maman, who was Empress of the Holy Roman Empire, that the phrase terrified me more than she could know. Every time she said it, my imagination painted a violent tableau of Abraham and Isaac.

Unflinchingly pragmatic, Maman prepared us to accept our destinies not only with grace and equanimity but with a minimal amount of fuss. Thus, I had been schooled to expect, as sure as summer follows spring, that one day my carefree life as the youngest archduchess of Austria would forever change. What I never anticipated was that the day in question would come so soon.

In the company of my beloved sister, Charlotte, I was enjoying an idyllic afternoon on the verdant hillside above the palace of Schönbrunn, indulging in one of our favorite pastimes—avoiding our lessons by distracting our governess, the Countess von Brandeiss.

A bumblebee hummed lazily about our heads, mistaking our pomaded and powdered hair for dulcet blossoms. Charlotte had kicked off her blue brocaded slippers and was wiggling her stockinged feet in the freshly cut grass. So I did the same, delighting in the coolness of the lawn, slightly damp against the soles of my feet, although we'd surely merit a scolding for staining our white hose. Affecting a grim expression and pressing my chin to my chest until I achieved our mother's jowly appearance, in a dreadfully stern voice I said, "At your age, Charlott-ah, you should know better than to lead the little one into childish games."

My sister laughed. "*Mein Gott*, you sound just like her!"

Countess von Brandeiss suppressed a smile, hiding her little yellow teeth. "And you should know better than to mock your mother, Madame Antonia."

"Ouf!" Startled by the bee, which now appeared to be inspecting with some curiosity the ruffles of her bonnet, our governess began to bat the air about her head. Nearly tripping over her voluminous skirts as she leapt to her feet in fright, Madame von Brandeiss began to hop about in such a comical fashion that it was impossible for us to feel even the slightest bit chastised.

Maman's scoldings were so easy to duplicate because they came with far more regularity than her compliments. From middle spring through the warm, waning days of September, she was a familiar presence in our lives, tending to affairs of state from the outskirts of Vienna in our summer palace of Schönbrunn, a grand edifice of ocher and white that resembled a giant tea loaf piped with *Schlag*, whipped cream. With scrubbed faces we were presented to her in the Breakfast Room, its walls, the color of fresh milk, partitioned into symmetrical panels by gilded moldings and scrollwork. Charlotte, Ferdinand, Maxl, and I looked forward to the day when we would be old enough to merit an invitation to join her, along with our older siblings, for a steaming pot of fragrant coffee and terribly adult conversation about places like Poland and Silesia, places I remained unable to locate on the map of Europe that hung on the wall of our schoolroom.

For the remainder of the year, when the prodigious Hapsburg family resided at the gray and labyrinthine Hofburg palace in the heart of Vienna, we, the youngest of the empress's brood, scarcely saw Maman more than once every ten days. We even attended daily Mass without her, a line of ducklings, dressed in our finest clothes, kneeling on velvet cushions that bore our initials embroidered in silver thread. Charlotte and I remained side by side as our pastel-colored skirts, widened by the basketlike panniers beneath them, nudged each other; our heads swam with the pungent aroma of incense while our ears rang with ritual—the resonance of the grand pipe organ and the bishop's solemn intonations in Latin.

And as the days grew shorter we began to forget the woman who had almost dared to have fun during those departed sunlit months. Mother became matriarch: a forbidding figure clad all in black, her skirts making her appear nearly as wide as she was tall. Marched into her study for inspection, we would stand still as statues—no fidgeting allowed—while she peered at us through a gilt-edged magnifying glass and inquired of our governess whether we were learning our lessons, eating healthy meals, using tooth powder, and scrubbing our necks and behind our ears. The royal physician, Dr. Wansvietten, was put through the same paces with questions about our general health. The answers were invariably in the affirmative, since no one would dare to admit any act of negligence or weakness, and so she dismissed us from her presence, satisfied that we were dutiful children.

I slid across the grass on my bottom, nestling beside our governess, adjusting my body so that I could whisper in her ear, "May I tell you a secret, Madame?"

"Of course, *Liebchen*." Madame von Brandeiss smiled indulgently.

"Sometimes...sometimes I wish you were my mother." The pomade in her hair, scented to disguise its origin as animal fat, smelled of lavender. I closed my eyes and inhaled deeply. The fragrance was so pleasant, it nearly made me sleepy.

"Why, Madame Antonia!" The countess managed to appear both touched and alarmed, her cheeks coloring prettily as her gray eyes stole a reflexive glance to see who might be listening. "How can you say such a thing, little one—especially when your *maman* is the empress of Austria!"

Madame von Brandeiss tenderly stroked my hair. I could not remember whether my mother had ever done so, nor could I summon the memory of any similar display of warmth or affection. It was enough to convince me that they had never taken place. I felt my governess's lips press against the top of my head. Somehow she knew, without my breathing a word, that the empress's demeanor rather frightened me. "I'm sure your *maman* loves you, little one," she murmured. "But you must remember, it is the duty of a sovereign to attend to great and serious affairs of state, while it is a governess's responsibility to look after the children."

I wriggled a bit. My leg had become entangled in my underskirts and had fallen asleep. "Are you ever sorry you didn't have any of your own?" I asked the countess. Inside my white stockings I wiggled my toes until the tingling was gone.

"Antonia, you're being impertinent!" Charlotte said reproachfully. "What did Maman tell you about blurting out whatever comes into your head?" I loved and admired my next oldest sister more than anyone in the world, but she had the makings of quite a little autocrat—Maman in miniature in many ways. Already her adolescent features had begun to resemble our mother, especially about the mouth.

Ignoring my sister, I tilted my chin and gazed earnestly into our governess's eyes. "If you could have, would you have had sixteen children, like Maman?" There were only thirteen of us now, owing to the ravages of smallpox. I'd contracted the disease when I was only two years old and by the grace of God recovered fully. Only a tiny scar by the side of my nose remained as a reminder of what I had survived. When I grew older I would be permitted to hide it with powder and paint, or perhaps even a patch, although Maman thought that women who covered their pox scars with *mouches* had no morals. "If you had a little girl, Madame, what would you want her to be like?"

Countess von Brandeiss swallowed hard and fingered the engraved locket about her neck. She was perhaps nearly as old as Maman; the brown hair that peeked out from beneath her straw bonnet and white linen cap was threaded with a few strands of silver. She tenderly kissed the top of my head. "If I had *had* a little girl, I would have wanted her to be just like you. With strawberry blond curls and enormous dark blue eyes, and a generous heart as big as the Austrian Empire." Tugging me toward her, she readjusted the gray woolen band that smoothed my unruly tendrils off my forehead. It wasn't terribly pretty but it served its turn, and was ordinarily masked by my hair ribbon. But that afternoon I had removed the length of rose-colored silk and used it to tie a bouquet I plucked from the parterres—tulips and pinks and puffy white snapdragons.

"Yes, *Liebchen*," sighed my governess, "she would be exactly like you, except in one respect." I looked at her inquiringly. "If *I* had had a little girl, she would be more attentive to her lessons!" Madame von Brandeiss gently clasped my wrists and disengaged my arms from her neck. Her eyes twinkled. "She would not be clever enough to invent so many distractions, and she would pay more attention to her studies. And, she would not ask so many"—she glanced at Charlotte, who was feigning interest in splitting a blade of grass with her pale, slender fingers—"*imperti-nent* questions."

"Now," she said, urging me off her lap and onto the lawn. "Enough games. Like it or not, *ma petite*, it is time for your French grammar lesson. You too, Charlotte." The countess clapped her hands with brisk efficiency. "*Allons, mes enfants.*"

In the blink of an eye, a liveried footman handed Charlotte our copybooks.

Before I could stop myself, I pursed my lips into a petulant little moue. Our governess stuck out her lower lip, playfully mocking my expression. "You mustn't pout, Antonia. It was you, little madame, who convinced me to move your lessons out of doors today."

Rolling onto my belly and propping myself on my elbows, I lifted my face to the breeze and filled my nostrils with the scents of summer. The boning in my bodice pressed against my midriff and my skirts belled out above my rump like a pink soufflé. "But I'm not pouting, Madame. It's how God made me," I said brightly. In truth, what Maman calls "the Hapsburg lower lip" gives the impression of a permanent pout, even when I'm not sulking. Our entire family looks the same way; with fair hair, a pale complexion, and a distinctly receding chin, I resembled every one of my siblings and ancestors.

And yet, if I'd had a glass I would have appraised my appearance. Was I pretty? Maman thought I was a perfect porcelain doll, but I'd overheard whispers among the servants . . . something about the way I carried my head. Or perhaps it was my physiognomy. Then again, I was a Hapsburg archduchess. I had every reason to delight in my lineage. Still—I wanted everyone to love me. If there were a way to please them, I wished to learn it. "Do you think my chin makes me look haughty?" I asked Madame von Brandeiss.

"People who have nothing better to do will indulge in idle gossip," our governess replied. Charlotte placed her hand over her mouth to hide a smile. "Your chin makes you look proud. And you have every reason to be proud because you are a daughter of Austria and your family has a long and illustrious history. And," Madame von Brandeiss continued, beginning to laugh, "you are doing it again."

"Doing what?" I asked innocently.

"Doing everything you can think of to avoid your books. Don't think you can fool me, little madame."

She clapped her hands again. "Come now, you minxes, you've dawdled enough. *Vite, vite!* It's time for your French lesson." She shook Charlotte gently by the shoulder.

Charlotte rolled onto her back and sat up; she was diligent by nature, but if I began to dally, she could become as indolent as I when it came to our schoolwork. Our moods affected each other as if we had been born twins. Her grumble became a delighted squeal as something caught our eyes at exactly the same moment. "Toinette, look! A butterfly!" My sister shut her copybook with a resonant snap. Joining hands, we pulled each other to our feet and began to give chase. Without breaking her stride Charlotte swept up her net from where it lay in the soft grass with a single graceful motion.

"*Ach! Nein!* Girls, your shoes!" Madame von Brandeiss exclaimed, rising and smoothing her skirts. Her boned corset prevented her from bending with ease; she knelt as if to curtsy and scooped up one of my backless ivory satin slippers.

"No time!" I shouted, clutching fistfuls of watered silk as I hitched up my skirts and raced past Charlotte. The butterfly became a blur of vivid blue as it flitted in an irregular serpentine across the manicured hillside, its delicate form silhouetted against the cerulean sky. It finally settled on a hedge at the perimeter of the slope. Charlotte and I had nearly run out of wind; our chests heaved with exertion, straining against the stiff boning of our stomachers. My sister began to lower her net. I raised my hand to stay her. "No," I insisted, panting. "You'll scare her off."

I held my breath. Gingerly reaching toward the foliage, I cupped my hands over our exquisite quarry. The butterfly's iridescent wings fluttered energetically, tickling my palms. "Let's show Madame," I whispered.

With Charlotte a pace or two behind me, limping a bit because she'd put her foot wrong on an unseen twig, I cautiously tiptoed back across the lawn, fearful of tripping and losing the delicate treasure cocooned within my hands. The rapid trembling of the butterfly's wings gradually slowed until there was only an occasional beat against my palms.

Finally, we reached the countess. "Look what I've got!" I crowed, slowly uncurling my fingers. The three of us peered at the motionless insect. Charlotte's face turned grave.

Catching the troubled expression in her pale blue eyes, "Maybe she's sleeping," I said softly, hopefully, stroking one of the fragile wings with my index finger. My hands were smudged with yellow dust.

"She's not sleeping, Toinette. She's..." Charlotte's words trailed off as she looked at me, her usually flushed cheeks now ashen with awareness.

My lips quivered, but the sobs became strangled in my throat. Drawing me to her, Charlotte endeavored to still the heaving in my shoulders, but I shrugged her off. I didn't deserve to be comforted. An enormous tear rolled down my cheek and landed on my chest, marring the silk with an irregular stain. Another warm tear plopped onto my wrist. I closed my hands again as if to shelter the butterfly in the sepulcher made by my palms, while the full weight of my crime settled on my narrow shoulders.

"I. Didn't. Mean. To. Kill. Her. I've. Never. Killed. Anything. I. Would. Never. Hurt . . ." My sobs finally came in big loud gulps, bursts of hysterical sound punctuated by apologies. With a look of sheer helplessness I threw myself into my governess's open arms.

"Shh, *Liebchen*," soothed the countess, caressing my hair. "We know you meant no harm." For several moments I remained in her embrace, my cheek pressed against the ruching at her bosom. Then Madame von Brandeiss knelt before me and used her lace-edged handkerchief to blot my tears. "Perhaps," she said, gently taking my clasped hands in hers, "perhaps she was too beautiful to live."

Even then I recognized that it was not the demise of an insect that troubled me to such an extraordinary extent, though Maman has always chided me for an excess of sensibility. It was my guilt that overwhelmed me. In my heedless haste to possess something beautiful, I had not considered the consequences. My covetousness had destroyed the very thing I had so curiously, passionately, impetuously adored.

In the aftermath of this little tragedy, our French grammar lesson took on an added significance.

"How do you say 'the butterfly is dead'?" Madame von Brandeiss asked us. She turned to look at me but I regarded her blankly. Aware that she would receive a correct response from my sister—which is why she inevitably began our instruction by offering me the benefit of the doubt—our governess addressed the better student. "Charlotte, what is the French word for 'butterfly'?"

"*Papillotte*," I interjected before my sister could draw breath.

"*Papill*on," Charlotte corrected with the smug satisfaction of an older sister regaining her superior place in the natural order of things.

"You are right, Charlotte. Very good. *Très bien*. And how would you say 'The butterfly is dead'? *En français*. Madame Antonia?"

This time Charlotte would not be permitted to provide the answer. I chewed on my lower lip—the protruding one. I had no head for rote memorization or endless conjugation of verbs in tenses I would rarely use. I preferred situations where there was no inappropriate choice: to wear the blue gown or the yellow; to play with the flaxen-haired wooden doll or the one with chestnut tresses.

Madame von Brandeiss began to feed me the words. "*Le papillon . . .*" she began encouragingly.

"*Le papillon tot ist,*" I volunteered.

"Well, *ma petite*," our governess chuckled, "you identified the butterfly in French but it died in German. Come, girls, what is the French for 'dead'?"

"*Mort,*" Charlotte replied with confidence. I gave her a mutinous look.

"Let's try again, Antonia, now that you know the French. *Le papillon . . .*"

"*Mort ist,*" I said, my nose beginning to twitch as I sniffed back tears.

Frustrated both by my inability to construct a simple grammatical sentence and by my tendency to mix French and German, especially when it came to the verbs, Madame von Brandeiss took a pencil from a red lacquer box and in a meticulous hand, wrote out the words in my copybook and then in Charlotte's. *Le papillon est mort.*

To our governess's consternation, I insisted on delaying the rest of the lesson while I scrabbled in the dirt to dig a grave; my *papillon mort* deserved a proper burial. As I tore away tiny fistfuls of grass and sod, two periwigged footmen waited patiently with my portable writing desk, their faces as expressionless as if they had been cast in porcelain. I crossed myself and said a little prayer over the new grave. Satisfied that the butterfly would now go to heaven, I wiped my hands on my gown and sank down beside Charlotte, my heavy skirts billowing out beneath me.

"Now I am ready for my lesson, Madame von Brandeiss," I said, playfully bumping my sister with my shoulder. A servant opened the tiny clasps on the rosewood writing desk and placed it on my lap while another attendant uncapped the ink bottle and sharpened my quill. Then, as always, I dipped my pen and meticulously traced the words that Madame von Brandeiss had lightly penciled in my copybook. And, as always, Maman would never know that I, no more talented than a parrot or a trained monkey, had not really written them myself.

While Charlotte and I copied our French sentence, tongues peeking intently from the corners of our mouths, a few feet away the footmen were setting up the easels for our watercolor lesson. Madame von Brandeiss suggested that we look toward the palace and paint the view, incorporating the imposing south façade and the gardens. From our vantage at the summit of the slope the flowers resembled a multitude of colorful spots arranged in perfectly symmetrical beds.

We had not been laboring long over our brushes and pots of color when I felt a tug at the lace on my sleeve. "*Hsst!* Look!" Charlotte exclaimed. I turned to follow her gaze. The countess had fallen asleep with her hands folded primly in her lap, her mouth slightly agape. A subtle snore emanated from her throat.

My sister's eyes were bright with mischief. Being older, she was always the ringleader in our games, and I never followed her with anything less than slavishly devoted enthusiasm. We loaded our brushes with color and cautiously tiptoed over to our slumbering governess. Falling to our knees on either side of Madame von Brandeiss, at Charlotte's silent signal we applied the brushes to our governess's face. Suppressing a giggle, I marveled that we had never thought of this girlish prank until now. The worst that might befall us, I ventured to surmise, was that the kindhearted countess would throw her hands up in the air and exclaim, as she tried not to laugh, "*Ach*, whatever am I to do with you children?"

I painted a red rose, a symbol of Austria as well as my favorite flower. Charlotte, with a surer hand than mine, artfully sketched a green climbing vine.

Madame von Brandeiss awoke with a start. "*Ouf, mein Gott!*" She bolted upright and began to bat the air, chasing off the flies that she thought had landed on her face. But Charlotte and I had already retreated to our easels and were intent on giving a magnificent performance as a pair of perfectly behaved archduchesses.

I was daubing blots of paint onto the watercolor paper, reds and purples intended to represent the parterre of tulips below us, when a distant shout claimed our attention. Franz, one of my mother's footmen, was panting up the winding gravel path, his steps increasingly belabored the closer he got to the hilltop. Breathless and wheezing, and doubtless a bit warm in his wool livery, he bowed deeply to Charlotte and me. As he deferentially nodded his head to Madame von Brandeiss, Franz noticed her comically painted face and dropped his gaze before our governess could wonder if something was amiss. My sister and I stifled our urge to laugh. Shoulder to shoulder, we nudged each other, feigning terribly innocent expressions by widening our already prominent eyes.

Rivulets of sweat traced pathways from Franz's white horsehair periwig along his meaty, flushed cheeks as he addressed our governess in halting gasps. "Countess von Brandeiss. Her. Imperial. Majesty. Wishes to speak. To Madame Antonia. Immediately." He bent over to catch his breath, resting his palms on his knees.

Within moments the footmen who had attended us all afternoon had packed up the copybooks, writing implements, and watercolor paraphernalia with the precision of a military unit. I scooped up the bouquet I had fashioned earlier in the day and began to skip down the slope as if I were a mountain goat.

"Madame Antonia, your slippers!" the countess exclaimed. Clasping a satin shoe in each hand, she started to give chase. I stumbled on the tip of a stone embedded in the hillside, catching myself with my hands as I fell forward, but my foot got caught in my skirts and I rolled toward the palace for several yards before I could right myself. At the foot of the hill, breathless but unharmed, I scrambled to my feet and tried to smooth my rumpled skirts. Perhaps Maman would not notice the streaks of dirt. Or the grass stains. Charlotte, Madame von Brandeiss, and our retinue of attendants had taken the more traditional route, trotting down the pathway at the perimeter of the lawn. When they finally caught up with me, Madame von Brandeiss grasped my elbow to steady my balance while I shoved my stockinged feet into my slippers. We descended the elaborate staircase to the pebbled walk beside the parterres; Charlotte and I followed dutifully behind our governess, the gravel crunching percussively beneath our feet. Several paces back, the footmen, laden with our school things, brought up the rear.

Just before we reached the south entrance to the palace, Franz caught up to Madame von Brandeiss and whispered something in her ear. She wheeled on us, her hands on her well-upholstered hips, her mouth a gaping O of surprised betrayal. "Madame Antonia, Madame Charlotte!" With an exasperated sigh she wagged her finger at us, scolding, "Whatever am I to do with you little monkeys?"

With no convenient looking glass, the countess rushed over to the Obelisk Fountain to regard her reflection in the water. "*Ach*, the little devils," she muttered, crouching beside the fountain, as her skirts belled out about her. She cupped her hands and splashed her face with the cool water until our artistic efforts were washed away.

The footmen inside the palace stood at attention, never lowering their gaze to acknowledge us. Their gold and black livery nearly shimmered in the highly polished parquet. Our heels clicked rhythmically along the floor as we strode through the high-ceilinged corridors that connected countless chambers like a string of pearls, our names announced each time we crossed another threshold. "Make way for the Archduchess Maria Carolina, the Archduchess Antonia, and the Countess von Brandeiss."

Some minutes after we entered the palace, I skidded to a stop just inside the ornate gilded doorway of the Chinese Room, where Maman was waiting with a guest to speak to me. My mother had caught the fashionable fever for all things Oriental and consequently had commissioned a room that would marry our Austrian décor with exotic images painted on inlaid ebony panels depicting scenes of life in China. Did people really dress so strangely on the other side of the world?

I had not troubled to check my appearance in the Mirror Room as we sped through it on the way to the Chinese Room. No wonder Maman's lips were pressed together grimly. What the Empress of Austria saw standing breathlessly before her was a ten-year-old hoyden, her rose-colored skirts a calamity of stained rumpled silk, her reddish-blond hair askew and missing the pink satin ribbon that had held it in place, grubby fingers (though she could see only my left hand; my other hand was behind my back), and filthy hose. The woeful state of my stockings she might have missed, had I not removed one of my slippers in order to shake out a pebble. Her eyes followed the tiny stone as it skittered along the floor, rolling to a stop a mere inch from her visitor's well-shod foot.

My mother was seated behind a large rosewood table, the width of her panniers obscuring the yellow brocaded upholstery of the armchair. Her writing desk, as always, was piled high with documents, writs, and decrees so fastidiously arranged that if a sheet of paper poking out from the rest had been one of her children, it would have received a rebuke for unruliness. The room smelled faintly of ink.

I made a low curtsy to her. "Good afternoon, Maman." Her plump figure was tightly laced into a black silk gown with an intricately embroidered stomacher; a small black cap trimmed with ribbons concealed much of her thick graying hair. She had rarely looked more imposing.

Maman's guest was a gentleman of her vintage with a narrow face, an aquiline nose, and arched brows that formed a double canopy for his small, restless dark eyes. His hair, perfectly curled and powdered, was tied in a tidy queue with a black domino. Upon my ungainly arrival, the stranger had risen from his chair and struck an *attitude* I had learned from our court dancing master: his feet turned out and his right leg thrust forward, so that his slipper jutted at an oblique angle that made the brilliants on his silver shoe buckles twinkle as they caught the light. From the way the man carried his head, he seemed terribly proud of his red velvet coat, which was ostentatiously embroidered with gilt thread all along the edges from neck to hem, as well as on the turned-back cuffs. Whoever he might be, his wardrobe proclaimed his importance. Perhaps he was someone official because of the broad cordon he wore across his chest—a diagonal slash of blue watered silk. Someone royal?

The visitor made a bow and smiled benevolently at me, unlike my mother, and I decided to like him. Besides, I might need an advocate, for whenever Maman scowled, it meant either that she was contemplating a declaration of war or that I had disappointed her.

By now Charlotte and Madame von Brandeiss had entered the room, making their deferential curtsies to the empress. Maman snapped open her black silk fan and held it between her cheek and her guest's line of vision so that he could not glimpse her cross expression at the sight of my governess's damp hair and the telltale stains of watercolor on her face. In a gesture of solidarity my sister stepped forward and placed her hand in mine, which comforted me and gave me courage to face the reprimand that would surely come. I sensed that Maman was struggling with herself, deciding whether to chastise us, which would abase us in the eyes of our visitor, or to say nothing, which might leave the impression that she condoned our disheveled state. The room was so silent that I imagined all the little Chinamen and Chinawomen on the illustrated panels had paused in the performance of their tasks, suspended in time, to see what the Holy Roman Empress would do. But the whole world knows that the empress of Austria does not mince her opinions or curb her tongue. So she chose to admonish our governess.

"Is this the way you present my daughter to me, Countess?" Maman's voice was stern and clipped.

Beside me I felt Charlotte's stolid presence, a sister's strength that would support me if I faltered. "It's not Madame's fault," I stammered. I could not lie to my mother; she would see right through me. At any rate, I could not stand mutely by while my governess was blamed for my conduct. "It was my idea. Mine and—"

"You will take Madame Charlotte from the room, Countess. At the precipice of fourteen she is too old to engage in childish pranks, and old enough to know better than to goad her impressionable younger sister into indulging in whatever she finds amusing. And Madame von Brandeiss, I will speak with you later."

Charlotte squeezed my hand reassuringly, then reluctantly let go. Our palms had been sticky with fear.

Madame von Brandeiss curtsied deeply and lowered her eyes. "My profoundest apologies, Your Imperial Majesty, for the young archduchesses' unkempt appearance. It will not happen again, I assure you."

But—excluding the visitor—we all knew it would. Still, as the footmen closed the imposing doors behind them, I wanted to make it all right. "I was the one who rolled in the grass, Maman. I was the one who soiled my stockings." I neglected to mention my ink-stained fingers, owing to my clumsiness with the quill and all the blots I had made in my copybook. But I did add, "I was the one who dirtied my nails by burying the butterfly." At that last remark my mother arched a graying eyebrow, then waved her fan dismissively. "*Le papillon*," I said proudly.

"*Papillon?*" muttered the stranger. But I don't think Maman heard him.

"Enough, Antonia," she said curtly. "What's done is done. My chief concern is that it will not be done again. Antonia, you will wear that dirty gown every single day until you learn the value of the clothing you mar. And that an archduchess, no matter her age, is expected to behave like a proper young lady. You must set the example for the rest of the realm."

My cheeks were hot with shame. I lowered my head. "I am sorry, Maman."

She peered at me. "What are you hiding behind your back, Antonia?"

She had been so harsh with me that I had nearly forgotten

about the bouquet. "A present for you!" I said brightly, smiling broadly at the prospect that the flowers might cheer her. After all, they always cheered *me*. If I had my choice my rooms would be filled with fresh blossoms and there would be flowers on every surface, painted on my walls and ceilings, woven into the fabric of my gowns, and embroidered on my shoes and purses. I would wear a garden in my hair.

I stuck out my arm and proffered the colorful posy. Maman almost smiled. Then she saw that I had tied the blooms together with my hair ribbon.

"Come closer, little one," she commanded. I knew I would be safe from any further chastisement because my mother had used her pet name for me. I approached the table, but she motioned for me to stand beside her. She took the bouquet from my hand and brought it to her nose.

The man in the red velvet suit smiled, but with his eyes, not with his mouth. His thin lips remained a hard slash of pinkish gray. "*Très charmante, Votre Majesté.* Very charming."

Maman clasped me about the waist and drew me toward her, replying to the man in French. "She most certainly *can* be—especially when she behaves herself. Or did you mean the charming posy, monsieur le marquis?"

She asked me to stand in the center of the floor, a flower within a flower within a flower that was a miracle of marquetry. I resisted the impulse to twirl about, as I always did when I stood at the heart of the inlaid rosette.

"Allow me, monsieur, to present you to my youngest daughter, Archduchess Maria Antonia Josepha Johanna of Austria," Maman said in what I privately referred to as her empress voice. The gentleman bowed to me in a most courtly manner and smiled his most engaging smile. So I gave him mine and, unable to help myself, executed a little pirouette in the center of the flower. Though my academic flaws were legion, I had always received compliments on my natural grace.

"Antonia, this is the marquis de Durfort, the new French ambassador, who has come all the way from Versailles to visit us." When I looked at Maman blankly, she added, "He is the envoy from the court of Louis Quinze."

"It is my great pleasure to meet you this afternoon, *madame l'archiduchesse*," said the marquis. "*Je suis très enchanté de faire votre connaissance cet après-midi.*"

"The marquis has come to Austria on a very important mission," Maman told me. "On his sovereign's behalf he has been instructed to request your hand in marriage for His Most Christian Majesty's grandson: Louis Auguste, dauphin of France."

I confess that my first reaction was confusion. Bewilderment. I clenched my nails against my palms so that I would not cry. Was I going away to get married now? I was relieved that Charlotte was no longer in the room. I could only imagine the look of surprise behind her wide, light eyes, a reaction tinged with envy; it was not the custom for younger daughters to wed before their elder sisters and there had been no talk of choosing a husband for Charlotte. I wondered if it was because she was not so desirable, not so pretty.

"Why are you not smiling?" my mother asked me.

"Because," I began sheepishly, my voice soft and small. *Because I'm only ten years old. Because I never want to leave my brothers and sisters. Because shouldn't someone else come first? Maria Christina? Maria Josepha? Even Charlotte?* "Because I'm not sure what it means."

The adults exchanged glances. "You don't know what it means, my little one?" echoed Maman incredulously. "It means that you have a glorious destiny before you. It means that one day you will be Queen of France."

TWO

I Will Never Get Used to Good-byes

～ 1767 ～

Fortunately I was not immediately packed off to Paris, or wherever Versailles was, to marry the grandson of Louis the Fifteenth. I had believed that the French ambassador, the marquis de Durfort, had come to take me away that very day, but as the days turned to weeks and the weeks became months I discovered that he had only come to *talk* to Maman. Talking, evidently, was what ambassadors did. They ate prodigiously, too. And received a lot of gifts. At least the marquis did so, because he never turned down Maman's invitations to dine nor declined a single present from her. There were so many I lost count: a lapdog that shed its silky hair all over Monsieur's velvet breeches; a trained monkey who had evidently learned how to relieve himself in a gentleman's chapeau; a gilt snuffbox bearing my portrait in enamel; an ebony walking stick with the head of a lion carved in solid gold; and a pair of shoe buckles with a matching stickpin studded with diamonds.

The French ambassador was still at court when we celebrated my eleventh birthday on November 2, 1766, and—on behalf of the dauphin, he said—he gave me a brooch in the shape of a butterfly. "*Un papillon bleu*," he added with condescension, as if I couldn't tell. It was covered with tiny coruscating sapphires, which he very diplomatically said reminded him of my twinkling, indigo blue eyes. The butterfly's eyes had been fashioned from a pair of diamonds. *Les diamants*. More words to learn. I thought it would please the marquis if I improved my acquaintance with the French language. French was the formal language of our court, too, but because so many people from all over the world lived in Vienna, it was not unusual to hear both French and German, and even something else, spoken within the same conversation. It wasn't quite so difficult to master when I was speaking, but to write in French without mixing anything was absolutely beastly, for I had never learned the rudiments of grammar in any language.

Meanwhile, Maman treated the marquis as though he were a prince. In the middle of the winter she offered him a pineapple. This was considerably more than a mere gesture of hospitality, as the fruit had to come from a place called the Indies, all the way on the other side of the globe. My little brother Maxl had worried that on their return the sailors might have had to do battle with fearsome, scaly sea monsters, but I chided him for thinking so. Hadn't Maman taught us that there was no such thing as ghosts or goblins or demons? There was no room for superstitious silliness among the Hapsburgs; we were not dwellers in the Dark Ages, but children of the eighteenth century—the Age of Reason.

I had been too naïve to realize that Maman's flattery of the French ambassador, the gifts and the grand gestures, were on my account. It was not until the spring of 1767 that I received my first lessons in the art of diplomacy from two of my older sisters, Charlotte and Maria Josepha. The three of us were enjoying a *fête champêtre* on one of the manicured grass *tapis*, or carpets, in the gardens of Schönbrunn. Madame von Brandeiss had insisted that we take as much healthful air as possible because a smallpox epidemic had infected the palace. Maman had fallen ill, which utterly terrified us—we had all thought her invincible and, being fatherless now, could not imagine ourselves without her. It had been painful enough to lose Papa so suddenly when I was only nine; my grief then had been so profound that I thought I should never smile again. But in her illness Maman would not countenance any tears, and demanded rather adamantly that none of us dwell on the state of her health, insisting that it would please her more if we went about our days with dry eyes and our thoughts fixed firmly on the future. The fate of the empire, she reminded us, rested on the shoulders of her children.

At present, Josepha and I bore a significant portion of this burden in the shape of her upcoming wedding to the king of Naples and my impending nuptials with the dauphin of France. Every day at Mass we prayed for Maman's swift recuperation while our eldest brother, Joseph, who had ruled alongside Maman ever since Papa died, saw to the business of empire. With what little I understood of politics at the time, I surmised that if it were up to her and not to God, Maman would recover from smallpox if only to forestall Joseph's progressive reforms from coming to fruition.

"Maman must maintain good relations with the French," Josepha told me, plucking the stem from a strawberry. Mindful of my youth as well as my general ignorance of world affairs, she explained that we'd recently concluded a lengthy military conflict called the Seven Years' War, and that France had not been entirely happy with Austria after the fighting ended.

"Why?" I asked. "Did we lose?"

Thoughtfully sucking on the sweet red berry, Josepha admitted that she wasn't exactly sure. Charlotte nibbled on her bread and cheese as if she were a little mouse. "Everything is about politics," she announced, more interested in the conversation than the repast. I would have laughed at her, but she displayed an innate aptitude for governing that belied her years. "Even our lives are about politics. Especially *our* lives," she added, flicking her hand to chase away a hovering horsefly. Then she batted away an equally pesky footman and availed herself of a slice of cold ham. "Think about the family motto: Others wage wars to succeed, but you, fortunate Hapsburg, marry!" Having altered it slightly to reflect our situation, Charlotte chuckled to herself. "Sometimes I think Maman had so many daughters because she has so many enemies! Austrian archduchesses are meant to marry well and create alliances with other kingdoms so that our borders can be safe." She mentioned two rulers who were Austria's biggest threats: Frederick of Prussia (whom Maman referred to as "the Devil") and Catherine of Russia. According to Charlotte, these "Greats" were intent on pecking away at our empire the way chickens gobble feed.

"Do you think I will ever become 'Antonia the Great'?" I asked, sticking my nose in the air with mock grandeur.

"Not if you marry the dauphin of France," Charlotte replied.

Josepha agreed. "Unlike Austria, the kingdom of France is bound by Salic law—which means that only a male heir can rule. The duty of a French queen is to make heirs by becoming *enceinte* as many times as possible. The more boys you produce, the more your subjects will love you. You'll be lucky enough to be known as 'Antonia the Great with Child.'" She began to laugh so hard at her own witticism that she gave herself the hiccups. Her lemonade trickled down the cascading bows that adorned her violet satin bodice like a mountain spring tumbling over a rill.

Unamused by any joke made at my expense—Josepha's

ruined stomacher served her right—I tugged off a crust of bread and tossed it to a little bird who had been eyeing our meal, insisting that I was very glad not to have been sent off to Versailles yet; although I admitted some confusion as to the delay. It beggared belief that the marquis de Durfort was lingering in Austria simply to partake of all the lavish banquets Maman invited him to. Surely there was good food in France. Didn't they get pineapples from the Indies, too? Did they have no lemon ice? My naïve questions only sent my sisters into renewed gales of laughter.

"You know how much I despise it when you and Josepha speak to each other in riddles I can't solve," I announced petulantly. I rose to my feet and flounced away, pretending to be more interested in one of the rose trellises than in anything my sisters had to say. The buds were just coming into bloom. I used my fingernails to remove a pale pink one, snipped off the thorns in the same manner, and worked the short stem into my hair.

"Come back here!" Charlotte shouted. "Please don't be snappish, Toinette!" I turned on my heels and slowly sashayed toward them, enjoying the heft of my swaying skirts, my hips made manifest only by the grace of a pair of panniers. My sisters shared a significant glance. "All right, we'll explain it to you. You can't get married until you are half a woman," Charlotte said sagely, brushing a crumb from the corner of her mouth. It landed on her lap; with her thumb and forefinger she deftly flicked it off her striped silk skirt. "Maman and the French ambassador are stalling for time because Générale Krottendorf has not arrived."

I was dumbfounded. Générale Krottendorf—the wife of Général Krottendorf, of course—was a friend of Maman's who used to visit us regularly. "But why would she have anything to do with my marriage plans?" I asked.

Charlotte and Josepha exchanged another conspiratorial look.

"What?" It irked me when they knew something I didn't and

then lorded it over me with the peculiar brand of superiority they assumed as an elder sister's prerogative. I picked at a strawberry stem and fixed a resolute gaze on the yellow damask tablecloth that served as our picnic blanket. A tiny red ladybird with five black spots on her back crawled across my skirts, like a living cabochon ruby. I tried to remember whether it was good luck or ill to see one. *Fly away home! Your house is on fire and your children are all gone.* What a terrible thing to recite to such a small defenseless creature.

Josepha daintily wiped her fingers on a linen cloth, staining it crimson. Unlike me, or Charlotte, Josepha never soiled her gowns or scuffed her slippers. Her lightly powdered ash blond hair never came undone from her coiffure. She never scrabbled in the dirt to bury a butterfly or romped with a mud-spattered pug-dog. The tension in her embroidery stitches was always perfectly even. And she was invariably the first to take pity on my ignorance. "Générale Krottendorf," she informed me with all the sagacity of the royal physician, "is the nickname Maman gives to our monthly flow—which should arrive with as much punctuality as the real générale!"

"When the générale makes her first visit, you are half a woman. And you become *fully* a woman on your wedding night!" Charlotte added.

"I wouldn't even know what to do on my wedding night," I replied. The liveried footmen, maintaining a discreet distance from the three of us, pretended not to hear, but one of them smiled and then quickly covered his mouth with his gloved hand. The musicians began to play a little louder. Even in our pastoral repose, privacy was merely an illusion.

Josepha blushed delicately. "They say it just comes naturally. But I wonder if *I'll* know. I wonder if Ferdinand will like me," she added reflectively, referring to King Ferdinand of the Two

Sicilies, one of the sons of the king of Spain. She and Ferdinand were to be married in Naples at the end of the year.

It was a cruel fate. Charlotte and I had overheard the most unpleasant descriptions of Ferdinand's character; and Maman herself had said terrible things about him. The king was only sixteen, the same age as Josepha, but according to the Austrian ambassador to Naples, he was little more than an uncouth boy with brown hair, beady eyes, and a bulbous nose—a youth who liked to play horrid tricks on people and who invited ambassadors to keep him company while he sat on the commode. I can't explain it, but what fascinated me most about this behavior was that his palace had a commode! We considered ourselves a far more elegant and sophisticated court, superior in every way to the boisterous Neapolitans, and yet we didn't have a commode at any of our palaces. Maman's attitude was that if porcelain chamber pots were adequate for her ancestors, they would do just as nicely for us. And with 2,500 servants in the Hofburg alone, there was no shortage of people to empty them.

It would only have made Josepha feel worse about leaving us to wed this loutish king if we told her all the awful things we knew about him. Charlotte was quite sure that if Ferdinand had been a peasant instead of being born into the Spanish branch of the Bourbons, our mother would not have considered him good enough to be a stable groom, let alone a bridegroom for Josepha, with her delicate features, pale complexion, and complaisant demeanor.

I concluded that our eldest brother, Joseph, must have known what to do on his wedding night with Maria Josepha of Bavaria, because he was already a widower with two little girls. Joseph had adored their mother, his first wife, Isabella of Parma. Isabella was a granddaughter of Louis XV of France (which, I realized, would have made her a cousin to my future husband, the dauphin). She was the prettiest woman I had ever seen; and like our mother, Joseph had been lucky enough to have married for love.

If Isabella had lived long enough, I would have asked her about Louis Auguste and whether we would please each other. Would I like him? Perhaps even more important, would he like me? But Isabella had died of smallpox in 1763, four years before I found myself desperately needing such answers.

Joseph had remarried only because Maman insisted that it was his dynastic responsibility to do so—which is how it came to pass that he wedded a woman named Maria Josepha. At first I found it terribly disconcerting that two people in our enormous family now had the same name. But in truth most of Europe's royalty were in some way interrelated and most of us likewise bore a combination of family and saints' names. After Joseph's second marriage, we Hapsburgs privately called my sister "Pretty Josepha" while our new sister-in-law, from the Bavarian House of Wittelsbach, was "Homely Josepha."

I felt sorry for Homely Josepha because my brother never loved her. She was rather short and plump and had ugly teeth. I could not say whether that was the reason she rarely smiled, or if it was because she was miserable in Vienna. I heard the servants gossiping soon after they were married that Joseph had refused to share her bed despite Maman's philosophy that it was healthy for the marriage when a man and wife slept in the same chamber every night. Even *I* knew that he had ordered a partition to be constructed on their shared balcony at Schönbrunn so that he didn't have to see her.

Two years ago, after our father's death, Maman had asked Joseph to formally share the imperial duties with her—which of course meant that, as his wife, Homely Josepha would officially be known as the Empress consort of Austria. Yet no one ever thought of her that way. Maman was still the empress and no woman could rival her power or her formidability. In fact, no one ever thought of Homely Josepha at all.

But now she, too, lay feverish in her bed, her body red and blistered with the telltale marks of smallpox—the disease Maman referred to as "the scourge of Europe." And my brother had an even better excuse for avoiding his wife. As the emperor of Austria he could not be exposed to the disease, especially because Maman, who had contracted it by visiting Homely Josepha's sickroom, was bedridden with it as well. Austria could not afford to lose both its reigning sovereigns.

Maman had always been candid with her children about illness and disease, and even about death and dying, because she didn't want us to be afraid of them. Nevertheless, we tiptoed around the subject of her indisposition, each of us certain that if we were to voice our fears they would undoubtedly come true. Instead, we spoke in self-conscious tones of other things—of dances and kite flying, boat rides and the pug bitch's new litter.

It was Joseph who found the three of us in the garden to tell us the end had arrived. He was perspiring heavily in his black silk mourning suit and gray brocaded waistcoat embellished with jet beading. Death was such a frequent occurrence that all of us had formal mourning clothes at the ready. A tricorn of shiny black beaver shaded my brother's eyes from the afternoon sun. Although his lips were grim, his eyes were dry. "She's gone to God," was all he said.

With a collective, terrified gasp, we jumped up—plates, platters, half-eaten strawberries, and goblets of lemonade tumbling from our hands and laps, haphazardly spilling their contents all over the yellow cloth.

I flew into Charlotte's arms and began to weep. She stroked my hair maternally, though within her comforting embrace I could feel her heart beating wildly against mine. "Maman is dead?" Josepha exclaimed, crossing herself and then shoving her fist to her mouth to stifle a huge, choking sob. Her nose began to turn bright red as it always did when she was trying hard not to cry.

Our brother looked startled for an instant. "No—not Maman. My wife. My wife is dead."

Time stood still, or so it seemed, while our minds grasped the information and all its implications. We would not be orphans. Yet Maman remained in danger. And Joseph had now twice been made a widower.

Although I was relieved and grateful that it was not Maman whose soul had gone to heaven, there was still reason enough for grief. Frustrated when I could not locate my handkerchief, I availed myself of my *engageantes*—the frothy layers of lace at my elbow—to wipe my runny nose. I didn't care. What was such a trifling thing compared to the snuffing out of a life? Homely Josepha—it now seemed too cruel to call her that; henceforth she would be "Angel Josepha"—didn't deserve to die, and especially so unappreciated. With all the innocence of youth and ignorance of the wide world I shot Joseph a reproachful look that bordered on contempt. He seemed puzzled by my expression. "She loved *you*, you know," I muttered.

Our *fête champêtre* in the grass now seemed a discordant frivolity. The musicians packed away their instruments and discreetly dispersed, and the servants cleaned up the remnants of our picnic while we unhappy Hapsburgs trudged solemnly back to the palace. The funeral, Joseph told us, would take place as soon as possible; a corpse rotten from smallpox was dangerously contagious and therefore had to be interred with great haste. Although she was born in Munich and had been Princess of Bavaria, because she was the Empress consort of Austria, Angel Josepha would be entombed in our family crypt and not be sent back to her homeland for burial.

The court was immediately directed to begin the observance of a three-month period of mourning. From now until the end of August there would be no concerts, operas, or dances. Aware that it would be stifling to endure almost the entire summer without any lively entertainments, Maman permitted the youngest of us—Charlotte, Ferdinand, Maximilian, and I—to enjoy our pastimes as long as our behavior was not unduly frolicsome. To alleviate some of the boredom I spent many hours indoors at Schönbrunn practicing the harp, embroidering a bevy of lilac blossoms on a firescreen, and undressing and dressing my favorite doll in the new clothes I had learned to stitch from Madame von Brandeiss.

How eagerly I anticipated the day when I would have a gaggle of lively children at my heels, tugging at my skirts, always keen to play games! For the time being I lavished my affection on my dog and my doll. As they had both entered my life when I was all of seven, I had given them the sort of spectacularly unoriginal names that young children typically bestow upon their playthings and pets. Poupée was the French doll with the pretty painted face that my sister Maria Christina had given me for Christmas; and Mops was my pug—*Mopshund* being the German word for a pug-dog.

Joseph did not attend his wife's funeral, nor did Maman, who continued to recuperate. And very few people followed Angel Josepha's tin-plated sarcophagus down to the imperial crypt below the Kapuzinerkirche, the Capuchin Church. I was all the more sorrowful after my request to accompany her bier was denied. She should have had a sympathetic friend there to say goodbye and to wish her soul a safe journey to heaven. And although she was not beautiful, she was virtuous; I never heard her say an unkind word, nor reproach anyone—even my brother—for their conduct toward her.

A few weeks after Angel Josepha's death, the imperial physicians reported that Maman had fully recovered and was capable of resuming her imperial duties. Naturally, we were grateful and relieved, and none of us more so than Maman. But I noticed a difference in her. It was not merely that she was thinner, and perhaps had even lost one of her three chins. She seemed weary, less patient, and even more attentive than ever to her deeply ingrained sense of duty. No longer did my mother appear to embrace life, although God had allowed her to live; instead, she seemed burdened by earthly cares. Even her beloved *Kammermusik* concerts no longer brought her joy.

While the court was in official mourning my sister Josepha's wedding to the king of Naples had been placed in a state of limbo. Naturally, it would not have been seemly to plan a joyous celebration, but in all sincerity, the only one who was looking forward to Josepha's impending union was Maman. Yet by the second week of October the three months of mourning had elapsed and my sister's bedroom in the Hofburg was as bare as a nun's cell. In preparation for her journey to Naples, nearly everything Josepha owned had been packed into heavy wooden trunks studded with her initials. I didn't much envy her trousseau. It consisted of dozens of gowns and robes made up in brightly colored silks and brocades and trimmed with everything one could imagine—spangles and beading and lace and gold fringe, and precious gems, of course—because Maman had been informed that the Neapolitans were fond of these unsophisticated, garish touches. She wanted to be sure that King Ferdinand would become smitten with Josepha immediately. The way Josepha explained it to me, "the sooner the baby, the stronger the alliance." She meant Austria's alliance with the Two Sicilies. The closer the days drew to October 15, the date of my sister's departure, the more I was forced to confront an ugly truth about our mother: It didn't matter to Maman if Josepha and her husband did not fall in love, just as it hadn't mattered to her when she urged Joseph to marry Homely Angel Josepha of Bavaria. And yet *she* had been so deeply enamored of our papa that she refused to wed any man but him, despite our grandfather's objections to such an unequal match.

I was no longer as cocooned from the harsh realities of the world as I had been only a year earlier. The passing of my unloved sister-in-law and the imminent departure of Josepha for an equally loveless marriage forced me to confront a painful lesson about the privileges of rank that I would have been just as happy to delay. Palaces and carriages and bejeweled gowns came at a high price. Gap-toothed Marta who emptied my chamber pot every morning may have envied my sumptuous wardrobe and my hours of leisure (and who would not prefer to caress the strings of a harp than dispose of someone else's urine?), but she had the freedom to follow the promptings of her heart and marry the man she loved because the fate of nations did not depend upon her union.

On October 12, after the family breakfasted together Josepha drew me aside and, with a catch in her throat, asked if she might speak to me alone. She had barely touched her food, nervously tapping her heavy silver spoon on her egg cup and only nibbling at her toast. Her pot of bitter chocolate, which she looked forward to drinking each morning with girlish enthusiasm and an indulgent spoonful of *Schlag*, was ignored and grew cold.

It was a long, labyrinthine walk to the wing of the palace where the archduchesses lived in what we laughingly referred to as "the convent" because our brothers all resided on the opposite side of the courtyard. Our skirts rustling, Josepha clutched my hand as we sped through countless cream-colored chambers embellished with *boiserie*—raised moldings and elaborate scrollwork—passing innumerable pairs of footmen standing as stiff and silent as statues at the entrance to every room.

Each of us had our own apartment consisting of a formal reception room, a salon, and a bedchamber. A stranger entering our residential quarters might have been surprised by their simplicity, a striking contrast to the rococo splendor of the state rooms that reflected the latest taste in décor and the grandeur of empire. Someone who had never seen the formal salons, and who had only visited the Hapsburgs *en domicile*, might have thought we lived like any large family of the German gentry—pious, industrious, and boisterous.

Josepha followed me into my salon, shutting the door quietly behind her. Mops eyed her curiously from his bed on the floor, sensing in his uncanny canine way that something was amiss. Clasping my hands in hers, Josepha drew me over to the blue velvet love seat. "I want to say good-bye to you," my sister told me. Her hands felt cold and damp. Her face was pale, the color drained from her cheeks.

"But you don't have to say it yet," I insisted. "You don't leave for another three days." I rested my head against her shoulder. "I wish you could remain with us for another three *weeks*, so you don't miss my twelfth birthday."

Josepha sighed heavily. "Even so, I think I would miss it anyway. In fact, little one, I'm afraid we may never see each other again."

I shivered at her words. "What are you saying?"

"Maman says I must pay my respects today to...to Homely Josepha—before I leave for Naples. She says that it's the proper thing to do." My sister's voice was hollow.

"You have to perform a take-leave for a dead person? Homely Josepha will never know."

"But Maman will."

I had little use, and even less patience, for empty ritual. "Well, what if you didn't do it?" I asked her. "Or what if you told Maman you would and then only pretended to go into the crypt?"

Josepha trembled. "You know I can't. I could never lie about something like that. It wouldn't be right. And even if Maman never found out, God would know. I could confess my sin and make peace with disappointing Maman, but I couldn't disappoint Him."

Although she was trying to appear brave, her eyes were filled with terror and tears. "Descending into the Kaisergruft to commune with the dead souls there, especially Maria Josepha's spirit, and our having the same name...I can't explain it, Toinette... but I have a premonition that you and I shall never see each other again."

She would not be consoled by my reminder, now halfhearted, that there was no such thing as ghosts.

"It's not Homely Josepha's *ghost* that I am afraid of." My sister shuddered. "I know her soul is in heaven, but her body...Joseph said she was buried quickly because the doctors didn't want the disease to spread. What if they weren't careful enough?" I placed my arm about her shoulder and allowed Mops to jump into her lap; if I was unable to allay her fears, surely the pug's warm, devoted presence would comfort her.

"Maman thinks I'm being childish about the whole business." Josepha reflexively stroked the dog's smooth tan coat, then rested her cheek against his thick neck. "To her mind, I have an obligation and it is my duty to fulfill it. Yet it is also my duty to become King Ferdinand's bride."

I squeezed Josepha's arm to reassure her. "I know you don't want to wed him," I said softly.

"It doesn't matter whether I wish to marry him or not—"

"Well, certainly not to Maman," I interrupted.

"—it's that I don't think I ever *will*." Mops hopped onto the floor and began to nose about the ruching at Josepha's hem. Finding no errant crumbs, he grew disinterested and pattered over to a comfortable spot on the rug. My sister impetuously threw her arms around me, holding me so tightly that I could feel the boning in her lilac silk bodice pressing into my chest. I had forgotten how much taller she had grown. Ever since I'd learned that I was to marry the dauphin of France, I'd begun to wish I could stop time and keep things just as they were. I would stop it at the picnics and the operas—before we ever got to the leave-taking and the funerals. When I was younger, maybe five or six, I'd made a wish that I would never be sad. It hadn't come true.

Josepha began to weep. "I'm afraid I will join Johanna," she sobbed as she held me even closer. In addition to Maria Anna (whom we all called Marianne), Maria Christina, Maria Elisabeth, and Maria Amalia, we'd had another sister—Maria Johanna Gabriella Josepha Antonia. Johanna was born five years before I was, and only one year before Josepha. The pair of them had been as close as Charlotte and I were. In 1762, two days before Christmas, Johanna died of smallpox. She was only twelve years old. Just a few months older than I was now.

That thought alone was so immense, so frightening, that my efforts to reassure my sister evanesced. What could I say to Josepha? How could I tell her, with any measure of honesty or certainty, that her fears were unfounded? I could not lie. So we perched on the edge of the love seat, our tears staining the blue and rose floral Aubusson as we clutched each other so tightly that the very impression of our bodies reaffirmed the physical, the corporeal, the fact that we were alive.

"Promise you will never forget me," Josepha whispered, her words warm in my ear.

"Never," I whimpered. I swallowed hard and blinked back a sob, forcing a brave note into my voice. "Never."

Always dutiful, pious, and obedient, Josepha did as Maman

instructed. After my sister took leave of me that morning, she descended into the dank and drafty Kaisergruft and knelt before the tomb of Angel Josepha. Our sister Elisabeth and I saw her that afternoon and kissed her good-bye once more. Already Josepha complained of feeling ill. Her cheeks were flushed with color, though she insisted she was cold. By the time Maman summoned us to the Rössel Room where the imperial physician somberly disclosed the worst, I was no longer allowed to see her.

I fixed Josepha in my memory as she was on the last afternoon I saw her: a frightened girl in a gown of violet brocade, a good sister and an even better daughter—one who placed a higher value on her pledge to Maman than on her own brief life.

October 15 was the day on which Josepha should have climbed into a grand traveling coach in the courtyard of the Hofburg. It was the day she should have ventured forth, clattering over the cobbles toward the unknown, a new life, first as a bride and a queen, and then as a mother, in a kingdom where a hot sun warmed a sparkling sea. But instead of waving our handkerchiefs, wiping our tears, and wishing my sixteen-year-old sister, Archduchess Maria Josepha Gabriella Johanna Antonia Ana of Austria, a safe journey to Naples, we were bidding her a final farewell as she took the ultimate unknowable journey, on her way to heaven.

Josepha's fears had been well founded, her terrified premonition correct. One of the Capuchins, his own face wet with tears, later admitted to Maman that in their haste to inter the corpse, Angel Josepha's tomb had not been properly sealed, which is how my beautiful sister caught smallpox. More than ever I wished it were possible to turn back the hands of the clock, stopping them at a moment when the clergy or the doctors or *someone* would have noticed the—the literal graveness—of the error. But I could not trick Time. Now there were two Angel Josephas. I had been too hasty in naming the first.

THREE

Stalling for Time

I knew better than to listen at keyholes and spy on people. I would have to confess my sin after Mass on Sunday. But I also knew that Maman and Joseph were discussing my future, and I would defy any twelve-year-old girl to restrain her curiosity under the circumstances.

The pair of them were in Maman's study, which she kept so chilly that the frosty air blew through the keyhole against my cheek. Outside in the Hofburg courtyard, the wind howled with alarming ferocity, swirling the late December snow in circular eddies. As I crouched beside the door and squinted into the room, I could see my eldest brother, tall and noble, known to the rest of the world as Franz Joseph of Austria, snap open his enameled snuffbox and place a pinch of tobacco in the crook between his right thumb and forefinger.

"You were saying, Maman?" he said before inhaling sharply.

Our mother scowled. "You know I think that's an ugly habit."

"You don't approve of anything I do." Joseph chuckled. "Snuff is all the rage among titled gentlemen. But whether it's progress, reform, or snuff, you have neither patience nor tolerance for modernity."

Maman sighed heavily, as if she knew her next sentence bore such import that it would require a massive exhalation to keep it hanging in the air. "I fear for the little one, Joseph."

"Many girls are wed at twelve."

Maman snorted. "Antonia at twelve looks ten. At her age, I had already begun to resemble a woman."

Our mother's expression was grave. I'd started to notice that ever since she announced my betrothal, the pouches beneath her eyelids had been growing darker with fatigue.

"You are aware, Joseph, that I am loath to admit an error in judgment. But it might have been a mistake to negotiate a treaty with the French when Antonia is so young. After all, the world—"

"You mean *France*, Maman," my brother interrupted. He availed himself of another pinch of snuff.

"—cannot be expected to sit back and wait until Antonia grows taller and begins to develop," our mother continued, as though Joseph hadn't spoken a word. "Did you know that the very first thing Louis inquired of his ambassador to Vienna was whether Antonia had good breasts? I tried to offer him Charlotte, but she is older than the dauphin by two years and Louis wouldn't hear of the match. Evidently the boy is as immature as Antonia. And as bashful as a violet. Louis feared that Charlotte would devour him."

I wondered what Charlotte would have made of Maman's characterization of her and debated whether I should tell her. After all, it had been her idea for me to eavesdrop. My sister had convinced me that there were occasions when politics took precedence over piety—such as when one's fate is in the balance.

A footman approached and I straightened up, seized by the momentary fear that he might tell Maman. Then I remembered the vast differences between my rank and his. Still, I gave him a wink and touched my finger to my lips. He inclined his head respectfully.

I knelt beside the keyhole again. Maman was speaking. "Austria cannot afford to delay much longer while Prussia and Russia rattle their sabers in earnest, threatening to carve into our territories as if the Hapsburg Empire were an enormous roasted joint. We need allies. We once had Parma. Now it is lost to us, and Lombardy with it, thanks to the English. And while the French have hardly been our friends, a strategic alliance with them will strengthen both our kingdoms by checking the ambitions of our enemies."

Joseph continued to pace anxiously. My eye began to twitch, and I drew away from the keyhole for a moment. "Then why not renegotiate the terms of the marriage treaty," I heard him suggest. "Elisabeth is twenty-four; perhaps *she* should be offered to Louis—not for the young dauphin, of course, but for the king himself. His Most Christian Majesty is a widower, yet he remains a vibrant and most vital man with"—Joseph chuckled—"an immense...joie de vivre. He is still quite the *roué*, you know."

"I know Louis has mistresses." My mother sounded like she had been sucking on lemon pastilles. I adjusted my position to get a better view of her. She looked equally sour. "All sovereigns have paramours. And no matter their feelings, it is not for their wives to make scenes. Although she may have already lost his love, she risks losing something far worse if she berates him. She loses his esteem."

Joseph spoke in a low rumble. "*Ça suffit*. Enough, Maman. Papa is more than two years dead." He rubbed his arms in an effort to massage some warmth into them.

My torso was growing pinched from crouching so awkwardly

within the carapace of my corset. *Come to the point!* I thought impatiently. Enough talk about husbands and wives and mistresses. What about my wedding to the dauphin! Moments later, Maman resumed the conversation. But her voice sounded strained. I imagined her thick body tensing beneath her black damask bodice. "I have already considered dispatching Chancellor Kaunitz to speak with France's Foreign Minister, the duc de Choiseul. Let the diplomats sort it out—our representative and Louis's. But there is no getting around the fact that your sister is no longer the beauty she once was."

A lump rose in my throat and I stifled a gasp. *Did Maman mean me? Have I somehow lost my looks? Is it because I still resemble a child?*

"Look at Elisabeth through the eyes of a politician, Joseph, and not with those of a devoted brother." My mother cleared her throat, endeavoring to suppress a telltale crackle in her voice. I knew that sound well; it was the harbinger of unwanted tears. "Elisabeth survived the smallpox, but her face is so ravaged with pockmarks that Louis would never have her. He might have done so once upon a time, but he prizes feminine beauty." Maman sighed with tremendous resignation. "And your sister Amalia is also too disfigured to make an acceptable queen of France. No, it will have to be Antonia and the dauphin. What is done must never be permitted to be undone."

She seemed to expect my brother to counterattack, but when he made no reply, she pressed on. "But at present, we have little more than badinage—empty words, an honorable promise—on which to pin the hopes of an empire. It is imperative that we hasten France's formal commitment to Antonia's marriage; for without a written assurance from Louis himself, the accord is too easily broken."

I had heard enough.

They were becoming impatient. *I* was becoming impatient. I was not growing up fast enough, betrayed by my own body. And by now I knew full well that my body was my destiny. My future was at stake, but no one would tell me anything.

Throughout the first months of 1768 I gained a clearer understanding of what Maman had meant when she'd spoken of pressuring the French to finalize my marriage plans. Her efforts to keep the marquis de Durfort entertained knew no bounds. The ambassador was an honored guest of the empress at every winter ball, even when there was more than one given on the same night. As always, there was a hidden purpose behind Maman's most innocent gestures. She knew how much I loved to dance, and if she was not especially proud of my academic efforts at least she could show the Frenchman my natural grace in all the formal court dances, from the stately pavanes to the lively polonaises.

Often, after supper, the imperial children would perform in concert. I would sit down at my harp and play for the marquis, accompanying myself in some pretty tune with a pastoral lyric, usually something rather silly in translation, praising the sunshine and the flowers. Privately, I fretted that the French ambassador might be growing weary of Maman's increasingly transparent efforts to demonstrate that I was worthy of one day becoming their queen.

On one evening, at her special request, my youngest brothers and I re-created the dance we had performed during the celebrations for Joseph's first marriage to the beautiful Isabella of Parma, she of the mild, sweet countenance and dark, shining eyes that death had closed too soon. Our original performance had been the divertissement in an opera written especially for the wedding by our court composer and royal music master, Herr Gluck.

Maman even insisted that the seamstresses make a copy of the gown I had worn when, as a five-year-old girl, I first danced the divertissement. The bodice of deep blue satin was very tight, and my ivory-colored sleeves and skirt were adorned with festoons of roses, each one fashioned out of petal pink silk. Because the robe was so closely fitted, Maman thought it showed how well made my limbs were (a tacit implication that I would bear healthy children), and there were no furbelows on the sleeves to distract from the graceful movements of my arms. She was proud, too, of my long neck and the way I carried my head.

As the music filled my ears, stirring my soul, I obeyed my feet, letting them take me through the intricate steps of their own accord. Out of the corner of my eye I noticed Maman nodding and smiling, her deep blue eyes glimmering with hope and pride. And as the pavane drew to a close, she subtly poked the marquis with her elbow, as if to say, "See, won't she make an enchanting dauphine of France!" In response, he raised his handkerchief, heavily scented with violet water, to his upper lip. I could not tell whether he was registering disapproval or ennui.

That January, during one of our winter festivals, my mother was somewhat more blunt, tact and diplomacy having yielded no stronger a reaction from the marquis than a series of wan smiles. One frosty afternoon Maman accorded him the honor of standing beside her on a balcony of the Hofburg to view a procession of twenty-two sleighs bearing the imperial family. Unbeknownst to her, that morning her youngest children had built a snow fort in the courtyard outside the Leopoldine wing of the palace, where we made our residence. Charlotte and I closed ranks against Ferdinand and Maxl, pelting them with snowballs from the safety of our frozen barricade. But when the boys retaliated, we squealed like piglets and pleaded our femininity as a defense, for we knew Maman would scold us most emphatically if we paraded before the French envoy with wet hair. Our brothers were quite miffed that we had claimed victory without permitting them to fire a single volley.

Just before the procession was to begin I hopped into my sleigh and drew the fur rug over my knees. The air, biting and brisk, smelled clean and fresh; a sharp inhalation stung my nostrils. As my team of four perfectly matched white horses drew near the balcony, I waved jubilantly to the distinguished onlookers, my passion for the gently falling snowflakes clearly written in my flushed cheeks and sparkling eyes. When Papa was alive, during the winters that were too mild for the snow to remain on the ground in Vienna for any length of time he would dispatch a small army of servants to transport it from the mountains to the Hofburg in heavy sledges, all in the name of indulging his children—and especially me, his favorite daughter—in our most beloved pastimes.

I raised my hand to my brow to shield my eyes. High above me, silhouetted in the sun, Maman stood near the balustrade as majestic as a statue. She was bundled in velvet and furs, her plump hands shoved inside an enormous ermine muff. The only indication she gave of not being impervious to the cold were the two bright spots of pink upon her cheeks. Another buried memory bubbled to the surface—the childhood certainty that my mother was the most powerful person in the world, so formidable that I genuinely believed God had given her permission to control the weather.

The poor marquis, who undoubtedly had never planned to spend the better part of the day out of doors observing a winter carnival, was shivering in his formal court costume, clutching his bright red cloak about his shoulders as though it were a flannel blanket. His thin lips had a bluish cast and he kept dabbing at his nose with his lace-edged handkerchief. His precious violet water was no match for a Vienna winter.

In my mother's words, I was "a vision in white" that afternoon, from my fur hat to my white leather boots. My sleighing costume was not only trimmed with marten and embellished with diamonds, but the jacket and skirt were profusely embroidered with silver thread. Maman had taken every precaution; in case I failed to scintillate, my garments would sparkle for me. By now I had grown a bit more astute about the intricacies of diplomacy and was aware that she had staged the entire procession on my account.

As my swan-shaped sleigh slowly glided below the balustrade, the bells on the horses' harnesses hushed to a faint rhythmic jingle. The four white mares tossed their heads as if to shake the snowflakes from their manes and I waved gaily to Maman and the ambassador, giving them my brightest smile. And then, in the stillness of the moment, I saw my mother gently nudge the marquis and utter (none too discreetly, as her voice carried in the nippy air), "The little wife."

Maman had the tenacity of a terrier. Not two days later she informed Durfort that she possessed portraits of every member of the French royal family. They had been a gift from my brother Joseph's first wife, the beauteous Isabella. My mother's announcement hung upon the air. I stole a glance at the ambassador, whose mouth twitched as if he had trapped a bee inside it and daren't swallow. The sun-shaped pendulum swung inexorably to and fro, the passing seconds audibly ticking by.

"I am certain that His Most Christian Majesty would enjoy the honor of owning likenesses of the entire imperial family as well," said the marquis, finally finding his tongue. Pretending to be overwhelmed by the compliment, Maman smiled benevolently, her eyes moist with happiness. Surely no finer actress trod the boards at the Burgtheater!

"Well, then, my brother's wish is my fondest command," she

replied, referring to the French king as if they were siblings—the manner employed by all monarchs to address each other. "I will place a portraitist at his disposal. Or perhaps, monsieur le marquis, your sovereign would like to select the painter himself," she added, the consummate diplomat herself. Turning to address me, she said in a manner at once formidable and maternal, "You would like to sit for your portrait for the king of France, would you not? After all, you were but seven years old the last time you were immortalized in oils."

They might have thought I was merely a silly girl, interested in nothing but flowers, dolls, and butterflies; but now that I was twelve, I was extremely conscious of being not quite a child and not yet a woman either. And just because, as an archduchess of Austria, I had been schooled to hold my head high no matter the circumstances, I was not impervious to the barbs of the backstairs gossips. I overheard their titters and whispers. I would not amount to much after all, they said; I would not fulfill Maman's grand ambitions. Everyone from the ministers to the chambermaids seemed to know that Générale Krottendorf had not yet paid her first visit. And there were some in Maman's government, my brother Joseph among them, who feared that she was wasting her energy, focusing too much attention on the political alliance with France at the expense of other, more immediate concerns.

One morning, she summoned Charlotte and me to the Rosenzimmer. Many paintings of the imperial family, executed by the court painter Martin van Meytens, graced the walls of our various palaces—the massive Hofburg with its thousands of rooms, Laxenburg (which had been my late papa's favorite because it was comparatively cozy and small), and Maman's beloved Schönbrunn. When I was seven, Herr van Meytens had painted me in a dress of pale pink satin with a rose in my hands. I remembered him as a very jolly man who perspired a lot. He made me laugh when he would remove his gray wig, blotting the sweat from his glistening bald head with the same smelly rag he used to clean his brushes.

But it was not our own court painter who was to render our likenesses in oils. The footmen opened the paneled doors of the Rosenzimmer to admit two gentlemen. One of them, dressed in a manner even more elaborate than that of the marquis de Durfort, was very kind looking with an open face and eyes that sparkled with intelligence. The style in which he wore his reddish hair, curled and powdered and tied with a broad black ribbon, did nothing to conceal his receding hairline. The gentleman's companion was by comparison quite coarse looking, although I could see that his fawn-colored frock coat, or *le frac* as the garment was nicknamed, was exceptionally well tailored.

Maman introduced the visitors. The gentleman with the pleasant countenance and wide smile was the duc de Choiseul, a special envoy from Louis XV. She informed me that it was the duc, in his capacity as France's Foreign Minister, who had conceived the plan to marry me to their dauphin. Maman greeted him with tremendous, almost giddy effusion. Gone, at least for the moment, was the melancholia that had characterized her demeanor since the death of my father and which had been exacerbated by her bout with the pox. Her glumness had been replaced with a glow that made her appear far younger than her fifty years. I'd seen that flushed expression before; it was a look of conquest.

The other man, Joseph Ducreux, was the portrait painter. He looked quite common, with a large flat nose that seemed as though it had been pressed with a great degree of force into his very red face. He bowed to us, of course, because of the difference in our stations. Maman had always taught us to be polite to people from every stratum of society; the implication of the lesson was that such gentility was reciprocated, but one could plainly see from Monsieur Ducreux's supercilious expression that he would have preferred not to acknowledge us with so much deference. Consequently, I saw no reason to impress him.

I was dressed in a rich shade of blue that mimicked the color of my eyes; Charlotte was in salmon pink with ivory bows at the elbows, intended to draw attention to her best feature—her pale and lovely forearms. At Maman's request we stood like Meissen figurines in the center of the parquet and permitted Monsieur Ducreux to inspect us, which he did by circling us several times, first clockwise, then counterclockwise. Then he stepped farther away as he held up his hands to form a frame. Finally, he moved uncomfortably close, peering into our eyes through the window made by his fingers.

The duc de Choiseul stood beside Maman, looking rather grand, except when he inserted his monocle and I realized he was studying me as well. I felt like one of the fantastical animals that Papa used to have in the imperial menagerie. A sultan had once sent my father a camel! It joined the colorful, and exceedingly voluble, parrots; the tawny puma; the furry red monkeys with their hairless derrières, which it gave them great pleasure to display to anyone who would pay them the slightest mind; and the baby rhinoceros that had arrived by boat up the Danube River.

Charlotte and I were holding hands. Our long kid gloves fit so snugly that we could feel the heat emanating from each other's palms. The portraitist glanced at Maman and she told us to separate.

"They are not twins; their individual personalities must shine through the canvas," said Monsieur Ducreux. "I do not paint empty dresses. I paint souls."

I winked at Charlotte and she shrugged, having less use for this man than I. When the painter turned his back to us to address Maman, I mimicked his vanity. "I do not paint empty dresses," I mouthed, sticking my nose in the air. Then I tugged at my bodice and made a pretense of peering down the front. Referring to the nonexistence of my bosom, I whispered to my sister, "I *am* an empty dress!"

"Which of them do you wish me to paint, Your Imperial Majesty?" the painter asked Maman.

"Why, both of them," she replied smoothly.

The portraitist looked somewhat confused. "I was sent here to paint the future dauphine of France. Monsieur le dauphin can marry only one of them."

What arrogance! He should have known better than to confront the Empress of Austria. "That's none of your affair," snapped Maman. "Antonia," she added, gesturing toward me, "is to wed the dauphin. And since you are determined to paint their souls, that one"—she said, indicating Charlotte—"is the pragmatic one. Carolina has a good head on those pale white shoulders and will soon make an exceptional queen. The little one," she added, meaning me, of course, "has a beautiful soul but she never settles on something for more than a moment. One could sooner teach a butterfly to fly in a straight line." Maman did not mince words; she never did. She sank imperiously into a chair. "Antonia, monsieur, is the giddy one."

At this, Monsieur Ducreux began to inspect me even more closely. He stepped back for a different assessment and, making a little *hmph*-ing noise, shook his head. He stepped forward and shook his head more emphatically as he muttered something to himself. Then he asked me to smile, at which point, accompanied by an insistent "*Non, non, non, non, non,*" he wagged his head to and fro so vigorously that it seemed ready to fall off his shoulders.

The painter strode briskly toward the duc de Choiseul and whispered something in his ear. The duc frowned, and in a voice too soft for me to hear, repeated it to Maman. She gestured for him to sit beside her. With tremendous elegance, he lowered himself into a capacious armchair of gilded fruitwood upholstered with an allegorical petit point. The pair of them began to converse in low tones with their heads bent toward each other, a tableau broken only by the occasional concerned glance in my direction. I was not sure what was expected of me, other than not to fidget, so every time they regarded me, I made sure to smile, both broadly and sweetly, as though marriage with the dauphin of France was the primary reason I drew breath.

"Of course," Maman said, after a lengthy sotto voce exchange with the diplomat, during which the only word I could make out was *dommage*—a pity. She did not look at me again. "Absolutely. We assure you we will do whatever it takes." And then, addressing Monsieur Ducreux, she said, "You will begin with the archduchess Maria Carolina's portrait. The archduchess Maria Antonia, it appears, is not yet fit to be immortalized."

FOUR

The Truth Is a Bitter Cordial

According to Monsieur Ducreux's appraisal—and his opinions were (with a regretful countenance) supported wholeheartedly by the duc de Choiseul—I was not the beauty Maman thought me to be. The French had decided to delay their formal request for my hand until Austria could assure them that I was the embodiment of loveliness and fecundity. Given the immaturity of my twelve-year-old body, the latter would be difficult to express in the portrait that Louis Quinze had commissioned. Even with a fashionable ladder of plump bows adorning my stomacher, my chest would never convey the illusion of womanly pulchritude. But what had truly thrown Monsieur Ducreux into such a flurry of anxiety was my general appearance from the neck up. To keep my spirits from plummeting, I allowed myself to take comfort in the knowledge that he considered my neck itself regal and swan-like.

"But something must be done with her hair," the duc said to my mother. "Have you not noticed that the archduchess has patches near her hairline that are nearly as bald as a peeled onion?"

Maman appeared taken by surprise. She beckoned me to approach. "Lean over, Antonia." She inspected my hairline and scalp, poking with her fingers as though she were looking for lice. "It's this," she said finally, tugging off the gray woolen band that the Countess von Brandeiss employed to keep my hair off my forehead. "This silly rag is pulling her hair out at the roots." To me, she added, "*Liebchen*, we shall have to find a more suitable way to keep your curls tidy and presentable."

The duc de Choiseul cleared his throat. "The hairline itself is a problem, Your Imperial Majesty. A high forehead is, *certainement*, a mark of distinction. But," he added, touching his own brow, "if you were to draw horizontal lines across your daughter's face, it would immediately be apparent that considerably more than a third of the child's physiognomy is taken up by her forehead. And for the French taste, the archduchess's *front* is somewhat *too* prominent. It is, as we say in France, *trop bombé*."

Maman gave him a quizzical look. "And how do you propose to remedy the problem? We cannot very well change her head," she added imperiously. And yet behind her large blue eyes I detected a look of anxious uncertainty, as if she *would* change my head if such a thing were possible and if it would mean a formal commitment from France.

They spoke of me as though I wasn't there. I stood before them obediently, mute and meek, as though I were merely a fashion doll whose wardrobe was being examined in contemplation of a purchase.

The duc saw my lower lip begin to tremble and offered a look of kindly reassurance. "Of course we cannot change the shape of the archduchess's head. But we *can* change her hairstyle, madame, so that it does not emphasize the unfashionable defect.

Allow me to contact my sister, the duchesse de Gramont, who will of course know the finest Parisian coiffeurs. I will dispatch a note immediately to enlist her recommendation." He paused for several moments of reflection, wondering how he might best broach the next, and evidently even more awkward, subject. "But fixing the forehead will not be enough, I'm afraid." His large brown eyes were as sorrowful as a beaten hound's. "Your Imperial Majesty, we must do something about the teeth as well."

"The teeth?" I exclaimed. "What is wrong with my teeth?" Were they less than perfect because Maman had been stricken with a terrible toothache the day I was born?

"Antonia," Maman admonished. "What have I said to you about blurting out your every thought?" Instinctively I covered my mouth with my hand. My teeth were nothing as bad as Homely Josepha's had been. Hers had been little and brown. Mine were mostly white, at least.

"But what *is* wrong with her teeth, monsieur le duc?" Maman asked him.

"In a word, madame, they are crooked." Receiving no immediate reaction to his assessment, the diplomatic envoy added, "They must of course be straightened before there is any thought of her traveling to France."

I felt as though I had been struck by lightning—stunned and queasy all at once. Maman regarded me with a look of utter horror. I had somehow failed her again.

When the imperial family sat down to dinner that evening, Maman made sure that I was seated at her left hand, with the duc de Choiseul directly across from me, in the place of highest honor to her right. Above our heads, the ornate chandeliers sparkled with two dozen candles apiece, casting a magical glow on the crystal goblets and highly polished silver. Low bowls of red and white roses, echoing the colors of the family dining room with its

ivory walls and crimson upholstery, filled the room with their
sweet fragrance.

Although she never did more than nibble at her food no matter who was present, Maman was famous for the way she entertained her most distinguished guests. When the family dined
alone, our chefs prepared simple, hearty fare—local dishes like
beef goulash, and my favorite, veal schnitzel with dumplings. But
on a formal occasion like this evening, the dishes—eel in beurre
blanc, sautéed kidneys, pineapple ices—were all concocted from
French recipes, an additional honor to the duc.

When I was not stealing surreptitious glances in the back of a
spoon at my woefully uneven teeth, I found myself wishing that
Maman had not boasted to the duc of the great care she took in
superintending her children's education because—well, because
it was not true, and it prompted him to bombard me with a multitude of questions. When, during the soup, he asked me what I
knew of Marie Leszczyńska, all I could do was stare blankly at
him, my open mouth incapable of forming a response, until
Charlotte needled me for looking like a carp. "Don't you know
who Marie Leszczyńska is?" she whispered incredulously. My
brother Ferdinand, who loved to tease me, pulled a face when no
one was looking; it was the vacant-eyed, slack-jawed expression
of a dullard.

As we were eating one of the fish courses, the duc casually
mentioned that there were a number of beautiful villages along
the border that France shared with the Austrian empire.

"Oh, yes," I enthusiastically agreed.

"Which is your favorite, then?" he asked jovially, delicately
prying a tender scallop from its shell.

And this time, when I could not give him a reply because I
hadn't the vaguest idea of any of their names, let alone where they
lay on a map, Ferdinand surreptitiously touched the tip of his fin-

ger to his nose, and Charlotte accused me of resembling a frightened fawn. I was turning into a veritable menagerie right before
her eyes. What beast would I remind her of by the time we got to
the pastries? Although I adored my sister, she was not always
kind. I knew Charlotte was still reveling in Maman's compliment
that she would one day make "an exceptional queen." Maman
had said nothing of the sort about me, and her palpable silence on
the subject sat in my gut like day-old mutton stew. Instead, I was
a problem. My hairline was a problem. My teeth were a problem.
And by the time the ices were served and the duc de Choiseul politely inquired whether I understood why the 1756 Treaty of Versailles was so important to Austria, I realized that my mind was a
problem as well. Perhaps I did indeed require a different head if
I was ever to be queen of France.

Throughout this awkward quizzing Maman was wearing
what her children referred to as her empress smile, a munificent
expression that masked all traces of mortification or unpleasantness, no matter the situation. Nevertheless, while Maman rarely
touched wine or spirits, I could tell that she wished there was
something other than lemonade in her goblet.

After the coffee and brandy were served in the adjoining
room and my siblings retired for the night, Maman insisted that I
remain while she conversed with the duc de Choiseul. The servants had discreetly closed all the doors, leaving only the three of
us to discuss my future—and my flaws. In truth, I was not part of
the discussion. I was there to listen—to hear the duc confess his
shock at my ignorance of what, to his mind, were the mere rudiments of an acceptable education for a future queen of France.
How was it that, with my marriage treaty under discussion for
the past two years, I did not know something as elementary as the
identity of Marie Leszczyńska?

The duc turned to address me, speaking as if I were still ten years old. "Marie Leszczyńska, *ma petite*, is the consort of our present king, Louis Quinze, who is known as the '*Bien-Aimé*' or Well-Loved. As we speak he is making improvements to the great palace of Versailles where one day, it is my fervent hope, you shall reign beside his grandson, your future husband, the dauphin." I nodded my head in shame. From now on I would know her name, even if I tied my tongue in knots trying to pronounce it.

My knowledge of geography, or the evident lack of it, was deplorable as well, according to the duc. He asked Maman to explain to me the importance of the 1756 Treaty of Versailles. Aware of my woeful retention of unconnected historical facts, she boiled it down to a broth that would fill a nutshell: The treaty cemented an alliance between Austria and France in which each realm had promised to aid the other in a time of war. As we had once been mortal enemies, this concord was important because it set the stage for my dynastic marriage with the dauphin.

Maman was clearly disappointed in me. It was in the set of her mouth, emphasized by the tiny lines that formed above her lips, and in the disquietude behind her cobalt eyes. Yet then, in an astonishing moment of vulnerability, my mother, the empress of Austria, admitted to the duc de Choiseul—a Frenchman—that she was in some ways responsible for my empty head. She explained that my sisters and I had been raised to present a pretty picture at all times, and never to be messy or untidy (a precept I still seemed incapable of upholding). Appearing in her Presence Chamber where she received visitors, or at meals, properly washed and scrubbed, with our hair combed off our faces, was more important than learning the names of the towns located along the empire's frontier.

Our governesses had been instructed to instill us with courage, self-confidence, piety, and good eating habits. We were taught to be respectful to everyone, including servants, and never to seem haughty or overly familiar—conduct unbecoming an archduchess of Austria. The fortunate Hapsburg daughters would impress people not with our ability to solve mathematical equations or recite the details of some half-forgotten battle, but with our musical talents, our needlework, and our strong devotion to morality.

Such a system was all very well and good, agreed the duc amiably, as Mama refilled his brandy glass with a generous hand. "And no one save yourself wishes to see the archduchess Antonia wed the dauphin more than I do."

A dreadful silence heralded the duc's contemplation of the best way to address the situation. "Your Imperial Majesty, I have hazarded my entire diplomatic career on this union. But Louis is a man of unpredictable temperament and is often led astray by the influences of others. Until His Majesty makes a formal written request for your daughter's hand on behalf of his grandson, the agreement reached between our countries two years ago is too easily broken. Nothing must be done—or not done—that will jeopardize the marriage."

I glanced at Maman, aware that months earlier, she had voiced identical fears. *Why must it be me?* I wondered. *When I am so clearly inadequate to my destiny?* And yet, precisely because it *was* my destiny, I also knew that it was my responsibility to rise to the occasion and embrace it. I had not emerged from Maman's belly to while away my entire life in Vienna, doing good works, dabbling with watercolors, and caressing lapdogs.

The duc smiled at me. "Are you willing, Madame Antonia, to do all that is necessary to prepare you for your future station?"

"Monsieur le duc, what a silly question," I heard myself say. Of course I was willing. Let them change my hair, straighten my teeth, stuff my head with geography and the names of French queens. The future of Austria was in my small, pale hands. I would not fail my family again.

Maman raised an eyebrow and glanced at the duc. "You see? I expected nothing less."

And so, within the month a veritable army of experts began arriving at the Hofburg, prepared to transform me into the dauphine of France.

FIVE

Another Sacrificial Lamb

Pierre Laveran had the largest hands I had ever seen. Even worse, his knuckles sprouted tufts of dark hair. But Maman, who did not have to submit to his sausage-sized fingers probing the recesses of her mouth, was prodigiously impressed by his credentials. After all, Monsieur Laveran had been a pupil of Pierre Fauchard, the most celebrated dentist in France.

On his arrival at the Hofburg one frosty morning in mid-February, Monsieur Laveran was immediately escorted to the breakfast room, where the sunlight was always strong. As usual, the tall windows were open, despite the nip in the air. Maman preferred to keep the rooms cold, insisting that the low temperature prevented her from becoming lethargic; and she could ill afford to fall asleep while there was always so much to accomplish. My brother Joseph would work alongside her, swathed in a fur-lined cloak, while she perused and signed state documents in her morning *négligée*, impervious to the chill.

Monsieur Laveran was inept at concealing his surprise at the room's lack of warmth. No doubt he assumed, as anyone would, that the empress of Austria could afford enough firewood to stoke the elaborate ceramic stove. Little did the dentist know of Maman's penchant for economizing in our family rooms. And she did not alter her system for those she considered tradesmen. I hoped that Monsieur Laveran could still be dexterous with cold fingers.

A footman positioned one of the striped silk chairs in front of the window where the light was the best, and Maman instructed me to sit. When I saw Monsieur unpack his instruments, including horrid metal pliers with pelican-shaped beaks that looked better suited to a carpentry shed, my stomach turned sour and I clutched the padding on the chair's upholstered arms until my knuckles went white. I began to shiver, more from fear than from the temperature in the room.

Maman stood nervously beside the dentist as he studied my teeth with a tiny mirror on a long handle that resembled a lorgnette. His breath smelled heavily of cloves, and his pocket watch ticked so loudly that I found myself enumerating the seconds. "*Eh bien, eh bien,*" he muttered to himself as he poked about my mouth. I'd counted to 132 before he finally pronounced my teeth in need of straightening.

"What will that entail?" Maman asked, her voice tense with trepidation. "And more to the point, how long will it take?"

"*D'abord*—first—I will need to insert an appliance that was developed by my esteemed mentor." He reopened his large black leather case and removed what appeared to be two small gold horseshoes, perforated with tiny holes at regular intervals. "Your Imperial Highness, 'Fauchard's Bandeau' is a crescent-shaped strip of precious metal that is set behind each row of teeth, upper and lower. We will begin today—*immédiatement*—and if all goes well, in three months' time the archduchess will have perfectly straight teeth." He stepped away from me and grinned broadly. His own teeth were not terribly good and my stomach gave another lurch. I recalled that Monsieur Laveran's father had been a celebrated dental surgeon as well; why had he not seen to his own son's smile? "And you, *madame l'archiduchesse,* you must remember to use a brush and tooth powder every morning and night, even when the inside of your mouth resembles a gold mine." He heartily laughed at his own joke.

"Are you ready, my dear?" he asked. How I wished I could shake my head no. But I nodded meekly, and Maman reached out and stroked my hair. A tiny tear formed in the corner of my eye, this time not from fear, but because I could not remember the last time my mother had shown maternal concern. Today of all days, as I faced these exotic instruments of torture, I wanted to be her baby, "the little one," and not a political chess piece. I nervously eyed the numerous bits of gold that Monsieur Laveran had placed upon a linen napkin. Were all of those tiny glittering rings and lengths of wire to be inserted into my mouth?

Apprehensively, I bit my lower lip. The dentist called for brandy. I feared he needed it to steady his nerves. So *I* called for Madame von Brandeiss, and to my surprise, Maman did not object. The reassuring presence of my governess would surely give me the courage to endure the ordeal. But when the countess obliged Monsieur Laveran by tying a damask cloth about my neck so that I would not stain my blue brocade with blood, she became so distraught that the dental process might cause me pain that I had to squeeze *her* hand.

The spirits, it transpired, were for me. After thoroughly washing his immense hands, Monsieur Laveran dipped his forefinger in the brandy and massaged my gums with it, a procedure he repeated several times until I assured him that I could barely feel his fingertip.

"*S'il vous plaît, ouvrez la bouche, ma petite archiduchesse*," he said. I obediently opened my mouth as wide as it would go.

Then, clasping one of the gold loops with an ugly-looking pair of pincers, he placed it around one of my teeth and squeezed with what I was convinced was all his might, pressing the band down into my gum line. Clutching the arms of the chair, I flinched and squirmed, my derrière involuntarily rising off the cushion. I yelped, but the sound was strangled by the presence of his hand inside my mouth. He repeated the process with every single tooth. When he handed me a mirror to appraise my appearance I was startled to see that my mouth resembled a double row of tiny ivory bandboxes, each encircled by a golden ribbon. There was a minuscule lock at the center of each tooth. My mouth felt heavy and numb, and tasted of nails, and I wanted to cry. The brandy had worn off. When the clock struck the hour of one I realized that I had been sitting in the breakfast chair for four hours, with more torture to follow: Monsieur Laveran had yet to insert the horseshoe-shaped bandeaux.

"Now, these will expand the arch made by her teeth so that they no longer push against one another," the dentist explained to Maman and Madame von Brandeiss as he pressed one of the bandeaux against my lower teeth. He took a length of golden wire, and began to thread it through the horseshoe's perforations. The wire was looped around the back of each tooth, leaving the sharp ends sticking out of my mouth until Monsieur Laveran snipped them off and secured them, with a tight twist, to the tiny lock on the golden band encircling the tooth. I never believed that I had thirty-two teeth until I counted every single excruciating twist and snip. The seconds ticked by ominously. I would willingly have been anywhere else but that chair. A *thousand* geography lessons could never have been so painful.

By the time the dentist had completed his work—through

considerable squirming, flinching, and countless silently shed
tears on my part, as well as admonitions from Monsieur Laveran
to keep still or the process would only take longer—the mechanical clock had long struck four. Outside the Hofburg the sky had
become a palette of blue and gold, the final burst of winter sunlight that heralded the violet dusk. As I had missed both luncheon and tea I was ravenous, but could not imagine ever eating
again. My jaw felt bruised from stretching my mouth open all
day. The gold bands dug into my tender gums. The screws on
each tooth punctured the inside of my lips until they began to
bleed. Clutching the mirror I appraised my appearance. "Be
brave, Antonia," my governess murmured. But I did not see the
future dauphine of France; I saw a monster. I tugged at the blood-
ied yellow cloth about my neck, inadvertently tightening the
knot. Yanking it over my head and hurling it to the floor, I ran
from the room and did not stop. When I reached my apartment,
I flung myself upon the canopied bed. Tucking Poupée in the
crook of one arm and Mops beneath the other, I ducked my head
under one of the bolsters and sobbed like an infant.

Although Madame von Brandeiss came to fetch me, I refused
to come down for supper. My mouth was puffed up like a fish's. I
was ugly and I was miserable. All alone, it was easy to pity myself;
had any other princess undergone such physical torment to prepare to wear a foreign crown? Yet by the time my tears had run
their course I was able to convince myself that perhaps it was better to view my predicament like a Christian martyr: Tribulation
could only strengthen the soul.

That evening, a gentle rap on the door drew me out of bed.
"Who is it?" I whispered.

"Me. It's important. Toinette, open the door."

I obeyed. Charlotte stood before me, clutching her white cam-
bric nightdress about her, honey-blond curls spilling out of her
cotton bonnet. She proffered a bowl-shaped glass half filled with

amber liquid. "Drink this," she urged. "It will help numb your pain."

I brought the snifter to my nostrils and inhaled the fruity, slightly astringent aroma: brandy. "But I don't like spirits," I protested.

"Then think of it as medicine," my sister replied.

So I swallowed the brandy in a single searing gulp. But Charlotte still looked unsatisfied. "What?" was all I needed to say before I saw her lip begin to quiver.

"Maman announced something at dinner. I wanted to tell you myself before you heard it from anyone else."

We seated ourselves side by side on my bed as we had when we were younger, swinging our legs and letting our bare feet graze the floor.

My sister clasped one of my hands in hers. Several moments elapsed before she could speak. "I suppose it was inevitable," she said, choking on a sob.

I grabbed her other hand. "What was?" My stomach tumbled over like an acrobat losing his balance on the wire.

"My portrait—the one Monsieur Ducreux is completing. It is being sent to Naples. To the king." Her voice broke. "To Ferdinand the . . . Ferdinand the idiot. It's been settled between Maman and his father, the king of Spain—I am to replace Josepha as his bride."

The room began to spin. "No, it cannot be so! Not you, too!" I threw my arms about Charlotte's neck and pressed my head against her bosom. Without stays she had become soft and round. Although she would not turn sixteen until August, she had grown into a woman. Fertile. And therefore ripe to become a queen.

I searched for an argument against the match. "But you do not even speak his language!"

"There is no need," Charlotte replied dolefully. "Court,

Parliament—like everywhere else, business is conducted in French; it is the common language of diplomacy. And I will have an entourage of good German maids to converse with in our native tongue. Even His Sicilian Majesty does not speak the language of Dante and Petrarch. We have been informed that he knows only the local Neapolitan dialect." She wrinkled her nose as though she smelled week-old fish. "It is the patois spoken by the peasants."

Charlotte apologized to me then, sorry to have teased me in front of the duc de Choiseul on the evening of his arrival at the Hofburg. Despite Maman's kind words about her talents and abilities, Charlotte admitted that she had felt a bit envious of my destiny, astute enough to realize that Monsieur Ducreux had come to Vienna on my account and that painting *her* portrait as well had at first been no more than a subterfuge, intended to deflect attention from the import of my role in Austria's future. Yes, Charlotte acknowledged, someday we would all become queens of somewhere—but I, the baby of the family (except for Maxl, of course), the girl everyone viewed as the silly goose, would eventually preside over the most elegant court in Europe, while her own fate would be far less glorious.

"So now *I* am being dispatched to a noisy backwater in order to shore up Maman's ties with the Spanish Bourbons, just as you will one day bring the support of the French branch of the house to our Hapsburg family tree." Never one to control her temper, my sister's tirade began to gain both volume and speed. "Do you know that when King Ferdinand learned of Josepha's death, the ninny staged a mock funeral procession through his palace in Naples? He dressed one of his footmen as a woman and stippled the man's face and arms with chocolate to mimic the ravages of the pox!" At my aghast expression, Charlotte paused for breath. "Oh, *ma petite*," she sobbed, "you cannot begin to imagine how miserable I will be."

"What sort of monster is this king? How can Maman let you go?" But I already knew the answer. We were expected to hold our heads proudly, roses in full bloom on the stems of our swan-like necks, and submit to whatever destiny Maman arranged for us. But it didn't begin to lessen the pain of parting. I was still grieving over the death of our sister Josepha. And we both knew that once Charlotte reached Naples it was entirely possible, if not probable, that we might never see each other again. "I can't bear to lose *you*, too," I told my sister, clutching her shoulders as if I might keep her there, at the edge of my bed, with the sheer power of my embrace. Oh, if only it were so! "It will be very grim here, after you've gone. And you must write to me every day." I managed a faint laugh. "You must promise to tell me what it is like to be a married woman."

We sat on the bed facing each other with our bare legs tucked beneath us. Charlotte reached over and touched an errant curl that had escaped my nightcap. She twined it about her finger, drawing closer. "I will also confess that I don't envy that lion's cage in your mouth!" she said, endeavoring to inject some levity into the bleakest moment of our lives.

I hunted about for a handkerchief and wiped a wayward tear from the tip of my nose. "And there is so much more to come," I said. "One day you might not recognize me! Now Maman intends to engage two French actors performing at the Burgtheater to teach me proper diction and elocution."

I mimicked what I imagined I might sound like after the players finished with me, enunciating every syllable and elongating each vowel with comical precision. "*Bon-joooour, Vo-tre Maaa-jes-téeeeee; je suuuuuuiiiis l'ar-chiiii-duuuuu-chesse Maria Antonia d'Au-triiiiiche.*"

I saw that my silliness cheered Charlotte, so I continued to regale her with our mother's elaborate system for turning an ill-educated caterpillar named Maria Antonia of Austria into a dazzling butterfly. *Un papillon*. "Monsieur Noverre, the great ballet master, has been invited to forsake the duke of Württemburg's court at Stuttgart and come to Vienna to improve my dancing. Not only that, the sister of the duc de Choiseul is dispatching her own *friseur* to alter my hairline somehow. At least you," I said to Charlotte, squeezing her hand, "have been judged perfection."

"Perfection for an ugly and indolent idiot who entertains ambassadors in the commode," Charlotte replied bitterly. "A *hideous and stupid* indolent idiot." A ponderous sigh escaped her lips. "Oh, *meine kleine Schwester*—my dear little sister—if I cannot find happiness in marriage, I hope at the least to learn that your union with the dauphin of France will be filled with radiant joy and many, many babies."

I nodded vehemently. "I love babies."

She glanced at my favorite doll. "Then may your rooms be filled with the joyous babble of real ones." Charlotte cradled Poupée in her arms. "Her face is dirty," she observed, then licked her finger before using it to remove a black smudge from the poppet's wooden cheek, a gesture Madame von Brandeiss had employed on my own face with a handkerchief a hundred times a year. Charlotte straightened the doll's yellow dress and fluffed her white fichu and cap.

I gazed lovingly at Poupée as if she were the child I would someday hold and coddle, whose every gurgle would send me into raptures. "I want sixteen of them. Just like Maman had."

My sister blushed. "Me too. Sixteen. So I have many others to love instead of my husband. And every one of them will be fat, healthy, and boisterous. With big pink cheeks and chubby limbs."

From that minute, and for the next few weeks until Charlotte's proxy wedding on the seventh of April, the pair of us treasured every moment we were able to share. Monsieur Ducreux had yet to complete my sister's portrait, which would be sent to

Naples in advance of her scheduled arrival there on the twelfth of May. Meanwhile, I had to endure the constant discomfort of the bandeaux and the wires that encircled my teeth like a golden fence; there was no thought of the painter commencing his portrait of me until the braces were removed. Once a week, Monsieur Laveran would inspect my progress, often tightening the tiny screws that held the wires until I was sure I felt my teeth shift, despite his repeated assurances that the process was not nearly as immediate as I imagined it.

While the plans for Charlotte's wedding proceeded with undue speed I was being put through my paces like one of the white stallions at the Spanish Riding School. One morning after breakfast we were joined by a fragile, plain-looking woman in a deep blue gown whose powdered hair set off an equally chalky complexion, relieved only by a pair of narrow, dark brows. Her colorless face also appeared barren of any humor.

Maman made the introduction. "Antonia, this is the Countess von Lerchenfeld. She will be superintending your studies from now on."

What? My mother might just as well have placed her hands about my narrow waist and squeezed all the air out of me. The past several weeks had brought me nothing but sorrow. First I discovered that I would lose my precious Charlotte to a world over the mountains and a man-child not fit to reign over a stable; and now my beloved governess was being replaced—the one constant I had counted on. "I don't understand, Maman." My eyes filled with tears, and I fought to blink them back. Maman had begun to chide me for childish displays of emotion that, on the brink of womanhood, she deemed me too old to indulge. In truth, Maman disdained excessive sentiment at any age.

Stubbornly, I stood my ground. "Madame von Brandeiss was so kind." I wanted to add, "I love her," but I didn't dare.

"Indeed," said Maman, ignoring my trembling lip. "She is kind. And her kindness, as well as her general deficiency in the subjects of history, science, and the classics are, I would hazard, two of the reasons your head remains so empty at the age of twelve. You will not find the Countess von Lerchenfeld quite so lenient." Her expression softened. "Nor will you find her an ogre if you concentrate on your lessons. I have instructed the countess to drill you every day in French, history, geography, and penmanship. Your studies with her will commence in the Rosenzimmer after Mass this morning."

We had been raised to acknowledge that Maman's word was incontestable. Madame von Lerchenfeld, with her outmoded starched cap that crowned an equally inflexible demeanor, had spent the past two months "finishing" Charlotte, in preparation for her role as queen of Naples. Prior to that she had been the Mistress of the Robes for our older sisters. Charlotte assured me that the new governess was no ogre, but she was no Countess von Brandeiss either. And if Charlotte had survived the woman, I could do no less, or I would never hear the end of it from my sister.

My first tutorial with the countess was unspeakably dull, a relentless litany of names, dates, and figures, few of which would remain in my head for more than a moment or two. By the end of the first half hour I found myself pacing about the room, tracing the patterns in the inlaid floor with the toe of my slipper, picking at the lint on the red velvet upholstery, and wishing that my new governess had a livelier disposition, while I was certain that she was wishing *me* to be considerably less exuberant and more attentive. More like Charlotte, perhaps. But try as I might—and I was truly making every effort to concentrate—I cannot learn when my mind is not entertained.

When the wearied countess decided that we had studied enough for one day, my relief was surely obvious. Lerchenfeld's frown illustrated her disapproval. The following afternoon I resolved to do better, but when my eyes began to glaze over during her recitation of the battles we fought during the Seven Years' War, I changed the subject by asking her where she was born.

"Bavaria," the countess responded, startled by my question.

"Do you ever miss it?"

Her eyes misted over, a reaction that surprised me. "It was a very charming place to grow up," she told me. I believe it was the first time I had heard her speak of anything with a degree of sentiment. I suppose a human heart pulsed within her humorless husk of a body after all.

I rested my chin in my hands and gazed at her. "Please tell me about it," I said. In the double blink of an eye, my question was no longer the diverting stratagem I had intended; now I was genuinely intrigued by whatever it was that had so touched my new tutor. "I want to know everything about Bavaria."

"There are many beautiful forests and the air is fresh and sweet..." she began, followed by several hazily romantic reminiscences of her birthplace. Before we knew it, the countess was glancing at the elaborate mechanical clock near the wall. "My goodness, the time!" she exclaimed. "Well, we will have to finish up with the Battle of Lobositz tomorrow."

I did not wish the Countess von Lerchenfeld to feel that we had frittered away another afternoon of instruction, so the next day I pleased her with my ability to locate Bavaria on a map, as well as the Schwarzwald, the Black Forest, recalling that she had proudly boasted of their clock-making and their cherry tortes. Perhaps, I suggested slyly, if I were to *taste* one of these confections, I might always remember our lesson on Bavaria!

The weeks flew by—which meant that my three months of purgatory in Fauchard's Bandeaux would soon end; but it also signified the imminence of Charlotte's marriage to King Ferdinand of

Naples. Outside the Hofburg, the frost was all but gone and tiny shoots of grass had begun to peek out from the cracks between the paving stones. Birdsong awakened me, and the afternoon light didn't wane quite so soon. For the first time in my life I dreaded the coming of spring.

On the seventh of April, as the trees were beginning to bud, my beloved Charlotte, clad in cloth of gold with a tissue overlay of white organza, her bodice studded with precious gems, and her hair threaded with seed pearls and dressed high off her forehead, was united by proxy with the king of the Two Sicilies at the Church of the Augustine Friars in Vienna. The elegance and majesty of Charlotte's bridal wardrobe could not have made a more incongruous contrast to the torment in her soul.

Our brother Ferdinand, who was only a year older than me, knelt beside Charlotte at the altar, representing his Neapolitan namesake. For one who was prone to boyish pranks, he took his responsibility quite seriously. My sister kept a glum but dignified gaze on the bishop during the entire wedding Mass. Earlier that morning Charlotte had warned me that she dared not glance in my direction for fear she would dissolve into tears. But she was made of sterner stuff than I, and I would do well to gain a bit of her mettle. With an impressive amount of confidence and maturity for a girl of fifteen, she was already determined to make the most of her destiny *in spite* of her new husband. That Ferdinand of Naples was a weak and indifferent sovereign was, to my clever sister, an asset she intended to turn to her advantage. She had heard he cared for nothing but hunting. "*Wunderbar!*" she'd told me. "*Magnifique!* While *he* amuses himself slaughtering innocent beasts, *I* shall consult the ministers and become the true ruler of the Two Sicilies. A king in petticoats and panniers."

Nevertheless, the mood at her wedding reception—a grand meal of more than a dozen courses served in the ornately mirrored Spigelsaal where we always dined on state occasions—was decidedly more funereal than celebratory, for once the toasts were over and the crystal goblets were drained, after the ices and cakes were consumed and the sticky dishes cleared away by a fastidious army of liveried servants, Charlotte would be bidding farewell to her family and her homeland. With every passing minute I grew more anxious, my heart beating faster, my stomach churning, aware that each second that had passed would never come again. By dusk, Charlotte's presence would be no more than a memory that would begin to fade by the following morning; an echo of slippered footfalls, the imprint of her head on the bolster.

Above the courtyard of the Hofburg, the sky was mottled with patches of gray, threatening thunder. Behind three teams of matched bays, the enormous berline that would convey Charlotte out of Vienna, past Laxenburg just to the south, and over the Dolomites into Italy stood at the ready. To Maman this luxuriously appointed black and green carriage, its hunter green wheels embellished with pure gold, was an emblem of imperial splendor. The bride and I saw a sarcophagus on wheels.

All of us—Maman, Joseph, Christina, Elisabeth, Amalia, Leopold, Ferdinand, Maxl, and I—were gathered outside to say good-bye. Charlotte's two ladies-in-waiting, her official chaperones, were already seated inside the carriage, their enormous skirts leaving little room for the reluctant bride. The horses, caparisoned and plumed in the Hapsburg colors of yellow and black, stamped impatiently as the coachman (indifferent to our sorrow as long as his purse was full) puffed away on his long-stemmed clay pipe. Charlotte's retinue of German maids would follow, their departure unheralded by anyone of note.

Each of us embraced Charlotte, as of the past few hours the queen of the Two Sicilies. When it was my turn, we held each other so tightly that neither of us could breathe with ease. So close were our torsos that I could feel my heart beating against the boning of her bodice. I twined one of her lightly powdered curls about my fingers in a gesture of girlish affection. "Do you feel any different, now that you are a queen?" I murmured.

Charlotte pulled away, just far enough to cup my face in her hands. "Just a little," she admitted, adding with a wicked smile, "Now that I am a queen, I can contradict Maman if I wish!"

We shared a chuckle, choking up as we realized that it would be the last time we would ever be two little daughters of Austria, a pair of rosy cherries on a single stem.

"*Mein Gott*, I miss you already," I whispered in her ear. A teardrop snaked its way down the side of my nose.

"Maman is watching us," Charlotte said softly. It was almost an apology.

"Antonia, *ça suffit*," our mother said. "That's enough. Farewells are a part of life."

Charlotte and I separated slowly, reluctantly, until only our gloved fingertips touched, lingering for one moment more as we pressed them together.

"Antonia. Enough."

"*Oui*, Maman." I stepped away from my sister, treading backwards, almost deferentially, afraid to meet Charlotte's eyes again for fear of erupting into sobs.

With great formality, Maman kissed Charlotte on both cheeks. "Godspeed, my daughter. Bring honor to the House of Hapsburg with your piety, your good sense, and most of all, your fertility."

My sister's eyes were moist. But when Charlotte was helped up the traveling steps and handed into the coach, the fullness of her emotions got the better of her. My heart was breaking as I stood on the cobbles, wobbling in my court heels. I lifted Mops into my arms and waved at her with his paw; his tawny coat soon grew wet with my tears.

A crack of the coachman's leather whip spurred the horses into action and the carriage clattered out of the courtyard, swaying side to side. But just before it reached the gate, the driver pulled up the teams and brought the berline to an abrupt halt. The door flew open. A footman scrambled to unfold the traveling steps as Charlotte vaulted past him onto the paving stones, practically losing her shoes. "Toinette!" she cried. Hitching up her heavy skirts, yards of fabric trailing behind her, she ran straight toward me as though her life depended on it. I handed Mops to Maxl and opened my arms to receive her. For several moments we remained in a fast embrace, motionless but for two pairs of gently heaving shoulders.

"I have not yet met my husband, and already I am unhappily married," Charlotte murmured, her words intended for my ears alone. "I cannot conceal my fear that your destiny will be the same as mine." She kissed me on the mouth. Her lips were soft and tasted of the salt from her tears. Charlotte drew back a few inches and regarded my own doleful face. "*Sois courageuse,* Toinette. Be brave." Her words were as much a reassurance to me as an effort to find that resolve within herself.

Charlotte turned and without another word walked back to the berline as if she were about to mount a scaffold—head raised, chin defiantly high. Her final, cathartic burst of emotion over, she was now a proud martyr to her fate. The courtyard was eerily silent. We watched as the footman handed her into the carriage once again, then heard the soft *thump* of the closing door, the click of the turning lock, and the coachman's command to "Drive on!" As Charlotte rode away from Vienna forever, I saw her face pressed to the glass, trying to capture one last glimpse of home. I would not see her again.

SIX

Becoming

Following Charlotte's departure, Maman declared the Rosenzimmer a permanent classroom, or perhaps more accurately a
laboratory, where with a good deal of alchemy an Austrian archduchess would be transformed into the French dauphine. The
enormous mechanical clock sitting regally in its four-postered
gilded case kept track of the time by striking once every quarter
hour and on the hour itself, when miniature likenesses of my parents emerged and danced a minuet with each other to the accom-
paniment of a music box embedded within the clock. It made me
feel closer to Papa to take my lessons in the Rosenzimmer and I
believe Maman, too, felt as though he was watching over my
progress. I often thought that she had spent her entire store of
sentiment on my father, and consequently had none to spare for
their offspring. With her singular combination of devotion and
precision, she even knew exactly how long she had been married

to Francis of Lorraine, having recorded the exact moment of
Papa's death in her prayer book.

> Emperor Francis I, my husband, died on the evening of the
> 18th of August in the year seventeen hundred sixty-five at
> half past nine o'clock. He lived 680 months, 2,598 weeks,
> 20,778 days, or 496,992 hours. Our happy marriage lasted
> twenty-nine years, six months, and six days, 1,540 weeks,
> 10,781 days, or 258,744 hours.

I liked to imagine that my marriage to the dauphin—should
it ever finally happen—would prove just as felicitous. And if God
should choose to take him before me, I hoped, too, that I would
miss him as much.

Among the thousands of rooms that lay within the vast Hofburg, the Rosenzimmer was one of my favorites—although I had
yet to see even a fraction of them because our family affairs were
conducted where we resided, in the Leopoldine wing, named for
Maman's grandfather. The Rosenzimmer derived its name from
the decorative oil paintings above each of the doorways—
glorious still-lifes of roses, in every size and hue imaginable.
When I was younger I tried to convince my sisters that the room
itself smelled of roses. It was years before I discovered that the
scent that clung to the crimson upholstery, the heavy velvet
drapes, and even the oils, was our mother's perfume.

It was the perfect location for my lessons, not merely for the
clock, but because the chamber was capacious enough to accom-
modate the musicians required to accompany my lessons with the
famous ballet master Monsieur Noverre. The room's highly polished parquet also provided the perfect surface on which to learn
the court dances that were popular at Versailles.

The choreographer's arrival in Vienna offered me a welcome

respite from the tedious hours I'd spent during the past several evenings at Maman's elbow, learning how to play the card games that were all the rage in France. I enjoyed piquet to some extent, and found Pope Joan to be an amusing diversion; however, there was one game that truly bored me to distraction. A board game similar to Lotto where one placed bets on the number the "banker" would draw from a bag, it was called cavagnole; and it was, unluckily for me, the most popular pastime at the French court. I could only hope that by the time I was married to the dauphin, they would have discovered something more exciting to occupy their evenings. Couldn't I simply practice being a good hostess instead? Maman, who was perfectly aware that I could never sit still for more than two minutes together, was beside herself with anxiety. It was imperative that I master the rules of cavagnole, and play round after round with avidity and skill. My sighs were heavy and unsubtle. With an alacrity that defied description I looked forward to my dancing instruction.

I had conjured the image of a dainty gentleman with a nasal voice and mincing gait, who wore far too much hair pomade and scent. In my imagination, Monsieur Noverre was as slender and graceful as a water reed and never left his apartment without the full maquillage worn by the courtiers at Versailles: a veneer of white lead cream meticulously applied over his entire face, a bit of kohl rimming the eyes, a bright circle of rouge on the apple of each cheek, and a dab of it at the center of his lips to form a cupid's bow.

But Monsieur Noverre was not at all what I expected. In the flesh he seemed far more English, or even German, than French; in fact, he didn't look like a ballet master at all. I struggled to mask my embarrassed relief at finding him to be a genial gentleman with a sturdy figure, a pointed nose, and powdered hair tied in a neat queue, his intelligent face barren of all cosmetics, and his person devoid of any cloying fragrance. No wonder Maman was so pleased with him. Our court was less formal than France when it came to matters of dress, except on state occasions. Believing that one's appearance was more attractive as God made it, my mother disdained heavy makeup and rarely even wore rouge. If we wanted our color to be high and to convey the impression of robust health, she had taught us to pinch our cheeks until they stung. And with the exception of holidays, gala days, and formal presentations, we went about attired as any other aristocratic family.

Although Monsieur Noverre had traveled the world and spoke several languages, Maman had instructed him to address me in French in order to improve my proficiency. According to her directives, our dancing lessons would always begin with the minuet because I was already familiar with the intricate steps and was confident in my footwork. Practicing a dance I had mastered as a child would give me the courage to tackle the quadrille and the gavotte.

I soon came to admire Monsieur Noverre and his amusing habit of keeping time by tapping his high heel against the floor and conducting the chamber musicians with the handle of his lorgnette as I danced from one end of the Rosenzimmer to the other. It was the only element of my comprehensive education in which I demonstrated a considerable aptitude, yet Monsieur Noverre still found room for improvement. Natural grace was not enough. Technique was imperative. The future queen of France would have to be *une danseuse nonpareille*—without equal in the entire kingdom. Certainly I would be complimented in public as the best dancer in France, but Monsieur Noverre was preparing me to garner those accolades on merit. It was up to him to make sure that there would be no cause for derision behind my back.

The ballet master maintained an incessant chatter as I practiced my steps. "And, *oui*, the head is held just so. *Parfait!*" he would exclaim. "But your carriage, your deportment, is up-up-up—shoulders down and back, chin up, very graceful, *oui*? Perfect. *Oup! Non-non-non*, don't forget the *port de bras*—the arms rounded, more grace, *oui*? No pointing the elbows; you do not wish to injure someone. Everything must be curved, from the tilt of the head to the way you hold your wrist." Monsieur Noverre crossed the floor to partner me. "And when you promenade forward, eyes face front with the shoulders down and the chest open, as if to show off your beautiful jewels. Imagine that you are wearing a gorgeous diamond necklace and you wish it to catch the light as you move. *Oui—c'est ça*—that's it! *Parfait! Très charmante.*"

Mastering the quadrille was much more difficult because there were so many variations on the dance for four couples. An archduchess of Austria could not dance with the servants, so my siblings were pressed into service as I was drilled in my maneuvers like an infantryman. My head became so stuffed with the names of dance steps that at night I would dream of the Chaîne des Fleurs, the Moulinet, the Passé-Passé, the Boulangère, and the Corbeille. The Basket, the Baker, the Reel, the Daisy Chain— I would awaken with a start, my heart beating wildly and my underarms moist with perspiration, having dreamt that I executed the Moulinet in the middle of a *bal à Versailles* when everyone else was doing the Boulangère.

The quadrille, the gavotte, and the minuet were performed at every European court, although at Versailles, particular attention was given to their execution. But I soon learned that at the court of Louis XV the manner in which one *walked* was as important as the way one danced. As a matter of etiquette, it was absolutely vital that I master a way of moving from room to room known as the "Versailles Glide," which had been performed since the time of the Sun King. Not only was I expected to perfect this unique skill, but since the death on June 24 of Queen Marie Leszczyńska, I, as dauphine, would have the rank of first woman in France unless Louis remarried. Consequently, as with my dancing, I would naturally wish to ensure that *my* glide exceeded that of all the other ladies at court in grace and beauty.

Only *women* glided, but in order to properly instruct me, the dancing master would have to don the aptly named *grand panier*—a large basket—as well. These ridiculously wide underpinnings, very similar to the farthingales worn by women of a bygone era, such as England's Queen Elizabeth, were long out of fashion in Vienna; but at Versailles, Monsieur Noverre assured me, the women still wore *les grands paniers* when full court dress was required. And so, with all due haste, a team of servants was dispatched to the royal wardrobe to locate two of the outmoded cages.

Meanwhile, Monsieur Noverre had somehow managed to locate a pull toy—a yoked team of little wooden horses that had once belonged to Maxl, but had long ago been given to the grandson of Frau Schwab, the little hunchbacked woman who emptied the ashes from our stoves. "*Regardez les chevaux, madame l'archiduchesse.* Watch the horses," said the ballet master. He grasped the string between his thumb and forefinger and drew the toy across the floor. "What do you notice about them?" he asked me.

I wasn't sure what I was supposed to see. "What *should* I notice?"

"How the horses move."

"But they don't," I insisted. "They're on wheels."

"Aha!" Monsieur Noverre triumphantly brandished his lorgnette. "*Exactement!*" He approached me, dragging the toy behind him. "And if *you* perform the Versailles Glide properly, you, too, will appear to be on wheels."

"Like this?" With tremendous enthusiasm I began to execute little *chasées* about the room. I resembled horses all right, but not the ones on the string. The effect I produced was far more gallop than glide. And I nearly kicked off my shoes. The backless slippers with their two-inch court heel, or—as it was known at Versailles, the "Louis" heel—were difficult enough to keep on one's feet without the added challenge of gliding in them as if they were the runners of a sledge.

"Not quite." The ballet master chuckled, amused at my energetic effort. "Would you like me to demonstrate, or would *madame l'archiduchesse* prefer to figure it out on her own?"

Duly chastened, I admitted that perhaps I might learn the movement more quickly if I paid attention to his lesson rather than endeavoring to guess, through trial and error, how to perform the proper steps.

Monsieur Noverre stood before me, quite naturally, with his legs together "*en parallel*," and bent his knees ever so slightly. Although his torso was completely erect, as if he had been laced into a corset with a long busk down the center, he pitched forward just a bit and rose up to a *demi-pointe* so that his weight was on the balls of his feet.

"*Maintenant, regardez-moi*—now watch me," he said, and began to shuffle forward in tiny, graceful steps, moving very quickly—an unbroken series of infinitesimal *pas de bourrées*. "You will notice, Madame Antonia, that my heels remain slightly raised, hovering just above the floor, while the rest of my foot never leaves the ground." It was the most comical movement I had ever seen.

I endeavored to imitate his stance, but when I glanced in the mirror, I looked a lot more like Königen, our spaniel bitch, right after she'd done her business and was trying to avoid soiling her haunches.

"Almost," said Monsieur Noverre diplomatically. He demonstrated the proper position again. "One does not squat, although one always keeps the knees bent and soft. Imagine that there are tiny wheels on the soles of your slippers. Have you ever seen a magician perform an illusion?" he asked me, and before I could reply, added, "You think you are seeing one thing, but your eyes are deceiving you. That is the Versailles Glide. No single step should be discernable. In fact, it should not look like steps at all. The woman must seem to *float* an inch or two in the air. And when it is done correctly, the beholder can only exclaim, 'It is surely done by magic!' "

While the glide *looked* relatively simple, it was not at all easy to perform with any degree of grace. In fact it was rather fatiguing, and after only a few minutes my legs were aching from trying to balance on the balls of my feet while struggling to keep my heels from touching the parquet. To my astonishment I discovered that I could not take the gliding part for granted. I stumbled when I shuffled with my right foot and the sole of my slipper momentarily stuck to the floor, causing me to lose my balance.

"You mustn't expect to master the movement in a single day," Monsieur Noverre said encouragingly. "It takes some courtiers years to perfect it."

"But I don't have years," I protested. After righting myself, I continued to practice the Versailles Glide until I began to feel more confident and my footwork became smoother. I could only imagine that with the necessary accoutrements in addition to the underpinnings—including an enormously wide skirt with a weighted hem that would increase the illusion of gliding and would mask my feet from view—it wouldn't look quite so silly.

I was mistaken.

The *grands paniers* finally arrived and I retired to an anteroom where Liesl, one of my maidservants, helped me dress. But first I had to remove my bodice and overskirt so that she could fasten the cumbersome cages about my waist—"hen baskets," we sometimes called them because they resembled the ones that peasant women would balance on their hips when they went to market. After Liesl tied the cotton tapes, the lower half of my body claimed an expanse of more than six feet; I was far wider than I was tall! Getting through a doorway would require a dainty side-step; descending, or clambering into, a carriage would be a feat of uncommon dexterity, even though the hoops were made to collapse. I imagined that two hundred years earlier, when queens had dwarves to entertain them the way we played nowadays with our lapdogs, the little people might have hidden beneath the panniers and shocked everyone by emerging and beginning to juggle or tumble when no one expected it—like during Mass!

But these underpinnings, while ungainly, were relatively weightless; and without the voluminous court dresses worn over them, it would be impossible for me to fully master the walk.

After an exhaustive search, Maman's old *robes de cour* were found, carefully preserved in paper tissue. She had been slender, like me, when they were in fashion at the Hapsburg court. I ran my fingers lovingly over her blue Lyon silk with gold lace, and then over the other gown—a still-vibrant shade of yellow moiré festooned with violet ruching and bouquets of lilac silk rosettes. Each had a long train that began at the shoulder. The dresses smelled of camphor and rosewater, a faint lingering aroma of my mother's perfume. She hadn't worn that scent since Papa died. I buried my nose in one of the bodices and thought of him, but drew my face away when a tear came to my eye so that I would not stain the silk.

I chose the celestial blue *robe de cour* and burst out laughing after Monsieur Noverre removed his frock coat and embroidered waistcoat and asked Liesl to help him lace the yellow court dress over his black silk breeches and full-sleeved chemise.

The beauty of the Versailles Glide, Monsieur Noverre reminded me, lay in perfecting the illusion that one could carry several pounds of opulently embellished fabric on one's frame and yet appear to be moving forward without one's feet touching the ground.

"My dear archduchess, this is what it should look like when you are wearing the appropriate garments." Monsieur Noverre glided across the polished floor with effortless grace. The gentle rustling of his, or rather Maman's, skirts masked the sound as he shuffled across the Rosenzimmer on the balls of his feet.

"Now, Madame Antonia, you try it. Keep your knees bent ever so slightly; the position will be undetectable beneath the *grands paniers*. The entire movement is created from the knee down."

He peered at me through his lorgnette with a practiced and critical eye. After a minute or so I began to feel like I was sailing across the parquet. "I'm flying!" I exclaimed as I executed a series of swirls about the Rosenzimmer.

"Now, follow me," Monsieur Noverre instructed. Because our formal trains trailed behind us for several feet, yards of silk separated us. "If the Versailles Glide is properly performed, you will not be able to trod upon or trample my court train, even accidentally."

It was my first lesson. But it would take hours of practice day after day until my feet no longer felt sore after only a few minutes, until I could traverse the vast halls, corridors, and chambers of the Hofburg while effortlessly sustaining the walk. I kept thinking about Maxl's little wooden horses, pretending that I had a mile-long satin ribbon about my waist while some unseen hand was pulling me forward. How much easier it would have been if my slippers had wheels! Poor Liesl massaged my calloused feet every evening after I soaked them in a bucket of bath salts. Were the women of Versailles in as much discomfort? And would I ever become used to their absurd, doll-like shuffle, gliding through the French court in my vast *grands paniers* as though I had never moved any other way in my life? What was wrong with a good German stride?

SEVEN

"A Particularly Egregious Faux Pas"

It would not be sufficient to perfect my skills in dance and movement; my tongue would have to become as agile as my toes. By the time I arrived in France—if I was ever to arrive at all—their language must come as willingly and mellifluously to my lips as my native German. With that in mind, Maman doubled her efforts, hiring *two* experts to train me. It was the only misstep she would make, but it was a grave one.

Although Maman spoke French fluently, she had never lost her German accent. Acknowledging that this was perhaps the one situation where her own talents and experience could not guide me, she had become determined to engage a French elocution instructor to tutor me in the correct pronunciation of the language. Evidently, as it was taking Louis an inordinate length of time to enter his formal request for my hand on behalf of his grandson, my mother had grown increasingly anxious—particularly after the duc de Choiseul admitted to her that there were still many at Versailles who spoke against the match. I had much to prove. Or *im*prove, as things stood.

Would it really happen? I wondered. And who were these un-named naysayers? But I had enough worries closer at hand. Deep inside my heart the fear grew stronger by the day that I would disappoint Maman, and, by extension, the Hapsburg dynasty and the entire Austrian empire.

I would have to endure the dental tortures of "Fauchard's Bandeaux" for another few weeks, but perhaps Maman had convinced herself that if I could speak French properly with all that metal in my mouth, I should shortly achieve linguistic perfection without it. Soon after Charlotte's departure a pair of actors from the Comédie-Française in Paris arrived at the Hofburg. Monsieur Sainville and Monsieur Aufresne were living at the time in Vienna where they were performing in a romantic comedy by Marivaux at the Burgtheater.

Chaperoned by the Countess von Lerchenfeld, I awaited their first visit in the Rosenzimmer. My new governess had suggested I practice my hostessing skills in front of the actors. After all, when I became dauphine I would be expected to hold court in my apartments every morning and to preside over card and gaming parties—oh, the dreaded cavagnole!—nearly every night. Consequently it was important to learn how to lead the conversation, to listen graciously—or at least appear to do so—and to make sure that my audience was always contented and entertained. I had ordered coffee with cream and cinnamon and was prepared to offer it in my very own service of ruby-colored Meissen ware embellished with a rose motif. A dish of marzipan rested on a rosewood half-table. It had taken more than one day of practice to be able to pour the coffee without the tips of my lacy *engageantes* dipping into the porcelain cups.

At first I thought the players had arrived in costume because their wide-cuffed velvet coats and full, curly wigs—in the style worn by my grandpapa, Charles VI—were so long out of fashion.

The buttons of Monsieur Aufresne's waistcoat, an affair that grazed his knees, were straining to contain his girth. In contrast, Monsieur Sainville was as slender as his colleague was portly, his uncommon height echoed by his beribboned walking stick. Their faces were highly rouged, embellished with patches here and there (on Aufresne's left cheek and above Sainville's right lip) to cover telltale pockmarks. Unfortunately, their heavy makeup, calculated to produce the illusion of youth, had the opposite of its intended effect, for the white lead foundation had settled into the fine wrinkles of their faces.

Monsieur Aufresne made a leg, such as courtiers did in the time of Louis XIV of France, thrusting out his well-turned calf. His hose—once white, I presumed—were a dingy dove-colored shade. Doffing his feathered hat with such a theatrical flourish that the plume swept along the parquet, he declaimed, "*Bonjour*, little madame," producing the greeting from deep within his barrel-shaped chest.

"*Bonjour*," echoed Monsieur Sainville, as he greeted me with the same outmoded court bow. His voice was considerably higher than Monsieur Aufresne's. His enormous hat—amber-colored velvet, accented with a vibrant yellow plume—had seen better days.

I smiled at the pair of players, forgetting that I had a mouth full of gold. I must have looked quite fearsome. My hand flew to my cheek to hide a blush. "*Bonjour, messieurs. Je suis enchantée de faire votre connaissance,*" I said, and immediately noticed that the men exchanged glances. Was my accent dreadful? Passable? Did my dental bandeaux frighten them? Although they were merely actors, I wished to make a charming first impression.

I gestured toward the armchairs and invited the gentlemen to partake of some coffee with cinnamon. I suppose we all had our parts to play, because they fell over themselves to praise my gown, my features, and even my carriage as I glided over to the table to offer them a nugget of marzipan. Monsieur Sainville made a point of mentioning that he had some familiarity with the manners of the nobility, as he had formerly been the Vicomte Clairval de Passy. I was at pains to imagine how a vicomte could tumble so precipitously down the social ladder, until his companion explained that the *ci-devant* nobleman, after falling in love with a celebrated actress, had adopted her profession so that they might never endure a separation. I had never heard such a remarkable—or romantic—story.

Although they seemed to take themselves quite seriously, I found messieurs Sainville and Aufresne to be quite a comical pair. I studied their faces as they drank their coffee, noticing how tiny the porcelain cup looked in Monsieur Aufresne's large, expressive hands. Suddenly I realized that the players reminded me of Cervantes's knight errant Don Quixote, and his squire, Sancho Panza. The Countess von Brandeiss had suggested that I read the novel in its German translation, but it was far too long and ponderous to hold my attention.

In order to discern the strengths and weaknesses of my speech, the actors asked me to converse with them. I glanced over at Madame von Lerchenfeld and she nodded her head, giving me her tacit permission to talk to the players as though they were my social equals. The countess surreptitiously stiffened her spine, a reminder to me to sit up straight. One of my shoulders is a bit higher than the other; when I become inattentive to my posture my siblings tease me for resembling the misshapen Frau Schwab. Maman had somehow become certain that the less forgiving corsets worn by the women of Versailles would disguise my physical flaw.

In the lucky absence of such an instrument of torture, I endeavored to emulate the result, sitting as stiff as a poker as I politely inquired of the players whether they were enjoying the fine weather. Not a cloud in the sky, I added, in my cautious French. Had they ever seen it so blue? After a few moments, I realized that I had been posing numerous innocuous questions and neither of these painted gentlemen had said a word. Was my accent so unintelligible that they could not make head or tail of my words? "I don't understand—why do you not reply?" I asked them. *Je ne comprends pas.* Of what use is a conversation when one party is doing all the talking?"

"We are *listening* to you, madame archduchess," said the portly one, Monsieur Aufresne.

"Oh." Suddenly I was too embarrassed to continue. "Another morsel of marzipan?" I exclaimed, reaching for the dish. The men declined the almond paste, but I couldn't resist. I nibbled the peach-shaped candy as I thought of something else to say. I feared I was not being a good hostess or a particularly exemplary pupil. It was difficult to conduct a dialogue in a foreign tongue with complete strangers who were there to assess me, and who would no doubt report their impressions to Maman.

"How do you find Vienna?" I finally asked, fairly confident that I had constructed the French sentence correctly. *Aha!* I had found a topic on which one could expound indefinitely.

"Vienna is a very beautiful city, madame," Monsieur Aufresne replied. "My wife and children are quite happy here as well." Patting his prodigious belly he added, "And the food is excellent. I have become quite partial to your schnitzel." He brought his fingers to his lips and kissed them with a loud smack.

"With potato dumplings?" I asked excitedly. "You have good taste indeed, Monsieur Aufresne, for that is my favorite meal in the world." He was the first rotund Frenchman I had seen. I imagined his family all shaped the same way—pink cheeked and round, like the nesting dolls the Empress of all the Russias had sent to Maman, or a fat Viennese burgomeister and his brood.

Another painful silence descended.

"Perhaps you would like to recite something for us," Monsieur Sainville suggested. From the deep pocket of his embroidered coat he drew a small book bound in red calfskin, its pages yellowed. "This is a copy of the play we are performing at the Burgtheater. *La Femme Fidèle*," he said. "*The Faithful Wife*."

"*Parfait!*" exclaimed Monsieur Aufresne. He snatched the little volume from his colleague's hands and placed it in mine, exclaiming in his rumbling voice, "You will kindly turn to the passage on page twenty-three, and read Céline's speech—she is the faithful wife."

This would be a treat; I loved the theatre. I was a natural mimic, and if I had not been born an archduchess, perhaps I might have dabbled in it. I was intrigued by the idea of playing at being a shepherdess without the fuss of farm animals, or pretending to be a carefree maidservant without having to empty a chamber pot. Every day a new play and a different costume. What fun!

I quickly glanced at some of the other scenes before returning to the speech that Monsieur Aufresne had assigned me. I dared not say so, but had I been asked to select a passage on my own, I would have preferred to read the role of Céline's saucy maid, Florette, who was so much cleverer and more interesting.

Evidently Monsieur Sainville thought so, too, because he read Florette's part in the scene with Céline, and it was all I could do not to laugh at his fluted tones and the way he fluttered and flounced about the Rosenzimmer.

He judged my interpretation of the faithful wife to be "*absolument charmante*—utterly charming." But they had not come to the Hofburg to teach me to become an actress. My accent was, "*malheureusement*, madame," regrettably deplorable. And that would never do for the future dauphine of France.

For the next two hours I sat opposite the pair of players and did nothing but mimic funny French vowel sounds—*eu, ou, eau, oou*—until my lips were tired. We then tackled consonants until the top of my mouth and the back of my throat felt raw from voicing so many R's—though they were really nothing to producing the German *ch* sound, as in *ach*. Despite my native partiality to my mother tongue, I was discovering that French was a profoundly beautiful language when properly pronounced.

The actors were pleased with my swift progress and assigned me a number of sentences to practice; a second lesson was arranged. Some days later, I stood in the center of the Rosenzimmer repeating the phrases they had given me to perfect.

The players' suits, rather threadbare velvet affairs, were just as outmoded as the ones they had worn at our first encounter, but I noticed that the men had moved their *mouches*; the black patches were stuck to different parts of their faces than they had been on the day we met. I tried not to stare.

I had been practicing my French on Mops and Liesl, and even on Liesl's little son (although neither pug nor maid nor moppet could understand a word of the language), so I was delighted by the players' assessment that my pronunciation was already improving. "But you must properly produce the sound as well," said Monsieur Aufresne. "After all, you will be speaking to people all day, from your morning *levers* to your evening *couchers*."

"And it will not do for the dauphine to suffer *mal à la gorge*— a sore throat," chirped Monsieur Sainville. "So we will teach you the actors' method to avoid fatiguing the vocal cords."

Apparently, learning this technique entailed lying on the floor and placing one's hands on the belly. Would *madame l'archiduchesse* be permitted to do so? The players applied to the dour-faced Madame von Lerchenfeld, who succinctly informed the pair that a daughter of the House of Hapsburg does not supinate her limbs. In that case, would madame the chaperone herself submit to the demonstration? "*Absolument pas!*" came her emphatic refusal.

After a brief and whispered conversation between them, the

players concurred that the only way to demonstrate the technique would be if they performed it themselves. Monsieur Aufresne doffed his tricorn and lowered his bulk to the floor, while Monsieur Sainville, with all delicacy, knelt beside him and placed his palm over his colleague's enormous gut. The slender actor explained how to breathe from the belly rather than from the lungs, instructing me to watch his hand rise and fall while Monsieur Aufresne inhaled and exhaled deeply, as he spoke several sentences in order to demonstrate how one sustains the sound without risk of injury.

Try as I might, I just couldn't see it. *"Excusez-moi, messieurs,"* I said, begging their pardon. I scuttled over to Madame von Lerchenfeld's chair, interrupting her reading. I had assumed she was enjoying one of her devotional works, but curiously, she snapped the book shut as I approached her. "I can't understand how to breathe properly because Monsieur Aufresne is so"— I puffed out my cheeks and surreptitiously pantomimed a rounded gut—*"dickbäuchig!* How can I tell whether his belly has expanded?" I whispered.

The countess placed the book in her lap and clapped her hands in three sharp raps that echoed off the paneled walls of the Rosenzimmer. *"S'il vous plaît, messieurs!"* She asked them to switch places so that I could better discern the breathing technique as it was demonstrated on Monsieur Sainville's considerably slimmer frame.

After watching the men for several moments I was determined to experience it for myself. The actors could never touch the royal person, but who was to prevent me—except my pinch-faced governess, whose attention I now imagined was immersed in some lurid novel—from lying down on the floor and feeling my own belly? So there I lay, swallowed up by my skirts, on a hard wooden floor, while above me an artificial garden was forever in bloom. However, despite my best efforts, I couldn't discern whether I was breathing correctly because my corset and stomacher restricted the movement of my torso—the very raison d'être of these accoutrements, but of no use to me now.

Too distracted by the roses overhead, I closed my eyes and practiced my phonetics. The actors had given me a few sample sentences to repeat. "*Le petit chien est bleu*"—the little dog is blue—I intoned with tremendous deliberation as I puffed out my lower belly, pushing it against my stays, then gradually deflated it as I spoke.

"Antonia, what is the meaning of this!"

My eyes flew open and I was treated to a view of somber black brocade festooned with lilac furbelows, my mother's skirts. I sat up with a start. Maman was shadowed by the duc de Choiseul, his customary benign smile replaced with a grimace of consternation. I will long remember their mutual expression of horror at the sight of Monsieur Sainville in a recumbent position on the polished floor, while his stout colleague bent over him in what must have appeared to be a somewhat compromising pose with his ample derrière, clad in dun-colored breeches, poking skyward like the rump of the rhino in the royal menagerie.

In a tone that could freeze fire, Maman announced that the lesson was over. Immediately.

Countess von Lerchenfeld had jumped up from her chair as though her skirts were ablaze. She colored furiously and endeavored to hide her book inside a pocket. Luckily for her, Maman's gaze was fixed on the pair of actors, who scrambled to their feet with as much dignity as they could muster and quickly donned their hats. With a "By your leave, Your Imperial Majesty" and a considerable amount of bowing and awkwardly ingratiating smiles, they departed the room in great haste.

"Actors," said the duc with icy disdain. There was a hardness in his eyes I had never before seen. "I had not believed it when it was first reported to me. The news defied everything I have come to recognize as Your Imperial Majesty's piety and correctness—particularly as it applies to your daughter's preparation to become the dauphine."

I rose to my feet and smoothed my skirts. Never before had I seen Maman speechless. Her fleshy chins trembled with apprehension.

"I-I was against it from the start," the countess stammered. Maman's glare could have penetrated iron.

The French diplomat wrung his hands. "Your Imperial Majesty, the court of Versailles, and most specifically His Most Christian Majesty, are extremely distressed to learn that you have engaged a pair of strolling players to educate the future queen of France. I have staked—"

"Yes, I know," Maman snapped. "You have staked your lengthy career on Antonia's union with the dauphin. There is no need to remind me, monsieur le duc." After several moments of hideously tense silence, my mother summoned her redoubtable equanimity. "It was my studied estimation that a pair of native-born speakers would be more appropriately suited to improving my daughter's French. True, they are actors—"

"*Undesirables*," the duc interrupted. He shook his head. "Versailles regards this decision, madame, as a particularly egregious faux pas. In fact," he added, measuring his words in a way that sent shivers along my spine, "when it is coupled with the archduchess's continued deficiency in intellectual pursuits and her poor acquaintance with basic academics, Louis has begun to question your judgment—as well as Madame Antonia's suitability to become dauphine. It will take a good deal of delicacy—and persuasion—to convince him otherwise."

I had never seen my mother look so pale.

EIGHT

The Really Hard Work Begins

My summer nights at Schönbrunn were consumed by cavagnole, sitting at card tables opposite countless Viennese courtiers playing round after round of the wretched game until my eyes were dry with sleeplessness. The hardest part was the arithmetic, for the player who placed the winning bet would receive sixty-four times his stake from the banker. I had to learn how to multiply countless combinations of currency, taking into account that the numbers on a cavagnole board ranged from one to seventy. However, even after paying the winners, it was really the banker who stood to reap the largest sum at the end of the evening, for he got to keep all of the losing bets. Yet the long nights were worth the effort; I was making Maman proud with my newfound skills. The empress of Austria was a woman who applauded those who took risks and I was proving myself quite the little gambler, bold in my bids when it counted and reticent at all the right moments.

By autumn we were back at the dreary, massive Hofburg, and because the bald spots near my hairline had finally grown in to Maman's satisfaction, she deemed it the proper time to engage the prominent hairdresser we had all heard so much about. The duchesse de Gramont, sister to the duc de Choiseul, had dispatched her own *friseur*, Sieur (short for "monsieur," they told me) Larsenneur. According to the duchesse, "Larsenneur dresses the best heads in France," a recommendation that was sure to please my mother. If it broke her heart to concur, even tacitly, with King Louis's view that the Austrian empire was incapable of supplying the necessary talent to prepare me for my new role, it was her private sorrow. My marriage was the greatest diplomatic alliance of her reign. For such grand stakes, she would try, however much it stuck in her throat, to swallow her pride.

Sieur Larsenneur arrived in Vienna with a massive number of leatherbound wooden trunks, identifiable in the grandest way. Even the Hapsburgs did not have their initials engraved on silver plaques affixed to the lids of their baggage! And for a man who did nothing but dress hair day after day, the monsieur had such a serious demeanor that I found him slightly absurd—as if coiffures were the most important things in all the world. Through the gauzy haze of retrospect, I suppose my little reddish-blond head *was* of international proportions!

Equally striking was Sieur Larsenneur's fancy for elaborate *perruques*. His hair was always hidden beneath a curled and powdered wig and he was most fastidious about maintaining them. Each *perruque* conjured a distinctive personality and I entertained myself by imagining that he gave them names and, in the privacy of his narrow and unadorned room, would converse with them as though they were his companions.

On the appointed day, Maman summoned me to one of the Hofburg's smaller but no less grand salons. So many chambers in the palace resembled each other, in their ivory-colored paneling accented with gilded moldings and heavy crimson draperies, that someone could easily become disoriented wandering amid the labyrinthine residence. As I entered the room my eyes widened in surprise, for it seemed as though every courtier in Vienna was present, wishing to see how this famed *friseur* would transform my curls into an elegant style befitting the dauphine of France.

Attired in a satin suit the color of oysters with a finely embroidered waistcoat, the hairdresser was announced to the assembled throng in a voice so stentorian one might have imagined him to be the most important man in Vienna. And that brisk November morning, I suppose he was. After making a low court bow to each of us, Sieur Larsenneur assured Maman that when he was finished with me, I would be the envy of every young girl in Europe. With an astonishingly haughty manner for a tradesman, the *friseur* informed us, "In Paris I am called *Le Chevalier des Cheveux*—the Cavalier of Hair—for I rescue the distressed tresses of damsels."

So puffed up was he with his own conceit that I nearly burst out laughing in front of the whole court; but feeling the sharp rebuke of my mother's gaze upon me, I tried to stifle my giggles behind my hand. When a chuckle erupted nonetheless, I had to bite the inside of my lower lip in order to regain my composure.

Maman instructed me to sit upon a low upholstered stool that would afford Sieur Larsenneur the best view of my head from all sides. After circling me a few times, he requested Maman's permission to touch the archduchess's person. No sooner did my mother assent than Sieur Larsenneur removed the lilac-colored ribbon and tortoiseshell pins that held my hair in place, allowing my locks to tumble down my back. A tingle coursed along my spine as he ran his hands through my hair to determine its weight and texture. In a single moment my hopes became rosier: perhaps the Frenchman could indeed work miracles.

"*Les cheveux, les cheveux*," the *friseur* muttered to himself as he rubbed a lock of my hair between his slender fingers. "The hair, the hair." Keenly observing Sieur Larsenneur's furrowed brow and murmuring lips, the courtiers leaned forward onto their toes and rocked back on their heels as one body, with the same sort of fascination they might have displayed were they witnessing the spectacular feats of a lion tamer. Baron Neny, florid and corpulent and prone to pronouncements that, to his immense delight, invariably proved correct, maintained a commentary on the hairdresser's every movement, from brushing out my long hair, to teasing it off my forehead and drawing it tightly back until I thought he was about to pull my scalp off, to—finally—plaiting the length into a queue that began at the nape of my neck and hung down my back like the tail of a piglet. Then, with a grand flourish the *friseur* draped a large white cloth about my body, pinning it shut. He opened a pot of pomade scented with attar of roses to mask the pungent smell of the bear grease, scooped a bit into his palm, and rubbed his hands together before smoothing them over my new coiffure. "Almost, *madame l'archiduchesse*. Almost!" he breathed, his hands fluttering in anticipation of the completion of his masterpiece. "We are now to put on the finishing touches!"

From his monogrammed leather satchel Sieur Larsenneur withdrew a device that resembled a bellows and puffed a very light dusting of powder onto my hair—not even enough to conceal the shade of blond beneath it.

"*Ach! Zehr gut; zehr schön*," Baron Neny intoned pompously. "Very good. Very pretty. It is such a simple style—deceptively so. And so decent; so elegant." A roomful of courtiers nodded their heads in immediate agreement.

The drape was removed and a gilded hand mirror was placed in my lap. The moment of truth had arrived. Despite what a chamber of sycophants thought, aware that they had been witnessing the handiwork of the man believed to be the finest *friseur* in Europe, I wondered if my head looked as painful as it felt after all that tugging. I stole a quick glance at my reflection and promptly dropped my hand into my lap again. I would be expected to smile. I would be expected to love it.

But I didn't love it. What was the point of "fixing" my disproportionately high forehead if the hairdresser's remedy was to yank my hair back, more tightly than any gray band of wool had ever done? My forehead resembled a convex slab of marble. And the high, severely close coiffure made me look old—significantly more so than my thirteen years. I hated it. While the courtiers cooed and crowed like a flock of plump, perfumed squab, I blinked back the stinging tears that had begun to form behind my eyelids. I would not cry. Archduchesses of Austria never cry—no, never—at least, not in public. My hands raised reflexively to loosen the coiffure and relieve some of the tightness that made my scalp feel like a snare drum, but everyone was ogling me, eyes wide, smiles broad. They loved it. And although it was *my* head, I was not expected to have an opinion about what had been done to it, or—more to the point—an opinion that contradicted that of the empress of Austria. And it appeared that the empress of Austria was quite pleased with the results. Maman even smiled (though she didn't part her lips) and permitted Sieur Larsenneur to kiss her hand.

Baron Neny was delighted as well. Speaking for the assembly of courtiers and diplomats he declared that my new hairstyle was so lovely, so à la mode, that "before long all the young women of Vienna will be demanding *une coiffure à la dauphine.*"

Well, I thought, if they do, they are foolishly following a hideous fashion. All they will get for their slavish mimicry is a dreadful headache. When I was given leave to return to my apartments I appraised my appearance in a standing cheval glass, and releasing the fury that had been simmering since I'd first beheld my new and improved hairstyle, I slid my fingers under the tight coiffure, tugging at the roots to soften the style and relieve the pressure from my aching scalp.

The following day Sieur Larsenneur worked his magic—Maman's word for it—and dressed my hair once again in the severe manner that the court had uniformly found so becoming. Was this how Monsieur Ducreux was to paint me? And what would Louis of France think when he saw my portrait? Assuredly His Most Christian Majesty would not believe that I was on the cusp of thirteen. The longer I gazed at my reflection the more I convinced myself that I sooner resembled an ancient hag of twenty-five!

But Sieur Larsenneur had been deemed such a genius that Maman awarded him a place within my retinue. It was a significant honor, and one he could scarcely refuse, even though devoting himself entirely to my tonsorial needs would mean the loss of his Parisian clientele. When the time came, he would be expected to pack up his boar-bristle hairbrushes, bellows, and curling papers and tongs and travel to France with my entourage to remain at Versailles as coiffeur to the dauphine. I envisioned many tugs of war with the *"Chevalier des Cheveux,"* for not a quarter of an hour after he finished dressing my hair, I had once again worked my fingers through it to reduce the severity of my hairline.

By now, the braces had finally come off, too. My teeth resembled a row of little pearls and I could not help admiring the result by stealing frequent glances at myself in the mirror and rolling my tongue over my smooth and even smile. I had nearly forgotten how wonderful food could taste without a mouthful of metal. And no more prying bits of spätzle out of the contraption with my fingernail! Maman was relieved to have done with the messy business of renovating my outward appearance, but she still regarded my insides as a work in progress. Thus my improvement continued apace, even as the dancing figures in her grand mechanical clock presented ninety-six reminders a day of the amount of time lost to us forever.

One evening after the completion of my daily lessons—harp instruction from Herr Gluck; dancing with Monsieur Noverre; and (under the strict tutelage of the Countess von Lerchenfeld) a dreadfully boring recitation of French grammar made all the more tedious by a nasty head cold and threats of a vile-smelling mustard plaster—I received a summons from Maman. I was to attend her in one of my favorite rooms in the entire palace, a colorful, nearly circular salon dominated by fantastical murals that the painter Johann Bergl had created for her just two years earlier. The dull walls had been transformed into an imaginative fairyland: Swans, egrets, and other winged creatures mingled with woodland animals in vibrant landscapes dominated by fantasy castles and follies, amid pools and skies of purest cerulean blue—a hue that made my heart soar just to look at it. What a treat for the eyes after chamber upon chamber of crimson, cream, and gold.

At the center of the exotic salon stood several wooden crates embossed in burnt cork with the fleur-de-lis of France. Around its circumference stood twice as many gloved footmen awaiting the empress's command to pry them open.

"This is all for you, Antonia," said Maman, gesturing expansively at the array of boxes.

"For me?" I echoed stupidly, my eyes widening. "What's in them?"

Maman smiled complacently, a cat who had found a sunny alcove in which to nap. "Let us open them, shall we?" Her words alone were enough to cue the servants, who pried open the crates with iron bars.

"Dolls!" I exclaimed with delight. Nestled amid layers of straw and cotton-wool were dozens of wooden figures with painted faces and miniature horsehair wigs, each garbed in a sumptuously crafted gown. Six crates contained but a single figure apiece, much taller and more elaborate than the other dolls, perhaps three-quarters of my own (admittedly diminutive) size, with inset eyes and mohair wigs. Their gowns—satins, silks, brocades, and figured damasks, and even the heaviest and most costly textiles of all, cloth of silver and cloth of gold—were the color of moonlight and pearls, festooned and furbelowed with the most exquisite *dentelle*: lace from Chantilly, Alençon, and Le Puy.

"How I would love to wear gowns like this every day," I murmured, cradling one of the smaller dolls as if she were a newborn.

Maman regarded me with an expression that, were it a pinprick on a map, lay somewhere between amusement and hauteur. "And so you shall, little one." She gestured proudly at the delicate contents of the crates. "These are fashion dolls—*poupées de la mode*. And the tall ones are the '*grandes pandores*.' Each of the *grandes pandores* is wearing a wedding gown; we shall inspect every gown, its color and embellishments, and determine which would be the most suitable for your marriage to the dauphin."

"But they are all so magnificent," I breathed, my voice hushed and reverential. Did Maman see in them what I did? Not so much in the robes themselves, but in the *grandes pandores*. The dolls' eyes ranged from cobalt to cornflower and from hazel to leaf green, their hair color every shade of blond from flaxen to strawberry to ash. It seemed as though each was one of my sisters come back to comfort me during the next stage of this great trial. There they were: Marianne and Christina, Amalia and Johanna, Josepha and Charlotte.

"Antonia!" The sharp rap of Maman's fan against the ormolu table disrupted my childish reverie.

"Do I have to choose one of the wedding gowns now? They

are all so beautiful." How could I disappoint my wooden sisters? It would be like picking a favorite among them, and although my real favorite had always been Charlotte, the companion of my girlhood, frankly I liked "her" dress least of all.

"You may choose two of them," said Maman, striking an odd balance between imperious and indulgent. "In one of them you will approach the altar in the chapel at Versailles; the other will be your gown for the proxy marriage."

"Proxy marriage." I parroted her words. I'd all but forgotten there would be a ceremony in our chapel, followed by a no less elaborate feast. Royal brides were first wed in their native kingdom; by the time they set foot in their husband's lands, in the eyes of the Church—although the rite was always repeated in the groom's country—they were already man and wife.

"Your brother Ferdinand will take the dauphin's part."

Oh, dear. I grimaced. Ferdinand had also stood in for his Neapolitan namesake at Charlotte's proxy ceremony. That day, he had been unable to misbehave. He was terrified of Charlotte; she'd freeze him with one stare and he knew he could expect retaliation. My relationship with my next oldest brother was somewhat different. How often had he hidden a tadpole in my shoe just to hear me squeal? Or switched my milled soap for bootblack? What sort of boyish prank might he be tempted to play when I was his "bride"?

"Four hundred thousand livres" (Maman nearly choked as she mentioned the sum) "has bought you an enviable trousseau, every thread of it from France. All the satin and furbelows in Europe will make you look like a dauphine, but you still lack the proper temperament, not to mention education." A heavy sigh escaped her lips as she brought a jeweled hand to her breast. "I have no one to blame for it but myself. Sometimes I despair whether you will ever become ready to wed."

She had said it again. I was a disappointment to her. True, I could dance, I could glide as well (so Monsieur Noverre assured me) as any duchesse at Versailles, I could play the harp like an angel (*danke schön*, Herr Gluck), and I was a confident and charming hostess during endless rounds of cavagnole. My forehead was no longer offensive to French eyes and my teeth were now as straight as God surely intended, had He not had so much to contend with on the day of my creation. My right shoulder no longer appeared higher than the left, owing to the most unforgiving of stays. But until my head was stuffed with knowledge and my bodice stuffed with flesh, I was as useful as a loaf of bread not yet risen; a malformed lump.

I meekly lowered my head and bobbed a shallow curtsy. "Yes, Maman."

"The Countess von Lerchenfeld is not equipped to finish you," my mother continued, her voice tinged with resignation. "Moreover, she is not French." She paused and brought her steepled fingers to her chin, reflecting. Only the most astute of observers would have noticed the woeful state of her nails, bitten to the quick with worry. The woman who could not stomach imperfection in others was herself a flawed being, although she would never admit to it. If there were ever another war, it was imperative that Austria and France remain, or become, allies. Maman had nobly fallen on the sword of her failure to fully transform me, but when all was said and done, success really rested within *me*. Would I ever be up to the mark?

Maman regarded me for such a long time and with such remarkable stillness that I began to shift in my shoes, rocking back and forth on my heels. "You are excused, Antonia."

And that was it. I curtsied to her again, for it was really the empress of Austria who had banished me from her sight.

My cheeks were damasked with shame. For the past several months my entire reason for breathing was to wed the dauphin of

France and bring additional honor and glory to the Hapsburgs. But my sister Charlotte's unhappy letters from Naples were all the proof I needed to recognize that being married was not the equivalent of being fortunate. Not if you were the bride.

Naples, November 13, 1768

My beloved Toinette:

You asked what it is like to become the wife of a man you have never met, let alone know if you can ever love. One suffers real martyrdom, which is all the greater because one must pretend outwardly to be happy, while unknown to all, your heart withers on its vine. I would rather die than endure again what I had to suffer. My husband has less sense than a pig, although his manners and habits are similar enough to one. The first night... was so unspeakably humiliating. He came to bed reeking of garlic and onions, hopped upon me as though I were a sack of potatoes and then, when his duty (and mine, we mustn't forget) was done, had the insouciance to accuse me of smelling rank and of having an ugly face! This from a man whose hair, even when he bothers to comb and powder it, has the color and consistency of dung-colored straw, whose vacuous countenance is marred with pustules, and who lacks the maturity of a simpleton.

You are either laughing as you read this, or you are terrified that I will be punished for writing such things about the king of the Two Sicilies. But no one here speaks German, so they cannot read my correspondence.

I must end this letter sooner than I had expected. A dispatch has arrived from the prime minister. Ferdinand is, as usual, off to the hunt. This leaves me to deal with Mr. Acton; and it will not surprise you to learn that I am making the most of this opportunity. Maman would be proud, I think. This little Hapsburg is fortunate in nothing else but in having a husband who cares even less for governance than he does for fashion.

Please keep me in your prayers, dear sister: I have much need of them.

Your loving sister Charlotte,
Queen of the Two Sicilies

Maman had granted my request for the fashion dolls to be placed in my suite of rooms. Sometimes I would invite a pair of playfellows—the daughters of my wet nurse, Frau Weber—to enjoy them with me. Although the Hapsburgs were a close-knit family, Maman fiercely believed that we should behave as any bourgeois brood might and mingle with "ordinary" children, the better to understand our subjects and to appreciate the benefits of our birthright. But this mandate only went so far. Commoners were not our *friends*, she would remind us. There would always be an unseen, but nevertheless impenetrable, barrier between an archduchess of Austria and the offspring of a servant or tradesperson. We might share our toys with Frau Weber's children, but never our secrets.

Consequently, in the absence of Charlotte the French dolls became my companions and confidantes. Their red painted lips could not reveal my fears; their tiny wooden ears heard only what I wished them to know. And the *grandes pandores* who so resembled my much older siblings, even down to the color of their eyes and hair—why, my imagination brought me closer to them than we had truly been. The smaller dolls, the *poupées de la mode*, were each a miniature marvel of mantua making. In the privacy of my rooms, I peeked up their dresses to inspect their undergarments, examples of the very things I would wear next to my skin. They were so delicate, so elaborate, so tiny! Silk stockings, as white as virgin snow, with reinforced toes and heels, enveloped legs no thicker than two of my fingers; doll-sized sets of stays, embroidered and embellished; frothy flounced petticoats—and, oh, the shoes! Every doll wore a different pattern. With so many garments being prepared for my bridal trousseau, I imagined that the most difficult decision of the day, once I became dauphine, would be choosing what to wear.

"Maman says she spent four hundred thousand livres to dress all of you," I whispered to the dolls one November night. I had taken to sleeping beside one of the *grandes pandores,* my arm crooked about her torso, crumpling her sumptuous wedding gown. Mops did not conceal his jealousy of my new bedfellows; several times I scolded him for gnawing on their legs and tearing at their skirts with his teeth.

"But," I confided to the doll I'd named Charlotte, "I overheard Maman tell the duc de Choiseul that Louis has not yet formalized his offer for my hand in marriage to his grandson the dauphin."

"Charlotte" looked at me with her pale blue glass eyes. Her lashes were tiny dots painted in a row beneath them. "Perhaps I won't have to leave Vienna after all." But that thought gave way to the fear of failing Maman. I knew she had done everything the French diplomats—as well as Austria's ambassador to Versailles, the comte de Mercy—had advised. Still, the expected commitment from Louis Quinze had not materialized.

A sharp knock at my bedroom door startled me. I blew out the candle in haste and pretended to be asleep. Then the door was flung open. I clasped "Charlotte" more tightly and buried my face in her satin-clad shoulder.

"Antonia!"

I bolted upright. "Maman?" I could not recall the last time she had visited my bedroom. *We* came to the empress, as bidden; she did not make it a habit to look in on her children, particularly in the middle of the night.

Behind her a servant carried a candle; the silhouette of the flame flickered ominously on the wall above my bed. My mother peered at me, her fist clutched to her chest to close her dressing gown. Even in shadow I could see her displeasure, evident in the set of her mouth, in her narrowed eyes. "What do you think you are doing?" she demanded, her voice and manner as alert as if it were already breakfast time.

"Sleeping?" I replied meekly. The word squeaked out as a feeble question.

"With *that*," Maman amended, pointing to the *grande pandore* beside me in the bed.

"It's 'Charlotte,'" I insisted.

"It's nonsense," my mother said sharply. "God and Louis of France willing, you are going to be a bride, Antonia; you are far too old to play with dolls. Some girls your age are already mothers."

"Because they have met Générale Krottendorf," I mumbled.

"What was that?"

"Nothing, Maman," I murmured.

My mother's rebuke fixed my decision not to inform her that I pretended that the *poupées de la mode* were my make-believe children by the dauphin, although I also had to imagine that some of the dolls were little boys, so that they could inherit the throne. Because boys wore dresses until they were breeched, it was not such an absurd conceit. When I was all alone I would speak to them as if they were my babies, scolding or coddling depending on the scenario I imagined. I knew nothing of what it meant to be a bride, other than to wear an enviably beautiful gown, like the *grandes pandores*. Was it a surprise that I should be afraid of the one-way journey to an alien court, where I would forever speak a foreign tongue? Maman, who brooked no weakness in anyone, least of all herself, would not have countenanced a word of my childish fretting.

"God has answered my prayer," she announced. "Of late I have been convinced that only divine intervention could prepare you to become dauphine, and through the good offices of the duc de Choiseul and the Archbishop of Toulouse, a savior has arrived. Your tutelage will commence immediately." She gestured to the brocade bellpull hanging alongside my bed. "Ring for Liesl and have her dress you in your blue striped *robe à l'anglaise*. In half an hour I will expect you to attend me in the audience chamber."

The "savior" was, at thirty-four, only a few years older than my brother, the Emperor Franz Joseph; but having just attained the age of thirteen, I found him positively ancient. He was introduced to us by a bleary-eyed duc de Choiseul who had ridden through the night to escort Abbé Jacques-Mathieu de Vermond to Vienna. This priest, with his unprepossessing manner and thatch of russet hair, was to mold my mind and finish my education.

In his long black soutane with its narrow white jabot at the throat, the abbé seemed at the time even older than his years. His pale eyes were, to my own sleepy ones, alert but not immensely intelligent, lacking the requisite fire I imagined would be the hallmark of a brilliant man of parts. As my mother peppered him with questions regarding his pedagogical qualifications, his morals, his manners, and the entire history of his family, I watched his face closely. Did such an interrogation (and before the sun had risen, no less) intimidate him? Evidently, it did not— and if he had been overwhelmed by the presence of the empress of Austria or by the interview itself, he possessed the admirable equanimity not to reveal his anxiety.

"The abbé is nothing if not patient," the duc de Choiseul asserted with a chuckle, tipping a nod to his new protégé.

"Then we shall test his mettle," my mother replied. Turning to address the raven-clad cleric, she added, "The archbishop speaks of you with the highest of compliments. Consequently I place my faith, and that of my entire realm, in your hands. I regret to admit that the archduchess has too many academic deficiencies to be blithely overlooked, and it will be up to you, monsieur l'abbé, to ameliorate the matter."

The stakes could not have been greater. My mother had placed the fate of an empire on the perfectly ordinary shoulders of a simple priest with nothing but a pair of recommendations and a certificate from the Sorbonne to commend him.

Abbé Vermond nodded his head and bowed respectfully. "*Merci*, Your Imperial Majesty. I thank you for bringing me to Austria and hope that God sees fit to make me worthy of the trust you have placed in my hands and of the education of *madame l'archiduchesse*."

Maman waved her hand dismissively; at that small hour of the morning she lacked the patience for obsequiousness. "You will be shown to your rooms where a pot of coffee or chocolate will await you. There will of course be a basin and ewer with which to cleanse yourself after such a long journey. At the hour of six I will expect you to be in the Rosenzimmer, prepared to begin your tutorials. I will also expect daily reports as to my daughter's progress. And do not mince words. Time will not wait upon her improvement." Maman looked from the abbé to the duc de Choiseul, as if to seek additional confirmation that she had indeed engaged a redeemer. Although the nobleman's mouth betrayed no emotion, his dark eyes were intense with meaning. "Well then!" she said briskly. "Good morning and welcome to the court of Vienna, Monsieur de Vermond."

It would be a trial by fire and I had been plunged into the caul-
dron. With so many other lessons occupying my time, Maman accorded the abbé Vermond just one hour a day in which to
improve my education. The abbé spoke no German, so my lessons would of course be conducted in French, making them all
the more arduous. The endless conjugations and grammatical ex-
ercises bored me to distraction. And as the wintry frosts began to
thaw and Vienna burst into bud, nothing could have been more
onerous than composing essays on French history and geography.
"I cannot learn on paper," I insisted. "My mind just won't retain it."

But the abbé was very clever; he would see my attention flag-
ging and turn a lesson into a game. One day he spread a large document on our work table. "Here is a map of Europe," he said.
"Show me Vienna."

I gave him my best smile. "I can show you Vienna better out
of doors."

"But then you will miss the journey," he replied cryptically.
Endeavoring to conceal his exasperation, he said, "We begin here:
Vienna." His pale finger pointed to a dot on the map. By the end
of the hour I had traced a line across Europe, marking my entourage's eventual excursion across the Hapsburg empire and
into Bourbon France, memorizing the locations of every destination between the Hofburg and Versailles. Cities and villages that
had been no more than unfamiliar names printed on a sheet of
colorful paper suddenly had meaning to me. Armed with the
knowledge that my carriage would clatter through countless
towns, I wished to know about each of them. What did they look
like? What did the people eat? How did they dress?

Some destinations held more mystery for me than others.
Near Strasbourg, the border between our realm and that of Louis

XV, I would make the magical transformation from Austrian archduchess to dauphine of France. In the forest of Compiègne, outside Paris, I would finally meet the king and his grandson—who by then would be my husband!

This lesson was augmented by a catechism of sorts: identifying the various men involved in arranging my marriage. For every correct answer, I was permitted to take a bite out of a raspberry tart dusted with powdered sugar.

"Who is the comte de Mercy-Argenteau?" Vermond asked.

"Comte de Mercy is Austria's ambassador to France." The abbé nodded and I bit into the pastry.

"And who is Prince Starhemberg?"

"Maman's Envoy Extraordinary—her special envoy—who will lead the Hapsburg delegation into France. His father was a great field marshal who brought glory to Austria, which is why Maman singled him out for the special honor." I took another nibble of the tart. "An Envoy Extraordinary is not as lofty as a minister—or even as an ambassador, like monsieur le comte de Mercy. His sovereign may send him on all sorts of assignments, and to many different places, depending upon what he is required to do at any given time."

"The duc de Choiseul?"

"France's Chief Minister," I replied, licking the sugar from my fingertips. "Maman says it was his idea—as well as hers, of course—to marry me to the dauphin of France." I marveled at how the duc managed to serve two masters with such agility. I once overheard Maman mention that King Louis "stirred up controversy even as he shrank from it"; and she herself was the hardest woman in Europe to please, I was sure of it.

"That is correct, *madame l'archiduchesse*. And for an additional bite of raspberry tart, tell me why your marriage is so important to the duc."

"An alliance between Austria and France will dissuade

England—France's enemy—from any notions of invading France, because Britain would then have our imperial army to contend with as well. And with the support of France on *our* side, Catherine the Great of Russia and Frederick the Great of Prussia will think twice about overrunning our borders and conquering part of our empire, like Frederick did with Silesia before we entered the treaty with France."

"Your tart, madame!"

Grinning my thanks, I made sure to savor my extra bite.

"And what about the marquis de Durfort? What is his role in your marriage plans?"

I reached for the pastry again, but the abbé deftly pushed it just beyond my grasp. "Durfort is France's ambassador to the Austrian court." Abbé Vermond moved the raspberry tart closer; I covered it with my palm as I lowered my voice to a conspiratorial whisper. "And he has developed a *tendre* for the Countess von Dorfli, even though he has a *wife* back in France. It's all quite shocking."

I could see that the abbé was trying to suppress a chuckle. "*Très bien, madame l'archiduchesse.* Except for that bit about the transgression of the sixth commandment." He cleared his throat. "And tell me about Prince Kaunitz."

The tart was almost gone. "Prince Kaunitz is Austria's chancellor—Maman's most important minister." It was Prince Kaunitz who had been in large measure responsible for our treaty with France in 1756. Our countries had been enemies before that. After the duc de Choiseul had embarrassed me so many months ago with his question regarding the treaty, I made it my business to learn all about it. "I do believe Prince Kaunitz has the most amusing nose; it swoops down at a precipitous angle and then rises up again at the tip. Do you not think so?" I grinned at my tutor.

"It is not for me to say," the abbé replied diplomatically.

Although he was no pinch-faced Countess von Lerchenfeld, abbé Vermond was far from doting. I still missed my beloved Countess von Brandeiss. And in those first few weeks I fear I sorely tested the abbé's customary patience. But in time, we achieved a mutual respect, albeit a begrudging one.

"You have the hand of a child," he said one day, referring to my immature, loopy penmanship. Herr Mesmer, my writing teacher, had failed me miserably, being more interested in his experiments on the workings of the mind than on the empty one of the youngest archduchess. I was considered by my family and tutors to be rather proficient with pen and ink, a tolerable artist (for an archduchess, of course); and yet my handwriting—which I agonized over—produced an ungrammatical, misspelled mess of blots and scrawls.

"Let's try this sentence, *madame l'archiduchesse*: The queen is kind and amiable."

I dipped my quill and began to write, *Le rein est gentille et*— Vermond halted my belabored progess by silently touching the tip of his pencil to the word *rein*. Glancing from my error to the abbé and back, a peal of laughter issued from my belly. "*Mon Dieu!*" I exclaimed. "I almost wrote 'the *kidney* is kind and amiable'!" I began anew: *La reine est gentille et aimable*.

Later, when the time came to stand before Maman and offer her a report of my progress, he did not toss me to the wolves. There was much he could have said, and perhaps he did so when I was not in the room. Or perhaps he recognized that my mother was taskmaster enough for two.

That progress report I recall above all others. Maman was taking coffee in her breakfast room. She questioned my tutor as if I wasn't there; it was often her way when she conversed with another adult in my presence.

"Your Imperial Majesty, it pleases me to say that Madame

Antonia is more intelligent than has been generally supposed," the abbé responded.

Maman raised an eyebrow.

"Your daughter deserves praise where it is due," Vermond conceded. "She has many fine qualities, traits that cannot be taught, but which are innate and genuine. Madame Antonia will make an exceptional dauphine in due time." He pressed on. "Physically, she is becoming quite a beauty. Even a man of my bent," he said, indicating his clerical soutane, "can see that she has a most graceful figure; holds herself well; and if (as may be hoped) she grows a little taller, she will have all the good qualities one could wish for in a great princess. Her character, her heart, are excellent."

I felt my cheeks grow warm. His words made me stand a little straighter, raise my chin a bit higher. If I could have become taller in that moment, I would have done so, knowing that it would please the abbé. As of that moment, I ceased to regard him as merely my tutor; the gentle cleric had become my friend.

Maman peered at Vermond, lifting her lorgnette purely for effect; she had no need of it to see him clearly. "Well, then, monsieur l'abbé. It is up to you, *n'est-ce pas*, to see that her mind flourishes with the same vigor." She lowered the lorgnette and leveled her gaze, direct and unyielding. "Do not disappoint me. The history of the world as we know it, you and I, hangs in the balance."

NINE

Closer and Closer Now

"You have so much enthusiasm, so much *charme*, when we converse about pastoral things—*les papillons, les fontaines, les belles fleurs*," Vermond observed one day. By then it was spring. The year 1768 was little more than memory and the crocuses and forsythia of 1769 were beginning to bloom. In another week or two, red and yellow tulips would dot the parterres and perimeters of Vienna's public parks.

"It's because I *like* butterflies, fountains, and beautiful flowers. Perhaps I am not made for correspondence and for books," I argued.

"That does not excuse you from perfecting both your writing and your reading," Vermond replied. "It is my duty to see that you excel in everything."

I lowered my lashes and smiled at him, noting the soft pink that suffused his cheeks. "But when I go to Versailles, you will read to me!" I added gaily.

Vermond chuckled in spite of himself. "Madame Antonia, the office of 'reader,' or lecturer, means that I would serve as your spiritual counselor, not as a nanny; bedtime stories and lurid novels on the order of *La Princesse de Clèves* would not be the topics of our discourse—rather the word of God, as it is written—"

I interrupted him with a wave of my hand. "*Tant pis*," I sighed with an air of mock resignation. "Too bad."

The abbé's hand flew to his chest. "You know, I almost believed you! Call it blasphemy to say so, but were you not born to wed the future king of France, you could have been an actress."

I stifled a giggle. "If my mother heard you, she would send you packing back to Paris on a mule with no provisions but moldy bread and contaminated water." I recalled the debacle over messieurs Aufresne and Sainville. "And don't think for a moment that she would hesitate to relieve you of your duties if you do not transform me from an Austrian caterpillar into a French butterfly."

Vermond scrubbed a hand through his russet hair. "I hope Your Royal Highness does not believe I would wish you anything other than what you are," he said with a bit of a glint in his light brown eyes. "With the exception of becoming a proficient and productive student. Therefore"—he cleared his throat—"touching on the subject of the future king of France, kindly recite the history of its queens."

Ahh! This I knew. It was right and natural that I should feel an affinity with these women, some of them no older than I when they departed their native lands to be yoked in matrimony to a stranger. If they were ever homesick I was sure they kept the secret locked within their bosoms, knowing it was not only their duty, but an honor, to bear the next king of France.

I began with Eléanore d'Aquitaine, who introduced tablecloths to the French court and who scandalized her mother-in-law with her extravagant wardrobe, her cosmetics, and her opulent jewelry. "And she bravely rode at the head of the French army on the crusade to the Holy Land. Bare-breasted and in red boots, too!" I had spent weeks trying to imagine the scene. I also tried to picture how she survived day to day, enduring a loveless marriage to her cousin, Louis VII, who had few interests beyond prayer and repentance, when she herself, who so adored music and dancing, was the very image of liveliness and sociability.

"Well," sighed my tutor, scarcely concealing his amusement, "you are correct; although you would do well to heed the lessons Queen Eleanor either flouted or forgot. Her own husband imprisoned her for more than fifteen years for daring to meddle in politics."

"Ah, but that was her English husband!" I countered. "I am to marry a *French* king."

And so my examination continued as I scampered down the branches of the royal family trees, from the Capets to the Valois and finally to the current reigning dynasty, the Bourbons. "Maria Theresa"—a name I could not possibly forget, as it was also my mother's—"was the wife of Louis XIV, the Sun King. She was the Spanish infanta and the three-times-great-grandmother of the dauphin, Louis Auguste, my future husband."

"And?" Vermond gently nudged.

I racked my brain. "Oh, *ja*—I mean *oui*—a silly phrase. The French peasants were starving for want of bread and she dismissed their hunger, saying, '*Qu'ils mangent de la brioche.*' But what's a brioche and why should they eat that, if they have no bread?"

Vermond laughed. "A brioche is a delicious breakfast bun baked with flour, butter, and eggs. And just a pinch of sugar, so it's a little bit sweet—like a cake."

I frowned, furrowing my brow. "Well it's a silly thing to say, then. 'Let them eat cake.' She should have gone out among the people and fed them. It's what I would have done."

April 27, 1769

Your Excellency:

You are much wished for here, comte de Mercy. I confess that no one awaits your return to Austria with more impatience than myself, for I am sorely in need of your talents.

Her Imperial Majesty has had the goodness to inform me that Your Excellency will devote some of his evenings to Madame Antonia. Nothing could be more useful at the moment, and I observe with pleasure that Her Royal Highness appreciates the benefit of your sagacity and experience of the world. "Austria could not have a finer ambassador," she has informed me.

Lesson plans were at first a challenge, but over the past several weeks I believe that my pupil and I have found our stride. I began with the history of France, but I merely employed it as a background on which I could work up all the objects it is necessary to know in the ordinary course of life. Excepting the history of recent times, I only called her attention to the important facts, especially those epoch-making occurrences in our habit or in the French government. When I came to a position that would have been embarrassing to a prince or princess (grain shortages in the countryside, for example), I always waited after explaining the circumstances, and made her say what she would have done in their place. I had to lay stress on this and I had the pleasure of remarking that she often gave the right view.

I come now to the subject that has produced no end of consternation—that of Madame du Barry. Her Imperial Majesty has learned of Louis's new paramour, and moreover, of the woman's immediate and overwhelming influence on the king. After a battery of imprecations ("gutter trollop," "mercenary vixen," "blond harridan"), the empress launched into her greatest concern; namely, that an influential royal mistress does not bode well for Austrian interests, particularly as those interests are embodied in the person of the virginal future dauphine, who will be compelled to contend with the *maîtresse en titre* for the king's attention, regard, and favor. Madame Antonia's rank, the empress acknowledges, may well be overshadowed by the grim reality of a conniving and alluring woman in Louis's bed—a woman who is already gathering about her a devoted coterie of courtiers with their own interests at heart.

I seek your counsel because the very existence of Madame du Barry renders our collective task that much more challenging. How are we (or perhaps the burden must be shouldered alone by your humble and ill-suited servant) to prepare the archduchess to become a formidable rival of the king's favorite? As a celibate man of the cloth I am hardly equipped to discuss with a girl of thirteen such thorny matters as the ramifications of her future grandfather's adulterous liaison with "a woman of low birth and even less breeding," in the words of the empress. Nor does Her Imperial Majesty, who fully ascribes to the teachings of our Mother Church on the subject of adultery, wish her daughter to know of the king's paramour. Your wisdom and worldliness on this score would be highly beneficial to all concerned.

Finally, although I admit my initial reluctance to act as Madame Antonia's confessor, feeling on sturdier ground as her lecturer, I can only assure Your Excellency that my original disinclinations for that function have been greatly diminished by the goodness and singular confidence shown me by Her Royal Highness. I began by hearing her confession during the Christmas fêtes and from the vantage of being privy to her inmost thoughts, I can state with certainty that she

wishes to do good in the world and to please God and her elders. Additionally, and not to be discounted, to a charming
face she unites every grace of deportment. As the matter currently stands, I am quite convinced that the French court and
the kingdom will be enchanted with our future dauphine.

> Your Excellency's very humble and obedient servant,
> Abbé Jacques-Mathieu de Vermond

There was great pomp and ceremony on the exceptionally
sunny day in May when Monsieur Ducreux's formal portrait of
me was dispatched to Louis XV of France. By then we had de-
camped to Schönbrunn for the summer months, although
Maman often left us to attend to affairs of state at the Hofburg.

The painter had in fact executed two portraits, but Maman
detested the first—in which I look flat as a board, laced into a teal
blue gown embellished with ecru ruffles. My hair, lightly powdered, is styled off my forehead in the mode that Sieur Larsenneur had fashioned for me; but my neck, accentuated by a ruched
choker, looks unnaturally long when compared with the expanse
of bosom revealed by the gown. Perhaps if I had had something
delectable and alluring to show for all that skin, the image would
have been more attractive. In my view, the artist had represented
my face rather accurately, but the balance of the composition conveyed the image of a physically immature child—hardly the mes-
sage Maman wished to send to France.

Appalled by Ducreux's maiden effort and livid at him for
wasting precious time, my mother refused to accept the portrait.
I was to sit for the painter again. And this time he was cautioned
in no uncertain terms to create the image of a nubile bride.

On May 13, the commission was unveiled, its protective white
drape removed for all to ogle. Well! I was surprised to see that I
looked quite the young lady. This time, the pose reflected an an-

gular jawline. *Did I ever look like that?* I wondered. Pearls were entwined in my powdered coiffure. Even my dress, silver watered silk with accents of royal blue and pewter gray, was a markedly more mature choice than the barely embellished deep blue gown I had worn in Monsieur Ducreux's previous effort. Standing beside Maman and the diplomats involved in arranging my marriage—the marquis de Durfort, the duc de Choiseul, and our ambassador, comte de Mercy—I regarded the second portrait. This time around, my doppelgänger's gaze was direct and confident. I stifled a giggle with my fingertips. I *would marry me*, I thought!

It fell upon the marquis to transport the canvas to Versailles—along with the portraits that Monsieur Ducreux had painted of the rest of the imperial family. Maman had no intentions of giving the impression that she was overtly anxious for my formal marriage proposal, although that was precisely how she felt. Yet Louis of France could never be allowed to suspect as much. My mother pretended that my portrait was merely one of many, a gift from the Hapsburgs to the Bourbons.

But there was not a person involved—not in the Mirror Room at Schönbrunn or in the Hall of Mirrors in the palace at Versailles, who did not see through the ruse.

A month later, the marquis returned, bearing with him the document that fulfilled all my mother's hopes and dreams for the Hapsburg Empire: King Louis's official request, dated the seventh of June, 1769, for my hand in marriage on behalf of his grandson, Louis Auguste, dauphin of France.

Although she imbibed but one celebratory sip, Maman commanded that hundreds of bottles of Alsatian wine be brought up from the palace cellars. The melodious sound of tinkling crystal resonated throughout Schönbrunn's lofty ceilinged rooms; by nightfall there would be nary a minister or ambassador, footman or maid, nor a single one of the fifteen hundred court chamberlains, who was not a bit tipsy.

I wished to see the document that spelled out my destiny, imagining that it would have a great golden seal affixed to it, or that it would be embossed with a lily, the royal insignia of France, bound in white ribbons to denote the House of Bourbon.

But the formal request for my hand was none of these things. Was it inauspicious that such vital news be conveyed in nothing more momentous than an ordinary letter? After such lengthy (and in truth ongoing) negotiations for my hand and improvements to every other body part, I suppose I had expected a fanfare of trumpets and something on the order of a royal proclamation or decree. I imagined that flags representing our two houses might be flown from some lofty vantage, announcing the royal union to all and sundry.

But the modest form of the offer in no way diminished my mother's relief. Her voice quavered with emotion—and something else: victory. "Oh, my little one," sighed Maman. She beckoned me into her arms and I found myself both grateful and confused at her rare display of affection. So tightly did she envelop me that the stiff ruching of her bodice prickled my cheek. Finally, after all I had undergone to become worthy of the title of dauphine, the goal was to become a reality. Louis had viewed Monsieur Ducreux's likeness of me and approved of the result.

Through the hot tears welling in our thankful eyes, Maman's private salon—the Millions Room—became a blur of red, white, and gold. Even the crystals in the massive candelabrum above our heads seemed to wink with joy.

"Easter, he says." My mother had released me from her embrace. A determined finger pointed to the formal commitment from France. "Louis proposes that the wedding should take place next Easter." Her eyes were dry now; no hint of sentiment remained, and Maman was once again every inch the empress. "Which would fall in the middle of April, would it not, monsieur l'abbé?" She directed her attention to my tutor, who commended her swift calculations.

"April? Why, that's nearly a whole year away." I felt tugged in two directions: happy that Maman's great plans for me would indeed bear fruit, yet secretly pleased that my departure for a distant kingdom to reside among strangers for the rest of my days would not, after all, be an imminent one.

But Maman appeared displeased by Louis's forestalling of the great event even as he confirmed my formal betrothal to the dauphin of France—heavens, he'd even sent her a fine set of Sèvres porcelain to commemorate the alliance! But she did as she always managed to do in such circumstances: turn the situation to her advantage.

She regarded the troika of men in whose trust she had placed my transformation and the success of her empire's foreign policy: the patient, russet-haired abbé; Louis's outspoken and impetuous minister, the duc de Choiseul; and our suavely elegant ambassador, the comte de Mercy.

"My fondest hope and my deepest fear," she began, "realized and recognized. Vermond, the archduchess's French remains deplorable and her proficiency with the written language far worse. Her moral character wants significant improvement as well; she is far too impressionable and naïve—*une vrai ingénue*—to navigate the hornets' nest that passes for the Bourbon court. The alliance rests on slippery terrain as it is, but it will founder in the mire of political intrigue if she does not develop the skills and the confidence not merely to hold her own but to dominate—and all without appearing to do so. In a manner of speaking, to be a king, you have to learn to be a king."

The men gravely nodded their concurrence.

"Ten months purchases us much time," she said, with a surreptitious glance at my nonexistent bosom and a note of panic in her voice. "You will be that much more prepared to kneel at the altar beside your husband and, upon a certain unhappy event, ascend the throne of France." She added sternly, "Make no mistake, Antonia, you still have much to learn."

Maman lowered her hand, an indication to kneel before her, as though I were about to receive a benediction. She made the sign of the cross and kissed me gently on the forehead. "I expect great things from you, little one," she said, and her tone made it impossible to offer any contradiction. "You will not disappoint me."

I knew, even as I softened my knees into a curtsy and left the Millions Room, its heavy door shut behind me by a silent pair of footmen, that her words were not in fact a blessing. They were a command.

June 21, 1769

My esteemed Brother:

Permit me to formally tender my thanks for the honor that the house of Bourbon has bestowed upon that of the Hapsburgs. May the uniting of our ancient and noble lines in the persons of my daughter Maria Antonia and your grandson Louis Auguste bring continued peace to our respective realms and the added blessing and benefit of an heir to the throne of France.

The acknowledgment that I am sending my youngest daughter into the care of the best and tenderest of fathers is a great consolation. In you she will find all the generosity, wisdom, and nobility proper to a monarch. Antonia has applied herself with diligence to the preparations for her future role.

In her, a fond and devoted mother trusts you will find all the effervescence and ebullience of youth united to an open heart and a trusting mien. I am certain you will comprehend me when I caution you: Her age craves indulgence.

Maria Theresa

TEN

Big Changes

July 28, 1769

My beloved Toinette:

So! It has come at last—the formal commitment from Louis of France for your hand in marriage to his grandson. Please do not be surprised that this news fills me with more dread than delight. For as much as it would gladden my heart, and those of all Austrians, to see you preside over the most sophisticated court in Europe, I cannot endorse with any degree of enthusiasm the state of holy matrimony. I despair for myself, knowing now that your turn will come soon enough.

I hope that your husband will honor you and not have an eye for every rustling petticoat that crosses his path. May his table manners be exemplary and his gustatory pleasures not extend to rising from his chair in the royal box at the opera house to toss bowls full of steaming macaroni onto the alarmed heads of the aristocracy.

Once again, I suspect, I have brought the sound of laughter to your lips, but I can assure you my husband is anything but amusing. Even the Neapolitan nobility, vulgar and boisterous as they are, find themselves mortified by the antics of their sovereign.

I do not ask for your pity. Like a good Hapsburg daughter, I am insinuating myself into the corridors of power. I have, quite by accident, discovered the most intriguing manner of obtaining Ferdinand's attention, as well as his assent to anything I propose. I have only to peel my kidskin gloves down the length of my forearms with agonizing, tantalizing slowness, and the king goes into raptures. My breasts are nothing to him, but my arms—*Mein Gott!*

Nonetheless, my ability to seize a political advantage when I see it (not so very unlike our dear Maman, *ja?*) cannot compensate for the most miserable marriage in Christendom. If our religion had not said to me, "Think about God," I would have killed myself rather than live as I did for the eight days that spanned our honeymoon.

I pity you, Antonia. You still have this to face. And when you have to confront this situation, I shall shed many tears on your behalf.

Do not forget me, *Liebchen*.

> Your doting sister,
> Charlotte

My sister's letter did more to frighten than to gladden my heart, though I expected nothing less than candor from her. Sugary effusion was not her way. Secretly I remained overwhelmed by the fact that in less than a year, I, too, would be a bride. And would Charlotte's unhappy fate be mine as well? I had never seen Louis Auguste; the king of France had yet to send a portrait, although he now had more than one likeness of me. Perhaps my husband would not be at all like hers. And yet, among Charlotte's many talents was the ability to think several moves ahead in any game of chess (a pastime I could never bend my mind to); when she assessed my future, what portents did she see?

"Do you think this must be what it's like to be in prison?" I asked Maman. At her insistence we had journeyed to the convent at Marizell. "Why are we here?" I asked petulantly.

"You know the reason perfectly well. And please do not shift your feet so; stand like a proper young lady. We are here because I made my First Communion at the shrine in the Basilica, and before you go to France, I would like you, too, to kneel before the statue of the Blessed Virgin."

But that was a hundred years ago, I thought, sighing heavily.

She gave me an exasperated look and, clucking with disapproval, continued to unpack her trunk. I was to do the same, as no servants had accompanied us. It was just to be the two of us: Maman and I. The walls of the cell were bare of embellishment, except for a wooden cross mounted on the white plaster above each of the two cots.

At least the chamber was cool, the thick, stuccoed walls prohibiting the August heat from permeating. It smelled slightly damp and fusty, like a boot that has not quite dried after being left out in the rain. The tiny, barred window was so high that it was useless for providing a view. I thought of my oldest sister, who presided over a convent in Prague. "Do you think Marianne enjoys being an abbess?" I said. How could anyone go from a life at court—so vibrant, so colorful, so gay—to a place so dull, drab, and so dreadfully quiet that the finches in the tree beyond the window seemed to deafen one's ears with their calls.

"Of course Marianne enjoys being an abbess," my mother

replied with a note of annoyance. She motioned to me to unlace her stays so she could exchange her corset and petticoats for a coarse shift.

"Must I do that, too?" Maman nodded mutely and placed her finger to her lips. "But if we must be silent here, then what is the point of our visit? I thought you said we came here to talk, woman to woman." Frankly, I felt like even more of a child—one in need of special attention, like a stray lamb being returned to the fold.

When she made no reply, other than to loosen my laces so that I could undress myself, I pressed on. "Do you think the Virgin will bless my marriage to the dauphin? Will she bring me luck, do you think?" The Virgin Mary was Austria's patron saint. It never made much sense to me that we were all supposed to make good marriages yet at the same time venerate a woman who had never wed. I unrolled my white stockings and tossed them on the floor. A look from Maman and I retrieved the hose and placed them in my wooden trunk. Then I slipped my bare feet into a pair of crudely made brown leather slippers.

Having jettisoned the costly trappings of empire—yards of black brocade richly embroidered, with an embellishment of gemstones around the neckline—Maman didn't seem nearly as formidable. The woman who stood before me, strapping leather sandals to her pale and slightly callused bare feet, could have been any dowager of a certain age, with tired eyes and a treble chin. I looked more closely at her feet, noticing for the first time the blue veins beneath her nearly translucent skin, and a yellowed, in-grown toenail. A shiver descended the length of my spine. I was not so sure I liked to witness the empress of Austria appearing so vulnerable. I saw then, in a fleeting instant, that my country's in-superability lay indeed within my hands; it had never before seemed as apparent to me.

"It is not about luck, Antonia; it is about faith," Maman said simply.

Like my pug Mops when he got a beef bone, I refused to shake off my present train of thought. Perhaps I thought it would bring back the Maman I was used to: formidable but familiar. "If Marianne had not been a cripple, would you have brought her here too, before her marriage?"

"Your eldest sister chose the religious life, Antonia. Now cease the impudent questions at once."

I didn't believe her. Maman was not the sort of mother to cheerfully allow one of her daughters to embrace God, instead of the prince of somewhere or other, solidifying a new alliance for the Austrian empire. *You, fortunate Hapsburg, marry* did not apply to becoming a bride of Christ. Marianne was nearly seventeen years my senior; she would be thirty-one in October. I was too little when she'd left for the nunnery in Bohemia to remember much about her. I wondered how many babies she would have had by now if she had not been born with a deformity of the spine. I wished I had known her.

"And don't say 'cripple,'" Maman added. "It is an ugly word."

The long white shift was scratchy against my skin. Had it been woven of nettles? The idea of wearing it for a whole week seemed like torture. Even my detested corsets were preferable.

For one week, my mother and I subsisted on water and brown bread with thick, chewy crusts, like the pilgrims we were. If any of the nuns knew that their visitors were the empress of Austria and her youngest daughter, they did not say a word. For that matter, they did not say a word at all. I don't know whether they had taken vows of silence, or whether they had nothing to say to us. I could not tell from their placid expressions whether they were happy, or even if they thought about happiness. *When did they stop feeling such pain in their knees?* I wondered every time we knelt on the cold slate floors. After only one day of repeated genuflection, my legs were purple with tender bruises.

With the exception of the communal meal, Maman and I were left to ourselves. Every evening, as we lay upon our hard cots, Maman lectured me on my religious obligations, which I was not to neglect, even as dauphine of France. She made me promise before the cross that at the court of Versailles, I would attend Mass twice daily, and always carry my Bible—the one Papa had given me, bound in white leather with my initials engraved in gilt.

But didn't the royal family of France attend Mass twice a day as well, I wondered aloud.

"Yes, of course, little one. But they don't mean it. Just like the Neapolitans," she added dismissively. "However, the French court is the most urbane in Europe. There, gossip takes precedence over God. You must develop the resilience of a willow and the sturdiness of an oak, resisting the temptations to become as frivolous and jaded and lazy as the lot of them."

Every day at Marizell, although I should have much preferred to stroll through the convent gardens, we visited the shrine inside the dark and dreary basilica and knelt before the silver grille that Maman herself had donated to the sisters. Behind the bars and ornate scrollwork—as though she were in jail—the wooden statue of the Blessed Virgin had rested in her niche since the twelfth century. And every day that week Maman and I offered her a silent prayer, eyes shut tightly, heads bent so low that our lips touched our raised, clasped fingers—fingers that clutched our rosaries. I think Maman prayed for peace throughout our empire, for Catherine the Great and "the Devil" Frederick of Prussia to keep behind their own borders, and for Our Lady to give me a bosom that would please the dauphin of France.

I prayed that he would love me.

———

After our return from Marizell the months seemed to fly by. Since the arrival of Louis's formal request for my hand I had begun to tick off the days on a calendar. It was now 1770, the year of my marriage. The short days of winter would soon lengthen into spring. In no time at all it would be Easter. The seasons were changing, yet my body was not, much to Maman's consternation. Although I had turned fourteen the previous November 2, Générale Krottendorf remained elusive. Twice a day at Mass my mother prayed for her arrival, numbering it among her orisons for the security of the Hapsburg empire.

Yet even as the time drew nearer, the fact of my impending marriage remained little more than a hazy illusion. True, I had seen the clothes I would wear as dauphine of France, fingered the sumptuous fabrics and admired the colorful jewels; but this lavish trousseau was represented by dolls, which I continued to regard as playthings.

Because my handwriting remained so abysmal, and my attentiveness to any form of written communication equally lackluster, the abbé Vermond had instructed me to write daily, maintaining a journal (in French, *bien sûr*) of my thoughts and impressions.

These musings might be private, but they were not secret, as I had to show him the journal every day to prove that I was fulfilling the assignment. "However, your thoughts shall go no farther than my eyes," the abbé assured me.

January 21, 1770

A ring arrived for me today, a gift from the dauphin. He writes that he hopes his modest present pleases me. It does indeed, and it fits my finger perfectly, even over my glove, which is how I would wear it in France (I wonder how he knew the size). It is a sapphire, very rich in hue, surrounded by a ring of small diamonds. When I turn my hand to the window to catch the light, the ring sparkles in alternate shades of orange, green, and blue, and makes tiny rainbows on the opposite wall. However, I do wish that Louis Auguste had sent me his portrait as well as the ring, because I should like to match his charming gift to a face and a body. Is he tall? Does he powder his hair? What color eyes does he have? Will he love me?

· · ·

February 6, 1770

The Countess von Lerchenfeld is dead. She fell ill before Christmas and her health had declined steadily since. I am made quite miserable by her passing, for I was not an easy pupil and I think she would have been happier had Maman allowed her to continue as the Mistress of the Robes to my older sisters. Annelise, the countess's waiting woman, discovered her cold body this morning when she brought the breakfast tray. I was gladdened to hear that she went peacefully and is out of pain. She is with God now and I am sorry that I gave her even a moment's displeasure. Her task was a hard one and I will strive to be a better pupil for the abbé Vermond.

· · ·

February 7, 1770

Sound the trumpets! *Finalement, la Générale est arrivée!*

Before long, the entire Hofburg had the news. It had buzzed from room to room, from the kitchen to the stables, from the royal wardrobe to the ministerial offices, like a bumblebee in a rose garden. Maman embraced me with tears in her eyes, declaring that she was now the happiest woman in Europe.

I was no longer a girl, but "half a woman" in my sister Charlotte's words. The consummation of my marriage in mid-May would make me wholly a woman, and then, within another year's time, a mother—the culmination of everyone's greatest wish, not least my own, for I could not wait to have children to coddle and cuddle and cradle.

But in all the excitement of Générale Krottendorf's first visit, my mother, as well as our maidservants, omitted to inform me about the pain. Why did they neglect to mention that my stomach would feel as pinched as if I had ingested poison, and my back would feel as though I had spent the night sleeping on the floor? And that every few hours the blood-soaked rag between my thighs that made me walk like a waddling duck would need to be exchanged for a clean one?

Still, I felt that I had finally succeeded in Maman's eyes. She swanned about the state rooms wearing a beatific smile, my hand tightly clasped in hers, demanding that everyone curtsy to the future dauphine. "We are so proud of her," she kept exclaiming, in a tone that managed to be both imperious and maternal. And then, with an abruptness that startled me, "You will sleep in my chamber from now on," she declared. It sounded more like a command.

I shuddered. "With you?"

"Who else? We have much to discuss, and the time has finally arrived." To my questioning glance she replied, "They are not the sort of subjects one speaks about in the light of day or in the state rooms of a palace."

Her boudoir terrified me. After Papa died, Maman had her beautiful draperies removed; sunny yellow damasked silk was ripped down and replaced with grim black velvet panels that puddled to the floor like liquid gloom. This suffocating cocoon, smelling of camphor, became my bedroom for the next two months. Poor Mops was left to his own devices in my apartments; he must have wondered where I'd gone off to every night.

A bed had been brought into Maman's chamber for me. I was close enough to hear her snore. As I lay shivering in my white linen nightdress, staring at the plasterwork on the ceiling with open-eyed terror, I was treated to a nightly diet of lectures designed to improve my moral fiber and to prepare me for my future role. These one-sided conversations were accompanied by a lengthy list of precepts. To be certain I would remember them, Maman had taken the trouble to write them down for me. She extracted my promise to reread these regulations for my conduct every month, lest I forget to apply them to my daily life.

"You must always present the appearance of acquiescing to your husband in all things, Antonia. Remember, you will enter the House of Bourbon as an honored guest."

"*Oui*, Maman."

"And never give the impression—or God forbid, *say aloud*—that 'we do such and such better in Vienna.' "

"But I would never—"

Maman ignored my protest. It was evident that she didn't trust me. "At the same time, do not forget that you are, first and foremost, a daughter of Austria. Your sister Charlotte has that booby of a husband wrapped around her little finger, and the interests of her homeland always take precedence over the Neapolitans'."

I wondered how I was supposed to be the servant of two masters. Charlotte was cannier than I; I lacked her guile, as well as her alluring forearms.

"And you are not to read novels or similar treatises of a morally repugnant nature. Such books may be all the rage among the French, but their principles are already corrupted and past redemption."

Read novels? I had no intention of reading *anything*. I hated to read, much to the continued consternation of the abbé Vermond.

"Vermond will approve your reading material," my mother continued.

"But if monsieur l'abbé is to accompany me to Versailles as my 'reader,' then why do *I* need to read anything at all?"

Thus went our nocturnal conversations. And every night she expressed her grave concerns regarding my susceptible nature.

"You are too eager to please, Antonia."

"*Oui*, Maman."

"That is exactly what I mean."

Although the room was dark I was certain she was frowning, her forehead furrowed with worry. But resignation was overpowered by resolve. In her view there was so much more to impart and so little time remaining. Maman not only lectured me nightly on the subject of my character, but was anxious to ensure that my body as well as my mind would obey her instructions.

"Always allow your husband to take the lead. But if he does not do so, then you must be prepared to school him."

"School him in what, Maman?" *How was I supposed to follow as well as lead?*

"The promptings of the heart," she replied euphemistically.

"But what if we do not love each other the way you and Papa did?"

Maman sighed heavily. Her breath hung like a storm cloud in the suffocating air of the chamber. "Don't be obtuse, Antonia."

"But I don't know what to *do*," I protested. Did the arrival of Générale Krottendorf signify that my body was supposed to feel certain stirrings? Desire, perhaps? All I knew was that the birth of a son, an heir to the throne of France, was the most desirable thing in the world to Maman, or for that matter to King Louis.

During those interminable sleepless nights in Maman's boudoir, as time crept inexorably toward my wedding day, her lectures assumed a more graphic tone. "You must view my union with your father as the exception and not the rule. Passion is not only rare but it is as fleeting as beauty. More important is a mutual respect between spouses. It is of far greater importance to be good than to be comely. If you and your husband can learn to look into each other's hearts, your marriage will be far more successful than if you merely regard each other's faces."

Then she explained where babies come from. To the consternation of my mother, the soul of pragmatism, I was alternately repulsed and frightened. Dying in childbirth was not uncommon. And *what* was supposed to go . . . *where*?

"Antonia, don't be ridiculous. It is the most natural thing in the world. Your body will tell you exactly what to do."

But what if I didn't know how to listen to it? If there had been a note of tenderness in Maman's words—some semblance of sympathy—I could have borne it better. But her voice was gruff, exasperated. After all, she had given birth sixteen times, so for her, nothing could have been more routine. With my coming she had even killed a pair of birds with the proverbial single stone, summoning her dental surgeon to extract a painful tooth while she endured the pains of labor. In the dark, I examined my body with tentative, fleeting palpations. No bosom, yet. Still. I suppose I had expected it to mushroom overnight after Générale Krottendorf made her maiden appearance. That's what happened to Charlotte. She had gone from coltish girl to voluptuous woman in a matter of weeks.

My torso was narrow and slender, my abdomen ever so slightly rounded, yet nearly as flat as my chest. How would a baby ever fit inside my belly? And the dauphin would do *what*? I touched myself down there, where the flesh was soft and moist on the inside, and on the outside where the skin was like that of a peach, downy and delicate. Two fingers wide, Maman had

guessed. Maybe more. And perhaps the length of my hand, fingertip to wrist. I tried to picture something matching those di-
mensions inside me, but I had a difficult time getting past the
strangeness of the whole idea. After all, that was where things
went *out*—liquid things like blood and urine—so how was something the size of a link of wurst going to go *in*?

The whole picture became even more of an exercise in futility
because I had not a face to put with the sausage, so to speak.
When we had inquired (on more than one occasion) as to his
looks, the abbé Vermond had assured us that Louis Auguste had
a "very pleasing countenance." King Louis's ambassador, the
marquis de Durfort, insisted coolly, between pinches of snuff,
that beauty was in the eye of the beholder. "Then I demand to behold him," my mother exclaimed. "Is the youth deformed? What
has His Most Christian Majesty to be ashamed of that he refuses
to send a portrait?"

Meanwhile, I tried to make certain that my final thoughts, as
I drifted off to sleep each night, were of Louis Auguste. In my
mind's eye he was tall and noble, with a playful expression in that
"pleasing countenance" of his. And of course he would move
with uncommon grace in a ballroom. The courtiers of Versailles—dozens upon dozens of glamorous men and women in
patches and paint, sparkling with jewels from their necks to their
shoe buckles—would become bilious with jealousy when the
dauphin took my hand to lead me onto the gleaming parquet in
the Galerie des Glaces, the Hall of Mirrors—our reflections mag-
nified not merely in the numerous looking glasses and the
weighty crystal pendants of the myriad chandeliers, but in hundreds of envious eyes.

ELEVEN

Renunciation

A pair of servants bustled about the breakfast room, clearing away the remnants of sweet rolls and chocolate. That morning my mother had violated her own strict dietary regimen and consumed two pots of the thick, bittersweet beverage. Her request of King Louis had been granted, but the result was worthless. Brandishing the engraving as she pointed with equal dismay to the other two very similar compositions that had accompanied it, she demanded of the marquis de Durfort, "What is the meaning of this?"

The emissary took a half step backward, striking a haughty pose by thrusting out his right leg as his chin tilted skyward. He held the *attitude* as though he expected Monsieur Ducreux to arrive at any moment with his brushes and easel, prepared to immortalize him. "Is there a problem, Your Imperial Majesty?"

"*Bien sûr*, there is a problem, monsieur! I engage one of your own countrymen to paint my daughter, not to mention several of her siblings—as a gift to your sovereign. We spend months in preparation for her sitting so that she will be depicted in the most flattering mode—proof to Louis that Antonia's abundant gifts will render her an eminently suitable dauphine. All I request in return is a portrait of the dauphin. And this is what Louis sends me?" She slapped the table with such force that the trio of engravings became momentarily airborne. "Fetch me Choiseul!"

Moments later the duc was admitted to the breakfast room. Diplomat that he was, he immediately sensed that something was amiss. "Madame." He bowed deeply to the empress, who dismissed the formality with a wave of her hand.

"Choiseul, does the king of France mock me?" my mother inquired in a tone that clearly indicated her displeasure. Before Louis's minister could formulate a reply, she added, "Is it not enough that I must contend with a sheaf of documents from the French disputing the order of precedence on the marriage treaty? Do you truly expect me to agree that the dauphin's name should be written before my daughter's, even on the formal proxy certificate—for a nuptial ceremony that is to take place on *Austrian* soil, in *our* Augustinian Church? It is too much to bear, monsieur le duc."

Maman leveled her gaze at the duc. "The archduchess takes precedence in her own country, Choiseul. On that account, there will be no capitulation from Austria; and, at this stage in the game," she added, scowling at the engravings displayed before her, "little room for compromise."

"Is it the wording of the marriage treaty that has so agitated Your Imperial Majesty this morning?" the duc de Choiseul inquired calmly.

By way of a reply, my mother continued to assail him. "It is *this. This* is what your sovereign has dispatched in response to my request for a portrait of the dauphin. What do you see here?" She cupped her hand and beckoned him. "Come closer."

Placing his pince-nez on the bridge of his nose, the duc de Choiseul peered through the spectacles and examined the three engravings. He cleared his throat. "Well...I see a pastoral composition bordered by trees at either edge...a good deal of sky, a sprinkling of coaches, mounted equerries, a trio of horses—"

"And what do the horses appear to be doing?" Maman acerbically inquired.

Choiseul raised his monocle and inserted it in front of his right eye. He peered at the engraving in question. "That appears to be a plow, Your Imperial Majesty."

"And who is the figure that appears to be pushing it—the one in the tricorn, dressed like a member of the lower gentry?"

The minister exchanged an awkward glance with the marquis de Durfort. "That would be—ah—that would be the dauphin, madame."

Silence descended on the room. I could hear the beating of my heart beneath my stays. Was I expected to say anything? I rose from my chair and tentatively approached my mother, who was still fuming over the highly irregular manner in which the dauphin had been depicted, sputtering like the hot oil used to fry *Schupfnudeln*. The engravings in and of themselves were charming; but I had to admit that Maman was fully in the right. We were certainly no closer to knowing what my betrothed looked like. They read my disappointment in my face. But it was my mother's displeasure that mattered.

Maman rang for a portable desk, which appeared within moments. Choiseul watched her remove a sheet of fine laid paper and dip a sharpened quill into a silver inkwell. With a fierce sense of purpose, she penned a torrent of words, barely pausing to refill the nib. A few flicks of her wrist sanded the letter from a sterling shaker. Passing a tiny spoon filled with nibs of red wax back and forth over a candle, she waited until the dripping wax pooled in a perfect circle the size of a coin, then sealed the missive by pressing into the soft wax with a stamp bearing the imperial crest.

"See that this reaches my royal brother without delay," she commanded, thrusting the letter at the marquis de Durfort. "I am to receive a proper portrait of His Royal Highness the Dauphin or it remains doubtful whether Antonia will marry his grandson by proxy next month."

A startled gasp escaped my lips, and I saw my shocked expression mirrored in the diplomats' faces. Was Maman bluffing, or did she really mean it?

April 9, 1770

He is so handsome! Imagine my delight when after so many months, nay *two years*, of wondering, a pair of portraits of Louis Auguste arrived at the Hofburg today. They were delivered by a stranger, as the marquis de Durfort had business at Versailles—preparing the French entourage's journey to Vienna for my proxy wedding ceremonies. Maman seemed pleased with the images, but no one could have been more delighted than I. I promptly requested one of them for my sleeping chamber, where, at long last, I have been permitted to return. Now I will be better able to picture sharing a bed with him. In the painting, the dauphin's hair is powdered, lending him a graver appearance than his fifteen years, but that is all to the good, as I shall depend upon him to guide me. If I must put a word to his face and figure, I would say it is "stalwart," for I find him neither slender nor stout. His eyes are a somewhat lighter shade of blue than my own, which

surprises me because I had heard that his hair in its natural
state is quite brown. Nonetheless, their expression is kind.
His mouth is on the full side. For weeks I have been trying to
picture kissing it, but as I have never kissed anyone on the
lips I'm unable to imagine whether the sensation would be a
pleasant one. I sat on my bed and gazed at the portrait for
some time, ultimately concluding that if I have to leave Austria and my family to marry someone for the benefit of the
empire, I could do worse than Louis Auguste of France. My
future husband is not ugly and stupid like my beloved Charlotte's *mari*, King Ferdinand of Naples, who cares for naught
but hunting and gourmandizing. And wenching, she wrote,
without bothering to explain herself.

I pity her. It is not Charlotte's fault that she had to marry
a lout with dirt under his fingernails and bid farewell to her
homeland to rule a provincial kingdom by the sea, while I
will one day be queen of the most exciting court in the world.
I have not had a letter from her in weeks; has she grown jealous of me? Frankly, I am afraid to ask.

My last week of anything resembling a normal life had drawn to
a close. On the fifteenth of April, Easter Sunday, the ascension of
Our Lord was overshadowed by King Louis's ambassador, when
our family Mass in the Kammerkapelle was interrupted by a
tremendous commotion. The marquis de Durfort had returned
to Vienna in state, at the head of the grandest cavalcade I had ever
seen. Hundreds of horses, meticulously groomed and splendidly
caparisoned, sporting feathered plumes of red, blue, and white,
and fine saddles tooled in gold leaf, pranced and tossed their
manes as if they somehow comprehended that a momentous
event was about to take place. The parade of carriages clattering
into the cobblestone courtyard of the Hofburg seemed never to

end; I counted forty-eight—all of them six-in-hand! And that sum did not even include the two massive berlines, traveling coaches that had been commissioned especially by Louis Quinze to conduct me from Austria to Versailles.

I had never been much enamored of the marquis de Durfort, with his *mouches* and his enameled snuffboxes and his pretensions to grandeur. Truly—did he need to ride into Vienna accompanied by an entourage of one hundred and seventeen servants, attired in the Durfort livery of yellow, blue, and silver, as if he himself were as lofty as a Bourbon? I was puzzled by such self-aggrandizement in a mere marquis, but Maman took a more pragmatic view. For the past four years, ever since our chancellor, Prince Kaunitz, and the duc de Choiseul had put their diplomatic heads together and conceived of a marriage between the dauphin and me—a union that would at long last create a vital alliance between our two realms—the king of France had sought to outdo Austria for pageantry and extravagance.

The marquis made a grand show of presenting the duo of traveling berlines to Maman—and me, of course. *Of course, of course, of course;* with him everything was always of course, a meaningless parenthetical peppering his sentences. Although the marquis spoke of the great expense to which Louis of France had gone to build the pair of carriages, thus doing the ultimate honor to the House of Hapsburg—because (of course) their archduchess could never be expected to travel to Versailles in anything less spectacular—what remained unsaid, suspended in the gaps between his flowery words, was that we Austrians were little better than bourgeoisie, ill-equipped to provide for the family's most celebrated bride in such glorious fashion as the French had managed to do without breaking a sweat.

Maman pursed her lips as she ran a gloved hand over the delicate crowns and allegorical images limned on the coaches' shiny blue exteriors. I studied her expression during Durfort's recitation of the berlines' numerous attributes—"built from two different rare woods, but of course the cost was nothing compared to the necessity of transporting the future dauphine of France in the manner to which His Most Christian Majesty anticipates she will soon become accustomed ... the body is coated with glass, which of course accounts for the magnificent shine, and of course the windows are glass; and in case the dauphine should become bored with one of the carriages, each interior is different. Here we have the crimson velvet, and of course in the other berline you will see that it is royal blue—colors found, of course, in the Bourbon coat of arms. In both of the coaches the upholstery is embroidered in gold and silver threads; in this one you will notice images of each of the four seasons, while atop the roof ..."

I had seen that look many times before when Maman grew annoyed at something. The marquis's self-congratulatory description of the carriages' superlative features was as the buzzing of a horsefly about her head. "Ah, *oui*," she agreed, masking her envy with an aura of appreciation at everything her sovereign brother had done for her daughter. "The gilded bouquets that garnish the four corners of the roof are indeed incomparable. You are quite right, monsieur le marquis, I have never seen anything like it."

Our carriages were nothing to the two berlines, and we knew it. Austria's most lavish conveyances, the imperial coaches for "all highest persons," meaning the sovereigns, Maman and Joseph, were distinguished from the carriages that were used by the rest of the royal family only by the color of their paint: black on top and a deep shade of green below. The golden bands that ornamented the circumferences of the deep green wheels were paltry adornments compared to the French berlines' numerous embellishments.

The unspoken competition was on. Maman became more de-termined than ever to overwhelm the French delegation with Austrian pomp and ceremony. After all, she had the hope of a vast empire at her back and the ability to harness their excite-ment. Was there a single soul in Austria who was not delighted that the archduchess Antonia would someday be queen of France? Many of our countrymen and women remembered well the havoc of the Seven Years' War. The alliance created by my marriage would ensure a lasting peace.

And yet, the bride herself was of two minds. In a few days' time I would be handed into one of those berlines, never to see my homeland again. And as the hours proceeded apace, Maman knew it was her last chance to dazzle. In those final giddy days I saw even less of my mother. She was meeting with dignitaries and entertaining the visiting French nobility. Perhaps she recognized that it was for the best, that within a space of time that could now be counted in hours I would lack her presence altogether. Or per-haps she was simply too busy hosting the grandest celebrations to grace the Hofburg in decades.

I caught her eye at one point and we held each other's gaze until I saw Maman's lips begin to twitch and she noticed my ef-forts to blink away the mist that heralded the onset of tears.

This was no time for sentiment, I knew. Each of us had our roles to play.

On the afternoon of the marquis's arrival, in another display of diplomatic protocol before the entire court, Durfort, on behalf of his sovereign Louis of France, made the formal demand for my hand in marriage to his Most Christian Majesty's grandson the dauphin Louis Auguste. It was only after Maman accorded her equally formal, and scripted, consent, that I was summoned to the mirrored Spiegelsaal, the grandest of the Hofburg's formal rooms of state, to receive my due: a miniature portrait of the dauphin surrounded by a wreath of brilliants. My mother pinned it to a red sash that she fastened diagonally across my torso. Sparkling and beribboned, I felt like a *Tannenbaum*.

"Hand in hand with a mother's fondest hopes are those of your motherland and of the land in which you will become a mother yourself."

I bent my knees and offered a shallow curtsy. "*Merci*, Maman," I murmured. She cocked her head as if to say "I'm the *empress* today," and my eyes widened in mute apology. I touched the sash and pressed my fingers to the portrait of my future husband. How magnificent it all was! And how overwhelming! I stood straighter and taller than ever and lifted my chin with pride.

Months earlier, I had attended the opera after the formal announcement of my engagement, an event that entailed four hours in the *friseur*'s chair while Sieur Larsenneur teased my hair to astonishing heights and affixed a number of false switches and plaits. I had to sleep with my neck on a wooden block so as not to muss his creation, in addition to being laced into a corset so rigidly boned I could scarcely breathe. In the imperial box at the opera house, the audience, from barons to wealthy burghers, rose as one to turn around and gawp at me as if I were a two-headed circus animal or some other accident of nature. They all wished to glimpse "the littlest archduchess," as I heard someone say—curious to see how I was dressed, the way I wore my hair, and whether I was a beauty.

Yet that experience, at once heady and horrifying (for I thought they would have taken a piece of me home with them, had it been possible), would be nothing in comparison to what lay ahead.

"But won't the archduchess enjoy being the center of attention?" Minding the difference in our stations my maid Liesl spoke as if I were not in the room, rather than directly addressing me—a ridiculous affectation when one young woman is lacing the stays of the other. She rarely remembered to refer to me in the third person, and I always found it jarring when she did so. As it was, I was feeling less and less like a living creature of flesh and blood the nearer we came to the date of my proxy wedding.

"Maman thinks I should rejoice, of course, because of the glorious future that awaits me. But to me the glory is Austria's, not Antonia's. They will dress my hair for hours; I will kneel before the altar in a resplendent gown that weighs as much as I do. But when the vows are spoken it will be an empire that weds a kingdom."

What better proof of this could there be, but the ceremony for which Liesl was now dressing me? Within the hour I would formally renounce all claims to the imperial throne. In accordance with my mother's directive, the corset had been laced so tightly that my spine felt like a ramrod. I slid my feet into a pair of backless brocade slippers and tied my panniers about my waist. Liesl, blinking back tears, pinned the frothy lace *engageantes* to the sleeves of my chemise. As loyal and kind as she was fastidious, Liesl was five years older than I and already a mother. Sometimes she would bring her little boy, Fritzi, for me to play with, and we would sit on the floor of my sleeping chamber for hours, because he loved to crawl about and get into mischief. One day I gave him a little wooden duck pulled by a string and he had never seemed happier, even though he tried to bite it. I dared not mention it to Maman, but I hoped that my servants at Versailles would let me play with their children.

"Beg pardon, madame." Liesl caught a falling tear with the cuff of her sleeve. I, too, sniffled a bit. She was not to accompany me to France and we both knew that in a few days' time we would never see each other again. She helped me into my sacque gown, a rich shade of blue (to complement my eyes), festooned with colorful flowers fashioned from gathered ribbon, carefully fastened the stomacher to my stays; then, humming to herself as she held the pins between her lips for safekeeping, affixed the gown to the stomacher. I was fond of trying to make her laugh so she would drop the pins, but nothing I could say today seemed to cheer her.

Liesl had already rolled up my gloves so that it would be easier for me to don them. One hand at a time, she held the glove open so I could work my fingers inside, then she rolled the glove back over my palm and smoothed it all the way up my arm to my elbow until the whisper-soft kid clung like a second skin.

A little jewel box, covered in royal blue velvet, rested atop the *demilune* beside my bed. I opened the clasp and removed the chest's only treasure, working it onto my finger. I took a step or two toward the window. A million motes floated on the beam of sunlight that filtered through the panes, and I tilted my hand, the better to catch the light in the facets of my new ruby ring. It was a gift from the dauphin, arriving the previous day with the marquis de Durfort and his resplendent entourage—just in time for me to wear it during the renunciation ceremony. Afterwards, I would place it in Ferdinand's care so that he, as my proxy bridegroom, could slip it onto my finger during the wedding ceremony.

The tiny diamonds surrounding the center stone winked as if to reassure me that everything would be all right. I wouldn't need Austria once I became dauphine. I would have *him*. The ruby, a crimson richer than ripe cherries, symbolized the depth of his affection for me. Of course, I had no inkling of whether such thoughts had entered the dauphin's head when he dispatched the ring, but it pleased me to ascribe such kind sentiments to the stranger I knew only from his portrait on my wall.

I admired myself in the pier glass as Liesl arranged the folds of the heavy silk train between my shoulder blades. She gently patted me on the back to indicate that I was dressed and ready to go. "And—we are finished! *Zehr schöne*, madame. Very pretty."

She handed me an ivory-handled silk fan and curtsied to me. I left my rooms and began the long walk through the Leopoldine wing from our residence to the official State Rooms.

The salon was crowded with men—dozens, perhaps; they stood too close to count, although the French nobles appeared disinterested in mingling with our Austrian aristocrats. Nearly every one of the inlaid octagons on the floor of the Pietra-dura Room was occupied by a dignitary—a riot of ribboned sashes, blindingly white hose, and polished black slippers. When they turned their heads to look at me as I entered the salon, a cloud of perfume, powder, and scented pomade wafted toward the doors. Their myriad conversations in a babble of German and French gradually diminished to a flurry of hushed murmurs, and then, as I stepped across the threshold, ebbed into a pregnant silence. The clusters of men parted, clearing a path along the parquet that led directly to an ornate table at the center of the room—and my mother.

She was wearing watered silk in an inky shade of greenish black, with a ladder of coral satin bows; her hair was dressed high off her forehead, increasing her majestic appearance—a redundancy, as she was wearing some of the crown jewels, including a ruby-and-sapphire diadem. The marble tabletop that separated us was dominated by a large document. Beside it lay a handful of sharpened quills and a crystal inkwell.

I lowered my chin and dropped into a formal curtsy. "Your Imperial Majesty," I murmured. My eyes met hers.

"Do you understand why you have come here, Antonia?" I nodded, and Maman continued her recitation for the benefit of the numerous ministers and courtiers. "This instrument before me," she said, leveling a jeweled forefinger at the enormous sheet of paper, "is called a Renunciation of Succession. In it, you pledge to give up all dynastic rights to the imperial throne of Austria and the Holy Roman Empire as well as to the territories held by your late father and his family, the dukes of Lorraine. Your marriage to the dauphin Louis Auguste, which will have full legal force and effect after your proxy ceremony in two days' time, will render you the future queen of France; and a French sovereign must have no claim, whether by birth or marriage, to the Hapsburg empire."

My brother Joseph, standing beside Maman, smiled benignly. I envied him. As a male, and as the eldest son, he didn't have to go anywhere; he was already emperor, ruling alongside our mother.

Austria's chancellor, Prince Kaunitz, then read the entire renunciation document, start to finish. If it was possible to be both bored and anxious all at once, I was the very picture of it. My knees gently trembled and my heart quavered like a snare drum, even as my mind wandered. While the prince droned on, something made me glance at the opposite wall; the Pietra-dura Room had derived its name from the myriad colorful mosaics that decorated the salon: large allegorical pictures, each fashioned from thousands upon thousands of tiny stone fragments.

They were *us*, those pietra-dura mosaics. And we were them. How fitting that my renunciation ceremony should take place in this salon. Maman, Joseph, my other siblings who had been wed or would be contracted to do so in a diplomatic alliance—and most of all myself—we were each one of us merely tiny pieces of stone in a much larger picture. Individually, we were just an irregular shard of marble, onyx, malachite, lapis, or coral, but together we formed a full and most recognizable image: one that represented the entire map of Europe.

As I took my solemn vow to renounce all claims to my birthright, I placed my hand on Maman's leatherbound copy of the Holy Scriptures, the same Bible that had belonged to her father, the emperor Charles VI, and upon which she had sworn to uphold and defend the Holy Roman Empire. All eyes were upon me. Would I manage to sign my name without smearing the ink with my lace *engageantes*? I didn't bother to read the proclamation; I would not have understood every clause anyway. All I knew was that even as a trail of black ink spelled out my name in bold, spidery letters, in reality I was fading away, less and less a part of Austria with each ceremony.

Maria Antonia Josepha Johanna von Hapsburg-Lothringen. I tried to remember to keep my tongue inside my mouth; Countess von Brandeiss used to tease me for sticking it out and touching it to the side of my upper lip every time I applied myself to something with any degree of concentration. Relieved to have written my name without any mishaps, I then added the date: *April 17, 1770.* It was all a formality, because with so many older siblings the likelihood of my ever becoming Empress of Austria was minuscule; nevertheless, as I placed the pen on the table and my mother sanded my signature, I was faced with the realization that I was, in one significant respect, no longer one of them. Nor was I yet a Bourbon. I had just set myself adrift, to dwell in a diplomatic no-man's-land.

The dignitaries applauded; a sea of crooked teeth formed innumerable brownish-yellow crescents of sycophantic smiles. Brava to Her Imperial Highness Maria Theresa. Bravo to Joseph, His Imperial Highness. Bravissima to the little archduchess.

That evening Maman was determined to outdo the French with a dinner these foreign visitors would remember for the remainder of their lives. The entire nobility of Vienna had been angling for an invitation, but my mother pared the guest list to fifteen hundred, a number that, according to the exigencies of state protocol, included the entirety of Durfort's delegation. Ordinarily, she would serve French cuisine at a state dinner, but this time she broke with tradition. My mother did not dare instruct the palace kitchen to compete with the sort of menu she imagined would be served at Versailles for fear we would suffer badly by comparison. Instead, in a stroke of diplomatic genius, she offered up Austria's most renowned and beloved culinary specialties. No rich sauces for us that afternoon; we served good honest meat pies cocooned in buttery crusts and crisp roast fowl by the hundreds, washed down with thousands of bottles of our local wines and brandies. Nothing in France, Maman averred, could possibly compare to the fruits of Vienna's own vineyards. Our pastries, too, rivaled all others, and thousands of confections from our *Konditorei*—tortes and nougats and strudels, filled with apples, nuts, and fresh berries—were devoured with gusto, accompanied by strong hot coffee topped with a dollop of cool, sweet *Schlag*.

I sat at Maman's right hand, through innumerable toasts, even though she and I merely pretended to sip from our wine goblets. My mother beamed so broadly—the ultimate "empress smile"— that I wondered if her face was growing tired from maintaining her grin. Reaching over the gilded place setting I rested my hand on top of hers, pressed it gently, and murmured, "Thank you, Maman." She lifted my hand to her lips and kissed it, a gesture that managed to seem both affectionate and formal.

Maman did not permit our guests to linger over a full stomach for long. That evening, all of Vienna was illuminated in an enormous celebration of my impending nuptials. Lanterns hung from the balconies; in nearly every window a candle flickered joyously. There was dancing in the streets, and inside the Hofburg, the crystal chandeliers twinkled above the thousands of revelers who had been fortunate enough to secure an invitation to the masked

ball. At midnight, the sky erupted with fireworks. As the last cascades of light disappeared into the velvety horizon I was still
dancing to the passionate strains of the violins. Although it was
my night, Maman had, with remarkable indulgence, granted my
request: to feign anonymity in the guise of a peasant girl, with my
red overskirt looped up on either side to expose my striped petticoat, a black velvet corselet, and a wreath of roses in my hair.
Below us, the Viennese rejoiced in the streets, giddy with free
food and wine. In the ballroom, stifling hot despite the open windows, a young man in a black domino mask and drunk on brandy
sidled up to me. "Did you know that all of this"—his expansive,
lugubrious gesture sent an elderly reveler toppling into a cluster
of giggling women. "Did you know that all of this is for the archduchess Antonia?" I nodded my head. "*Bien sûr*—of course," I
replied in French.

"Oh. You're one of *them*." Replying in *Hoch Deutsch*—High
German—the man sounded disappointed.

"*Oui, oui*," I said, enjoying my joke. "What do you think of
her?" I coyly asked him. My gifts of mimicry did not fail me. I
posed my question in German, but with a deliberately appalling
French accent.

"Oh, I have never met her. But I wonder what sort of a wife
she will make," the masked gentleman added. He made a lewd
gesture with his hands, placing them over his chest. Lowering his
voice and leaning toward me, he said, "I hear she has no bosom.
Well, that won't be much fun for the dough-*fan*."

I turned my face away and waited until he disappeared into
the crowd so that he would not see the crestfallen look I had not
been swift enough to hide behind a smile. Despite the crush of
people imbibing and making merry on my account, I had seldom
felt more alone.

TWELVE

A Bride Without a Bridegroom

∽ VIENNA, APRIL 19, 1770 ∾

My last full day in Austria. My last day as an unmarried girl. My last day as an archduchess.

The day began with family Mass in our private chapel, the Kammerkapelle. Interminable Latin. Kneel. Stand. Kneel. Sit. My head swam with the heady aroma of incense. I found it difficult to concentrate on the Mass when I knew that the next time I entered the chapel, in less than twelve hours, it would be as a bride.

The celebrations had been lovely, even the one hosted the previous evening by the marquis de Durfort at the French embassy, the Liechtenstein Palace. He had hired designers from Vienna's Burgtheater to build a Temple of Hymen adorned with replicas of cupids and climbing vines entwined about the fluted columns. This unabashed tribute to the forfeiting of my virginity embarrassed me, although most of the guests, particularly those from the French delegation, found it a huge joke.

But the frivolity dispersed with the advent of dawn; the next step was all solemnity. As the countless hands of numerous attendants flurried about me I had plenty of time to reflect upon my state. That the vast Austrian empire was relying upon me to fulfill my destiny with dignity was daunting enough, but amorphous. However, Austria, as embodied by my mother, a woman who did not countenance failure, was enough to fill me with trepidation. As much as she beamed with pride in public, Maman remained unconvinced that I had completed the transformative journey from unlettered archduchess to future dauphine. My mastery of both the French language and the country's history remained wanting, hard as I tried to learn them. But there could be no further setbacks: my courses had begun—the event that she and Louis had tacitly awaited for so many months. My body was now able to produce a Bourbon heir.

I knew my mother had fretted constantly over the delays in my marriage plans. "The king is perfectly capable of changing his mind," she'd remarked on more than one occasion. "Dangle the prospects of a Portuguese or Spanish infanta under his nose, or tout the advantages of a daughter of Savoy or Parma, and he's liable to break our concord in favor of another bride." In fact, she was eager for my proxy ceremony to be over and done with. "Until the vows are exchanged, I'll always be looking out of the corner of my eye for a chevalier to ride up to the Augustinerkirche and interrupt the wedding, still booted and spurred, with a letter from Louis calling it off!"

Everything had led to this moment.

Sieur Larsenneur devoted more than five hours to dressing my hair for the ceremony. Mops rested on my lap while switches of the same pale strawberry shade as my own—most likely shorn from convent novitiates—were fashioned into fat sausage curls with a pair of hot tongs and worked into my tresses until it was impossible to discern where my own hair ended and where the false locks began. The thick curls formed horizontal rows along the back of my head, the lowest ones grazing my neck and tumbling over one shoulder. After it was all lightly pomaded with rose-scented unguent, I nudged my pug onto the floor and submitted as usual to being draped beneath a cloth while the *friseur* blew the powder onto my coiffure with his little bellows.

Maman herself helped dress me in my wedding gown, a different dress from the one I had chosen for the ceremony at Versailles. One of the half dozen selections modeled in miniature by the *grandes pandores*, it was fashioned from heavy cloth of silver, and after I was laced into the gown and the heavily embroidered stomacher was pinned to the sides of my robe, I felt as though I were wearing a medieval suit of armor. It would have been nigh impossible *not* to walk in a slow and most stately manner. I regarded myself in the mirror. With the French court panniers tied beneath them (the silhouette an homage to the lineage of the absent groom), my skirts became nearly as wide as my sleeping chamber. Between the silver of my gown and the powder in my hair I resembled some fantastical creature from a sylvan grove, or perhaps the goddess of the moon.

At half past five the imperial family assembled in the Spiegelsaal. "How does it feel to be the proxy bridegroom for *two* of your sisters?" I asked Ferdinand, poking him in the ribs. Not yet sixteen, he was nearly a year and a half older than I, and the closest in age to Louis Auguste, yet he seemed so much older somehow. Perhaps it was because Ferdinand was now engaged himself; he would marry the daughter of the Duke of Modena in the fall.

As the clock chimed the quarter hour, Maman took her place with Joseph at the head of the wedding procession. We began the long walk down the marble corridor that led from the state apartments of the Leopoldine wing to the Augustinerkirche, where I would make my wedding vows. The next time I entered these rooms it would be as a married woman.

The grenadiers had taken their places along either side of the long corridor that led directly to the church, smart and noble looking in their carmine-colored coats. As we passed through the gallery, they remained impervious, chins lifted, unseeing gazes facing forward.

Unlike the Kammerkapelle, the Augustinerkirche was a parish church—a vast structure that dwarfed even the loftiest of supplicants. It was precisely six o'clock when the ornate doors were thrown open and the entire edifice resounded with organ music. Herr Gluck himself had composed it and it was he who was making the soaring strains reverberate from the inlaid marble floor to the vaulted roof. Joseph led the procession of the imperial family. Then Maman—for this was truly *her* moment—traversed the length of the nave, her heavy velvet mantle of state trailing for several feet behind her. As she had preceded me, I regretted not being able to see her expression, for everyone in the pews—the entire Austrian court—knew that my marriage was the culmination of her grandest political ambition to date. If Monsieur Ducreux had been there to sketch her with his pastels, the composition would likely have been named "Maria Theresa Triumphant."

The aroma of incense began to fill the sanctuary, musty and acrid and sweet. Ferdinand and I walked side by side, nearly shoulder to shoulder. He was clad in white watered silk with a blue order draped across his chest. Under his breath, he was counting the steps as if we were dancing, matching them to the pattern in the floor so that he wouldn't get ahead of himself in the carefully measured wedding march. "One two: coral. Three four: gray. Five six: coral. Seven eight: gray."

I glanced at him out of the corner of my eye. "Shhhhh." All right, I was never a good scholar, and maybe I still mixed up Burgogne and Bretagne even after the abbé Vermond had drilled me incessantly on the regions of France, but at least *I* never had to look where I was going when I danced.

As we processed toward the altar I tried to think of anything except the import of the occasion, for to do so would only result in a childish flood of tears or the paralytic inability to continue. *Don't tremble*, I told myself. *Think of something light and pleasant. Baumkuchen*. At Christmastime the imperial bakers would make a special confection—the *Baumkuchen*, or tree cake. It was really a series of cakes, each level slightly smaller than the one beneath it, stacked into an enormous tower and iced with a bright white sugar glaze. With each step toward the altar of the high Gothic Augustinerkirche, with its soaring ceiling and pristine white walls supported by fluted columns, I thought of a *Baumkuchen*.

In this way I reached the base of the ornate gold retable before I knew it; the trip had been sweet. As Archbishop Visconti, the papal nuncio, made the sign of the cross above our heads, Ferdinand and I knelt beside each other on purple velvet cushions rimmed with golden fringe. How silly it did seem at the time, and certainly so in retrospect, to be wed to one's brother!

The wedding ceremony itself was not a lengthy one. We recited our vows in Latin and the archbishop pronounced me the bride of the dauphin of France. Ferdinand placed Louis Auguste's ruby ring upon my finger, then raised me to my feet and kissed me on both cheeks. The church bells pealed in exultation. And the whole imperial court erupted into song as the first notes of Herr Gluck's "Te Deum" wafted down from the choir loft. A psalm of thanksgiving was appropriate to the culmination of a wedding Mass in any case, but that evening it was particularly resonant.

I overheard Maman reminding the comte de Mercy that she had the greatest reason to be thankful. That her fear of the ceremony being called off at the last moment had not come to fruition was written in her smile.

The Church had offered its congratulations in music, and the

State was not to be outdone as the Hofburg's cannons emitted a thundering salute.

After the ceremony, the crush of people in the Hofburg's Audience Chamber nearly gave me a headache; the red and white salon had never been intended to host so many visitors at once. Yet Maman chose the room deliberately for its modest size, for it lent an atmosphere of exclusivity to the reception. Vienna's loftiest citizens, as well as the highest-ranking members of the French entourage, offered their congratulations as dozens of gloved servants bearing trays of iced wine endeavored to thread their way through the throng. My hand was kissed so many times I feared the kidskin glove would wear away.

It was not until nine o'clock, when the imperial family sat down to a comparatively modest supper in the Spiegelsaal, that I found the time to exhale, or so it seemed, and the freedom to be myself. The first thing I did after being seated as the guest of honor at Maman's right hand was to surreptitiously slip my feet out of my shoes. The long day had been the first of many celebrations to come; I would have to grow accustomed to standing for several hours at a time without shifting from hip to hip to relieve my sore feet.

All of my favorite dishes had been prepared. My head swam with the familiar, mouthwatering aromas of Austria: roasted joints of pork, beef stew and dumplings, strong coffee. When I thought no one was watching me I closed my eyes and inhaled deeply, wishing I could store the scents within my memory for a day when, in a kingdom far away, I might secretly crave the tastes of home.

I looked around the long table at my family. My boisterous younger brother Maxl, with his round face and rosy cheeks—always the loudest one of us because he was the youngest and never thought he was being listened to—insisted on sharing the most shameless jokes, which he had heard from the stable grooms, earning a stern rebuke from Maman. Ferdinand got drunk and jested that he no longer feared the state of wedlock, as he had survived two dress rehearsals, although he admitted that his wedding would likely be more like Charlotte's—not nearly so grand as mine. Then he chided me for eating too many potato dumplings, insisting that the real dauphin would not want a fat wife. "*Je te déteste*," I told him, sticking out my tongue. He speared a dumpling from my plate and popped it into his mouth, before taunting me to grow up in two languages.

"In that case, I hope that your Maria Beatrice d'Este becomes a *monstrously* fat wife," I teased, puffing out my cheeks. "*Oink, oink.*"

"Children!" Maman exclaimed—but I could see that her eyes were laughing. She took a celebratory sip of wine. "I have a riddle for all of you." Aware of what was about to come, she suppressed a rare chuckle. "How many Hapsburgs does it take to rule the world?"

Joseph regarded our mother with both curiosity and amusement. "All right then, you've got me. How many?"

"As many as Her Imperial Majesty has children!"

Maman convulsed with laughter at her own joke. My younger brothers joined in, but I didn't think it was so terribly funny. Joseph noticed that I wasn't smiling. He disappeared into a world of his own, contemplating something that left him with a troubled countenance. For the remainder of the meal, every so often he would regard me and sigh deeply without saying a word.

I glanced at my mother, my eyes raised appreciatively, and received a warm smile. I had made her proud, which filled my own heart with gladness. I had not failed her that day and would not do so as the dauphine of France. My family toasted my good health and when Ferdinand raised his glass to my fertility, I could not suppress a blush. No one knew as well as he how to mortify me in company. Nevertheless, I would not have bartered that meal for any crown in Christendom. It was rather a lark to have been the center of attention for so many celebrations, but the feast that evening carried a special significance. I traced the golden rim of my dinner plate with the tip of my finger, and touched the imperial crests etched into the wine and water goblets as if to imprint them into my flesh. My childhood, my home. A Hapsburg archduchess. All of it could be measured in the imposing table laden with fragile porcelain and crystal bearing the marks that distinguished us from every other family in the world. It was a bittersweet repast we enjoyed that evening, laughing and jesting as if it were any other supper; and yet, if one paused for a moment to listen more closely, our gay voices sounded perhaps a bit too forced, the jibes a tad too hollow, because in truth we knew full well that it *was* a night like no other; it would be the last time we would ever dine *en famille*.

THIRTEEN

Auf Wiedersehen to Austria

VIENNA, APRIL 21, 1770

I rose the earliest I ever have awakened on a Saturday morning; it was still dark outside, and Mops, who had fallen asleep heavily across my chest, grunted and snuffled through his short muzzle at the gross inconvenience of having been disturbed. I would be compelled to witness my final Vienna dawn while having my hair smothered in mutton suet pomatum scented with lilac to mask the odor, and then dusted with orris root powder. Four hours of aromatic tedium as Sieur Larsenneur tugged and plaited—just to say farewell. In one moment I admitted to myself that I would have been much happier had I rolled over and gone back to sleep. In the next instant, I grew excited about my destiny. For this was it! Since my proxy wedding I had been referred to as Dauphine, which pleased me as much as it made me uncomfortable. The servants' increased deference saddened me. I had known them all my life, but they had grown remote, as if they tended to the needs of some strange Frenchwoman. Only my beloved Liesl remained the same. She was practical as always, utterly uncowed by my newly exalted status, cautioning me about putting on too many airs.

"Remember what your *mutti* says: Your job is to make everybody love you," she said, giving me a playful nudge in the ribs as she fastened my stays.

I blinked away the moisture in my eyes. "What shall I do without you in France?" I fretted. "And in all those other places." I had been studying the small map on which the abbé had plotted each of our destinations from Vienna to Versailles. I despaired of making a misstep. What a gaffe it would be if I were asked to say a few words to the villagers and I greeted the good people of the wrong one!

"I am certain King Louis will provide you with a maid to dress you," Liesl chuckled. "But I hope you will not come to like her as much as you like me!" None of our domestics would be allowed to accompany me to France, for they were considered too lowly; instead, I would be separated from those who had cared for me through my childhood, and attended along the journey by countesses and duchesses who were my mother's friends, courtiers of the loftiest ranks in the Austrian empire—women who scarcely knew me.

I would not be permitted to bring many of my cherished belongings either. It was expected that I would begin a fresh life in a new land with an entirely different set of accoutrements. I dug into one of my jewelry boxes and fished through a tangle of gemstones and pearls for something that might delight Liesl's little son. I found a little brass medal affixed to a ribbon of red, gold, and blue and pressed it into my maid's hand. "For Fritzi," I said. "Tell him it's from Toinette." Then, feeling badly for not having thought of it earlier, I shoved aside her cap and slid a small jeweled comb into Liesl's hair, as if I were dressing her for a ball. "To remember me by," I murmured, fighting the catch in my throat.

Then I stole one last look at myself in the cheval glass as Liesl, blinking back tears, arranged the folds of my peau de soie gown—cascades of sea foam silk. She handed me my fan, a gift from King Louis, painted with pastoral images of peasants at the plow and buxom shepherdesses at leisure. "They are all downstairs waiting," she murmured.

Impulsively I kissed her on both cheeks. "*Danke*" was all I could manage before I choked up again. "Thank you for everything." I drew a deep breath and thrust my chin into the air.

They were indeed downstairs. All one hundred and thirty-two of them, the grandest specimens of the Austrian aristocracy—attired in satins, silks, and damasks; trimmed with ribbons, rosettes, and furbelows; periwigged and powdered; panniered and perfumed; swathed in sashes dripping with medals and orders and self-importance—representatives of the glories of the Hapsburg Empire. I scanned their faces. I could name those I truly knew on both hands without running out of fingers.

In the courtyard of the Hofburg, gleaming in the morning light, King Louis's pair of enormous traveling berlines awaited, each driven by six flawlessly matched horses sporting blue and white plumes. Charlotte's leave-taking for Naples was nothing compared to this; suddenly I felt sorry for her. She had received very little fanfare for her swift dispatch to a coarse, ugly idiot of a husband.

Maxl ambled over. In the last few months my younger brother had grown quite round. I was startled at how much he now resembled our late Papa in miniature. How had I missed it? "Antonia, guess how many horses are here? I'll tell you: three hundred and forty-two! Imagine that!" According to Maxl, who assured me that he had counted each and every one of them—twice—my cavalcade comprised, all told, fifty-seven carriages. Thirty outriders, smartly garbed in blue and gold, their dull gray cloaks warding off the morning chill, were already in the saddle; their mounts stamped impatiently on the cobbles. The marquis de Durfort and the balance of his vast entourage were grouped about the various equipages that would convey them from Vienna to Versailles. To anyone else, all the bright colors would have suggested a carnival atmosphere. To me—no. Rather, it was yet another dot on a map of sorrows, sorrows that marked all the recent leave-takings of my short life: Josepha's death, Charlotte's departure, and now my own.

I felt my heart begin to tremble; my eyes once again misted over. I scanned the courtyard for my mother, finally locating her, with the rest of my family, gathered together near one of the berlines. Maman interrupted her conversation with Joseph and the abbé Vermond to regard me. Her dark blue gaze was unwavering, almost hard. In her eyes I read but four words: *Do not disappoint me.* I imagined in that moment trying to hold a line with all my might against an onslaught of Russian and Prussian cavalry bearing down on Austria, their sabers aloft, glinting with menace and the rage for conquest. So as I walked toward my mother I looked at her with the expression she wished to see, full of Hapsburg dignity and pride. But it was a mask, my eyes distracting her from the lump in my throat that would not go away, along with the thrumming that begins in my cheeks when I am about to sob.

Two footmen in Bourbon livery unfolded the traveling steps and stood stiffly on either side of the carriage door, their expressions impenetrable. The blare of a trumpet pierced the morning air.

Maman pressed a packet into my hands and closed hers around them. With every ounce of my determination I willed myself not to weep in her presence. Then with great formality she kissed me on both cheeks, as what seemed like the whole world—*my* whole world, in any event—stood watching. She smelled of lavender dusting powder. And when she spoke, it was for the ears of her ministers and courtiers, not mine.

"Farewell, my dearest child. A great distance will separate us.... Do so much good to the French people that they can say that I have sent them an angel."

My knees buckled. I knew they were the last words I would ever hear her speak. An anguished sob escaped my lips and everything became a blur of noise and color as I sank toward the ground. I knew Maman would have wanted me to depart with dignity; but even Charlotte, who is made of sterner stuff than I, had faltered and rushed back for a final farewell. And for better or worse, as my mother would willingly acknowledge, I am ruled by my emotions.

"Come now," I heard someone murmur, as a man and a woman I had never seen before clasped me by my elbows and gallantly raised me to my feet. They escorted me to the coach and handed me inside. With swift efficiency the footmen folded the traveling steps and shut and bolted the carriage door, imprisoning me in the most glorious gilded cage ever designed to transport a human being. Silk lined the soft, padded walls of the interior. Beneath my bottom was an elaborately embroidered representation of spring. On the opposite banquette, summer and winter were depicted with equal elaborateness, while beside me was autumn, obscured by the derrière of Countess von Waldheim, an elegant, if silly, woman who had received the great honor of being one of my traveling companions.

Trumpets announced my departure. The coachman gave the command to walk on. I turned back to gaze at my mother through the large glass panes and waved good-bye, hoping she would return the gesture, but she did not permit herself to be ruled by so much as a moment of womanly emotion. Her image was fuzzy and unfocused, filtered through my tears. I brought my handkerchief to my swollen eyes to hide them from the prying gazes of the palace servants who lined our route.

"Madame la dauphine, you must think of France." A gentle rebuke from the countess. She reached out, as if to touch my elbow, but I pulled away. I gathered my skirts about me and turned around again, adjusting my position on the plush crimson upholstery, this time craning my neck to glimpse Maman. The Countess von Waldheim suggested once again that *la dauphine* might want to face her future rather than her past, but I had no interest in her metaphors. A third time I turned, linen handkerchief clasped in my hands, and fixed my moist eyes on the throng of well-wishers that had gathered in front of the Hofburg until they, and the imposing palace that had been my childhood home, receded entirely into the horizon.

Only one soul could soothe me. I opened the large, beribboned wicker hamper at my feet and lifted Mops onto my lap. He immediately began licking my hand and nosing about the new jewelry on my fingers.

"I hope you will love your husband the dauphin as much as you love that dog," the countess sniffed. I glowered at her and she reflexively flinched, realizing her place, although she was easily three times my age. "I mean—*Austria* hopes..." She bit her lip and trailed off. I could not wait for her to fall asleep. If only the rocking motion of the coach would have the same effect on Madame von Waldheim as it did on my pug. I cradled Mops in my arms as I turned my head to and fro, gazing out the windows so as not to miss a single image of my beloved homeland. So many people were gathered to catch a glimpse of the processional and to wish me Godspeed that we rode through the crowded streets of

Vienna at a snail's pace. I felt bad, as the cobbles they had carpeted with spring flowers were now being heedlessly trod upon by hundreds of horses. Eager faces pressed forward to see me, eyes shining, cheeks rosy and flushed with excitement. An elderly man, violin tucked beneath his chin, serenaded me from an iron balcony. Regaining my poise as Maman would have wished, I smiled and waved to everyone, especially the little children who skipped alongside the coaches with posies in their hands. They would never see how frightened I was, never know that my stomach was tumbling like an acrobat and that I was drowning in a sea of perfume and perspiration that trickled from my hairline down the back of my neck toward the yellow ruching on my gown.

By early afternoon, the outskirts of Vienna were a memory and our route was a banner of brown through woods and pastures. I took advantage of the monotony of the landscape to open the packet Maman had given me. Inside were two lengthy letters, one with the ink nearly fresh, the other yellowed with age.

I read the newer one first:

My daughter:

It is a great journey you undertake and as much as I have endeavored to prepare you to accept your destiny I acknowledge with clear eyes that I have not entirely fulfilled my duty and that a lesson taught is not always a lesson learned.

I winced and swallowed hard. Why had I expected kind and loving words? The admonition continued.

Do not forget that when all is said and done, although you will be the first woman in France, you are a stranger in a strange land. Do not be ashamed to ask for advice and do nothing on your own. Always inquire as to whom you should receive and the nature of your intercourse with them. Avoid consorting with those who are underlings, for their trust may be both fleeting and fickle; and grant no requests unless the abbé, Comte de Mercy, the duc de Choiseul, or the king himself has sanctioned your ability to hear them. In this way you will avoid becoming an unwitting participant in the *petits scandales* of the French court.

If one is to consider only the greatness of your position, you are the happiest of your sisters. In Louis of France you will find a loving father who will also be your friend if you deserve it. Love him, trust him, try to decipher his thoughts.

As to the dauphin I say nothing; you know how highly I subscribe to the opinion that a wife must be completely submissive to her husband and must have no business other than to please him and obey him. The only true happiness in this world is a happy marriage. All depends on the wife, on her being willing, sweet, and amusing.

There was more—much more—reminding me to remember her in my nightly prayers; to commemorate the date of Papa's passing every eighteenth of August; and to be wise in my selection of reading material, once again invoking the licentiousness of Louis's court and their penchant for unsuitable literature.

Until now you have been sheltered from animosity and gossip. But at Versailles, you will be dancing on the head of a pin, and it will take every ounce of cleverness and strength not to tumble from your perch. This pin may be the most exhilarating, but it can also be the most dangerous ballroom in the world.

Only a missive from my mother could fill me with such dread when I was already the picture of trepidation. How was I to gain the respect of the French and become one of them if Maman constantly warned me against them? How would I reconcile our good German morality with the debauchery that Maman claimed infested the court of Versailles, gnawing at its fiber like an army of persistent moths?

She urged me to write to her during the journey. And of course I was to correspond with great frequency after I arrived at Versailles, as she longed to hear of my new life there and how I was managing my husband, as she put it. I was also to place my complete trust in the comte de Mercy and the abbé Vermond, for they had nothing but my best interests at heart.

> At the beginning of every month I will send a courier from here to Paris: In the meantime, get your letters ready so as to dispatch them as soon as he arrives. Mercy will be ordered to send him off promptly. You may also write me through the post, but only touch upon what anyone might know. Tear up my letters; it will allow me to write you more freely. I will do the same with yours.

Dancing on the head of a pin. Her words sent a shudder down my spine. I reread Maman's entire letter and caught myself holding my breath at her references to the "*petits scandales*" of the French court. Would I recognize them enough to avoid them? I refolded Maman's letter and placed it in my silk purse, then turned my attention to the second item in the packet. My eyes misted over as I recognized the clear strong hand, even though the ink had faded from black to grayish green. At the top of the first page, the title, "Instructions to my children both for their spiritual and temporal lives," gave a hint of what was to follow. When had Papa written it, I wondered. Had he penned a fair copy for each of us, knowing that someday it would accompany us on the passage from adolescence to adulthood? Did Charlotte, too, receive the same letter before she set off for Naples?

I herewith commend you to read these instructions twice yearly (at least that was less onerous than Maman's insistence that I read hers on the twenty-first day of every month!); *they come from a father who loves you above everything.*

I pictured my father as I perused his little guide, envisioning his open countenance and jovial mouth with its full, soft lips that so often had kissed me good night, and imagined that his small dark eyes were observing me from a higher plane. I'd lost track of the number of times he'd carried me on his sturdy shoulders, up to bed, or through a field of wildflowers as I wielded my butterfly net in search of elusive prey.

Remember, my children, to keep your Catholic faith, in your deeds as well as in your souls. This would not be difficult as I believed myself to be a dutiful Christian in every way. But his exhortation to *above all, have no particular passion or affection for any single thing* would be a harder precept to follow, for I was nothing if not ruled by my passions.

Like Papa. Did he write those words in the company of his mistress, the Princess Auersperg? Did she emit that high-pitched giggle of hers at his efforts to demonstrate his piety to his numerous progeny? Did she laugh just as hard when he counseled us to *have a horror of high play*, even as her throat, wrists, and fingers were bedecked with the jewels purchased by his winnings at the gaming tables?

Inside my little purse I carried the gold watch and chain that had been Papa's, one of the few personal possessions I had been permitted to take with me to France. And it was all I had left of him, save this letter—the thoughts of a doting father who loved life and all it offered, even as he (puzzlingly) instructed me to *take two days in every year to prepare for death, as though you were sure*

that those two were the last days of your life; and thus you will accus-
tom yourself to know what you ought to do under those circumstances,
and when your last moment arrives, you will not be surprised, but you
will know what you have to do. At the age of fourteen and on the
brink of my future, his morbid advice seemed superfluous, a
storm cloud on an otherwise sunny afternoon.

Had Papa done as much? I wondered. He had written these
lines as a healthy man in the prime of life, when the idea of dying
was no more than that. Death had taken him unawares, much
like a hawk taking down a field mouse. In those terrible final moments, there had not been time for reflection and repentance.

I read on:

The companions we select are of great importance, for frequently we are drawn by them in spite of ourselves into
temptations, which would never have otherwise assailed us.
Friendship is one of the joys of life, but we must choose our
friends wisely and not lavish affection carelessly.

I thought again of the Princess Auersperg. Did Papa regret
lavishing affection carelessly on his paramour? And if he had,
was it because he saw how much his affair pained Maman? Had
he ever paused to consider her feelings? I studied his list of precepts. Was Francis of Lorraine encouraging his children to heed
his words rather than follow his deeds? As much as I loved Papa,
in that moment I despised his hypocrisy. But if I were to apply
Papa's words of caution to my own life, how would I know a true
friend in a court filled with people vying for my attention and
favor? I, too, was too hasty with my trust.

As we left Vienna the procession behind my berline clip-
clopped at a surprisingly sluggish pace for a journey of such momentous import. My entourage was so large that I would arrive at

the center of a town while my cavalcade of diplomats and secretaries, courtiers and cooks, laundresses and stable grooms, snaked along the rutted roads for a mile behind me. We traveled from dawn to dusk, pausing to change horses every few hours and finally stopping for the night at a prearranged destination along our route. Lambach; Nymphenburg (my favorite place-name!); Augsburg; Riedlingen; Donau-Eschingen on the river Danube at the edge of the Black Forest; and Freiburg. Often I would be asked to say a few words to the local dignitaries who were puffed up with pride that one of their own would someday be queen of France. Maman would have been proud of me for never neglecting to thank our hosts for their hospitality and generosity. Townspeople and villagers carpeted the modest public squares with colorful spring flowers; ruddy-cheeked girls with wide eyes and flaxen hair offered me gifts of marzipan and other confections. We filled every local inn to capacity, delighting the tavern keepers who could barely keep up with the flow of beer my train consumed; we commandeered entire castles and manors, displacing their lofty tenants, who were only too honored to offer us their kitchens and wine cellars. We traveled with our own linens, quilts, and bolsters; so at least any fleas we transported would be our own! My ladies were considerably fatigued by the end of each day, an exhaustion that accumulated with each passing sunset, but they lacked my youth and curiosity—not to mention my nervous stomach, which would turn a little fillip every time I despaired of making a gaffe. I would lie wide awake, trying to count the number of French knots in the embroidered tester above my head, cradling Mops in the crook of my arm and wondering what the next day would bring, even if, for more than a fortnight, the routine was much the same. Sunny days were a fragrant joy, but, being May, we encountered a good deal of rain, which engendered no end of grumbling from my women of honor because they could not open the windows of the coaches without chancing the ruin of their garments. Particularly susceptible was the Countess von Waldheim, who suffered from a horror of being shut inside. She would begin to mutter incessantly "I am dying!" and gasp for air like a carp, fishing about her purse for a vial of vinegar-water.

On the sixth of May, two and a half weeks after we kicked up the dust between the cobbles of the Hofburg courtyard, we arrived at the Abbey of Schuttern on the Austrian frontier. Here, my nerves nearly got the better of me. I had enjoyed my progress through our empire, proud to be a Hapsburg archduchess despite being addressed as "la dauphine" at every destination. These fields, these woods, these farms and villages, these cities and towns filled with learning and laughter—all of these were ours. My mind was crowded with silly questions I daren't pose to anyone, not even to the abbé Vermond. Would the trees look different on the other side of the border, in France? Would the sky be another shade of blue?

And what must the Benedictines have thought of the bustling riot of sound and color and chaos that had descended upon their contemplative life of order and ritual? The modest cell in which I was to spend my final night on Austrian soil was a hive of activity. Father Barthlem, the abbot, greeted me clad as any of the monks under his jurisdiction, in a simple brown cowled robe belted with a length of cord. Although we spoke but briefly, I saw such tenderness in his mien and a sense of utter contentment with his life, surrounded as he was by hundreds of guests for whom wealth and privilege was their raison d'être, and who cared little for spiritual nurturing, that it moved me nearly to tears.

One such person was a *très distingué* Frenchman, presented to me by the marquis de Durfort. His white periwig, fashioned into a pair of tight, sausagelike rolls beneath each ear and tied into a queue at the nape of his neck, sat high off his imposing forehead. I had seen heads like his—proud, veering on disdainful, reeking with self-importance—in picture books of Roman antiquities.

He introduced himself with a bow, touching the blindingly white froth of lace at his throat. *"Madame la dauphine, je suis très honoré de faire votre connaissance. Je suis le comte de Noailles, envoie extraordinaire de la cour de Versailles et de son très grand majesté, Louis Quinze."* With a pompous flourish, King Louis's Envoy Extraordinary, the comte de Noailles, drew a lorgnette from the pocket of his watered silk coat and peered at me down the length of his aquiline nose. I certainly hoped he liked the view.

The comte and the marquis exchanged a few words; I strained to overhear them, but like so many French, they scarcely opened their mouths when they spoke. From their gestures, it became apparent that the marquis deferred to the comte, who was, for the specific events of the next few days, the more senior diplomat. The comte de Noailles would be acting for Louis in the same capacity as that of my countryman, Maman's Envoy Extraordinary, Prince Starhemberg.

"You are comfortable, I hope," the comte de Noailles inquired stiffly, turning his attention back to me.

"Oui, monsieur le comte. Je suis très confortable," I assured him.

At this, the comte put away his lorgnette and pressed his lips together grimly. *"Ah, bon,"* he said. "Good." The men resumed their conversation. I heard the word *remise* mentioned more than once, and saw the comte de Noailles furrow his brow into a frown. At length, Louis's envoy addressed me again. "I will see you then in two days, perhaps," he said tersely. Followed by the marquis de Durfort like a dutiful spaniel, the comte withdrew from my presence with another bow, this one less florid than his first.

My stomach seized.

Perhaps?

May 5, 1770

Your Imperial Majesty:

Perquisites of political office notwithstanding, I have had no greater honor in my life than that of escorting your youngest daughter to her destination, as well as to her most illustrious destiny. Over the last two weeks she has made you, and the empire, proud with her grace and gracious manners. Universally she is thought a great beauty and the embodiment of charm and delight. In fact she has utterly beguiled the French entourage, although my counterpart, Philippe de Noailles, would seem unmoved by the sun were it to shine only upon his person.

And, I regret, even as I hasten to inform you, that on behalf of his king and country whom he feels have been grossly insulted, he has continued to balk at the precedence of your august majesty's name and that of the Emperor Joseph before that of his own sovereign on the formal documents connected with the dauphine's *remise*. I fear that the comte's refusal to accept, let alone countenance, these arrangements vis-à-vis the *remise* have resulted in an impasse that at present is insurmountable. The dauphine will remain on Austrian soil until the issue has been resolved.

The chain of couriers is in place, ready to proceed with the requisite haste. I await your instructions.

> Imperial Envoy-Extraordinary,
> George Adam, Prince Starhemberg

· · ·

May 6, 1770

My dear Prince Starhemberg:

I have been under the impression, after speaking with

Choiseul some weeks ago regarding the identical issue, that it had been fully resolved. And now I learn that, like Sisyphus, we have pushed the boulder nearly to the mountain's summit only to see it roll back to the base, bringing us with it.

We have come this far, and to have the fate of Europe stalled by the petty complaints of a pompous bureaucrat is intolerable. While it is neither in my policy nor my nature to make concessions of any sort, disaster may be averted within a matter of hours. It will take the secretaries that much time to make a fair copy of everything: Insist that they do so, yielding two versions of the documentation, one in which Louis takes precedence and the other according that status to Joseph and myself.

I place my faith and trust in your ability to resolve this calamity; the *remise must* proceed as planned tomorrow.

Maria Theresa

FOURTEEN

The *Remise*

≈ MAY 7, 1770 ≈

"I suppose Your Royal Highness must be very excited about this afternoon," Countess von Waldheim inquired politely. I forced a smile and resisted the impulse to deride it as one of the silliest questions I had ever heard. Mops, who was resting against my chest as Sieur Larsenneur tugged and teased and pomaded and powdered my hair, sneezed mightily, enveloped in a bergamot-scented cloud of orris root. My pug knew the truth, for he could feel the rapid beating of my heart against his dense tawny coat.

Who was I—Maria Antonia or Marie Antoinette? Arch-duchess or dauphine? We had reached the Rhine, the watery boundary that separated Austria from France, Hapsburg from Bourbon. In the center of the river, near Kehl, lay a tiny island, the Ile des Epis, named for the spiky cylindrical flowers of wild wheat that grew there in abundance—or so I was informed by the abbé Vermond. My very own atlas, I called him. However, by the time we arrived, all traces of wildness had been tamed and turned to artifice, courtesy of my future *grand-père*. The island was dominated by a five-room wooden pavilion, constructed for the sole purpose of my handoff, or *remise,* from the Austrians to the French. When the formalities were over, the structure would be dismantled and all the splendid treasures within it returned both to the royal storehouses and to their rightful owners, the prominent citizens of Strasbourg, on the French side of the Rhine.

The *friseur* had completed his handiwork and removed the cloth that protected my rose-colored *robe à l'anglaise*. Mops began nosing about the striped underskirt; I hoped that no one would notice that my lap was already frosted with dog hair.

Two of the pavilion's rooms were located on the Austrian side of the island, and another two, identical to the Austrian chambers, were situated on the other side of the imaginary dividing line, in France. The center salon was considered neutral territory, and it was there, in the *salle de remise*, where I would first set foot on French soil, never to retreat or look back, toward my homeland. I tried not to think of Orpheus making his fateful descent into Hades.

Outside, the torrential rainstorm created a curtain of sound; I was grateful to be inside the wooden pavilion, despite the dampness. A bevy of imperial courtiers had watched the preparation of my coiffure, glancing and gossiping as they sipped their coffee and chocolate, and picking daintily at sweet rolls that resembled the cinnamon bun queue of Mops's tail. From time to time the aristocrats would shift their position to avoid ruining their silks and velvets, when an occasional splash from above revealed gaps in the roof. I imagined they would tell their children and grandchildren about this day; yet what would they recall of it? That the dauphine wore pink and was caught biting her nails by the

Countess von Waldheim? That she poured the coffee for her entourage and was relieved to be able to speak to them in her native
German? The palpable anxiety in the room reminded me of our
family performances at the Hofburg and at Schönbrunn, as we
prepared, behind the painted scenery in the theater, to dance or
sing for our guests.

As he was the only one of my train who was familiar with the
makeup worn at the French court, Sieur Larsenneur applied my
rouge, dabbing my cheeks with carmine and deftly blending the
powder from a small splotch on each cheek into a pair of perfect
circles. The doll-like circles were an essential element of the toilette for women of the highest rank; as rouge was costly, its pre-
dominance was an indication of great wealth and status. The
addition of a heart-shaped smudge of lip rouge completed the
picture. I was deemed too young and my flawless complexion
pale enough to forswear the creamy foundation of white lead favored by older courtiers. I appraised my reflection in a hand mirror. A stranger gazed back at me—older, more sophisticated, yet
equally anxious about what lay ahead, a future for which no
amount of rouge could prepare me.

The Countess von Waldheim approached my chair, her humorless reflection hoving into view. She had doused herself with
lavender water that morning, and the aroma made me wish to
close my eyes and go back to sleep. She extended her hand to me.
Mops explored her fingertips with his moist black nose. "It is time
to change, madame."

I grinned and attempted a jest to relieve some of my own jit-
tery nerves. "Haven't I changed sufficiently for His Most Christian Majesty and Her Imperial Highness?"

"Your garments, madame."

I gave my minder a puzzled look. "What is wrong with the
ones I have on? Are they not pretty enough?"

"It was agreed that you must be reattired."

"By whom?" I demanded. "Who has the right to tell me how to dress?" She did not answer me. Instead, I was escorted into the antechamber of the *salle de remise*, where I was surrounded by women of honor and ladies' maids, garbed in peach and lilac, robin's egg blue, buttercup, and apple green, like so many colorful spring blooms.

Three wardrobe trunks were opened, revealing only a fraction of my costly trousseau. With the sort of reverence reserved for vestments and chalices, my noble attendants removed a pair of silk stockings from Lyon, panniers and petticoats stitched in Tours, and a preposterously heavy *grand habit de cour*, a formal court gown fashioned of cloth of gold with a deep, square neckline that enhanced my still-modestly sized bosom. A ladder of blue silk bows descended the length of the stomacher and accented the fitted sleeves at the elbow, drawing the eye to the filmy and delicate *engageantes*.

A pair of gloved hands fitted the clasp of a choker fashioned from a triple strand of pearls as large as peas; this was a mere backdrop for the enhancer—a sapphire the size of a walnut, which was a gift from King Louis. Another minion knelt at my feet, sliding my insteps into slippers of shimmering satin with high heels and pale blue rosettes on the vamp. Long white gloves were smoothed over my arms.

My Austrian garments—the petal pink *robe à l'anglaise* and underskirt, and the underclothes I had donned upon awakening, as well as my ivory damasked shoes and pink kid gloves—disappeared into grasping hands, eliciting gleeful cries from those who succeeded in claiming them as souvenirs.

The women positioned a trio of cheval glasses enabling me to admire my reflection from all sides. I resembled a coruscating cream puff. Wide blue eyes gazed back at me, wearing the expression of a frightened fawn. Mops sniffed about the hem of my new gown in search of a familiar scent. I sank down into a deep plié, for I could scarcely bend at the waist, and scooped the pug into my arms. The bows on my bodice must have looked like bones to him and he began to take one of them in his tiny teeth.

"*Ach, nein!*" exclaimed the Countess von Waldheim, and reached for the dog. Mops flinched and I cradled him more tightly. "That, too," said the countess, attempting another effort to remove him from my arms. "He is not among the possessions you are permitted to take with you into France."

"What?" My voice was small and horrified. "But he is the dearest thing in the world to me." Tears began to form in the corners of my eyes. If I gave them free rein they would snake down my cheeks like watery vines, marring my maquillage. Maman would have been appalled and embarrassed. But I couldn't help it. Except for the abbé Vermond, I had traveled to France in the company of strangers; Mops had been my only comfort. "But he is my pet—my companion!" I clutched his sturdy body to my chest as a half dozen hands reached for him, stopping just short of my person.

"Your little *Mopshund* is a German dog," someone said, as if to talk some sense into me. Well, *of course* he is German, you silly man (I very much wanted to reply).

"They have dogs in France, you know, madame la dauphine. I am sure that the king will make certain you are given a *French* dog to delight you."

"But I don't want a French dog. I want Mops," I insisted. My lower lip trembled. They were really going to do it; they were going to take him from me.

"You may bring the gold watch your father gave you, but you may not take the hound."

"Why the timepiece, but not my dog?" The words choked in my throat.

"Because your father was a Lorrainer—born in France," the Countess von Waldheim replied testily, sensing the onset of a storm. "Well, what is *now* France," she muttered under her breath. I was certain she was not relishing the idea of informing my mother that *la dauphine* displayed a violent fit of pique on the threshold of the *salle de remise*, humiliating the Hapsburg empire and staining her bodice with her tears.

For an instant I imagined upending Maman's grand plans and changing the fate of an empire—if not all of Europe—for refusing to part with my pet. I could envision the shrieks and tears, the threats to immure me in a convent for the remainder of my days before yoking me, with tremendous embarrassment, to some minor prince from Saxony. Maman's anger would be so enduring and intense that I would have *wished* myself a novitiate instead. But of course I was not permitted to alter my destiny. And of all the sacrifices I had made thus far, this moment was, if not the most painful, then surely the most shocking.

I feared they would do Mops some injury if they applied force to remove him from my arms. I buried my face in the thick fur of his neck stifling my sobs and darkening it with my tears. Inhaling his musty scent for one last time, I kissed the top of his boxy little head and gently, if reluctantly, handed him to the countess. In exchange I was given a linen handkerchief and a few minutes to compose myself.

The door to the *salle de remise* was opened by our chief envoy Prince Starhemberg, and I entered the center room of the pavilion. Ahead of me lay two more rooms—and France. Here was where the formal handover would take place. "You can thank the Archbishop of Strasbourg for the loan of these magnificent tapestries," said the prince, gesturing to the elaborate, and enormous, wall hangings. The thick carpets, too, came courtesy of His Excellency, as did the ornately carved chairs and the grand table, draped with a heavily embroidered blue silk cloth, that sat at the

precise center of the room, marking the symbolic border between
Austria and France.

On the far side of the table sat Starhemberg's French counterpart, the comte de Noailles, the man who had paid me so little
mind when he greeted me two days earlier on behalf of his
monarch. And behind the count stood a phalanx of French
courtiers, dressed like popinjays in shades of putty and puce and
wearing more powder, patches, and paint than the actors at our
Burgtheater in Vienna.

In order to be able to thank the archbishop for his generosity
with more than platitudes, I gave his tapestries a closer inspection. The theme was a popular one: classical allegory. At Maman's
insistence the abbé Vermond had tutored me in the myths and
legends of the Greeks, with specific reference to the moral lessons
contained within them: Pandora's box; Icarus's hubristic flight
and fatal fall. I stole a closer glance and blinked in disbelief. Here,
in the very room where I would become a bride of France, hung
the story, told in silks, of the marriage of Jason and Medea. Even
I, with my rudimentary schooling, knew that the tale ended in
the most horrific tragedy imaginable—a fiery murder and a double infanticide after Jason abandons Medea for a princess from his
own domain! I might have considered it an ill-starred omen, had
I not been Maman's daughter. She taught us to place no stock in
superstition. But truly—the choice of tapestry was in the poorest
taste. I wondered if anyone else had noticed the theme. Then it
struck me: Had the archbishop chosen it deliberately? In any
event, accidental or otherwise, it was a cruel joke and an even
meaner welcome.

Two versions of the *remise* documents rested on the table. In
one of them, King Louis's name was written before those of the
Hapsburg rulers; the opposite was true of the other set of papers.
In accordance with the protocol of the *remise*, after offering a few

words of greeting to me and to the Austrian delegation, the comte de Noailles read aloud from the documents. It was dreadfully boring and stilted and much of the formal language was outside the still-limited scope of my French vocabulary. But when the comte asked me if I understood the terms of the agreement, I made sure to nod my head sagely and favor his entourage with a warm smile of appreciation.

I heard a creak and glanced in the direction of the noise. The door at the far end of the room—the portal to France—had been opened by someone; someone who craved a peek at the proceedings, or me, or who was too impatient to wait a few minutes more for my entry into the next room. For the briefest moment I caught a glimpse of a woman's face: heart-shaped with perfectly arched brows framing an alert, almost unforgiving, gaze.

Finally, the comte de Noailles completed his recitation of the formalities concerning my *remise*. With an efficient flourish he rolled up the individual sets of documents and secured each with a length of black ribbon and a wax seal before handing them to a deputy who gave them to a second deputy, who then placed them inside a lockbox.

Now came time for the formal farewell and leave-taking. In a procession as choreographed as a minuet, each of my Austrian attendants approached me and kissed my hand as they genuflected in a bow or curtsy. Then, with studied grace and infinite slowness, as if they were wading through mud, they retreated backwards through the open door of the *salle de remise*, into Austria. The last of the German courtiers and dignitaries to bid me farewell was Prince Starhemberg, his great mission completed. Was it my imagination or did I detect an expression of intense relief suffusing his face as he raised his head from my fingertips?

The door to the Austrian side of the pavilion closed with an audible click. My entourage of countrymen and women had ex-

ited the chamber, leaving me entirely in the company of foreigners. A sour bubble of panic and dread formed inside my mouth.
Never had I felt more vulnerable and small, and less certain that
I could manage the weighty burden that had been lowered upon
me. And never was I more aware of the importance of not revealing that secret. The comte de Noailles walked to the edge of the
table and offered me his hand. As I accepted it I felt a lump rise in
my throat and the tickle behind my eyes that heralded the onset
of unwelcome tears.

Others wage war, but you, fortunate Hapsburg, marry! Our family motto resounded in my ears. A crucial alliance hung in the balance. Duty and destiny summoned, beckoned with the firm hand
of the comte de Noailles. Maman and her vast empire of tradesmen, artisans, and farmers, ministers and milkmaids, relied upon
me to fulfill it. A strong bond that would keep both Russia and
Prussia at bay would also keep sons and sweethearts, fathers and
husbands in the countinghouses, at the forges, and behind the
plows.

The door to the nearest of the two French chambers was
opened to its fullest by a pair of unseen hands, and I was promenaded through a gauntlet of gaping French courtiers who offered
their reverences as I passed. As I no longer heard the sound of
rushing water, I guessed that the torrential rains of the past few
hours had ceased. The only way to move was forward; a few
more steps and I would receive my first glimpse of the French
sunlight. I would embrace my new home, family, and kingdom.
Besides giving my husband the dauphin a son, I had but one office: to make them love me. I swallowed hard, then thrust my
chin into the air, proud, as Maman used to say about me, of my
swanlike neck on slender shoulders.

But the magnitude of the event proved all too overwhelming.
For more than two weeks I had been traveling across the Aus-

trian empire. King Louis's berlines were the epitome of comfort but I had never imagined I would often be spending as much as ten hours in a single day inside the conveyance—alongside the Countess von Waldheim who had the tendency to snore and wake up with a start, finishing the sentence she had begun before she dropped off to sleep. My journey was punctuated by myriad speeches in town squares and taverns, and long nights of card playing and conversation. I had scarcely slept, although I always remembered to favor everyone—hosts and gawpers alike—with my warmest smile; they would long recall seeing the dauphine's procession and I wanted them to think well of me and of Maman and Joseph, their rulers. The morning's preparations for the formal handover had unnerved me; and then, in the final moments left to me before I was to quit my homeland forever, they had taken Mops.

Poise and dignity failed me.

Inside the *salle de remise*, the periwigged old men with their red court heels, long-winded speeches, formal documents, and big words; as well as the thorough scrutiny of my person—my gait, my gown, my hair, my eyes, my hands—by dozens of faces, both jaded and curious, reminded me how much I was the object of a bargain, an exotic curiosity to be added to King Louis's *Wunderkabinett* of treasures.

At the center of a cluster of French dignitaries stood the woman who had stolen a peek through the doors. Surmising quickly that she was a welcoming soul in a sea of strangers, and realizing at the same instant how much I missed my mother, I launched myself into the woman's arms, clasping her about the waist and sobbing against her bosom. As my hot tears stained her pale blue-and-fawn-striped bodice, I felt her stiffen in my embrace, her own arms remaining firmly at her sides.

"This is not *comme il faut,*" she said. Her voice was soft but her tone and manner were as rigid as the boning in her stays. I disengaged myself and stepped back a pace or two, touching my fingers to my eyes to blot away my tears. "It is not at all the proper etiquette. My husband is the highest-ranking personage present and he must be the first, not I, to formally greet the dauphine."

Confusion, humiliation, and rejection filled my senses. "Who then is your husband, madame?" I inquired timidly, momentarily feeling like a whipped dog.

"Why, the comte de Noailles," she replied, gesturing graciously to her spouse.

"Ah." I smiled with delight and recognition, sniffling back the tears. "But we have already met! Monsieur le comte and I are old acquaintances by now, are we not?"

Neither of them was amused by my impish grin. The woman drew me closer and sternly whispered near my ear, "It will not do for you to mock that which you do not know or understand, madame la dauphine. The etiquette instituted by our sovereign's great-grandfather—the Sun King—is the backbone of the court of Versailles, the stays that bind our conduct and behavior."

A poor comparison, I thought. If only the woman knew how much I hated to wear corsets—or anything that constricted the movement of a supple spine! "*Oui, madame, je comprends*," I replied, though I really didn't understand a thing about their manners and protocol—or etiquette. The comte de Noailles bowed to me, though not as deeply as others had done. I wondered if he was so old—I was certain he must have been at least in his forties—that his knees bothered him too much to make a leg.

"Why does everyone bow or curtsy to different degrees?" I asked the woman, who had by then been formally presented to me as the comtesse de Noailles. She had not sunk as deeply into a curtsy as did some of the other women in the entourage.

"One abases oneself according to one's rank, and the difference in rank between themselves and the person to whom they are showing deference," answered the comtesse. Even my late governess, the Countess von Lerchenfeld, had not lectured me in so priggish a tone. "Do not despair of learning the proper etiquette, for I will teach it to you."

I gave her a grateful smile. "*Merci, madame.*" *Madame Etiquette*, I wanted to call her.

"You are most welcome, Your Royal Highness," the comtesse replied. "As your *dame d'honneur* and titular guardian—given your extreme youth—I will always be at your side to offer you corrections whenever I see that you are faltering or neglectful."

Oh, dear. So this was the lady who would be superintending my royal household, the highest-ranking woman in my retinue. I had hoped for someone much younger, one who could be my friend and companion, or at least someone who had adorable little children I could play with in my rooms—not a nanny or governess, or worse, a surrogate mother. I managed another smile, this one a good deal more wan than the first. "I look forward to it," I lied.

I craned my neck to see what had become of the abbé Vermond and Sieur Larsenneur; not spying them, I imagined they had been ushered back into one of the coaches transporting the minor members of the French entourage.

The comtesse de Noailles took her seat beside me in the traveling berline. Just across the river from the Ile des Epis lay Strasbourg, the first city I would visit within my new homeland. Everyone was out of doors as if it were a state holiday or festival; the air was filled with music, as though the gates of heaven had been thrown open for my arrival. Colored banners and pennants snapped in the breeze like dragons' tongues. The balconies of the stucco-and-half-timbered houses were bountifully hung with flowers or trellised with creeping vines of ivy. Children, charmingly garbed as shepherds and shepherdesses, danced in the street with beribboned crooks or skipped alongside our procession, rolling wooden hoops. Mothers with infants cradled in their arms lined the roadsides and waved to us or hoisted their precious darlings high into the air to catch a better glimpse of me as I passed. We paused for several minutes in front of a hostelry to watch women, clad in regional costume, performing a traditional peasant dance in my honor.

I was charmed beyond measure; my smile became broader with each passing moment. Waves of mirth and merriment—of laughter and (dare I say it?) *love*—emanated from the citizens to my coach. Had there ever been a warmer or more joyous welcome for a foreign princess?

A brass fanfare announced my entry into the main square. Strasbourg's dignitaries had gathered to greet me on the steps of the Gothic cathedral. Shielding my eyes from the bright sunlight that filled the square, I followed the church's lacy tracery skyward. Surely God was pleased with such a breathtaking monument to His might. Among the Swiss Guards standing stiffly at attention were a number of little boys attired in miniature uniforms; the oldest could not have been more than ten or eleven. My carriage halted in front of the cathedral; the door was opened and I emerged to a thunderous cheer and ascended the steps of the grand church to cries of "Brava, la Dauphine!" I turned and waved to the throng; unable to resist a chubby-cheeked tot with the blondest hair I had ever seen, I blew her a kiss.

The mayor of Strasbourg bowed so enthusiastically that I feared he might do himself some injury. *"Wilkommen, madame. Ich bin hier der Bürgomeister, Monsieur d'Autigny."*

Placing my hand on the mayor's arm, I gently interrupted him before he got too far into his speech. *"Pardon, monsieur le maire."* I regarded the cluster of distinguished gentlemen, including

Strasbourg's elderly archbishop, Constantine de Rohan-Rochefort, a distant relation of mine, and added, "*Messieurs, s'il vous plaît, ne parlez pas l'allemand. Dès aujourd'hui, je comprends—et je parle—seulement le français!*" For it was true—as of today I was a Frenchwoman and would speak only their language, feigning, for their sakes, an inability to comprehend a word of my mother tongue.

The crowd erupted into cheers. They were *my* people now. And, with tears of gratitude in my eyes, I could have hugged every one of them.

The welcome ceremony continued for another hour, followed by celebrations in every street. That evening, the houses were gaily illuminated with lanterns and the entire city sparkled with life. I attended a state dinner at the archbishop's palace, after which a chamber play was performed in my honor. Then, I was escorted to the center of the river, tripping lightly across a bridge of barges, impervious to the weight of my skirts, to watch as night was turned to day by a grand fireworks illumination. Fortunately, I was far too giddy with delight by then to find solace in sleep, for no sooner did the last of the pyrotechnics cascade into the river with a sizzle than I was whisked back to the palace to change clothes, only to descend the archbishop's grand marble staircase in a ball gown of salmon pink moiré. They had expected me to sit on a throne and observe the dancing like some elderly and enfeebled relic, but how could I remain still when the sweet soaring strains of the violins beckoned me to step onto the parquet?

The churchbells had long since tolled the hour of midnight when the comtesse de Noailles, unsuccessfully stifling a yawn behind her fan, escorted me to my bedchamber and supervised a bevy of attendants—no lady's maids for me, but baronesses and marquises—as they undressed me and prepared me for slumber.

Each one seemed to have her own task and behaved so deferentially, genuinely honored by the duty of unpinning the dauphine's coiffure, unclasping the dauphine's jewels, unlacing the dauphine's corset, removing the dauphine's gloves, chemise, shoes, and on and on. And did it really take so many women to handle a water basin, ewer, and facecloth? Madame Etiquette herself had the great honor of handing me my nightdress because, as she explained, she was the highest-ranking lady in the room. What would Liesl have thought, I wondered, having been the only attendant to see to my wardrobe and toilette in Austria? She would have laughed out loud, I believe, and then have apologized (hiccuping) for having been so irreverent.

I climbed into bed and closed my eyes. Someone blew out the candles and I heard their muffled footsteps on the carpet as they left the room. I was alone, finally. Alone to replay all the events of the day, my first hours in France. My lips curled into a smile. They loved me.

Maman, I have done it already!

FIFTEEN

Louis

Awakening to a gray and misty dawn, we attended Mass the following morning at the cathedral, where I was greeted with tremendous effusiveness by the archbishop's nephew and clerical coadjutor, Louis, the prince de Rohan. He was a prince of the church in every way, yet I could not begin to imagine him, even at first glance, dedicating himself to God and His holy works.

Small dark eyes, avid with intensity and ambition, shone in a face as round as a full moon. Strands of hair the color of walnut ink peeked out from the edges of his wig, as if to advertise his youth, in contrast to his aged, and most eminent, uncle. Beneath his clerical robes, which reeked of scent, peeked the elegantly tailored cuffs of a green silk damask coat. "At long last," he exclaimed, extending his arms, the better to display the costly lace that dripped from his pale wrists. "We have awaited your arrival with bated breath." His own smelled of cloves.

The prince de Rohan grabbed my hands, clasping them in his. His heavy rings, made more so by the pressure of his palms, nearly bruised my fingers. "Madame la dauphine, you are too young, too *enviably* young, to know how much I admire Her Imperial Majesty, your mother." His hands were moist, almost oily; I slid mine out of his grasp and surreptitiously wiped them on my skirts. "You will, for us, be the living image of the beloved empress whom Europe has so long loved and admired."

Living image? As far as I knew, Maman was not dead. But my distant relation had not finished pontificating.

"The *embodiment*, dare I say, of the beloved empress whom Europe has so long loved and admired—and whom posterity will continue to venerate." He peered into my eyes as if he wished to add me to his collection of rings and scent bottles; it made me feel queasy. And in the endless period before the Mass began the prince de Rohan made sure that I was fully aware of the extent of his erudition—to wit: his vast library (in which reposed one of Gutenberg's Bibles), his collection of art and antiquities, and his passion for gilt and enamel snuffboxes. I knew not what Maman thought of this man, who clearly cared much for worldly treasures while his devotion to God hardly appeared to be a higher calling from the Divinity. I was not eager to encounter him again; moreover, I hoped that His Unctuousness would remain forever in Strasbourg, a part of France I never expected to revisit.

After my encounter with the prince de Rohan, I could not depart the city quickly enough. I felt as though I'd eaten something unpalatable, and the taste had lingered on my tongue. The traveling berline rumbled on, making its way across the narrow dusty roads of France.

"When will I finally meet the dauphin and the king?" I asked Madame de Noailles. Ever since I had awakened my thoughts had been occupied with this encounter; I was anxious, yet eager to greet in the flesh the pleasant-looking youth portrayed in the miniature sent to me by his grandfather. "Must I wait until we arrive at Versailles?"

She laughed at my naïveté and reminded me that the formal introductions would take place once we reached the Forest of Compiègne in Picardy. "Would you like to see a map so that you may see how many more miles remain?" Though I would have much preferred to nap, I nodded my assent, so as not to appear rude, or (heaven forfend!) transgress some bit of etiquette as regards the transportation of a dauphine and her *dame d'honneur*. I missed Mops. "Do you think I will get my pug back after we reach Versailles?" I asked the countess.

"Shouldn't *la dauphine* be looking forward to greeting her husband instead?" she replied with asperity.

"I am—of course—eager to see *mon mari*," I assured her. *My husband*. How strange it felt to say those words while our wedding ceremony would not take place until the sixteenth of the month—another week away.

Finally, on May 14, as the afternoon sun began to wane, dappling the trees with amber light, we crossed the river at the Bridge of Berne and reached the Forest of Compiègne. I knew we had reached our destination when the sharp, strident blares of trumpets and buglers and the rat-a-tat of drums pierced the relative silence, save for the monotonous, soporific rumble of the coach. Suddenly, a splendid carriage approached mine from the opposite direction, and the coachman halted his team in the middle of the road.

Out sprang a pair of men, both somewhat taller than average. The older man was quite obviously the king, recognizable not merely from his accoutrements, but from his portrait. It was less easy to surmise the identity of his traveling companion. My initial thought was that the younger, rather stocky gentleman must be some sort of lackey, as he was clad in a dun-colored jacket and breeches that suited a tradesman, or perhaps a farmer in his best attire—but why would such a hireling travel in the presence of the king of France?

I alit from my coach and nearly leapt down the traveling steps. "*Grand-père!*" I could see him more clearly now, and did not wonder why he was still considered the handsomest man in France. Such a noble profile! Such bearing! His lively black eyes flashed with joy upon seeing me; and his lips, a perfect Cupid's bow, curled into a broad smile. I ran to him with the lightest of hearts, as though I were gamboling in a field of strawberries, and flung myself into a deep curtsy at his feet.

From above my head I heard a deep chuckle. "*Eh bien, c'est finalement la dauphine!* You are finally here!" His Majesty took my hands in his and raised me to my feet with ease and grace. Only after he kissed me on both cheeks and we stepped back to better regard each other, did I notice that his shoulders were slightly stooped. But it was to be expected, I suppose. After all, at fifty-nine years of age he was older than Maman.

The lackey hung back near the king's carriage, appearing entirely uninterested in the sovereign's first encounter with his new granddaughter. His gaze was cast downward, and now and then he scuffed the toe of his leather shoe against the dusty ground.

In short order the king's procession arrived and his courtiers began to alight from their coaches. What a pleasure, after all this time, to spy a familiar face among them. Although his mien was that of a diplomat, the duc de Choiseul's avuncular expression immediately set me at ease. Certain that Madame Etiquette would scold me for bending my knee to an inferior, I could nonetheless find no finer way of expressing my gratitude. "I will never forget, monsieur, that you made my happiness," I told the duc as I rose from a curtsy.

"Ahhh ... is she not *charmante*, your little bride?" The king was beaming. "As lovely and graceful as a nymph. A *wood* nymph," added His Majesty, gesturing theatrically toward the sylvan clearing.

The shambling boy raised his head as though it was a great inconvenience, and I caught a better glimpse of his face beneath his farmer's hat. Good heaven—it was the dauphin! He tilted his head and gave me a sidelong glance, which over the next few seconds slowly metamorphosed into a full gaze. Yet he seemed too paralyzed to move.

"Come, boy, embrace your beautiful wife!" the king exhorted.

He seemed utterly terrified, a large frightened rabbit with watery blue eyes. I smiled warmly, hoping to assure him that I would happily accept such a greeting. Or at least that I would not bite. But nothing happened; his feet might as well have been planted in the dark earth where he stood.

Well! If the dauphin would not come to me, I would have to take matters into my own hands. He could not know that my heart was beating rapidly, as much from anxiety as from excitement, but perhaps a proper greeting would set us both at ease. So I picked up my skirts and rushed over to him, pitching onto my tiptoes to plant an impulsive kiss on each of his ruddy cheeks; then I stepped away to gauge his reaction.

Louis Auguste answered with a horribly pained look. I felt my heart sink, my stomach plummet. He did not care for me! Was my face unattractive? My coiffure unflattering? My gown not to his taste? Perhaps he did not favor blondes. It would never do for him—and the king—to see my disappointment, so I masked it behind a gracious smile. But it was too late; Louis of France had noticed the awkward moment.

"Forgive my grandson's shyness," said the king. I detected annoyance in his voice. "He is unaccustomed to feminine charms."

I approached Louis Auguste again and took his large hand in mine. I hadn't realized until then how truly diminutive I was beside this boy; although he was only fifteen, he was two inches short of six feet and built as sturdily as any peasant. I could have hidden in his shadow! My husband's palms were as wet as if he had just washed his hands. The pain in his pale eyes remained so obvious that my heart reached out to him in sympathy. I wished I could have told him then and there that I was sorry he had been unable to choose his own bride, but I would try to be the best wife a man could have—once I knew what that entailed, besides giving him as many sons as my body could bear.

I swallowed my chagrin, for I was sure he did not fancy me. "I am certain we shall get on famously," I declared. I tried to remember the history of the kings and queens of France in order to make some clever favorable comparison to an illustrious couple, but my memory failed me.

King Louis diplomatically steered the conversation in another direction. "Well then, madame la dauphine," he exclaimed, clapping his hands together and pointing toward the royal coach, "shall we meet the rest of your new relations?"

The three of us clambered into the carriage, which would have been quite capacious for one, or even two people, but between my voluminous skirts and the dauphin's bulk, we were squeezed together like too many hens in a coop. With all the pride of owning every tree and leaf and woodland creature we surveyed, the king gestured as expansively as our rolling cocoon would permit as we rode through the forest toward the Château de Compiègne. He inquired with genuine interest as to whether I had enjoyed my travels across the Austrian empire and how I liked France.

"It is incomparably lovely," I replied diplomatically, though it didn't really look all that different from most of the Hapsburg terrain. But Maman had cautioned me not to compare my homeland to my new kingdom, and since I adored every inch of my beloved Austria, at least I spoke the truth. As the carriage rumbled on, His Majesty maintained a steady stream of small talk, as if the conversation were a ball he was compelled to keep in the air lest it deflate upon hitting the ground. I admired his ability to find something congenial to say over the course of our little journey, which (as I discovered after a surreptitious glance at my father's gold watch), was upwards of two hours in duration.

Apart from a few words that were mumbled too softly for me to hear, the dauphin did not utter a sound during the entire excursion. I sensed that his grandfather was growing testy from prompting him to offer an opinion or reply to one topic or another.

Louis Auguste was no more voluble when we reached the meticulously manicured lawns and gardens of the château, apart from an odd comment regarding the number of locks on the doors (well into the thousands) of the royal hunting lodge modeled on the architectural designs of Palladio. It all meant nothing to me, although I appreciated the king's tact in raising the subject, the way one might offer a bone to an old dog to draw it out of its lethargy.

We dined at the château that day and were conducted to separate sleeping chambers that evening. The dauphin paused at the head of the stairs and drew a small book from his pocket. He gave me one last, shy glance, and made a quick note with a stub of pencil. "My hunting journal," he said diffidently.

"But you didn't hunt today," I said gently.

"I know." His voice was soft and somewhat nasal. He seemed disappointed.

"Then what did you write? May I see it?" With an inexorable look, he clutched the book to his chest. He seemed like a large, frightened animal. I softened my tone even further. "Forgive me, monsieur; forgive me for being so bold."

"No . . . *C'est bien*. It's all right. You can see it." He thrust the leather-bound book in front of him. I gently took the journal from him. I opened it to the page marked by a crimson ribbon and read, in meticulous cursive, *Entrevue avec la dauphine.*

Interview with the dauphine.

Nothing else?

At least he'd been courteous enough not to record his impressions. How would he have put that first, dreadfully pained expression into words? I tried to suppress a flush of mortification.

If my mother inquired about our initial meeting, and she would, I would tell her what she wanted to hear. I would tell her that I had completely charmed and captivated Louis. I just wouldn't reveal *which* Louis. It would break her heart to know that after everything she had done to transform me from archduchess to dauphine, none of it had mattered. Louis Auguste had as much use for me as a pig has for a hairbrush.

That night, in the company of the comtesse de Noailles, I received a visit from the royal jeweler. He opened a case made of leather and velvet and displayed a number of rings; I was to select one of them for my wedding band. One after the other, I tried them on. They were all quite similar—circlets of yellow gold set with brilliants. Only one fit my finger; the others were all too large. I suppressed a faint smile. I had not been afforded the choice of bridegroom; why should my wedding ring be any different? I removed the ring from my finger and looked at it. This time it was not a mere sample from a jeweler's case. It was mine. I slid the ring on again, pushing it past my knuckle. *Mine.* It felt like an embrace.

The following morning at dawn, we climbed back into the royal coach and began the journey from Compiègne to Versailles. Around midday we reached the Carmelite Monastery at Saint-Denis where Princesse Louise-Marie, the youngest of the king's four daughters, now dwelt, having entered the Carmel three months earlier. We met her in the cloistered courtyard rather than in her cell, although she pointed to a dormer window in the upper story, behind which lay her modest chamber. I had imagined the former princesse, now Soeur Thérèse-Augustine, as a humble, pious woman, one whose higher calling had led her to eschew all worldly goods, like the brides of Christ that Maman and I had seen at the convents during our charitable visits. Instead, a hard face, devoid of humility, greeted us. Soeur Thérèse-Augustine still possessed all the hauteur of rank and privilege despite her postulant's habit of black serge, though the white cap she wore beneath her black veil lent her an even more severe air than a powdered coiffure could ever have done.

The former princesse was tiny, barely reaching my nose; I felt like a giant standing beside her. At her suggestion, we took a promenade about the garden, pausing to admire the vegetable patches and the distant orchard. She walked with a pronounced limp, though she did not let it impede her. I did not know what to say to such a personage, so I heeded my mother's advice and remained silent. Nuns were comfortable with silence anyway, I reasoned. I noticed that few words were exchanged between the king and his daughter as we walked; neither seemed particularly fond of the other. *How strange.* Although I feared Maman, and she'd even had her points of disagreement on policy and governance with my brother Joseph, it could never have been said that she actively disliked any of her children. Maman was exacting and unyielding, and occasionally unforgiving; but I knew she loved all of us.

We paused in front of a plot of carrots. A brown rabbit darted out of view as a slight breeze caught the edge of the sister's wimple and fanned it away from her face. She had lovely skin. Perhaps there was a kind person underneath it. After all, who would choose to walk with God instead of with kings if she lacked a pure heart? Soeur Thérèse-Augustine tilted her head to peer up at me and pointedly asked, "Are you a frivolous girl?"

"N-no, madame," I stammered, although Maman might have disagreed. "I believe in God and His Miracles and I attend Mass every day."

"I am glad to hear it," replied the sister, giving her royal father a hard look. "There is entirely too much frivolity at Versailles."

"And speaking of Versailles," said the king, "we must make haste. Rag, Piggy, and Snip, and the rest of the family, await the arrival of the dauphine; and I am sure she will want to avail herself of a good night's rest. For tomorrow night," he added with a lascivious glint in his dark eyes, "she will repose in her bridal bed!"

Soeur Thérèse-Augustine glowered at her father. "Lust. It is always about lust with you, Papa," she muttered. She took my hands in hers and held them firmly. "*Prenez soin,*" she told me, looking deeply into my eyes as if she were searching for something behind my irises. Her voice was low, for my ears only. "Be careful, my child." She gestured toward the apiary. "Do you see those bees? They are industrious and fruitful; from the nectar of flowers, they make honey with which we sweeten our tea. Each bee knows her place and what is expected of her. The queen has a natural, innate ability to control them." She stole a brief glance at her father. "But there are other hives, hives in which the ruler has lost control because he cares only for his own pleasure, rather than the industry at hand—the industry of governance. And so the bees no longer know their place. When a bee is not occupied with his own task and with the collective industry of making honey, he does not know how to use the hours in his day. An idle bee will sting."

Her warning was like a gust of ill wind. Several minutes had passed before I was able to put it, and the nasty little shiver it had provoked, behind me. So I fastened onto another element of the recent conversation—an exceedingly odd remark uttered by His Majesty.

"Begging your pardon, Papa Roi, but who are Rag, Piggy, and Snip?" We were once again in the royal coach, the road from the Carmelites a ribbon of brown behind us. It had begun to rain. Spatters and dashes darkened the earth and beat erratically on our roof. Rag, Piggy, and Snip! Of course, they must be three of the king's beloved dogs; after all, back home we considered Mops a member of the family—or I did, at any rate. Poor Mops. I wondered what he was up to. Had he arrived in Vienna yet? Did he miss me as much as I did him? Was Maxl still trying to feed him marzipan? I was sure my pug, were he with me now, would take to Rag, Piggy, and Snip immediately. Unless they were pigs, and not dogs. Mops tended to cower whenever he came near a pig.

"Rag, Piggy, and Snip are my aunts," the dauphin said sullenly. They were the first words I'd heard him utter all day. "They all live together in one wing of Versailles."

"*Ses maris aussi?*" I was glad to be able to engage my husband in conversation. Sticking to subjects he knew something about and could discourse upon with ease seemed like a tactful way to draw him out of his diffidence and lethargy.

"They have no husbands," replied Louis Auguste. "*They* never married," he added with a note of envy that made me wince.

"But why does Papa Roi call them by such silly names?"

The dauphin looked to his grandfather for an answer; clearly my question had been either too ponderous or too taxing.

The king laughed jovially. "Aha, then, *ma petite*! You will meet them soon, and you will just have to guess for yourself!"

The sky darkened ominously, becoming increasingly overcast as we neared our destination. As the king wished to show off the pride and joy of France that was Versailles, we had entered the palace grounds from the north, bypassing his favorite hunting

lodge, the Grand Trianon. The six horses clip-clopped along sylvan lanes for more than a mile, until we reached the château itself. Perhaps the atmosphere would have been a bit more gay if
lanterns had been hung out to welcome us as we rode through the
streets. I found myself suppressing an astonished gasp at the
gloominess of the view. What a contrast to the flower-bedecked
balconies of Strasbourg! The canals that (to hear King Louis
rhapsodize about them) I had imagined as meandering pools of
liquid blue were choked with mud. The figures on the allegorical
fountains extolled by the abbé Vermond were cracked and
chipped and the basins themselves were littered with debris:
apple cores, empty wine bottles, shards of splintered wood; I even
spied the fragments of a lady's silk fan. Ornamental statues lay on
the wet grass where they had been left to repose after toppling
from their pedestals who knew how long ago.

It was midmorning when the carriage clattered through the
gilded gateway—designed by the great Mansart, said the king
proudly—and the horses turned into the gravel expanse of the
Ministers' Courtyard. The dove gray façade of the château was
stained brown with rain. In my mind's eye I had envisioned
Versailles as a veritable fairyland, to which the grandeur of our
Hofburg, and even Mama's beloved Schönbrunn, paled in comparison. My head had been filled for the past two years or more
with the notion that the French court was the most sophisticated
and glamorous in all of Europe. Instead, I was about to enter an
edifice that at first blush appeared both shabby and unkempt.

I was grateful that neither my new *grand-père* nor my husband
saw fit to solicit my impressions of the great palace. Then again, I
doubted that the dauphin thought one jot about my reaction to
anything. I sighed heavily behind my fan, hoping that the château
would look much prettier in the sunlight.

But I was only fooling myself. The decrepitude was so shocking, particularly as I had been inculcated to expect no less than

paradise, that it only served to deepen my longing for Austria. Why, Versailles was a pigsty compared to Schönbrunn! I blinked back a threatening flood of homesick tears. It would serve no good purpose to weep; Versailles would be my home from now on and I would do well to appreciate it.

Our entourage entered the palace through a side door and I stepped over the well-worn marble threshold onto the black and white tiled floor of a high-ceilinged vestibule. Noticing my beleaguered expression, the comtesse de Noailles told the king, "I am certain *la dauphine* must be exhausted. Perhaps she should be conducted to her apartments right away."

Louis complimented my *dame d'honneur* on her astuteness and turned down a long corridor, beckoning for us to follow him. Several women in formal court maquillage, their faces primed with creamy white lead, large circles of rouge on their cheeks, reddened lips, and black *mouches*, swished past me along the black and white tiles, swiveling their heads to catch a glimpse of my appearance before gliding on, tittering to each other behind their fans. Was that the Versailles Glide? I stopped, mid-step, to admire their grace. Could I do as well? Dare I try it now? Yet perhaps my maiden efforts might be scoffed at, and I would be more successful if I were not so fatigued. Tomorrow then, I promised myself.

A few feet farther along, I spied a very grande dame, attired entirely in lavender silk with the powder in her hair tinted to match, who had paused for several moments beside a magnificent vase of porphyry mounted on a pedestal as high as I was tall. At first I thought she was engaged in rapt contemplation of the enormous urn, hands by her sides clutching her vast skirts as she raised them ever so delicately above her well-turned ankles. Then she stepped away, leaving a pool of liquid on the golden parquet where she had been standing.

I raised my hand—first as if to hold my nose, but I quickly

transformed the gesture into one of polite surprise, placing it over my open mouth. I hoped I had successfully disguised my disgust and managed instead to feign sweet curiosity. How could such splendor and squalor exist in a single place? Even in Vienna, which the abbé Vermond once confided that he found provincial compared to Versailles, we had no end of chamber pots and we availed ourselves of them in the privacy of our rooms! "Madame, is it the proper etiquette to piss in the corridor? And in the presence of the king?" I asked the comtesse de Noailles.

She gave me a cool look as if to say, *What a silly question.* "*Il n'est pas défendu,*" she replied succinctly. "It is not forbidden."

I had expected to float through the airy rooms but our efforts to reach my residence were impeded by a number of obstacles. With an imperious twitch of her skirts, Madame de Noailles shooed aside a gray and white tabby that nonchalantly meandered across our path in search of something. Her owner? A morsel to eat? I noticed that the cat wore a silver bell about her neck, suspended from a chain of diamonds. I thought of Mops and a lump came to my throat.

With equal dexterity my *dame d'honneur* brushed aside a ribbon seller. What was a tradesman doing inside the palace, as if the passages traversed daily by the highest personage in the kingdom, one whose right to rule had been sanctioned by God, were no grander than a marketplace or town square?

We jostled past clusters of courtiers engaged in animated conversation, as though the halls of the palace were a modern-day Roman forum or Athenian agora. Some paused to regard us with varying degrees of curiosity; others, to my astonishment, with scarcely a jaded blink. And yet we passed several nobles who, it seemed, had been waiting for hours just to glimpse *la dauphine,* and who greeted me with broad smiles, although such yellow-toothed grins were rendered slightly macabre by their painted lips. Were they always so splendidly attired, I wondered, or had they dressed so grandly to welcome me? At the Austrian court, we only glittered that much on gala days.

My suite of rooms was on the ground floor overlooking the gravel courtyard. Just outside my windows the palace guards were practicing exercise drills. How was I to get any repose with the incessant *tromp-tromp* of black leather boots on the pebbled ground? But the rooms were only my temporary quarters, the comtesse assured me. After the wedding ceremony my trunks would be moved into the dauphin's apartments, which, although they were situated on the same level, were much farther removed from the bustling entrance to the palace. Workmen, their linen smocks wet with perspiration, were busily installing several boxed hedges outside the windows to mask some of the cacophony and obscure my temporary rooms from inquisitive eyes. Well, it was only to be for one night.

I made sure to thank the king nonetheless for the lovely accommodations. "I am certain I will be quite happy here," I assured Papa Roi. "Surely I will want for nothing here; and with such kind people to attend me," I added, with a sweep of my arm that encompassed my magnificently attired attendants.

"Your happiness and comfort are my greatest concern," the king replied, and from the gentleness in his voice and the warm expression in his noble face I could believe it. My *grand-père*'s familial welcome gladdened me, especially in contrast to that of the dauphin, for Louis Auguste, trailing behind us, remained silent. Would it always be this way, I wondered. Yoked to a sullen and indifferent husband who lacked even the rudiments of polite conversation? The dauphin evinced no interest in knowing anything about me. "Did one of the cats make away with your tongue?" I gently teased. His full cheeks reddened into a blush. Gazing up at him, I took his hand in mine and gave it a little squeeze. "I meant

what I said before. You need not be afraid of me." Then I playfully pantomimed chomping my teeth together. "I do not bite."
My husband looked relieved, as if he truly might have thought I
was capable of it.

But the dauphin's reticence did not disappear, even at supper.
According to the comtesse, the extended royal family was present
that evening, as well as the highest-ranking members of their various households, seated at the lengthy, and lavishly spread, table
according to rank. The king was at its head while I, the guest of
honor and their new relation, was accorded a place at the opposite
end. To my right, the comtesse de Noailles, avid as ever to catch
any faux pas I might commit, reminded me to ask her and her
alone any questions I might have with regard to the given etiquette of a situation. If I did not observe another of equal rank
doing something, I was not to do it myself. I hastened to mention
that I was the first woman in France and as such had no social
equal.

"*Exactement*," the comtesse replied. "You must rely entirely
upon me to be your arbiter of what is and what is not *comme il
faut.*" She had explained to me during one of our lengthy carriage
rides that the Sun King had rebuilt Versailles more than a hundred years earlier, transforming a modest hunting lodge into a
vast château that would rival all others in Europe for grandeur.
The multitude of nobles thronging the corridors and state rooms
and generally milling about resided here, the comtesse now clari-
fied. "When he transformed Versailles it was Louis XIV's express
intention to keep the aristocracy in his sights, and under his
thumb. Of course, everyone was aware of the king's intentions,
but it created a way of belonging and of knowing one's place in
the world. And, *naturellement*, every courtier is eager for royal
preferment because it sometimes translates into gifts of property
and perquisites of power—a ministerial appointment, for exam-

ple. As for the king—by doling out such largesse, or removing it at whim, he preserves the loyalty of influential members of the nobility."

The way I understood it, the Sun King's establishment of rigid court etiquette, down to the most ludicrously minute detail, kept the aristocracy too busy remembering such things as how deeply to bow to one another to consider revolt or revolution. Instead, the king let them argue over the tiniest particulars of protocol, such as the proper length of a cloak on a given occasion; and he awarded them honors that cost the crown nothing to bestow, yet meant everything to a courtier: hence the right to hand the king, or the dauphin and dauphine, a water basin or a chemise.

My head throbbed. I hoped I had taken up the proper fork.

I glanced over at the dauphin, seated at my left elbow, head bent over his plate of oysters. He was slurping them down like a thirsty dog with a bowl of cool water. Among his siblings, although he was the oldest and their future king, Louis Auguste appeared to have little to say, intimidated by their liveliness and volubility. He barely looked at me, while his two brothers commandeered the conversation at our end of the table, eager to learn all they could about me. His next youngest brother, Louis Stanislas, the comte de Provence, who was my age though already running to fat, discoursed wittily on everything from music to politics to literature as if he himself were the host holding court, while the youngest of the three Bourbon brothers, Charles Philippe, the comte d'Artois—thirteen, and the only one fortunate enough to have inherited his *grand-père*'s black hair and flashing dark eyes—repeatedly asked me if I liked to dance and whether I enjoyed gaming.

I quickly discovered that the comte de Provence was fond of gossip, and discretion was not among his virtues. The numerous celebratory toasts had loosened his tongue and he rather injudi-

ciously let it slip that the dauphin's tutor, the duc de la Vauguyon—who, evidently, was not terribly fond of women, and for
some reason was even less so of Austrian ladies—had spoken
against our marriage to the bridegroom himself. I stole a glance at
Louis Auguste, who at that moment appeared to be focused on
nothing but his helping of pigeon pie. Was that the reason he had
been regarding me with such discomfort, even fear? What sort of
dreadful notions had his tutor stuffed into his head? What a challenge it would be to make him love me—or even esteem me—
when his tutor had already taught him to despise me!

Although my appetite had fled, my new relations were impervious to my dismay. While my new brothers gaily dominated the
conversation, Clothilde, the elder of their two younger sisters,
gorged herself on cream puffs.

"Clothilde is such a pretty name," I said to her, hoping to
make another friend. Having a ten-year-old sister to play with
would be infinitely preferable to spending those hours in the
dreary company of Madame Etiquette.

"They call me 'Gros-Madame,'" the girl replied, daintily dabbing at the corners of her mouth with a white damask serviette.
"Oh, I don't mind it," she added when she noticed my look of
shock. "I *am* fat. And," she said cheerfully, "I *like* to eat. The
dauphin is the same way, and he will be king one day, so how
could it be bad?"

I looked across the breadth of the table, laden as it was with
dishes both savory and sweet. A servant ladled deep spoonfuls of
strawberry mousse onto Louis Auguste's plate until the floral motifs that rimmed the porcelain were completely obscured. *Like a
pig at a trough*, I thought ruefully. *Quel dommage*. Such a pity that
the only activity that yielded him any pleasure during our first
meal together *en famille* was gorging himself on confections.
Then I remembered how his manner had brightened earlier, at

the mention of another subject. "Tell me about all the locks, monsieur le dauphin," I said brightly.

"I lost a toof!" six-year-old Élisabeth announced, coming around the table before her oldest brother could formulate a reply. She opened her mouth wide to show me the dark gap. Seconds later, she was on to another topic, tugging on the ruched furbelow above my hem. "Do you like pink? *I* like pink. It's my favorite color."

"I love pink!" I told the child, scooping her into my arms and lifting her onto my lap.

"Madame Élisabeth, don't be rude," admonished the comtesse de Noailles. "It is not becoming of a young lady."

Heavens, she was barely older than a tot! "Oh, it's perfectly all right. She's a darling," I said, kissing the top of the child's head. "And she smells so sweet, too! You're just a little *bonbon*," I told Élisabeth.

She giggled. "I'm *not* a bonbon; I'm a *girl*."

"Ho, really?!" I tickled her under the chin, and before I could ruminate any further on the realization that these five royal siblings had been orphans for years, I discovered that I was being watched by Mesdames *tantes*, the dauphin's maiden aunts, Adélaïde, Victoire, and Sophie—or Rag, Piggy, and Snip, as their father inexplicably called them. Having never wed, King Louis's daughters seemed quite miffed by the antics of the energetic young child.

The three princesses, born in consecutive years, were now in their thirties. They seemed terribly worldly, and had opinions on everything, which they proffered as general pronouncements. The duchesse de Penthièvre looked sickly in puce (said Sophie, who was somewhat gaunt herself); the chamber musicians played flat (according to Adélaïde, who was proficient on the French horn and the mouth organ, so she told me); the bishop's sermon at

Mass that morning had been dreary to the point of deadliness (Adélaïde again); the current price of Lyon silk was absurd (insisted Victoire, who needed many more yards of it to cover herself than did her sisters); and only Sèvres porcelain was suitable for, well, anything (a general agreement, along with the princesses' unanimously shared view that spaniels were far and away the best sort of dog). Eager to introduce me to life at court, Mesdames *tantes* made me promise to visit their apartments daily, where they would share the latest news.

Little Princesse Élisabeth announced that she could balance a spoon on the tip of her nose and proceeded to demonstrate her new talent, to the delight of her brothers and sister. I could see the dauphin wrestling with whether he dared hazard the trick himself. I might have encouraged him if I thought it would have made him laugh. If he did not know how to have fun, I supposed that it would fall to me to show him. But the comtesse de Noailles, grim-faced and thin-lipped, looked as though she would turn blue with horror.

"Who is the corpulent gentleman seated to the left of the king?" I asked, in order to distract her. The man's ceremonial sash strained to contain his girth.

"One does not point with one's fan, madame la dauphine." Madame Etiquette then proceeded to demonstrate the method of selecting someone from within a crowd with the most subtle of gestures. "That is the duc d'Orléans," she said, with an almost imperceptible tilt of her own fan. "He comes from another branch of the Bourbons. And so you will never refer to it, the Orléans *famille* does not get on very well with the royal family."

At my insistence, as I wished to know the names of everyone at the table as well as their functions at court, the comtesse identified the ducs de Penthièvre, Chartres, and Bourbon, the comte de la Marche, and the princes of Condé and Conti, all of whom were interrelated, most often by marriage. Because their names sounded so similar I was sure I would confuse the titles of Condé and Conti forever, and so I would have to remember them by their looks. The prince de Conti had a supercilious air, and seemed fond of various shades of green. The prince de Condé had the look of the aesthete about him, an opinion I was quick to share with Mesdames *tantes*, who lauded me as a sharp judge of character and informed me that Condé was indeed exceptionally passionate about gardens. I made a mental note to inquire about the *hameau*, or little village, and the follies he had designed for his newly constructed Château d'Enghien.

Thus far, the prince de Condé, although I had not been able to converse with him as he was seated so far from my chair, was (with the possible exception of Princesse Élisabeth and her silver spoon) the most intriguing person at the table.

Above the strains of the violins and the tinkling of crystal and porcelain, a silvery laugh pierced the air, drawing all attention toward the head of the table. The woman seated at the king's right had grabbed a morsel off the royal plate with a heavily jeweled hand and popped it into her own mouth. She wore no powder in her flaxen hair, a shade or two more yellow than my own. Her complexion was the color of fresh dairy cream—the better to show off her enviable *poitrine* in a gown of silver tissue spun with gold and spangled with rubies, from a sprinkling of them on her sleeves to a crimson crust that framed her deep décolleté. The sapphires in her ears and the triumph in her eyes lent her more airs of an empress than Maman ever had. My eyes strayed downward. Immediately I felt inadequate and wished that my own bosom was as pulchritudinous and had been molded to such perfection.

I gazed at her coiffure, which sparkled with emerald combs. Perfectly applied circles of rouge enhanced her natural blush. I

surveyed the length of the table; here sat the highest-ranking nobility of France and yet none of the women were so bedecked in
brilliants as this fascinating creature, who was so bold as to eat off
the king's plate. I could not take my eyes off her. She took another
bit of squab from His Majesty's dish and fed it to him. Louis took
not only the pigeon but her fingers into his mouth, enjoying both
with gustatory relish. He shared a full-bellied laugh with the
woman.

"What an intriguing person!" I exclaimed. I turned to address
Madame de Noailles. "*S'il vous plaît, madame la comtesse, dites-
moi—qui est cette belle dame-là?* Tell me, who is that very beautiful woman—and what is *her* office here at court?"

My dining companions grew silent. Madame Etiquette's back
stiffened perceptibly. At the far end of the room, Louis of France
and his personal guest of honor paid no heed to anything other
than their amusing little game of feeding each other. Mesdames
tantes muttered behind their fans in voices too low for me to discern the gist of their discourse. All I could hear, and the word was
uttered repeatedly with a derisive intonation, was "*elle*"—*her*.

The aunts looked to the comtesse de Noailles to furnish a
reply; after all, I had posed the question to her directly. All three,
Adélaïde, Victoire, and Sophie, had screwed their mouths into
odd little smirks that I did not understand. The dauphin coughed
quite audibly into his napkin. His younger brothers stifled a
snicker and collectively regarded my *dame d'honneur* through
narrowed eyes, waiting with undisguised amusement for her answer.

"*That woman,*" began the comtesse, speaking with painstaking deliberateness—and I had yet to hear her speak so slowly—
"*that woman* is Madame du Barry, *ci-devant*—formerly—the
lowly Jeanne Bécu, although some knew her as Mademoiselle
l'Ange of the rue de la Jussienne; and *her* office is to . . . to amuse
the king!"

Her nickname, Mademoiselle l'Ange, intrigued me. The Angel. Surely I appeared more seraphic; and it would be my pleasure to charm His Majesty and make him laugh. "Well, then!" I clapped my hands with glee, for nothing would have made me happier than to delight my new *grand-père*. "I shall be her rival," I exclaimed.

The dauphin, his brothers and aunts, and most particularly Madame de Noailles, froze as if a portraitist had asked them to hold a pose—cutlery and crystal goblets held aloft, halfway between the table and their lips.

Was it something I had said?

SIXTEEN

Finally!

⤳ MAY 16, 1770 ⤶

"They say it is a sign of good luck when it rains on your wedding day." I was being laced into my gown by a duchesse (of all things!) who offered me this platitude, although I'm sure her words were intended to reassure me.

"It's only a spring drizzle," I said, making polite small talk. Then I realized I had made a pronouncement and because the duchesse was my inferior, she could not disagree.

"*Ah, oui*. Only a drizzle," she echoed.

Sieur Larsenneur, a familiar pair of hands, was waiting patiently with several lengths of pearls to be threaded into my coiffure. It had taken him two hours to frizzle my hair with his heated wand and curling papers, after which he teased my tresses over a cage fashioned from wood and wire that had been precariously perched atop my head. Then, having swathed me in a length of muslin to protect my gown and shielded my face with a little mask, he had pumped powder onto my towering hairstyle with his little bellows.

I heard my *friseur* murmur something to the duchesse de Ventadour. The two of them stepped away from me to better regard the back of my gown.

Turning my head, "Why the frowns?" I asked them. They beckoned to the comtesse de Noailles and solicited her opinion, which was offered without a moment's hesitation.

"*Il n'est pas comme il faut.*"

I felt my stomach clench. *What* wasn't right? They referred to something behind me, so I tried to get closer to the mirror in order that I might see for myself.

"It will not close; there is not enough fabric," the duchesse de Ventadour said ruefully. "*Regardez.* I have pulled the laces as tight as I can, but you can still see the dauphine's shift."

"And the wide bands of *diamantes* on either side of the grommets emphasize rather than distract from the problem," observed my *friseur*.

Madame de Noailles allowed herself a rare moment of unchecked behavior. "How could they have gotten it so wrong? They had her measurements."

I heard the trio whispering among themselves, and the worried murmurs from the noblewomen who had been accorded the honor of witnessing the dauphine's bridal preparations. *No*, I wished to say to them, *I did not eat two desserts last night and I did not grow broader in these last few weeks and I do not know why the bodice of my wedding gown is too small and how the measurements provided by my mother months ago could have been so misconstrued.* The nervous butterflies that fluttered in my belly became as large as hummingbirds.

Was this little last-minute mishap supposed to bode good luck as well? Maman would have scoffed at such superstitious nonsense. But—after all the money she had lavished on my trousseau and all the pains she had taken to prepare me for this day—she most certainly would not find a single note of amusement in the current state of affairs. I thought of the crate of fashion dolls that had been sent to us in Vienna so that I might select one of the bridal gowns. The robe I had fancied most was modeled by the doll I had named for my beloved sister Josepha and was fashioned from cloth of gold and cloth of silver with a rose-colored under-skirt and a lavishly embroidered train several feet long. But had the silkmakers, weavers, and royal seamstresses fitted the dress to the figure of the four-foot-tall *grande pandore* instead of me? We had not been all that dissimilar in size, especially then.

The comtesse de Noailles tutted and sighed and muttered under her breath. She ticked off a number of possible solutions on her fingers and, with the acknowledgment that time was of the essence, ultimately resolved to turn an embarrassing gaffe into a display of glamour. "We will remove the dauphine's chemise," she announced.

"*Quoi?*" I was shocked. Was there to be nothing under my wedding gown but my whalebone stays, and beneath that, naught but bare skin? Evidently, *oui*. In France, the most fashionable women, though admittedly those who tended to be rather outré, had taken to exposing themselves beneath a bodice deliberately designed to leave an expanse of flesh in the back, in order to call attention to their pale skin. In transforming a disaster into a tri-umph, albeit a risky one, my *dame d'honneur* deemed it better for the dauphine to appear au courant with the newest fashion than a country bumpkin in a wedding dress that had been cut too small. Nevertheless, Madame Etiquette cautioned me that her decision was bound to elicit comment among the more conservative ele-ments of the aristocracy.

I hoped the gap would not become the subject of international gossip; if Maman were to hear that after all we had undertaken, my gown had not been properly made, there would be no end to her displeasure.

For so many months a great part of me had dreaded the day I would wear my wedding gown, yet since my arrival in France I had anticipated this moment with something closer to excitement. The events of the previous evening—the sumptuous dinner with my new relations, and in particular the visit I received later on in my apartments from the king himself, had truly set my stomach thrumming with exhilaration.

The king had presented me with an enormous chest covered in crimson velvet, so large that it took two liveried servants to wheel it into my salon. "As you know, I am a widower," Louis began.

I thought about the voluptuous blond woman with whom he had flirted during the meal. Madame du Barry.

"And with no queen, the dauphine is the first lady in France, and must own the most beautiful jewels," Louis continued.

Then I recalled the multitude of vibrant gems that had adorned the du Barry's throat and arms, her hair, and her gown.

His Most Christian Majesty regarded me with a chuckle as he gestured grandly to the jewelry chest. "Yet I have no doubt that you will outshine all others whether you wear these or no."

The doors of the massive coffer were unlocked and the drawers, lined in pale blue silk, were tugged open to reveal treasures beyond compare, resting on their own cushions—among them an ivory-handled fan encrusted with precious gems, and a choker of pearls the size of filbert nuts that was first worn by Anne of Austria, the mother of the Sun King. Perhaps being of noble birth myself, I was expected to react to such a magnificent gift with a sense of innate poise, but I was unable to suppress a gasp of awe. The necklace had been worn by every dauphine since Anne herself became the bride of the future Louis XIII. In that moment I felt like a part of history, a tiny fragment of a great whole. And one day, I would be fastening that same choker about the throat of the wife of my oldest son.

There was yet another gift from Papa Roi—a pair of bracelets fashioned from gold and enamel. Their clasps were decorated with sapphires that spelled out my cipher: MA.

Overcome, I slipped the bracelets over my wrists and fell to my knees before my *grand-père,* promising to be all he had hoped I would be, as dauphine of France, and some day as her queen.

Now I surveyed myself in the looking glass. From the front, at any rate, I was pleased with my appearance. Anne of Austria's necklace had been clasped about my throat. I also wore a pair of diamond bracelets and ear bobs. They were perfectly white and when I stood in just the proper way, they refracted the light into colorful sunbursts that appeared to emanate from my limbs.

When Sieur Larsenneur's back was turned, I tugged at my coiffure to soften the look of my hairline. For years now, the *friseur* and I had performed our little comedy: He always yanked my tresses tightly off my forehead and I routinely loosened them. I never asked him to style my hair differently and he would pretend not to notice my improvements.

My head felt heavy from all the pearl adornments, but it was nothing compared to the weight of my gown and train. Cloth of silver and cloth of gold were hardly flimsy textiles and I was both encased and enveloped in yards and yards of it. Would I be expected to glide across the floor as Monsieur Noverre the dancing master had taught me? I softened my knees, rose onto the balls of my feet, and took a few stuttering steps. I would not want to appear clumsy during the wedding processional. After a minute or so I began to grow accustomed to the heaviness of my accoutrements, taking several turns about the room as my train swished like a mermaid's tail behind me. It became a game to avoid knocking over the delicate tables and footstools, and the distraction helped to calm my nerves.

The marble clock on the mantel struck the half hour. At the chime, the comtesse de Noailles began to coordinate the journey from my temporary apartments to the State rooms above them. A bevy of noblewomen assembled with military precision to manage my train as I glided through the corridors and climbed the ornate marble staircase. From the Grande Salle des Gardes, we proceeded through the State rooms until we reached the Oeil de Boeuf, the antechamber to the king's suite, named for its oval-shaped "ox eye" window. I gazed up at the window, which led my eye to the heavily gilded figures carved in deep relief—cupids cavorting with garlands. *A fitting image for a wedding day*, I thought.

Here, on an ordinary day, explained my *dame d'honneur*, was where courtiers and ministers would gather with the hope that His Majesty would hear their petitions. "Sometimes they wait all day," the comtesse added with a perceptible sniff. "And sometimes longer."

I sniffed, too, but not out of hauteur as my minder did. I was smelling something rank that seemed to emanate from the corners of the room, something that had permeated the parquet. I thought of the lavender-clad lady who had relieved herself in the vestibule yesterday. Were the French too proud to use chamber pots, I wondered. Or was everyone at Versailles too lofty to empty them, even as they vied for such ridiculous tasks as handing a member of the royal family a facecloth or hairbrush?

With each passing moment my nerves began to get the better of me. As the members of our entourages mingled, a cacophony of conversations bounced off the gilded friezes and marble walls of the Grande Salle des Gardes like the chatter of a flock of magpies. Standing a few feet from me, alone, the dauphin looked uncomfortable—no; more than that—*resentful*, his bulk stuffed into his wedding suit of white satin and cloth of gold. I hoped his glum expression had naught to do with that awful duc de la Vauguyon, poisoning his mind against an Austrian bride. I had spent hours convincing myself that the comte de Provence should never have divulged such a thing, let alone to the bride herself . . . unless the young comte had his own schemes? We had just been introduced; how should I know whether to trust him? Perhaps he had lied to me after all. But if that were the case, why did Louis Auguste look so unhappy?

My fifteen-year-old groom pouted sullenly. "I feel like a trussed bird," he murmured. He regarded his reflection in the large mirror that hung over the enormous mantel. Fingering the fabric of his heavily embroidered coat, he made a helpless gesture that encompassed his entire person. "The comte d'Artois bet me that all this weighs as much as the plate armor worn by the knights in our European History books." He sneaked a surreptitious sniff at his armpits and wrinkled his nose. "Forgive me, madame la dauphine," he said, his cheeks coloring, "I perspire a lot."

By 12:45, the dauphin's siblings had arrived, as had Mesdames *tantes* and all of the ducs and comtes I had seen at dinner the previous day. Ten minutes later, Louis entered the Oeil de Boeuf and we offered His Majesty our bows and curtsies according to our rank. I had asked the comtesse de Noailles to write out the etiquette regarding the specific curtsies, or reverences. I intended to keep the scrap of paper in a reticule or a pocket, stealing glances at it until I had memorized the entire protocol.

"Madame la dauphine, you look radiant," observed the king, raising me to my feet and kissing me on each cheek. "Tell me, how are your nerves this afternoon?" He glanced at the dauphin, whose complexion was as pale as his wedding suit.

"I am quite well, *merci*," I lied, and quickly changed the subject. "My husband looks so handsome today, *oui?*" In truth, Louis Auguste, despite his pallor, and the fact that he had not stopped anxiously chewing his lip, did look extremely *distingué*, even with a little black *mouche* masking a ripe pimple on the side of his chin. His unruly chestnut hair had been hidden under a fashionable *perruque* styled into a queue that hung down past the nape of his neck; and the formal attire lent an air of majesty to his tall, stocky frame. I was suddenly struck with a frisson of pride. Were he to dress with such formality every day of the year, it would not overburden one's imagination to envision him as king of France.

"*Bonjour, monsieur le duc!*" Papa Roi had turned to jovially clap a much shorter man on the back. "Your pupil looks quite the grown man today, *eh bien?* Up to the mark, I hope. *Regardez!* The poor boy looks like he bears all the weight of France on those broad shoulders."

The shorter man, clad in mustard-colored moiré, lifted a monocle from a ribbon dangling at his breast and inserted it in the crescent-shaped hollow above his cheekbone. This must be the dreaded duc de la Vauguyon. Our gazes locked. In his eyes I read a look of pure disdain. So I decided to confound him by favoring him with my broadest and most disarming smile. I relished my little victory, although the entire exchange was over in a matter of seconds and I don't believe the king noticed a bit of it.

A flash of lightning illuminated the oval window and was followed seconds later by a sonorous clap of thunder. "Well, well, Jove has seen fit to attend the royal wedding!" His Majesty declared with a laugh. "A little rain is a sign of good luck."

I grinned at him. "So I've heard, Sire." He would never know that beneath my skirts my knees were knocking together like a pair of drumsticks.

The murmurs of countless conversations were overtaken by a

hush that filled the room. All eyes turned toward the windows to regard the torrential downpour.

In the way that boys of a certain age are wont to do, the dauphin's younger brothers began to joke about how uncomfortable it would be for the aristocratic spectators—those lucky thousands who had been granted the privilege of witnessing the royal wedding—to stand about the chapel with their silks and satins stained and dripping all over the marble floor. "And imagine all the muddy footprints!" sniggered the comte d'Artois.

"They'll consider it another honor," the comte de Provence sneered. He was dressed almost as lavishly as the dauphin, but his costume did not lend him the same regal aura; to me, he merely looked rotund. "They'll wipe up the mud with their handkerchiefs to show to their grandchildren."

"The lottery winners will be jammed together like sardines as well," said Artois.

"Lottery winners?" I echoed.

"Six thousand," the dauphin explained, "selected from the general populace, who have the honor of witnessing part of our wedding procession and ceremony. Versailles is the most democratic palace in the world," he added proudly. "Almost anyone can gain admittance, so long as the men are wearing a hat and sword."

"On any day you can see the vendors outside the gates renting them to visitors!" Artois added.

"Enterprising peasants," sniggered Provence.

Artois grinned. "Even loose women are welcome, as long as they don't try to . . . well . . . ply their trade, so to speak, in the private *appartements*."

What did a thirteen-year-old youth know of loose women, I wondered. Had my brothers Ferdinand and Maxl spoken of such vulgar topics in the company of their sisters and other ladies of quality, they would have received the sternest of rebukes from Maman. These Bourbon orphans lacked a firm parental hand, or that of an astute governess or tutor. Mentors such as the nasty little duc de la Vauguyon were apparently too busy prejudicing their charges' minds to prevent them from speaking like the residents of a barracks.

I despaired of ever understanding the intricacies of the French court. Even at its most rudimentary, it presented so many contradictions. For all their formality here at Versailles and all our simplicity in Austria, Maman would never, with the exception of state occasions, of course, dream of opening our doors to the riffraff.

At the stroke of one o'clock the bridal procession commenced the long walk from the State apartments to the chapel. Hand in hand, Louis Auguste and I walked together behind the Grand Master of Ceremonies with his tall staff. Thinking about how contented Maman would be to see me now, minutes away from taking my wedding vows, I found myself smiling, and out of excitement and impatience I squeezed the dauphin's hand. How tall he seemed beside me! He gave me a shy smile, then turned his head away with a wince that made my stomach dip. On this day of all days, I wanted him, if not to be able to love me, at least to *like* me. I did not love him, of course; I scarcely knew him. But there was something about his plodding and deliberate manner that put me in mind of a horse yoked to an overburdened cart and made me wish to slip under the harness myself so that we might lighten the load by pulling it together.

Out of the corners of my eyes I watched our reflections as we passed through the twinkling Hall of Mirrors. Tiers of chairs had been placed along the entire length of the room. For two hundred and fifty feet on either side, five thousand invited guests sat elbow to elbow to witness our parade. They looked so splendid in their *grands habits de cour*: the men in their silk coats, hats, and swords, and the women in their enormous panniers and deep décolleté. And everyone, absolutely everyone, was wearing formal court maquillage, their faces so heavily painted that some defied recognition. I prayed I wouldn't falter (or worse, trip) as I passed this aristocratic audience!

A magnificent procession snaked along behind us. Smartly dressed pages—such adorable children, I could have hugged each one for an hour—carried my voluminous brocaded train. In their wake followed the comtesse de Noailles, chin raised, with her angular nose in the air. The royal princes walked behind her—all the ducs and comtes who had dined with us, with the comtes de Provence and d'Artois at their heels, red heels, quite literally, a courtier's privilege since the days of Le Roi Soleil. The king was the last of the men in the procession; from mirror to mirror I glimpsed him beaming, the only ray of sunlight on an otherwise inclement day.

The dauphin's sisters, as excited to participate in the processional as Mesdames *tantes* were blasé about it, walked behind Papa Roi; and finally, a panoply of ladies of the court, sparkling with jewels from their powdered *perruques* to their shoe buckles, brought up the rear. We passed through the Salon de Guerre and the numerous rooms named for the gods of Roman antiquity— bright Apollo; clever Mercury; warlike Mars; chaste Diana; and finally, fittingly, the chamber named for the goddess of love, the Salon de Venus.

Some members of the bridal train were still on the marble staircase when the dauphin and I reached the cream-colored doors of the chapel, adorned with the gilded image of a Cupid. I smiled at the putti's unseeing eyes, then impetuously touched my hand to his golden wing for luck. The Grand Master of Ceremonies threw open the doors and rapped his staff against the floor three times.

"They do that when a *play* is about to begin, too," the dauphin whispered to me.

"Perhaps we are all actors in one way or another," I replied. I squeezed his hand again. "Only today, you and I are the leading players." By now I was eager for the whole spectacle to be over. I was seized with the sudden fear that the dauphin would glance at his tutor as we knelt before the altar; that a secret signal would pass between them and that Louis Auguste would suddenly exclaim, "I cannot wed this Austrian woman!" and run screaming from the chapel.

I stole another peek at my bridegroom to make sure he was still beside me. From the frightened expression in his pale blue eyes he seemed far too intimidated by the magnitude of the event to be contemplating flight.

We entered the chapel to a fanfare of flutes and drums. My husband's brothers had hazarded correctly; the entire nave as well as the galleries high above the soaring Corinthian columns were tightly crammed with the highest nobles in the land, craning their necks for a glimpse of us and looking a bit the worse for the weather. Their watered silk was truly so; and adornments of jewels and feathers drooped from dripping wigs.

"Do you think they can see that my knees are shaking?" murmured Louis Auguste.

"Surely they are looking at your face. And your magnificent ensemble," I assured him. I didn't admit that my own limbs shook with fright, though at least my legs were hidden from view.

The enormous pipes of the organ filled the rococo chapel with melody as the dauphin and I traversed the length of the nave and knelt before the Archbishop of Rheims on silk cushions beneath a silver canopy. I was sure I overheard whispers regarding the back of my bodice, as well as about my general appearance. "She looks so young! Are you sure she is really fourteen? I would have staked the entire contents of last night's cavagnole banker's bag against a wager that she isn't a day older than twelve."

The dauphin fidgeted all through the Mass, tugging at his lace cravat, picking at his nails, and touching his cheeks and chin as if to discern whether we had been on our knees so long that he had begun to grow a beard. We recited our vows and he slipped the little golden wedding ring I had chosen onto the fourth finger of my left hand. "I'm yours forever," I whispered. Our eyes met and his pale cheeks flushed with crimson.

The vows completed, the archbishop recited the paternoster. I mouthed the words silently, because the prayer has always stirred me. *Give us this day our daily bread, and forgive us our trespasses, as we forgive them that trespass against us...* For a moment, my eyes became dimmed with tears. And then, some of the butterflies in my belly mercifully departed, leaving me with a sense of joy and relief. As the archbishop spoke the final words of the prayer, countless rays of sunshine beamed through the windows of the galleries, as if they had responded to some divine cue. Now that the Mass had been consecrated, and our vows had been exchanged, the wedding ceremony was over, at least from God's perspective. But from the vantage of Vienna and Versailles, there were formal documents that had to be executed in order to seal the bargain, not with a kiss but with pen and ink and sand. Like all royal brides I was married not so much by an archbishop but by an international treaty.

The king signed his name with a flourish; then the dauphin did, writing with methodic precision. Now it was my turn. Behind me stood Louis Auguste's brothers and Mesdames *tantes* as well as the ducal cousins, ready to add their names for posterity. I dipped the quill. Oh, for the Countess von Brandeiss to write my name in pencil for me to trace! It was not such a silly wish; I was expected to sign my new name, Marie Antoinette Josephe Jeanne, with all the francofied spelling. I froze. I had never written it. And I couldn't spell for all the world. Not only that, the Countess von Lerchenfeld had once scolded me for my childish hand, insisting that a *chicken* would have had nicer penmanship.

They were waiting for me. The entire royal chapel was silent. I dipped the pen again and began to inscribe my name on the marriage document. It was difficult to keep my hand from quivering. *M*...I made it through Marie and had gotten halfway through Antoinette when I realized I needed to leave space for the rest of my names. As a result, the *ette* became too squashed together; "There is not enough air between the letters," as Lerchenfeld would have said. I panicked, trying to figure out a way to remedy the situation. But while I pondered my predicament, I made the error of leaving the nib of the quill on the paper instead of raising it. The result, to my extreme mortification, was an unsightly blot in the middle of my signature. I hastily scrawled my last two names—Josephe, which came out smaller than I had planned, followed by Jeanne. What an unholy mess!

But I had done it. I was now married—to my real husband, not a political proxy. It was no longer a mere courtesy to address me as "la dauphine." The dauphin clasped my hands and leaned over to whisper in my ear. "I'm so glad it's over!" He sighed heavily. "Finally, we have the part of the celebration I've been looking forward to ever since I woke up this morning."

Could it be? I smiled at him nervously. "And which part of the celebration is that?"

"The wedding banquet!" he exclaimed with more energy than I had seen him display all day.

I tried to conceal my disappointment. I had no stomach for a meal, but clearly my husband had been thinking of little else all day. "Is it really true that we are to dine on the stage of the new opera house—in the presence of six thousand spectators?" I asked him.

Louis Auguste nodded. *"Grand-père* commissioned the opera house just for our wedding banquet. *La Salle de Spectacle*, he calls it."

"La, then!" I forced a chuckle. "If we are to sit upon a stage like mummers, while the whole world watches us eat our oysters and pigeons and pastries and sip champagne, it will certainly be a spectacle!"

"That part happens every day," said the dauphin. I had discovered that if a topic had anything to do with food, hunting, or locks, like a curious turtle he emerged from his shell. "Eating in public, I mean. It's called a *grand couvert*, and it takes place at one o'clock in the afternoon—at *déjeuner*, luncheon. But tonight, a voyeur must have a coat of arms that goes back several centuries in order to gain admittance to the *salle*."

What an absurd custom! "Don't people have better things to do with their time?"

My husband regarded me as if I had asked whether horses could fly. "No," he replied succinctly. "And in any case, I never pay them any attention. Once you're busy eating, you forget they're there."

Perhaps you *could forget*, I wanted to say. Just imagining thousands of people staring at me while I ate was enough to rekindle my anxiety. What was the purpose of such an assembly? Did they memorize the menus and ask their own chefs to re-create them the following week? Did they wait for members of the royal family to spill food onto their garments or grow tipsy with wine, and then go home and tell their friends all about it?

The wedding dinner was not scheduled to commence until

dusk, and I was grateful for a few hours' reprieve. Rather than returning to my temporary apartments, I was escorted to the
dauphin and dauphine's rooms, a double suite of salons and bedchambers, with its own music room and library. Here was where
we would live and entertain as husband and wife until that fateful day when we would no longer be the heirs to the throne of
France, but her king and queen. This, too, was a great deal to ab-
sorb. I was now a bride, but more than that—a *wife*. Becoming
dauphine was no longer the speculative topic of conversation at
Schönbrunn and the Hofburg; I had fulfilled Maman's plan for
me. It was real: in the marble floors and fluted columns; in the
painted screens and sparkling chandeliers.

My trunks were already in the Salle des Gardes, the guard-
room where the men who protected our persons ate, played cards
and other games, and waited until their services would be required.

Apart from the dauphine's bedroom, which was capacious,
but dreary—the heavily embroidered tester and bed hangings
had belonged to my husband's late mother—I found the rooms to
be bright and airy with a charming view. Most of the salons
looked directly onto the landscaped parterre at the rear of the
château.

Launching myself onto a chaise of pale blue damasked silk, I
kicked off my slippers with gusto. One of them landed in a corner
of the room; the other lodged itself in the andirons, where it
would surely end up smudged with months-old soot once it was
retrieved. I already detested the *grand corps*, the beastly corsets
worn every day by Frenchwomen of the highest rank, for they
were the most unforgiving, having no shoulder straps and being
laced in the front with rows of diamonds. They were much more
severe than those we wore in Austria, but of course I was not to
compare the two. "Would someone kindly unlace me?" I in-

quired of the dozen aristocrats and fourteen maidservants who
hovered about the chaise like bees at a hive. My *dame d'atours*, or
Mistress of the Robes, the duchesse de Villars—who made sure to
tell me that she had performed the same office for the late queen,
Marie Leszczyńska—glanced warily at my guardian.

But the comtesse de Noailles nipped in the bud my attempt to
enjoy a degree of comfort. "It is not proper etiquette for the
dauphine of France to lounge about like a courtesan or some loose
woman from the Parc aux Cerfs."

"What's the Parc aux Cerfs?" I inquired. She gave me a dark
look, then wrinkled her nose at my errant slippers. I grinned, if
only for my own amusement. Would she scold them, too?

"It is not the time for relaxing. You must greet the members of
your household now. It is the proper etiquette."

Under my breath I muttered that last sentence along with her.
A noblewoman, one of the few who was young and pretty, smiled
knowingly at me. I gave her a wink. "*Et alors*, bring them on," I
told the comtesse. How I would rather have taken a nap before
the command performance of a wedding banquet!

A maid fetched my slippers and I was reshod by the duchesse
de Picquigny, who, I was gladdened to realize, had a sense of
humor. The sweet-natured comtesse de Mailly placed a small bolster behind my back to make me more comfortable. And there I
sat for well over two hours while a parade of men and women
paid their homage as if I were some sort of monument, or vestal
virgin, with a deep bow or curtsy, and—if their rank permitted
it—touching their lips to my raised hand. The comtesse de
Noailles remained at my right elbow for the duration of the presentation, informing me of the name and duty of each member of
my household entourage and whether I should offer them my
hand to kiss. Yes to the gentlemen and women of honor; and yes
to my controllers general, who would superintend my expenses.

Yes to my maître d'hôtel, or chamberlain, and yes to the equerries. No hand kissing was appropriate for the nineteen *valets de
chambre*; the almoner, who would dispense my charitable
largesse; or the five chaplains and the pair of preachers. No to the
four surgeons and the duo of doctors, and of course the fencing
master deserved no such honor. *Absolument pas*—absolutely
not—for any of the tradesmen and women: the dauphine's tapestry maker, clock maker, apothecaries, and wigmaker, as well as
the kitchen attendants, a panoply of cooks, butlers, wine bearers,
and scullery maids.

All told, one hundred servants would see to my personal
needs from now on, including a young woman whose sole office
was to be my bath attendant. Was everyone in France employed
at Versailles? Whatever would Liesl have made of all this...this
superfluousness of servants? Even the Hofburg, with 2,500 to attend the royal family, paled in comparison. With so many people
bustling about me every moment of the day, not to mention all the
gentlemen and women of honor who were expected to keep me
company during my hours of leisure, how would I ever get a moment's peace?

After the thirty-third introduction (or maybe it was earlier
than that...or later...) my mind stopped focusing and it all became a blur of bows and curtsies, and "I'm so honored, madame
la dauphine" and "I wish you joy and good health, madame la
dauphine." Oh, *Gott im Himmel*—I mean *Sacré Dieu*—oh, God
in Heaven, I was bored!

By the time the twenty-two members of the royal family gathered
in the new opera house, or Salle de Spectacle, for the wedding
banquet, the skies had opened once more and the wind was blow-
ing the rain sideways in horizontal torrents.

"Papa Roi says the fireworks celebration will have to be canceled," said the dauphin. He glanced at me out of the corner of his eye but dared not look me full in the face. "I am sorry for it, because I think you would have liked to see them, madame la dauphine."

"They will have more illuminations later in the week, I am sure." The comte d'Artois seemed unable to refrain from participating in any discussion that touched on a pastime or entertainment. "Might I escort you to one of the incendiary celebrations, madame la dauphine?"

Had my new brother been more than thirteen years old I might have thought he was trying to flirt with me. "I should be honored, monsieur le comte," I said politely. I caught Madame Sophie, the youngest of Mesdames *tantes*, and the one her father called "Snip," giving me an odd look. Then again, she seemed to regard everyone with sidelong glances, like a hare darting through a vegetable garden, expecting at any moment to be brained with a shovel.

A table set for twenty-two had been placed upon the raised stage of the Salle de Spectacle; it sparkled with nearly a hundred cut-crystal goblets and innumerable items of silver flatware, épergnes, and other serving dishes. The theater was bathed in the amber glow of thousands of candles, from the enormous silver candelabras to the gold and crystal chandeliers that ringed the opera house's horseshoe-shaped interior.

No expense had been spared in its construction, although, like the trappings of a stage play, the finishes were faux. Wood painted to resemble marble, particularly the fluted Corinthian columns of coral-colored "stone" that echoed those in the royal chapel, fooled the eye into believing they were the genuine article—a masterpiece of trompe l'oeil. The boxes along the sides of the *salle* were adorned in gilded relief. Above our heads, at the apex of the proscenium arch, a pair of winged angels flanked the Bourbon coat of arms—all in blazing gold. The king sat directly beneath the escutcheon, while on either side of him the dauphin and I echoed the position of the seraphim. And there we were, the royal family of France, all lined up like a row of hens. In the candle glow, everyone, even Mesdames *tantes*, looked radiantly beautiful. Surely there had never been nearly two dozen people so gloriously arrayed. I had to admit that our formal court costume in Austria, ornate as it was, paled in comparison. Maman placed more value in what lay within the heart and in the head.

The wedding banquet could not have been more unlike the dinner *en famille* of the previous night. For one thing, no one spoke a word. Instead, forks were lifted, goblets were raised, and comestibles were served and consumed in terrifying silence, except for the strains of the eighty-piece orchestra and the dauphin's energetic slurping of two dozen oysters. Indeed, as he had told me, he was oblivious to the presence of the spectators when there was a plate of food in front of him. His eyes were cast downwards, intent on peeling, shelling, slicing, or spooning, depending on the course.

I could not stomach a morsel, nor touch a drop of wine, even in celebration. What if I spilled something on my gown or used the wrong fork? The entire nobility of France would witness and remember it. They might think me provincial or clumsy. Better to sit still and stately with my neck long and elegant, and smile prettily as if there was nothing in the world I would rather have been doing. *My new home*, I thought. *My family. My kingdom. My people*. And when I paused to regard the daunting sea of faces avidly watching me as "my people," the knot in my belly began to untie itself.

The orchestra was playing an odd sort of melody—exotic and percussive. "What sort of music is that, Papa Roi?" I whispered.

"It is the sort of music that is the height of fashion," the king replied with a wink. "Turkish."

"Who is Monsieur Turkish? Or is it Maestro Turkish?" Perhaps the composer was Italian. He certainly wasn't German—no good German would write such strange sounds.

The king laughed out loud, and suddenly all eyes were upon him because they had not heard our discourse. "*Ma petite*, the Ottoman Turks command a vast land to the east. Surely you have heard of the Ottoman Empire?" I blushed furiously, crimson to the roots of my hair. "Or perhaps you have trod upon Turkey carpets?"

"Begging your pardon, Your Majesty. Sometimes I can be a little fool."

The king leaned toward me, so close that I could smell the garlic on his breath. "Oh *non*, *ma petite*. *Vous êtes absolument charmante*. Absolutely charming and utterly captivating."

A pyramid of featherlight puff pastries filled with sweetened whipped cream was placed on the table and the dauphin began to heap them onto his own plate. Although he had already consumed enough food for three men, he dove into the dessert with such enthusiasm that one might have mistaken his appetite for that of a half-starved beggar. I felt embarrassed for him; I did not want the loftiest souls in France to see my husband, their future king, in such an unflattering light.

I cannot imagine what went through their powdered heads, but Papa Roi did not stint on his opinion. "Ho, there, my boy! Don't overload your stomach tonight!"

The dauphin glanced up, between mouthfuls. "Why?" he asked, somewhat confused. "I always sleep better after a good supper."

The king turned his head away from his grandson and gave me a look that brimmed with both sorrow and sympathy. I was certain that every eye in the opera house saw it.

SEVENTEEN

Rien

The dreaded banquet finally ended; but for the thousands of voyeurs whose noble lineage entitled them to witness the events of the royal wedding, the real spectacle had just begun. A grand processional led by the king and the Archbishop of Rheims conducted my husband and me from the Salle de Spectacle to the dauphin's apartments where a table had been set up in the music room. There, like the monkeys in my father's zoo at the palace of Laxenburg, whose antics were displayed for the delight of the Austrian elite, Louis Auguste and I were expected to amuse the crush of ducs and duchesses, marquis and marquises, and comtes and comtesses whose rank accorded them the privilege of watching the heirs to the throne of France play a few rounds of cavagnole with members of the Orléans branch of the Bourbons. I was too anxious to acknowledge the exhaustion in my body. I knew I must play, and play deftly. And of course, because the courtiers loved the game so much, I tamped down all feelings of tedium, as one ticket after another was drawn from the banker's bag, and the players held their breath to see if anyone had backed the winning number and whether the wager had been prodigious. Why they enjoyed such a dreary pastime remained a mystery to me.

Eventually, Louis Auguste stifled a yawn behind his hand. The archbishop, his fingers reflexively clasped, as if in a permanent state of prayer, glanced expectantly at the king, who regarded the pendulum clock on the mantel. Midnight had come and gone.

"*Et maintenant*—and now—it is time for the *coucher*," said Papa Roi. The glimmer in his eye unnerved me. He took my arm and nestled it in the crook of his elbow as he escorted me to the dauphin's bedchamber. My husband lagged behind us like a sullen puppy.

During one of her many interminable lectures on the etiquette of the French court, the comtesse de Noailles had explained that certain members of the nobility (only the highest, of course) were entitled to spend their mornings attending the rising and formal dressing, or *lever*, of the king and of the dauphin and dauphine; and at the end of the evening, to attend the ritual of our undressing and getting into bed, or the *coucher*. But the explanation of it and my experiencing it were worlds apart. It was our wedding night! Were the dauphin and I to have no privacy?

A pair of intricately painted folding screens shielded our view from each other, but I suspected that my husband was enduring a similar agony. Every jewel in my hair and on my body and each article of my clothing—shoes, gown, panniers, pockets, petticoats, and stays—was removed with painstaking exactitude and humiliating *longueur* and passed hand to hand by a chain of women, including my ladies in waiting, Mesdames *tantes*, and Madame de Noailles. But some of these aristocratic handmaidens were unknown to me; as strange fingers touched my skin, it pebbled with modesty and cold. After my stays were removed, behind the rococo screen I crossed my arms over my bosom. This was one occasion on which I was grateful that my bare arms could completely cover my breasts.

Madame Etiquette tugged at the blue satin ribbons encircling my thighs. I began to protest, but her stern expression—the "*il n'est pas comme il faut*" look—cautioned me that it was the proper etiquette to submit with dignity to the humiliations of the *coucher*. My garters were untied and my white silk stockings were rolled down, as I extricated my feet with as much grace as I could muster. My legs were now bare as well.

I was as naked as the day I emerged into this world. What sort of a country had I come to—where every action was prescribed and proper, yet perfumed courtiers piddled in the palace corridors and the future queen of France was compelled to display her chaste limbs to the prying eyes of strangers? I could not bear to tell Maman about this ritual; she would be horrified! But she had enjoined me to make them love me, so for her sake I would try to endure it.

Salvation arrived in the form of my nightgown, a white-worked shift with a high collar and delicate lace at the wrists, white embroidery on fine linen of an equally virginal hue. I reached for it but the women might as well have been playing a game that I used to enjoy with my brothers and sisters where we would use any means necessary to keep an object out of the hands of the designated "seeker." The embroidered nightgown passed through the grasp of several women who handled the garment as if it were a holy relic. Meanwhile, I did not have enough hands of my own to conceal my modesty.

Finally, a sweet-faced woman with a halo of blond hair and almond-shaped eyes slipped the shift over my head. It reached the middle of my calves in the front and was a few inches longer behind. The comtesse de Noailles, not immune to my look of despair, explained that etiquette dictated (but of course!) that the most recently wed, and highest ranking princess of the blood, could have the honor of handing the bridal nightshirt to the dauphine. This privileged attendant was the duchesse de Chartres, who had become a princess through marriage. I vaguely remembered her presence at the dinner *en famille* the previous night. So much had happened since then, my mind was blurry. I certainly recalled her husband, for the duc de Chartres had a very red nose and bad skin.

Our respective retinues must have arranged a mutual signal, because the dauphin and I emerged from behind our screens at the same moment. And what a comical sight! Louis Auguste was dressed in an identical nightshirt, although the royal seamstresses could have stitched three of mine out of the fabric used to construct my husband's. In a rare moment of spontaneity for the French court, we exchanged a glance and burst out laughing. The comtesse de Noailles frowned. So did the Archbishop of Rheims. He invited the dauphin and me to face the matrimonial bed, which he then sprinkled with holy water—mattress, hangings, tester, and bolsters, blessing our union and praying for our connubial success.

The king and cleric, and all of the aristocratic assemblage, watched as we climbed into bed. Were they going to watch us consummate our nuptials as well?

We were as pallid as our nightshirts. I noticed that Louis Auguste was holding his breath. So was I. *What were we supposed to do next?*

After an interminable, and tremendously uncomfortable, silence, the hangings were finally drawn. Someone extinguished the candles. "*Bonne nuit,*" came a chorus of murmurs, as the king and courtiers exited the chamber. "We leave you to it, *eh bien?*" a man's voice chuckled. I hoped that it wasn't the archbishop. My husband and I lay in the dark, side by side on our backs with an ocean of fine white linen between us. It was the first time we had been alone all day.

"Who handed you your nightgown?" I whispered.

"The king," my husband whispered drowsily.

"I got a duchesse." Silence. "Don't you think it's silly that so many people have to touch something as simple as a nightshirt before we may put it on?" Silence. "Monsieur le dauphin? Louis Auguste?"

"What?" he grumbled. "And call me Louis. I hate Louis Auguste."

"But the king is Louis. You have to be Louis Auguste, at least until . . . well, you just have to, so no one is confused when I mention 'Louis.' "

"All right, I suppose." Silence. "Why are we whispering?"

"I don't know," I whispered. "I asked you a question. I asked if you thought it was silly that such common things as our nightgowns are treated with so much reverence."

"I'm tired," he whispered. "And I never thought about whether it's silly or not. I just do it. I've been doing it all my life. Besides, it's not about the nightgown. Everything we touch, everything we wear, is a reflection of our glory and divine right."

"Do you like it?" I asked my husband. "The etiquette, I mean."

"No," he replied groggily.

"Then when you're king, can you make it stop? Because I *hate* it."

"I don't know."

"Don't know what?"

"Don't know if I *want* to make it stop."

"Why not?"

"Because we've been doing it for nearly a hundred years. It's what makes our court special. And if I stopped it, who would we be?"

I thought about it, eyes open, gazing at the underside of the tester and a ceiling I couldn't see. My body was stiff with fear. Our banter had helped me to relax a little bit, but now Louis Auguste was silent. I wondered if he would try to touch me. Maman had explained what was supposed to happen on a wedding night, particularly between two royal spouses.

Aren't we going to make a treaty? I mean—a baby. I didn't voice my thought. Instead I let my left hand creep, inch by awkward inch, toward my husband's snoring frame. My fingers found his right arm, grazing it. He flinched, already asleep, and I yanked my hand away, heart pounding furiously.

I dared to admit to myself that somewhere deep inside I was relieved that Louis Auguste had not leapt on top of me. And yet I had not fulfilled my duty as a bride. Guilt mingled with relief. I stared into the blackness overhead. I had always imagined that after today everything would begin to fall into place and my fears about becoming the wife of a stranger and the future queen of a foreign land would begin to evanesce. But my husband winced nearly every time he looked at me, and had little interest in any discourse. If he did not *like* me, or even find my companionship tolerable (and if his gustatory enjoyment would always result in the snoring bulk beside me), how were we to give the Bourbons an heir?

The golden ring on my finger was an indication that our goal was only half completed. It would take a baby boy in my belly to fully satisfy Maman's alliance with France.

When the hangings were drawn open the following morning I awoke to a sunlit day and an empty bed. The dauphin was gone—but where?

"Hunting, madame la dauphine," said the maidservant who brought me a Sèvres chamber pot. "Monsieur le dauphin always goes hunting in the morning. Except for the special occasions... like his wedding yesterday." I could not fathom the reason for her sly grin until I glanced back at the bed and realized that a half dozen maids were inspecting the linens for telltale smears of carmine. *Oh, mon Dieu*, I realized with a gasp. There would be no blood. Nothing had happened during the previous night. My bridegroom and I had slept together as chastely as if we had been siblings.

While the maids bustled about the bed, clucking over the sheets that remained mortifyingly *un*soiled, I noticed that the dauphin had left his hunting diary on a pretty little fruitwood table. *Dare I?* I was insatiably curious to see what he had written on our wedding day. I already knew that he was not one for long-winded descriptions. As he was unable to go hunting, what might he have written about all the festivities?

The red ribbon marked the current page; and, taking full advantage of a rare moment when no one was looking at me, I stole a peek.

What?

I blinked in surprise. On the page was but a single, solitary word: *Rien*. Nothing. Years from now people would read Louis Auguste's journal and think that *rien*—nothing—had occurred on the sixteenth of May in the year 1770. My face reddened. Bad enough that I was poking my nose into my husband's business, but oh, how humiliating to read what I had found.

Rien. Nothing. No hunting, yes, but it equally applied to our wedding night, when we dashed the great hopes of both our kingdoms, because nothing happened in the matrimonial bed, either.

I *knew* he didn't like me! But it was up to me to figure out how to do something about that. No one must know—except for the chambermaids, who had already discovered that I remained a virgin. Perhaps I could purchase their loyalty. I hunted for a reticule and gave each of the women a gold louis. I had no idea how much such a coin was worth, but from their gasps and blushes and "madame la dauphine, *merci mille fois*"—a thousand thanks—and their deep curtsies of gratitude, I must have been extremely generous, even for a member of the royal family.

I began to write to Maman about the extraordinarily rigid etiquette that, according to the comtesse de Noailles, would dictate the events of my every waking hour at Versailles, starting with my *lever*, at which numerous privileged members of the French nobility sat or lounged about my salon while I was dressed, coiffed, and made up. My mother would either be tremendously impressed by the godlike way the royal family was regarded here, or else she would burst out laughing at the absurdity of the customs.

I was *en négligée*, attired in a loose-fitting, beribboned gown of ivory satin, in the midst of my first public toilette when the comte de Mercy entered my salon with a large wicker hamper embellished with a pale blue bow. Tall and elegant in his meticulously curled and powdered wig, his dark eyes appearing to take an immediate inventory of the scene before him, he made a deep bow, displaying his calves through white silk stockings. "Madame la dauphine," he said, offering me the basket, "behold one of the most difficult diplomatic endeavors of my career."

I heard a sound from within the basket, quickly untied the ribbon, and lifted the lid. Into my arms flew Mops, licking my face with enthusiastic kisses. "*Mon Dieu!* How did you get him back?" I asked the ambassador incredulously.

"Extensive negotiations," he said with a wink. "We may have to partition Poland."

"I don't care if you had to agree to partition Heaven," I exclaimed. "Ohh, how's my *petit chou*?" I cooed, cuddling my pug. "Did you miss me?"

The courtiers chorused their astonishment. "*Qu'est-ce que c'est?*" inquired the marquis de Mont Blanc of his wife, who had been too busy flirting with the young comte de Fleury to notice anything.

"Eh?" she replied.

The marquis then directed his question to the elderly duchesse d'Arpagnan. "*Quoi?*" she shouted, raising her ear trumpet.

The comte d'Artois, who had exercised his privilege as a member of the royal family to attend my *lever*, caught my eye, and we exchanged a mischievous glance. What fools; you think they'd never before seen a dog! "*C'est le petit chien de la dauphine*," my new brother said, loudly enough to be heard in Strasbourg. I burst out laughing. "Just a dog, *mesdames et messieurs!*"

After another cuddle, Mops bounded off my lap in search of mischief and adventure. He found it aplenty under the ladies' voluminous panniers, nosing about their beribboned garters, a basket of embroidery silks, and a carelessly tossed pair of shoes. My attendants stepped back and waited patiently, while the courtiers expressed their bemusement, as I found myself crawling along the floor after him, but Mops was having more fun with a leather slipper than responding to his name, or repeated entreaties to "come." After all, there were so many new smells at Versailles! He would be none too pleased about all the stray cats that roamed the palace, marking their territory at whim. My pug finally came to rest in the workbasket with a ladies' cap perched on his squat head. The lace-edged lappets dangling from either side made him resemble a droop-eared basset hound. My peals of laughter were now echoed by several of the courtiers present, and suddenly I recalled Papa's admonishments regarding false friends.

Did they, too, find my pug adorable, or were they merely endeavoring to ingratiate themselves with me? How would I come to know the difference?

"Madame la dauphine, you must control your dog." The comtesse de Noailles regarded me sternly. Nervous in his noisy new home, Mops impudently relieved himself against the curved leg of an ormolu table. I could not control my amusement. If Madame Etiquette thought I'd needed to discipline him *before* she uttered her remark . . . !

I cast my eye about for a servant. Surely *I* was not expected to clean up the mess! But the tolling of a bell interrupted my question to Madame Etiquette about the proper protocol regarding pet defecation. Instead, as my attention was diverted, I inquired, "What is that for?"

"It means the king is on his way to visit his daughters. You, too, are expected. Every morning, a bell rings to indicate that His Majesty is on his way to their apartments, where he takes his morning coffee. This will be part of your daily routine, as dauphine."

I glanced in the direction of my husband's bedchamber, the scene of *rien*. "Monsieur le dauphin went hunting this morning. Should he not join me as well?"

The comtesse gave me a cockeyed glance that, were she a warmer soul, I might have said was sympathetic. "The women of the royal family enjoy a different daily routine from the men," she said.

"Tell me—*we* have prayer and needlework and music lessons, while *they* go hunting!"

Her lips almost stretched into a smile. "*Everyone* prays. Mass is at noon every day. You and the dauphin's aunts will go directly from coffee with His Majesty. Your husband and his brothers will most likely join you in the chapel fresh from the hunt. And then afterwards, at one o'clock, everyone eats."

Coffee, then chapel; the afternoon meal, too—my first *grand couvert*—seemed a rushed affair on this first day. A long table was set up in the room that had been the Queen's Antechamber, behind which sat the royal family, like a line of clay pigeons, while privileged courtiers and members of the public watched us dine. Fortunately, it was over very quickly because the dauphin practically inhaled his food; and I remained too intimidated by the hundreds of eyes upon me and by the ritual itself to do more than eat a morsel or two.

"What next?" I asked the comtesse de Noailles, realizing that every hour in my day was choreographed and accounted for.

"Now you return to your rooms," she informed me.

"And play with Mops?"

"If you like," she sniffed.

If I *could*, would have been more accurate. At Versailles, one high-ceilinged room flowed into the other much like those within our palaces in Austria, but unlike the Hofburg, here the state rooms were perpetually crowded. At first my entourage had to navigate its way through the maze of courtiers, tradesmen, and other visitors, like maneuvering an embroidery needle into an intricate stitch. How was one to glide through the halls amid such obstacles? And I had truly been looking forward to demonstrating my agility and grace. But as people realized it was the dauphine's train passing, they began to fall back and let us pass, genuflecting into a curtsy or bow. I led the way with my head held nobly high, even if I was unsure where I was going. But Madame de Noailles was right behind me, murmuring commands under her breath in case I got lost on the way to the dauphin's apartments. My ladies, dozens of comtesses and duchesses, fell into line behind my *dame d'honneur*, as we glided airily through the halls, the soles of our delicate slippers needlessly polishing the glossy parquet. I wish I could have looked behind me at the sight, for I'm sure we resembled a colorful armada in full sail. I had done it without a misstep, arriving in my First Antechamber flushed with pride at my achievement. If only Monsieur Noverre had been there to see it!

Mops greeted me with a look of pure indifference, then presented me with the reason for his apathy: one of my husband's riding boots. The comtesse de Noailles knelt down, and with a look of pure distaste, reached for the boot, but Mops threw his bulk on top of it quite possessively, then made a dash with it under the nearest chaise.

Shrugging my shoulders, I grinned at Madame Etiquette and before she could utter a reproach, declared, "I am sure monsieur le dauphin has many more boots."

The comtesse regarded the carved and gilded clock on the mantel. "At three you must return to your aunts' apartments. So—you have a little bit of time in which to sew or read. Or," she added, with a sour look at Mops, "play with your little dog."

I had decided to embroider a waistcoat for the king, but with a constant stream of visitors to entertain, it would appear that I was never to have so much as a moment's peace or privacy; this period of "leisure" that would be allotted to me every afternoon between the end of the *grand couvert* and the three o'clock visit with my aunts and the king was filled with a barrage of interruptions. Would there always be so many callers, I asked the comtesse.

"Oh, yes," she replied. "And there will be more of them as time goes on and you gain greater influence with the king."

I was certain that Maman would be delighted to hear that last part.

My visitors that afternoon had come to introduce themselves and to offer their felicitations on my nuptials. Those conversations I could handle with a gracious nod and a warm smile. But I worried about future afternoons; what would people ask of me, and would I be able to help them—or *should* I help them? I re-called my mother's advice in the letter she had given me on my departure from Vienna: *Always inquire as to whom you should re-ceive and the nature of your intercourse with them ... grant no re-quests unless the abbé, Comte de Mercy, the duc de Choiseul, or the king himself has sanctioned your ability to hear them. In this way you will avoid becoming an unwitting participant in the* petits scandales *of the French court.* Was the comtesse de Noailles the correct per-son to ask about such things? Should the comte de Mercy be pres-ent; or, as an agent of Austria, would it be unseemly for him to be shadowing the dauphine? Was the abbé Vermond worldly enough to advise me, if a duchesse or vicomte implored me to in-tercede on their behalf with the king? Who could I turn to for counsel?

The answer, it would seem, was right in front of me, or would be at three o'clock. Maman had instructed me to regard Mes-dames as mentors; who better than the three princesses to guide me through the intricacies of the French court? As it was, many of my daylight hours were to be spent in their company. As I had correctly guessed, much of our time was devoted to the womanly pursuits of needlework and gossip, although Papa Roi's mid-afternoon visits were usually occupied with banalities—inconse-quential conversations that lightened the burdens of kingship. Such was the etiquette at Versailles that His Majesty had a special hour of the day during which nothing of import could be touched upon.

Much like my own brothers, the dauphin and the two young comtes had their own prescribed activities. Perhaps they still had lessons of some sort with the odious duc de la Vauguyon. And when he was not hunting, my husband, who it seems dreamt of becoming a tradesman the way a tradesman might dream of be-coming king, pottered about his very own forge, which the

comtesse de Noailles told me was located on the distant grounds
of the château, or he would help the stonemasons with their burdens, for the king was always adding improvements to the palace
and its grounds.

If the hour of three in the afternoon was set aside for the emp-
tying of the royal mind, at four o'clock every day, mine was to be
improved when the abbé Vermond visited my rooms to read to
me for an hour. That first afternoon, he whispered discreetly,
"They informed me that I am not to act as your confessor."

I glanced about to see if any of my ladies could overhear us, although they appeared to be engrossed in their own conversations.
"I heard the same," I whispered. My voice was colored with both
anger and regret. "They say the dauphine's household already has
more than one father confessor. I think the truth is that they want
someone French. I mean—I know you are French-born, but you
are *mine* and not *theirs*."

"It is for the best, you know, madame la dauphine. *Non, non*,
don't cry." The abbé offered me his linen handkerchief, which I
used to dab the corners of my eyes. "It is for the best," he repeated.
"I am trained as a scholar. As long as they still permit me to read
to you, *c'est bon*." I brightened at this. "So, what will it be this afternoon? A homily? A Bible lesson? Perhaps something from
your devotional."

"*Quelle bonne idée!*" I exclaimed. A wicked smile stole across
my lips as I turned away to fetch the devotional, bound in white
leather tooled with gold leaf. Flouncing back to the abbé, I
pressed the volume into his hands; it was held open with bands on
either page. "Begin where I have marked it, please."

Abbé Vermond cleared his throat and started to read. "There
appeared at this time a lady at Court, who drew the eyes of the
whole world; and one may imagine she was a perfect beauty, to
gain admiration in a place where there were so many fine
women..." His cheeks became damasked with crimson, and he

snapped the volume shut as if the words were about to leap from the page and bite him. "What is this?"

"*La Princesse de Clèves*," I giggled.

"You—you promised your mother you would not read lurid French novels!" the abbé stammered.

"But I wasn't reading it—*you* were!" My laughter got the better of me. Behind their painted fans my ladies tittered in amusement. I reached out and touched the abbé's hand with genuine affection. "I'm sorry. I did not mean to mortify you. It is just that...I am so far from home...and everyone is telling me what to do every minute of the day...and I just wanted to do one thing that would be spontaneous."

I felt so bad about having embarrassed poor abbé Vermond that I allowed him to spend the remainder of the hour lecturing me about the Good Samaritan. How foolish I felt for not having known that Samaria was a real place that one could find on a map!

My daily music lesson (harp, clavecin, or singing—at least the instrument changed) commenced at five. At six-thirty I returned to Mesdames *tantes;* and according to the comtesse de Noailles, I would do so every day at that hour. By that time the dauphin had returned from whatever it was that occupied his hours and accompanied me to their apartments. Except for the *grand couvert*, during which my husband's mouth was devoted to something other than conversation, he and I had not seen each other all day. How would we ever become close?

But my daily routine was far from over. At first I had not believed the comtesse when she explained that the royal family's every hour was accounted for. I had wondered if I was subject to so many restrictions because I was still only fourteen years old, but in truth, very little of my time was allotted for instruction of any kind.

"Unless you are attending a dance or fête, cards or cavagnole are played from seven to nine in the evening," the comtesse informed me, "either in your rooms or *chez* Mesdames. Gaming is followed immediately by supper at nine P.M. If the king is in residence at Versailles, the meal is served in his daughters' apartments."

That night, to my delight, there was no cavagnole as the dauphin and I attended a masquerade ball in our honor. My hair was powdered in a shade of pale lilac that matched my gown; and my ears, wrists, and throat sparkled with diamonds and amethysts. I danced until my satin shoes wore through, but my toes were sorer than my soles, because my heavy-footed husband trod upon them mercilessly. "I know that I am petite compared to you, but am I invisible?" I half teased.

Louis Auguste mumbled something incoherent. I believe it involved the word *lorgnette*. "*Je m'excuse*—I am so sorry," he said sheepishly, coloring to the hairline of his wig. "To me you are just a big blur—I mean a smallish blur. I can't see your feet."

"Well of course you can't, silly." I was grinning despite the pain because I didn't want him to think I was insulting him. "No one can see my feet under all these skirts."

Papa Roi did not arrive in Mesdames *tantes*' apartments until nearly eleven—which evidently was most often the case, according to Madame Adélaïde. By then the dauphin looked positively ravenous and I was straining to keep my eyes open after such a long day. How would I ever become used to so many activities—and so many changes of clothes—with so many people watching me disrobe each night? "At least when our father is away, you may retire at eleven," Madame Victoire informed me sympathetically. She had taken pity on her nephew as well, opening her private larder to reveal a fantastic trove of sausages, bread, and ham. At least he would not go to bed with a grumbling belly.

But no matter the hour at which we returned to our apartments, there would be no avoiding the dreaded ritual of the *coucher,* my husband in his bedchamber and I in mine. At least we were not expected to get undressed in front of each other.

That night, after our respective *couchers,* he came to my bed. As Louis Auguste swung his bare legs onto the pile of feather mattresses, I was struck by the prodigious size of his feet, a subject on which my mind was still engaged when he said, "They told me I have to do this every night until we … until you are …"

I finished the sentence for him. *"Enceinte."*

Even in the safety of the musky darkness, ensconced behind the bed hangings, I was sure he was blushing again. But I wasn't ever going to become *enceinte* unless we did what married couples do at night. He lay beside me in his nightcap and gown, exhausted from another day of hunting, eating, and dancing, motionless except for his heavy breathing, a slight wheeze that issued from his nose with each exhalation.

I waited for him to do something—every muscle in my body rigid with both anticipation and fear. Finally he murmured, "Did you know that you and I are related?"

A silly question, I thought. Of course I knew. Even if Maman and the abbé Vermond had not thoroughly schooled me in the dynastic connections between the houses of Hapsburg and Bourbon, any ninny could have hazarded an intelligent guess. Rare was the royal couple that shared no ties of blood. "We're not *very* related," I whispered. Is that why he did not dare touch me? "It's not like we are brother and sister. Your mother was a Hapsburg and we both descend from Louis XIII, with *famille* Orléans blood besides."

"Second cousins once removed," Louis Auguste murmured.

"How quickly you calculated our degree of consanguinity." I was impressed.

I felt a shift in the mattress as my husband shrugged. "I knew it already. Ever since they told me we would be married. Didn't you know it?" When I didn't answer him, he continued. "Although I would have figured it out anyway. I like mathematics. And science. And history. The duc de la Vauguyon says that if you do not study the effects of history it is doomed to repeat itself."

"I am glad, then, that one of us is an astute student," I said softly, despite feeling suddenly anxious. "Does this mean you will not be like Papa Roi?"

"I will not be like him in that I will be true to my wife, if that's what you mean," he said earnestly.

I imagined he was referring to the king's lengthy, and infamous, dalliance with the marquise de Pompadour. I'd heard there were many others besides. "You will remain true to me even if I am dead and you become a widower?" I asked.

"*Oui*. Even then."

We lay in silence like a pair of carved statues on a medieval tomb. "I think Madame du Barry is quite handsome," I said. I was not even certain why I had uttered the words. I envied the woman her bold beauty, admired her vivacity.

"Do you think she is beautiful?" It had taken all my courage to pose such a question. For all I knew, the dauphin preferred a certain sort of voluptuousness to my innocence.

"It is not for me to say," he replied, after a long silence.

But I need to know. "Darest say it anyway," I urged. "I won't tell anyone your answer."

The quiet was almost unbearable. The air inside our silken cocoon was becoming stifling. Could I draw open the hangings about the bed or would it not be *comme il faut*?

"All right, then. My answer is no: I do not find Madame du Barry attractive. I am not fond of artifice."

I gasped in surprise. "But your whole life—life at Versailles—the lives of everyone in the royal family, their courtiers—it is nothing *but* artifice!"

"You have seen how I prefer to dress." I recalled with clarity the portraits of the dauphin pushing a plow, and what a poor impression they had made upon Maman. Louis Auguste had worn the same unprepossessing attire on the day we met in the forest of Compiègne. "And you know that the pastimes and sport that bring me joy or solace—apart from hunting—are hardly aristocratic pursuits. Just ask Papa Roi!"

True; I could scarce imagine any of my brothers or, for that matter, either of the dauphin's brothers, dripping sweat over a forge or carting paving stones about in wheelbarrows in full view of the court.

We readjusted our positions on the bed, turning onto our sides to face each other at the same moment. As our arms extended, our long, full sleeves brushed together. His arm was warm, his stocky body emitting a musky heat. I imagined him as a sort of great bear.

Within moments he was snoring, while I lay awake staring at his silhouette in the dark. For the second consecutive night—*rien*.

The next day, Louis Auguste left at dawn to go hunting again and did not return to our apartments until late afternoon, his garments reeking of perspiration. I was in my drawing room in the middle of my hour with the abbé Vermond, playing on the floor with Mops, who was enthusiastically wrestling with a satin ribbon. I gazed up at the dauphin's grimy face. I would have welcomed him more effusively, but I was just as offended by his odor as I was by the awkward flinching gesture he made every time I endeavored to embrace him. "My, you've been gone nearly the whole day."

"Yes—and it was excellent sport today. I am quite fatigued. Did you sleep well?" he inquired politely, as if I were one of his maiden aunts, rather than his wife and bedfellow.

"Yes," I lied.

"Good then. I am glad of it." He turned toward the door. I hoped he intended to bathe before we joined Mesdames and his *grand-père* for supper.

I snatched the ribbon from Mops and pretended to scold him, mostly for the abbé's benefit. "Naughty dog. We don't eat ribbons." The chastened look in the pug's big black eyes was only momentary. He went for a slipper of pink brocade, changed his mind, and scampered off to gnaw upon a fan he found lying on the carpet.

The dauphin was already in the doorway. Leaving me again. "I missed you, today," I said glumly. Softly. Tentatively. He didn't hear me. Or if he did, he paid my words no heed. A second later he was gone.

Was this to be part of our daily routine as well? Two nights had come and gone and I was no closer to bearing an heir. Charlotte had become fully a woman on her wedding night. Even if the experience had been an unpleasant one, she knew her duty and had begun to accomplish it from the outset. Already I felt the weight of my responsibility.

A plan began to take shape in the corners of my mind. Louis Auguste would not dare touch me even when he couldn't see me. But perhaps if what he saw by day intrigued him . . .

He had indicated a preference for simplicity to fripperies and furbelows. Although my conduct might violate countless precepts of Versailles' etiquette, and the comtesse de Noailles would undoubtedly become apoplectic, I was the dauphine, the highest woman in France—and I needed to entice my husband into consummating our marriage. Who would dare gainsay me?

EIGHTEEN

Uncertain Footing

May 19, 1770

Your Imperial Majesty,

I am of two minds as I write this, for the dauphine is so lately a wife that perhaps it is too soon to address the issues that may concern you. Nevertheless as my brief is to observe and report on the dauphine's conduct, I regret to begin with the news that the royal marriage has yet to be consummated. Chambermaids learn such things sooner than diplomats, but Vermond confirmed the fact. The abbé has madame la dauphine's trust and confidence and although she did not say as much, he concluded from her melancholy looks that nothing whatsoever has come to pass in the *lit matrimoniale*. The linens on the bridal bed remain as pure as does your daughter. We all know the dauphine to be as charming as she is beauteous; therefore, I may speculate upon the reason for the behavior of Louis Auguste thusly: His Highness's constitution has been weakened by his sudden and rapid growth because his body has only in recent months become that of a man. His development is late; it is not yet time to despair.

There is another matter, one that I suggest be taken in hand sooner rather than later, for bad habits left unchecked grow like an untended garden. Although Madame de Noailles as the dauphine's *dame d'honneur* endeavors to instill in her every precept of the exacting etiquette that defines one's life at Versailles, the comtesse remains a social inferior. At her own peril the dauphine can willfully choose to ignore court etiquette and no one in the kingdom, saving her husband and the sovereign, can chide her for it.

Such laxness has taken the form of inattention to her toilette. At her *lever* this morning, in the presence of several courtiers of the loftiest rank, she refused to be laced into a corset. She then dismissed Sieur Larsenneur from the salon, insisting that she wished to wear her hair *au naturel*—sans powder, or even a proper coiffure! The ripples of shock have already reverberated throughout the palace.

I regret to be the bearer of unpleasant tidings; but we have not come this far only to hazard losing all.

> Respectfully,
> Comte de Mercy-Argenteau

. . .

May 24, 1770

Comte de Mercy, regardless of the opinions of Prince Starhemberg or Chancellor Kaunitz, whom I understand have been pressuring you to share the contents of your correspondence, *by my orders* the journals that you send on the subject of my daughter are for me and me alone and are not to pass through any other channel. For further safety you might send them by the messenger who will be dispatched monthly to Brussels, from there to you, back to Brussels, and then here. A complicated route, but a necessary one.

Every two or three months you will transmit me an ostensibly private report that I can show to Joseph and to Starhemberg in his new capacity as my foreign minister, but the journals will be for my eyes alone. I will burn them myself, for they will contain particulars that would make many people unhappy.

I have been obliged to write this letter in great haste, having my room full of ministers. I apologize in advance, as I fear you will have some trouble in succeeding to decipher it, and I am obliged to hurry to catch the messenger before his scheduled departure.

Maria Theresa

. . .

May 26, 1770

Private report from the comte de Mercy to Prince Kaunitz, Chancellor of Austria

Monseigneur:

As you may be aware, I am under orders to send my dispatches from France directly to Her Imperial Majesty. But I cannot in good conscience deliberately withhold information that may be of use to the man who is the head of government. I hazard my own employment by sending you any report, but I believe Austria's Chancellor should not remain in a state of ignorance with regard to the present situation.

It would be impossible to be more interesting than the dauphine, owing to her numerous endearing qualities. But these very attributes also constitute a striking indictment of her husband. At the time of the wedding, he appeared to be on the point of some development; but he has now relapsed into the disagreeable state to which he is inclined by nature. To assure you that it is not Austrian prejudice that colors my assessment of his character, I pass along the words of the esteemed duc de Choiseul, who is himself one of the architects of the royal marriage, and who is truly the governing power in France while the sovereign indulges in the delights of the comtesse du Barry. Choiseul has prophesied that if the dauphin grows to become as embarrassing a man as he is a boy, he will one day be the horror of the nation. It therefore rests on the shoulders of the dauphine to bring him about. However, since their first interview Louis Auguste has not shown the slightest predilection for his wife, or any anxiety to please her—whether in public or in private.

Fortunately, his indifference and incivility do not appear to intimidate the young princess. Her behavior is such as an experience far beyond her age might prescribe, and does her great credit. What at first I considered a gross dereliction of etiquette on her part may upon reflection be a stroke of cleverness. It may cost the dauphine the amity of her elders but may very well win her the attention and affection of her pedestrian-minded spouse. I admit my astonishment at how a girl so latterly backward has become so wise. Naturally, it remains to be seen whether such a risk will reap its intended rewards.

Two weeks after my wedding, during an otherwise unremarkable afternoon of conversation and embroidery, I received a visit from a most extraordinary quarter. No sooner had the guest been admitted than I requested the ladies attending me to retreat to the antechamber. Nonetheless, I could overhear their astonished whispers: What business, they wondered, could the comtesse have to transact with the dauphine?

I remained standing in the center of the room, the mistress of my world. According to court etiquette, as a member of the royal family I was compelled to speak first, or my visitor would be prevented from uttering a word. Endeavoring to mask my surprise I inquired warmly, "To what do I owe the honor of your call, Comtesse du Barry?"

"I have come to offer my felicitations on your marriage, madame la dauphine." She spoke in the same soft girlish voice that seemed to enrapture the king. The comtesse sank effortlessly into the deepest of court curtsies while I stood in the center of the room. She was wearing a gown of cornflower blue silk, a shade almost identical to that of her eyes, with a stomacher and underskirt heavily embroidered with silver thread. Her pale hair was dressed with diamond aiguillettes. My dress of sea foam green satin accented with pink ruching seemed childish by comparison. In that moment I wished that I was taller, more sophisticated, more commanding. My recent efforts to appear less artificial to the dauphin seemed even more out of place beside the most glittering, glamorous creature at court. Yet when the comtesse rose from her reverence I detected a throbbing in her ample chest. For all her feigned composure, she must have been as nervous as I.

"*Merci bien*," I said.

The comtesse could not have known, unless someone told her—and I hoped they hadn't—that I had declared myself her rival that first night I saw her. Since then I had often spied her in the company of the king—never during the day when he visited Mesdames *tantes* in their apartments, although her presence as His Majesty's favored companion at the formal state events celebrating my marriage was the talk of the court. People seemed shocked, yet no one criticized it openly. Apparently, the lady was extremely influential.

Maman had cautioned me that nearly everyone at Versailles

wanted something from the king. Clearly the comtesse had already managed to gain his ear. Regarding her now, so splendidly garbed and jeweled, I wondered if it had been a mistake to simplify my appearance in order to appeal to the dauphin's more rustic tastes. For if it was the *king's* attention I hoped to secure in order to strengthen Austria's alliance, I would surely not obtain it looking more like a petite bourgeoise of fourteen.

I felt myself flush. I knew that my attire had given rise to gossip among the court. Although I was the highest woman in the land, it had been a mistake to risk my credit, and so soon after my arrival, when such a vibrant woman had the honor of being seated at the king's right hand. I sensed that Madame du Barry's slightest desire would be made manifest by His Majesty; and wasn't that what Maman expected me to garner on Austria's behalf? I raised my chin a little higher, a reminder that I was a Hapsburg.

The comtesse regarded me from beneath her thick lashes, a gesture I read as an attempt at humility. "If I may, madame la dauphine—I have a wedding gift for you ... *un petit cadeau.*" From one of the pockets she wore beneath her skirts she withdrew a small box tied with a blue satin ribbon. "I would be honored if you were to open it in my presence," she urged.

Inside the velvet box was a tiny jeweled hummingbird, its throat encrusted with rubies of the richest hue I had ever seen. The body was pebbled with diamond pavé and the eye was a tiny sapphire. I smiled. "It's very lovely."

A chasm of silence opened between us. Neither of us quite knew what to say next.

On more than one occasion I had noticed the du Barry in conversation with the duc de la Vauguyon. Taking a second look at the little hummingbird I wondered if she was among those at Versailles who had secretly been against my marriage. Yet she had made such a kind and open gesture by visiting me that I began to regret my suspicion; after all, it must be difficult for a beautiful woman to be a favorite companion of the king. No wonder she was the subject of so much gossip—I was learning as much myself about the power of rumor and innuendo at Versailles.

We assessed each other for what seemed like an interminable length of time. My ladies' customary chatter wafting in from the antechamber had grown strangely silent, as if every one of my attendants was eavesdropping intently. The golden pendulum on the mantel clock swung to and fro, and I found myself counting the seconds as they ticked past. Finally I asked whether the comtesse planned to attend the *bal champêtre* in the gardens of the Palais Royal that evening. This ball was yet another nuptial celebration, although the king and my husband had declined to attend it, for reasons I did not fully comprehend; the dauphin had mumbled something about Papa Roi not being on good terms with the local officials. Nonetheless, I found it difficult to contain my excitement, for this would be my first trip to Paris, even if I was to be chaperoned by Mesdames *tantes*, and even if I would see little of the city beyond the environs of the Palais Royal. "I hear that the duc and duchesse de Chartres will open their gardens to the public for the fireworks illumination."

"And may I express the hope that this time they will not be postponed on account of thunderstorms." Madame du Barry smiled politely, and sank to her knees again with astonishing *longueur*. I would have to practice my own curtsies so that hers were not better. "Allow me to take my leave of you, madame la dauphine."

I nodded my head, and she rose gracefully. The du Barry smiled. I smiled. Then she backed out of the room with studied dignity, like an actress called upon to sham the behavior of a great lady.

My warm smile remained until she had disappeared from

view, trailing a cloud of essence of orange flower behind her. Then I allowed the corners of my mouth to relax. If the comtesse was a party to the same anti-Austrian faction as the duc de la Vauguyon, and was also a confidante of Papa Roi, perhaps I would do well to cultivate her acquaintance. Yet I would show her nothing but *douceur* and amiability. Madame du Barry would find me always sweet and kind; therefore, she would be unable to speak a word against me to her friend Monsieur de la Vauguyon without appearing churlish.

But potential palace gossip and *médisance*, backbiting—an art in itself, I was warned—paled in comparison to the genuine tragedy I witnessed in Paris that evening. The *bal champêtre* began as a joyful celebration, but for many, it turned into a nightmare.

I was still convulsed with sobs when Louis Auguste came to my bed that night. My hysterical recollections, punctuated as they were by ragged breaths, sniffles, and hiccups, must have sounded to him like the ravings of a madwoman. "I wish I could have stopped it. But there were so many. Crushed. *Petits enfants!*— innocents!—who turned out for the spectacle on their parents' shoulders."

My husband looked confused. "What happened tonight?"

"Death. Death happened." I clutched the bed linens with angry fists. "The carriages." I gulped for air. "The carriages fell in the trenches. Even the horses screamed."

"Trenches? What trenches?" The dauphin struggled to comprehend my disjointed outbursts.

"And so many people!" They'd been crowded like sardines into the colonnaded square and all along the Champs-Elysées. Trenches had been dug around the perimeter of the square, but the workers had somehow neglected to cover the ones at the entrance to the rue Royale. When the fireworks ended the thousands of spectators began to disperse. But there were not enough torches to light their way. Unable to see clearly in the dusk, they forged ahead nonetheless—straight into the open trenches.

"We shall be blamed for the chaos," I told my husband ruefully. "You and I specifically, because the *bal champêtre* was given in our honor. It is like the story of Caesar dancing while Rome burned!"

"Nero fiddling," the dauphin mumbled.

"What?"

"It was Nero who fiddled as Rome burned—but I take your meaning. The citizens will believe that their rulers only cared about having a fête, and were impervious to their suffering."

"*Exactement!*" I nodded vigorously. "They'll think we should have been able to protect them. There weren't enough watchmen to control the crowd," I added. The screams of the injured and their cries for aid had brought more people running, but in the dark the panicked citizens ignited a stampede, trampling several of their brethren in the process.

"If Papa Roi was angry with the Paris authorities before now, imagine how it will pain him to learn that the mayor was too penurious to pay the Garde Française the thousand *écus* it would have cost to maintain order." I knew nothing of the quarrel between King Louis and the Parisian officials, nor (I was certain) did the six hundred souls who were crushed beneath the coaches that fell into the open trenches.

"I saw their terrified faces," I told Louis Auguste, reliving the awful events in my mind. "I heard their cries—and there was nothing—nothing I could do!" I hugged my knees to my chest and sobbed into my nightgown. "You should have heard the screams. Their entreaties." I held my head in my hands. "I can't get the sound out of my ears."

"*Mon Dieu,*" the dauphin murmured. He inched toward me

on the mattress and tentatively placed his hands on my shoulders, as if the touch of my flesh might sear his palms. I nestled against his chest and drew his arms about me like a shawl. We remained like that for several moments, then I turned toward him and threw my arms about his neck, nestling my cheek in the hollow of his collarbone. My husband held me gently, rocking me like a child. "My heart is breaking, too," he murmured into my night-cap. "We must find a way to make it right."

I fell asleep in his arms, his heavy breath warming my ear. The following morning he rose early, but it was not to go hunting. "Allow me to show you something, madame la dauphine," he said, dismissing our attendants from our apartments. They departed with raised eyebrows, but any expectations of romantic intimacy they might have harbored would have been upset.

"I made this lock," he said proudly, opening the facing doors of a mahogany highboy. From a hidden compartment he retrieved a small casket.

"What is it?" I asked, peering over his broad shoulder.

"My monthly allowance." The dauphin unlocked the box, revealing a cache of gold louis. Then he sat down at his writing desk, sharpened a quill, and penned a brief letter to the Minister of Police.

> This is all I have to dispose of. Use it as best you can. Help those who need it.
>
> Louis Auguste

"Aren't you supposed to consult the duc de la Vauguyon before doing something like this?" I asked him. "Or at least ask your aunts if the gesture is, well, *comme il faut?*"

The dauphin emphatically shook his head. "I do not need the imprimatur of my tutor to aid those in distress," he said resolutely. "If I have learned anything, should I not have learned that it is the duty of a good Christian to succor those who are suffering in their hour of need?"

Finally, in this foreign court with all its arcane rules of conduct, I saw a glimmer of the humanity I had grown up with in Austria, one's charitable duty expressed and fulfilled. Pride welled within my breast. Although in so many ways we remained strangers, I had never felt closer to my husband. And I was pleased that he had obeyed his instincts rather than immediately run to the duc de la Vauguyon for advice. "I shall do the same," I said, glad to be able to contribute something as well. "After all, I have an almoner in my retinue."

But when he left our apartments to go hunting, like a spaniel I followed him through the suite. At the doorway, he turned to regard me, his simple black tricorn in hand. "Whatever are you doing?" he asked me. His bemused expression made me laugh.

"I am your wife!" I exclaimed with forced cheer. "And I so rarely see you for much of the day. I wanted to wish you a good hunt and to tell you that I will miss you today."

He seemed surprised. "Oh." Shyly, he dropped his gaze from my face to the floor and shifted his weight from foot to foot. "I suppose I will miss you too, then. But we will see each other at the *grand couvert*!" At the thought of the afternoon meal his mood brightened, and as a pair of footmen swung open the door, to my astonishment, the duc de la Vauguyon was standing right there on the other side.

I covered my queasiness with politeness. "Were you expecting your tutor this morning?" I asked the dauphin.

My husband looked confused. "N-no," he stammered. I tried to read his face, but I could not discern whether he was lying.

The duc reddened guiltily. "I was merely passing your apartments, madame la dauphine, heading—"

"Heading for those of Madame du Barry, *peut-être*?" I suggested sweetly.

"*Oui*—I mean *non*—I mean *oui*," said the duc, displeased that I had confounded him. He hastened away, and when he was beyond our hearing, I clasped my husband's hands and drew him closer. "I will wager tonight's banker's bag that he was trying to listen to our conversation through the door."

Louis Auguste shook his head, refusing to believe me. "He is a very honorable man, Toinette."

I felt something soften in my core at his use of the nickname Charlotte had given me. It emboldened me. "Did you know that the duc was against our marriage?"

My husband's face twisted with discomfort, as though he were straining over a commode. He'd known. It was more than I could bear. "Is that why you have never wanted to—to hold me; or even to kiss my lips? Is it because monsieur de la Vauguyon has poisoned your mind against me in some way?"

"N-no; of course not," the dauphin replied. He lowered his eyes to avoid my imploring gaze. "I mean, it's not that. It's just that..." He lapsed into a ponderous silence.

"Just that what?" I was frightened and frustrated, and my words tumbled out of my mouth in a more demanding tone than I had planned. I dreaded the prospect of a letter from Maman, once she learned that my marriage had not been consummated, chiding me for what she would doubtless assume to be my chilliness when it came to matters between men and women. I was painfully aware of my duty; and I wanted Maman to understand that I was doing everything I knew how, to be patient and kind. But I could never allow the empress of Austria to learn that because the dauphin's mind had been turned against Austrian women, he dared not make me his true wife!

"Never mind," mumbled the dauphin. "I don't want to talk about it."

His moods could be so changeable. "But *I* want to talk about it. There must be some reason for your aversion to . . . your repugnance for *me*. You said that you disdain artifice. So I have gone without powder in my hair and I have forsworn rouge in order to entice you. It is the talk of the court, and yet I do not think you have noticed! And when I see the duc de la Vauguyon skulking about our apartments at an hour when you have no lessons arranged, I am inclined to believe that perhaps the man does not have our best interests at heart. The comte de Mercy—and even my mother, as well as the abbé Vermond—think that the duc is a malign influence on you and that he is somehow contriving to make matters difficult between us."

"That's nonsense." Louis Auguste shoved his hat onto his head and turned his back to me. "I said I didn't wish to discuss it. And in any case, it's impolite to just blurt things out whenever you feel like it."

I felt the muscles in my neck begin to clench. "But we are talking about our marriage! And I apologize if I was blunt, but that can be my way sometimes. I say what I feel—*when* I feel it— which is better than keeping everything stopped up inside you like a bottle of undisgorged champagne."

"No, it isn't," the dauphin argued, still facing away from me. "You cannot just say whatever pops into your head, or act however you please. Not at Versailles."

I hate it, I thought. But for once I kept it to myself.

"And if you think it's all right to say whatever's on your mind, *I* think that your abbé Vermond is malign."

"*Vermond?* Malign?" I began to seethe. "I have known him for nearly two years and he is one of the only people I can trust here."

"What does he do?" Louis Auguste asked me, turning. "What is his purpose in your retinue? You already have two preachers, five chaplains, and an almoner in your household. What need have you of another?"

"He reads to me," I said flatly.

My husband snorted. "Reads? You don't even like books! All you do with him is sit and gossip! I can't think of a more superfluous fellow." Then he administered the coup de grâce. "And Papa Roi agrees with me."

Hot tears welled behind my eyes. "Vermond is my friend," I said quietly, fighting the urge to lash out, to strike with all the anger inside my breast. "I am surrounded every day by strangers. Foreigners. No one cares about *me*; they care only for the privilege of being in my proximity. You are out hunting all day and come to my bed out of obligation—there is no sense in pretending otherwise. True companionship I receive from the abbé Vermond. Because he genuinely cares for my welfare, I can confide in him and derive comfort from his judgment and advice. We can speak of *home*."

"You are dauphine of France. This is your home, now," the dauphin said sullenly.

I swallowed hard. He was right. But not about everything. I had a hit of my own to score. "And the only affection I get is from my pug!"

Although our daily routines were ritualistically prescribed, with every hour accounted for, most days I was terribly lonely. Maman was pleased that I spent so much time in the company of the dauphin's aunts, for she was convinced that they offered a stable moral influence as well as proximity to the king. The more time I spent in His Majesty's presence, the more opportunities I had to charm him; and the more I charmed him, the more fondly he would think of me. And the more fondly he thought of me, the more likely he would be to favor Austrian interests in his policies. But even though I understood why Maman wanted me to profit from Mesdames' influence, the princesses were on the northern side of thirty and I missed the companionship of people my own age. The dauphin's brothers were my only contemporaries, but most days they accompanied him on the hunt.

The following afternoon I was admitted to my aunts' apartments by the marquise de Durfort, wife to the pompous ambassador who had spent so much time in Vienna during the negotiations for my hand. Her face colored when she saw me, and I wondered if she was blushing because she guessed that I must have known about her husband's affair with the Austrian countess. I pretended not to notice her embarrassment. She curtsied deeply and retired to an adjoining room, leaving me alone with Mesdames.

Madame Adélaïde poured the hot chocolate into my cup, then refilled those of her sisters. As I sipped the thick, bittersweet brew I glanced about the room, appraising the sanctuary the princesses had created for themselves. As the king's maiden daughters, their rank prevented them from being compelled to observe court etiquette when it didn't suit them. Consequently, the women spent the better part of their days in dishabille, wearing loose-fitting morning clothes; when it was necessary to leave their grand suite of apartments—such as to attend Mass—they would tie a set of panniers and skirts about their waists, affix a lengthy court train, and conceal the entire haphazard ensemble with a voluminous black taffeta cloak. Trailed by an entourage of dozens of noblewomen, the princesses would glide along the marble corridors like a trio of enormous crows: Adélaïde (the oldest), always moving with purpose, was followed by Madame Victoire, huffing and puffing, her forward progress hampered by her girth; and Madame Sophie brought up the rear, torso pitched forward, gliding first left, then right, as if she expected something to dart out and grab her from one of the chambers that lined the corridors.

It didn't seem fair that Mesdames' singular attire drew no

comment at court (or perhaps it had, when they first began dressing that way), while my efforts to eschew the artifice the dauphin so despised caused titters of derision to reverberate throughout the palace. The king evidently had more important things on his mind (whatever they were) than the dauphine's toilette, because he said nary a word. And my husband hadn't even noticed the change. So I abandoned it. However, I lorded my one triumph over Madame Etiquette and refused to wear a corset. I remained as slender as a water reed, and I had nothing to constrain. And if Mesdames would submit to the *grand corps de baleine* only on state occasions, so too would I!

But to make matters worse, through no design of my own, my trousseau was already becoming the worse for wear. Boating on the Grand Canal was one of my favorite pastimes, but a single splash of water could leave a permanent stain on a silken gown. I loved to stroll amid the groves and gardens and along the pebbled allées, and naturally my long trains would drag behind me in the dirt, dredging the paths with every step I took. Satins, silks, and brocades were delicate and could not be washed, nor did they remain particularly pleasant to wear during the long hot weeks of summer.

Versailles was odiferous enough as it was. Mesdames' apartments—high-ceilinged, spacious, and filled with light from the tall windows that overlooked the parterres—were just about the only rooms within the palace that did not stink of stale urine. Chamber pots were hardly the sort of objects to be found in the public rooms, but it was where they were most required. Courtiers would mill about in search of the latest gossip (for knowledge was a form of currency) or to catch the eye of the king; or they would wait for hours on end in the Oeil de Boeuf for an audience with His Majesty, a summons that often never came.

Commoners occasionally brought a petition, in the hope of

being heard. Assured of having a captive audience all day, tradesmen and women hawked their wares in the corridors and antechambers. And where could they all relieve themselves but behind a painted screen or marble column, in a hidden stairwell, or potted orange tree?

Each of the aunts had her own spacious six-room apartment, although the women seemed to roam with impunity throughout one another's rooms. The princesses' six spaniels had the run of the rooms, but their dogs were well tended and did not relieve themselves on the colorful, elaborately woven carpets. The canines themselves had a noble pedigree, having descended from the litter sent as a gift from England's Charles II to his beloved sister Henriette Anne, the sister-in-law of Louis XIV.

That afternoon, my tête-à-tête with my aunts took place in Madame Adélaïde's cozy Interior Chamber. My back faced the great mirror over the onyx mantelpiece. Opposite me sat Mesdames, like the three Fates of ancient mythology, their capacious armchairs arranged in a demilune around the delicate fruitwood tea table.

"So! We hear you entertained a visitor recently." Madame Adélaïde peered at me over the rim of her porcelain cup, her expression avid as ever for new gossip.

I lowered my saucer into my lap without taking a sip of chocolate. "*Mon Dieu!* Please forgive me. How could I have been so forgetful?" Then I shared the details of my interview with the comtesse du Barry.

Victoire reached for a sweet roll, placing it on a Sèvres plate with a pair of silver tongs. A moment later, she added another bun to her plate, although she was still consuming the first. A plate of duck sausages rested by her elbow. "We would have thought better of you," she said between mouthfuls.

"Don't look so confused, my pet," Madame Sophie said. "We

are here to set things right." She glanced nervously from one sister to the other.

"So that you do not make the same gaffe twice," affirmed Madame Adélaïde. "You couldn't have known," she added, with a hint of condescension. She looked down her nose at me—the aquiline nose of the Bourbons.

"We should have told her much earlier," said Sophie, fidgeting with her lace *engageantes*. "But of course we never suspected she would be so—"

"Unwise," interjected her eldest sister.

"*Oui, c'est ça.* That's the word, Adélaïde. But what is done must be undone," insisted Madame Victoire. She dabbed at the corners of her mouth with a serviette, staining it with lip rouge.

I wondered aloud what was so wrong with the du Barry. After all, if she was a confidante of the king and I was expected to maintain his love . . .

"Do you know what a *maîtresse en titre* is?" Madame Adélaïde enquired pointedly. I allowed that I did not, so she explained it to me.

I gasped. *Oh, dear*. Perhaps referring to the woman as the king's official whore was putting too blunt a point on it. But it was an apt definition. Of course I knew what a mistress was; my own father had had one, although, like Maman, I could never reconcile his conduct with God's laws against adultery. But had Madame du Barry really sold her favors to other men before she became the king's paramour? I felt dirty for having associated with the comtesse, for having smiled at her, for having accepted her wedding gift. And such a loose woman wore the most luxurious gowns and the finest jewels in the kingdom on her wicked person! As if to show that the king condoned such lascivious behavior. Was France entirely immoral? "Why did Maman not teach me how to handle such things?" I agonized.

My mother had advised me to look to Mesdames for guidance in all things. And evidently I had made quite a misstep in allowing the comtesse to cross my threshold. Gently, but firmly, the dauphin's aunts explained that before Madame du Barry came to court she had been lowly Jeanne Bécu, the natural daughter of a friar and a seamstress. Jeanne had become a *grisette*, or milliner's assistant, but had really earned her livelihood by selling her body to the milliner's patrons. Her procurer, the comte du Barry, retailed Jeanne to various noblemen, launching her career as a courtesan. She met the king in 1768 when she came to Versailles on some errand, throwing herself on the mercy of the duc de Choiseul, but he'd not been enamored of her charms, nor had he believed her tale of woe. The widowed Louis, however, was instantly smitten, although Jeanne could not become an official royal mistress unless she bore a title—so he married her off to her procurer's brother Guillaume. A year later Jeanne was installed as His Majesty's *maîtresse en titre*. "Our father even had a false birth certificate created for her, so that she would appear not only to be younger, but descended from a noble lineage," Madame Adélaïde said acerbically.

What a disastrous state of affairs! I dreaded the barrage of criticism from Vienna once Maman learned that I had welcomed such a creature in my rooms, where, so I was told, only those whose conduct was above reproach were to be admitted. I threw myself on my aunts' mercy, craving their advice. "What shall I do? The entire court now knows that I have entertained—entertained a *harlot*!" It was imperative that I earn not only the support of the king but that of the courtiers as well.

"She is just a naïf," Madame Victoire observed, speaking to her sisters as if I were not present. "Her spirit is so unguarded; such candor and openness will only bring her unhappiness here."

Madame Sophie nodded in agreement. Wagging her finger at

me, she scolded, "You are far too trusting, *ma chère*." She blinked repeatedly; it was one of her nervous tics.

"That is why you have us," Madame Adélaïde said, her voice dripping with sympathy. She retrieved her pince-nez from her workbag and placed it on the bridge of her nose. Then she picked up her embroidery and resumed work on an elaborate rose that she had begun to stitch earlier in the week. Most of the upholstery in the room—painstakingly detailed pastoral scenes executed in millions of infinitesimal stitches of petit point that it had taken her years to accomplish—was the work of her own talented hand.

"*Pauvre petite*. Poor thing; look how upset she is." Madame Victoire placed a sweet roll on my plate, in an effort to cheer me.

Madame Sophie clasped her hands to her chest. Her knuckles were white with anxiety. "We are so glad you told us all about your interview with that creature." She glanced at the windows and noticed a dark cloud hovering above the gardens. "Oh, dear. I hope it will not rain today," she added nervously.

"Not today, *ma chère*." Victoire turned to me. "She is terrified of thunderstorms," she whispered, loud enough for Sophie to hear.

"My two younger sisters spent their childhood in an abbey," Madame Adélaïde explained. "The nuns would lock them in a closet when they misbehaved or showed fear. Victoire's constitution, being hardier, withstood the deprivation. Sophie has always been more delicate."

Victoire nibbled at the end of a croissant. "*Ça suffit, ma soeur*. Enough! There are matters more pressing. You have well and truly put your foot in it, madame la dauphine. And we must extricate you."

"Yes! We shall save you from yourself," Madame Adélaïde declared, licking the end of a strand of silk, the better to rethread her needle. "But you must solemnly promise to share with us everything that transpires—"

"And seek our counsel on all matters," Victoire interrupted.

"—so that we may be able to advise you, and keep you from doing further damage to your reputation." Madame Adélaïde surveyed me coolly. "We have naught but your best interests at heart, madame la dauphine. I hope you will permit us to school you with regard to your conduct here at Versailles."

Confused, I raised my hand to protest. "But I thought the comtesse de Noailles—"

"When all is said and done, your *dame d'honneur* is merely a glorified servant." Madame Adélaïde touched her bosom with her fan, then used it to gesture gracefully toward her younger sisters. "*We* are your relations."

"Madame du Barry gave me a wedding present," I reminded the aunts. "Although I am certain it was Papa Roi who really purchased it; surely that means he must approve of an acquaintanceship between me and his—his *maîtresse en titre.*"

An entire conversation transpired in the silent looks that passed among the king's daughters. Finally, Adélaïde, who usually spoke for the trio, said, "Although the divine right of kings states that a monarch is subject to no earthly authority, the credo does not negate the fact that my sisters and I do not approve of everything our father does. It breaks our hearts to see our kind and generous papa abase himself so. But you need not encourage his ill-conceived passion."

"But wouldn't Papa Roi be more pleased if I countenanced it? Or at least appeared to approve of it, in order to maintain his favor?"

"If His Majesty cannot bring himself to do so, then you must be the one to take the moral high ground," Madame Victoire said, concurring with her sister as she reached for a third sweet roll.

She licked her fingers with uncommon delicacy before smoothing her serviette over her broad lap.

Madame Adélaïde urged me to avoid the comtesse du Barry at all costs from now on. "And your conduct cannot be too subtle, or it might be misinterpreted or misunderstood. No—the only way to remedy such a woeful false start is to shun the creature entirely, to cut her so emphatically that the whole court cannot help but notice that you desire to have nothing to do with her."

Madame Sophie darted her eyes from one sister to the other as though she were viewing a *jeu de paume* on the royal tennis court.

"But what about Papa Roi?" After all, "the creature" was his lover. How could I make it a point to snub the du Barry without insulting my *grand-père*?

Madame Adélaïde raised an eyebrow. "Why, we must all band together to save the king from himself as well," she insisted. "It is difficult enough to see one's father make a fool of himself over a coarse woman of the gutter, but I cannot imagine how it must feel to be the first lady in France, and idly watch while a common harlot enjoys her suppers at the sovereign's right hand, holds court in her apartments like a queen, and wears the wealth of the kingdom on her back. There are many nobles whose morals are not so nice as ours who crowd her salon and super-praise her parts, from her false hair to her falsetto lisp, in the hope of gaining favor from our father through her influence. If I were you, I know I shouldn't bear it. And I would certainly wish to put her in her place in the most public manner possible and to assert my superiority in every way." She brought her chocolate to her lips and took a long, satisfying sip.

"Fear not, *ma petite*," said Madame Victoire reassuringly. "You will not be offending His Majesty by cutting the comtesse du Barry. In actuality, you will be doing him a great favor."

Armed with my aunts' enthusiastic assurance that Louis

would thank me for it when all was said and done, I firmly resolved, from that moment on, not only to snub Madame du Barry,
but to ensure that every minister, courtier, and servant would
know I was doing so. I left Mesdames' apartments with a light
step, on surer footing now that I'd seen what a gaffe I had made,
relieved that I had been able to set my moral compass to rights before it was too late.

NINETEEN

Taking the Bull by the Horns

The dauphin's brothers joined us at cards every night, but his sisters were considered too young for such activities, although their governess Madame de Marsan was often at the gaming tables in the company of the comtesse du Barry and her coterie. In the back of my mind I vowed to spend more time with Madame de Marsan's charges, for I would do well to number my little sisters-in-law among my friends at court, particularly when their governess kept company with my rival.

Dutifully obeying the dictates of Mesdames *tantes*, during my first few weeks at Versailles, when everything was so new to me and I was struggling to learn the correct etiquette and memorize every nuance, I would make it a point to navigate the room, pausing at every table to greet the players. The flames flickered and guttered in the ornate silver candelabra, casting a spectral glow on the painted faces of the courtiers.

My silk skirts rustled as I glided between gaming tables covered with green baize, my panniers so wide that I almost appeared to be floating. A tilt of my fan to the marquis de Durfort;

a nod of my head to the duchesse de Gramont; a half smile to her brother, the duc de Choiseul who, as I peered over his shoulder, seemed to hold a winning hand of *Écarté*—and on I glided to the next table. A close-lipped nod to the duc de la Vauguyon, looking as bilious as the shade of his waistcoat; the same to Madame de Marsan; and then, as if there were no one occupying her chair, I looked straight over the du Barry's head to say *bonsoir* to the duc d'Aiguillon, who I knew was enjoying a clandestine love affair with someone (or so I'd heard)—if I could only recall the woman's identity!

The courtiers pretended not to notice my slight. It was all part of the game. But the act of silence itself, the absence of a smile or nod, spoke loudly enough. And I was proud of my actions. My mother's court was respected far and wide, known the world over as the most moral court in Europe. Mesdames *tantes* appreciated the same virtues; and, grateful for their guidance, I could see that in Maman's absence they were striving to keep me from becoming tainted by the vices that were all too prevalent at Versailles. The king, when he was in attendance, never gave me the slightest indication that he wished me to behave in any other manner toward the comtesse du Barry; therefore, I interpreted his silence as an acknowledgment that his liaison with a former prostitute was not the sort of thing to flaunt before an impressionable girl of my tender years.

Before long, however, I was employing another one of Mesdames *tantes*' skills: *médisance*—the art of the snide remark, at which the aunts excelled.

It was a sultry night in late spring. The tall windows had been opened to the parterres; any breeze would have been welcome, as we were sweltering in our silks and brocades, and many courtiers had begun to perspire beneath their wigs, creating rivulets in their white lead makeup.

At times like these it was infinitely more fun to be an observer than a participant. I hovered near the wall of Madame Victoire's Large Chamber with two of my attendants, the duchesse de Picquigny and the comtesse de Mailly. We snapped open our fans for a bit of privacy, although from time to time we languidly used them to cool ourselves. "Don't they look like a couple of broken statues?" I whispered to my ladies, pointing to the ruined maquillage of two elderly marquis. I believe they were ministers of some sort.

The comtesse de Noailles sidled over to me, frowning with disapproval. "Remember, madame la dauphine, you must greet each of the players," she murmured in my ear.

"But I greeted them last night. Every one of them was here—and seated in the same chairs, too!"

Now she was at my elbow. "But they are very distinguished guests, and you offend them not only by ignoring them, but by refusing to mingle."

"*Bzzz*," I hummed, for the benefit of my ladies-in-waiting. "*Mon Dieu*, she is like a housefly." I pantomimed swatting at a fly that was buzzing about my ear, my elbow, my head.

But Madame Etiquette would not be shooed away so easily. "The marquis de la Chapelle and the marquis de Saint-Cyr have served the kings of France since the sixteenth century; you insult their ancestors as well as the gentlemen themselves by hanging back by the wall, and giggling with your ladies like a group of village maidens at a country dance."

But a bit of mockery at the expense of a few terribly self-important souls had not really been my aim. What I craved, in truth, was to return, if only for a few hours a day, to a time when not so much was expected of me. I missed the way my sisters and I played together during those golden days at Schönbrunn. I was fourteen; where was the harm in being giddy?

————

One afternoon, when the abbé Vermond arrived for our hour together, he was brandishing a letter. "From your mother," he said.
I jumped up from the floor, where I had been teaching the
princesses Clothilde and Élisabeth to play at knucklebones. I had
not heard from Austria in weeks. "*Gott sei dank!*" I exclaimed.
"Thank the Lord!" I broke open the seal and retired to a chaise to
savor the correspondence. But as I read Maman's words, the corners of my mouth inverted from an elated smile into a rueful
frown.

> Madame my dear daughter,
>
> If you wish to shock me, you could do no better than your
> present disregard for your appearance. After all the prepara-
> tions we undertook, not to mention an upbringing of the
> strictest respectability, it alarms me to discover that you are
> disporting yourself like a wanton—to wit: What is this non-
> sense I hear about your refusal to wear a corset? Every
> woman at Versailles does so without complaint and the stiffer
> French stays will do wonders for your posture. You are now
> at the critical time of life when you are developing your
> shape. I worry for fear, as we say in German, of *auseinan-*
> *dergehen, schon die Taille wie eine Frau, ohne es zu sein*—for
> fear of letting yourself gain a woman's fuller waistline with-
> out having the excuse of being a wife. If you insist on dis-
> paraging the French corsets I will have some Austrian stays
> made for you, which are not as stiff as the ones in Paris.
>
> I hear also that you are not taking care of yourself, even
> when it comes to cleaning your teeth, and that you are often
> badly dressed; even your ladies are aware of it.
>
> Furthermore, you *must* curb your tendency to make fun
> of other people. If others should discover this weakness in
> you, it will make you a tool in their hands. Do you wish to

lose the respect and confidence of a public who currently adores you? You cannot overestimate the value of such currency. You began so well; what happened? I now see you striding with nonchalant calm toward a certain ruin.

My eyes widened with each phrase. If there was a single gray cloud in a sky of purest blue, my mother was sure to find it and predict rain. "How does she know this?" I shrieked.

Vermond gave me an inquisitive look. "Is something amiss, madame la dauphine?"

"Well, Maman was right that I should be careful where I place my trust," I muttered. "Apart from you and Mercy, I have no friends here. I can't say what reason they may have to inform upon my habits, but there must be someone in our midst who wishes me ill and might even have a desire to see me humiliated." I slapped the letter against the palm of my hand. "I am met with rebukes such as these, and what does the Judas get for betraying me?"

The abbé looked anxious. "Surely no one at Versailles wishes you ill, madame."

I narrowed my eyes. "I regret to say, monsieur l'abbé, that I cannot entirely believe you. Did you not admit to me last week that there were members of the Bourbon royal family that had spoken against my marriage?"

The abbé's cheeks colored so deeply that the blush blended into the russet hue of the whiskers alongside his ears. "I thought I asked you not to repeat my words, madame la dauphine. And surely you don't suspect—"

"No, I don't," I interrupted. "Though perhaps it is why Papa Roi does not accept invitations from his cousins the duc d'Orléans and the duc de Chartres to attend events at the Palais Royal." But the threat to me lay closer, I believed. Much closer. Not a relation to the king, but someone I saw every day. I ticked off the number of waiting women whose motives were dubious by drawing lines with my fingers in the layer of dust on the pink marble tabletop. My rooms were filthy. The aristocratic attendants at Versailles were too haughty to perform menial labor, and the servants were too busy to be terribly fastidious about cleanliness. The duchesse de Ventadour gave me dark looks; I was sure that the comtesse de Bois-Passy gossiped behind my back with the comtesse de Perigord; if the maids who changed the linens were not lining their pockets with *écus* by disclosing my still-virginal state to foreign ambassadors or to courtiers who paid well just to have the latest *scandales* before anyone else heard the news, then why did I draw their rude smirks?

Beneath my skirts I wore a pair of pockets tied about my waist in which I kept the keys to my jewel chests, to my escritoire, and to the drawers in which I locked away the journal I'd begun writing under the abbé's instruction back in Vienna, as well as the letters I was in the process of composing. I wrote with relative frequency both to Charlotte and to my former governess the Countess von Brandeiss. I was now convinced that my keys were taken from my pockets at night while I slept none the wiser behind the bed curtains. My mother's letter had put me into such a fit of pique that abbé Vermond's efforts to reason with me came to naught.

Learning whom to trust at court was a perpetual obstacle course. The ladies and gentlemen of my household had been assigned to my retinue and I had no notion of why they had been selected or who had chosen them; most likely their three-hundred-year-old coats of arms entitled them to serve a dauphine. I might *hope* to secure their loyalty, but I did not *expect* it.

There was one person I needed to win over more than any

other. And once I did so, I hoped that the tongues would cease to wag. Therefore, if the dauphin would not come to me, I would bend my hours to his will and come to him.

My husband's workshop lay about a mile from the palace. I had chosen to walk there, rather than ride in a carriage, because I knew the decision would disgruntle several of my ladies. They hated to soil their hems and slippers, and shunned the sunlight with even greater vehemence, despite the benefit of fashionable silk parasols. In this way, my unnecessarily large entourage winnowed itself, leaving the most friendly of my attendants, as well as a few hardy souls possessed of a sense of humor (except for that mother hen, the comtesse de Noailles). I was thus spared the backbiting comments I often overheard, even from my own women, as they whispered behind their fans that I was transgressing some aspect of etiquette. Their red lips, perfect Cupid's bows, unleashed as many darts as kisses. Were they unaware that their voices echoed off the hard surfaces of marble, stone, and mirrors, and bounced off the soaring ceilings? Or did they intend for me to hear their barbs and jests that passed for wit at my expense? The worst had brought tears to my eyes that I had been hard-pressed to conceal: "*l'Autrichienne*," their nickname for me—a corruption of the French word for an Austrian woman and the word for a female dog.

The long walk to the dauphin's smithy and forge cleared my head, banishing much of my ill humor. I had forbidden all idle conversation and the charming weather had a salubrious effect on my soul.

The workshop was housed in a modest hut with a quaint thatched roof that could have easily been mistaken for a laborer's cottage. "*Bonjour*, kind sir!" I called out gaily as I stepped through the door. "Would it be too much trouble to build something for me?"

Startled, the dauphin spun around from his work table. An iron ring of keys clattered to the stone floor.

Clad above the waist only in his chemise and a linen vest, my husband looked so surprised to see me, and even more so by my request, that I moved to embrace him, but my touch only made him pull away. Momentarily miffed by his rejection I nearly forgot the reason I had come to him.

"I would like you to design a little chest for me—about yea high," I said seriously, describing it with my hands. "Large enough to house my correspondence—but I wish to conceal it as well."

The dauphin thought for a few moments, his lips twisting about in contemplation. Then, mopping his brow with his lace cuff, he seated himself on a high stool set before a slanted draftsman's table, sharpened a fresh quill, dipped it, and began to sketch a pretty cabinet with a cunningly placed false drawer. In the corner of the sheet of paper he drew a cylinder and scrawled a few notations beside it. "This," he said proudly, tapping the diagram with the nib of his quill, "is a lock that no one will be able to pick!" He then sketched the decorative elements for the chest—roses, upon my request—and we made our way to the rear of the hut, where together we selected the variety of woods he would employ; ash and cherry, rosewood, ebony and birch. I slipped my arm through his, enjoying the deliciousness of a shared venture, especially one that would in itself conceal secrets. Louis Auguste's enthusiasm was so palpable that he didn't even recoil from my touch.

Two weeks later, beaming with delight, the dauphin presented me with the finished cabinet. It was a masterpiece of marquetry. Recognizing that the little correspondence chest had begun to strengthen our fragile bond, I resolved to evince an interest in my husband's other favorite pursuit.

So one day, I joined the dauphin on the hunt. I secretly commissioned a riding habit consisting of a blue jacket with white facings, piped in red trim and embellished with silver buttons; a red skirt; and shiny black boots. A jaunty white panache, the gift of a snowy egret, fluttered gaily from my blue tricorn. I surprised the royal hunting party in mid-morning by riding up to the pink marble portico of the Grand Trianon in a carriage filled with all the necessaries for a proper *fête champêtre* on the grass. Liveried servants traveling behind me hopped off their postilions and began to unpack the chests, setting up the pavilion and the little wooden chairs, and unpacking the wicker hampers that were filled to bursting with bread and cheese, cold meats, ripe strawberries, and iced wine.

I adjusted the angle of my hat and lifted a spyglass to my eye. In the distance, I spotted the dauphin and the king on horseback and waved to them. "Surely you are fatigued from your exertions!" I cried gaily. "Come enjoy an outdoor repast!"

They rode up, perspiring profusely. The dauphin dismounted, removed his tricorn, and mopped his brow with the sleeve of his coat. A pair of grooms helped the king from his horse and led the mount into the shade where it would be fed and watered with the other horses. I had no doubt that as soon as they had eaten, the men would be eager to resume the hunt, so that they could kill a few more animals before Mass.

Papa Roi tucked a serviette into his neckcloth and allowed himself to be served a slice of peppered beef. "What an angel of mercy you are, *ma petite*!" He glanced at his grandson who was greedily devouring a roast leg of chicken. "Isn't she, my boy?" Louis Auguste nodded, never diverting his gaze from his greasy fingertips. Later, Papa Roi invited me to sit in his lap and feed him a strawberry. I took the stem between my fingers and playfully placed the fruit into his mouth. The king chewed thoughtfully on the berry, not at all, thank goodness, the way he had devoured the food Madame du Barry had fed him, and then pronounced me "absolutely charming." I could see why His Majesty was still considered the handsomest man at court, despite his advanced years. His smile always appeared genuine. When he looked at you, it was with such avidity that you felt there was no one else in the room, even when it was so crowded with people that you could not see the walls or the floor. That is the hallmark of a fine monarch, I thought.

"Tell me, what is it you wish for?" he asked me.

I smiled broadly and toyed with the yellow rose I had tucked into my bodice. "To please you in all things, *Grand-père*." It was the truth, but there was so much more I left unsaid.

"Such a sweet sentiment!" he exclaimed. Then he whispered something in my ear, nodding discreetly in my husband's direction. "But you know you must also please *him*." For a moment we observed the dauphin's absorption with his repast. Papa Roi sighed heavily and patted my hand. "This is a good beginning."

That night, when he came to my bed, my husband thanked me for my surprise visit. "Next time, I think I shall join you on horseback!" I told him. "I am quite fond of my new riding habit and should like to wear it again. Perhaps I shall even order several more of them. Although I don't believe my mother wishes me to join you at all." I wondered what she would do in my stead to win the affection and trust of a shy and terrified *mari*. "I look with such joy toward receiving her letters," I said quietly. "But her pages are always so full of chiding. Of course I have never been her favorite child," I sighed.

Safe and warm behind the heavy bed hangings, I began to tell my husband more about my parents, aware that he would never meet my mother. "When I was very little, I remember we were at war with Prussia and Maman was very busy with affairs of state.

So every week or thereabouts, my governess, the Countess von Brandeiss, would present me to her. Even though my father bore the title of Holy Roman Emperor, it was Maman who had inherited the crown through her papa. But because the Hapsburg lands were bound by Salic law, like those of France, where only a male can inherit, Maman ascended the throne as the sovereign only because my grandfather, Emperor Charles VI, issued an edict that named his only child—my mother—as his successor."

I chuckled, knowing what happened next. "So you can imagine that my *Grossvater* was none too pleased when Maman announced that she intended to wed a nobody, Francis of Lorraine—who would bring next to nothing to the marriage! And not only that, said my mother, she was going to marry for love!"

In a world ruled from ornate rooms of state, amity was the sauce on an already flavorful dish; it was not necessary for the transaction of affairs. But perhaps the dauphin and I needed to become friends before we could become capable of bringing a baby into the world. "Did your parents love each other?" I asked him.

"They were devoted," said Louis Auguste. "Like yours, I imagine. People would remark upon how rare it was for a husband and wife, particularly in France, to be so *sympathique*. But no one can give a compliment here unless it is tempered with a drop of acid." I heard the catch in his throat. "They said that it was a blessing that Maman outlived Papa by only two years so that she did not have to mourn him for very long."

"I agree; it was a thoughtless remark," I said gently. "*My* mother counted the number of *hours* that she had been married to my father! Her empty coffin has already been placed beside Papa's sepulcher in the Kaisergruft, where all the Hapsburgs are laid to rest." It felt strange to speak a German word; perhaps I had already become more French than I thought. "Papa died when I was nine years old. After that, Maman spent hours every day sitting beside his coffin, weeping and praying. I still remember the day it happened. August 18, 1765. My parents—with my older siblings—departed Vienna for Innsbruck, where my older brother, Archduke Leopold, was to wed the Infanta of Spain. No sooner did they leave our palace at Laxenburg when Papa suffered an apoplectic fit. He died in the arms of my oldest brother, Joseph."

"The French would have said he was lucky to have expired in the bosom of his family," the dauphin murmured. "I hope you were at least able to say farewell."

I swallowed the beginnings of a sob. "He had breath enough to send a messenger back to the palace to fetch me. My father held me tightly in his arms"—I wound my own about my chest, reliving the moment—"and said to his servants, 'God knows, gentlemen, how I wanted to embrace this child once more.' It was the last time I saw him alive."

The dauphin gave my calf a reassuring caress with his foot. "At least you can sleep at night with the knowledge that someone you loved loved you very deeply in return. Neither of my parents thought much of me." His voice was glum. "My older brother was handsome and quick-witted and golden-haired. In short," he said with a rueful chuckle, "everything I am not. I am the dauphin because Louis Joseph died. He was only nine years old."

I reached over and took my husband's hand. This time he didn't flinch. Instead, my touch might have given him courage to continue his train of thought. "Sometimes I think the king regrets that Provence, or even Artois, is not dauphin. They don't become tongue-tied in a room filled with dignitaries. My witty brothers always have a bon mot on their lips. One look at them and you know that they are princes. Papa Roi is disappointed in me. I see it in his face every day. As if he wishes to say 'It's a good thing your parents didn't live to see what a clumsy, stupid oaf will one day sit on the Bourbon throne.' But I cannot be other than what I am."

"I do not find you stupid," I replied. "It's just that your tastes do not accord with others'." In truth, they did not accord with my own, but I was willing to partake of them—the hunt, for example—if it meant that he would be comfortable enough in my company to make me a true wife. And perhaps, although we had not begun as our parents had, love—while not a requirement for a royal marriage by any means—might someday blossom, and our marriage would flourish and bear fruit, cultivated by the nourishing soil of companionship and esteem.

TWENTY

Soon?

⁂ SUMMER 1770 ⁂

Little by little, we were growing closer, the dauphin and I. But it was an exhaustive uphill climb. Every night, although we shared our thoughts, nothing else transpired between us. After nearly two months of marriage, still *rien*.

With between three and four thousand courtiers dancing attendance on the royal family and dashing about the château on any given day, privacy was scarce at Versailles. Yet I had little else to do but adorn myself with ceremonial garments. I was bored: bored of the women who fawned upon me, bored of the obsequious drawling courtiers with their *mouches* and their cavagnole, bored even with my music lessons and my hours in the company of the abbé Vermond. Every day seemed a tedious repetition of the last. The only thing I found myself looking forward to was the one aspect of my life at Versailles I would never have anticipated enjoying.

I noticed a change in the dauphin after the night we confided in each other about our parents. He started to invite me into his rooms, beckoning me with a crook of the finger, and dismissing his attendants. Their arched eyebrows were countered with our triumphant smiles. Oh, how they hated to discover that my husband and I were becoming friends! Life at the French court thrived on intrigue and scandal; when people, particularly spouses, got along amicably, there was nothing to gossip about.

At first, my husband would seek me out just to ask a question in matters of taste; he knew I wished to see him dress a bit more formally than he liked, if only to silence his detractors. His noisiest critics were his two brothers, who cared a good deal about appearances. What did I think of the designs for a new vest, the dauphin would say. Did I prefer blue or puce? Embroidery or brocade? Silver thread or gold? And then he would take pains to compliment my hair, which I had taken to wearing lightly powdered so that the reddish-blond shade still showed through—a pleasing option for a girl of my age. Every day at Mass I prayed that soon, perhaps, our casual discourse might turn to weightier subjects. I knew Maman was counting on it. In her most recent letter, my mother had asked whether Louis Auguste and I spoke of political matters, for I was never to forget that the primary reason for my marriage, at least from her vantage, was to further Austrian interests here in France.

Thus, even in our apartments we were not entirely alone. Through her letters, which arrived every two weeks or so and were delivered to me by either the comte de Mercy or the abbé Vermond, my mother's presence loomed, more political than maternal.

The monkey on my husband's back was his tutor, the duc de la Vauguyon. I had come to realize that whenever Louis Auguste became evasive, it was because something I had said, or wished him to do, did not meet the approval of the duc; and Louis Au-

guste remained too cowed by the man to contradict him. One afternoon I decided to take the situation into my own hands. It was
the first week in July. Perhaps I was testing the dauphin; I truly
cannot say, but I had been thinking about the matter since the arrival of my mother's latest letter.

"Maman thinks I should become more aware...of Papa Roi's
opinion on certain subjects—and yours, too, as you will be king
one day. Sometimes I overhear men from Paris waiting in the
Oeil de Boeuf with petitions for His Majesty—shoemakers,
clerks, actors from the Comédie Française. They complain their
taxes are so high that they cannot afford to put bread on their tables. I hear them grumbling that the nobility and the clergy don't
have to pay taxes at all. Is that true?" Louis Auguste looked away,
mumbling something. "Would you repeat that?" I asked.

"The duc de la Vauguyon..." he began, then broke off, embarrassed.

After several moments I wormed the remainder of the sentence from my husband's tortured conscience. His preceptor vehemently disapproved of females knowing the slightest things
about the subject of politics. Moreover, the duc had transmitted
his profound mistrust of Austrian women to his pupil.

"Why does your tutor think we are all so formidable?" I
asked, holding out my hands in a gesture of supplication. With a
giggle meant to dispel the dauphin's anxiety I added, "Am I such
an ogre?"

"Monsieur de la Vauguyon says that you are—are—" His
hand flew to his mouth to stop his words.

I clasped his wrist. "Say it, I beg you. Say it, even if it is unkind."

Louis Auguste lowered his gaze, scarcely daring to utter the
unpleasant words to my face. "'Austrian bitches,' he calls them."
His voice was barely above a whisper.

There it was. That word again. *Autrichienne*. I swallowed hard. "*Merci*. Thank you for telling me."

The dauphin clasped my hands in his. "I apologize for having hurt you. I did not want to do so for all the world."

I reminded him how necessary I felt it was for us, so newly wed, to present a harmonious image. I recognized that our elders were more experienced, more cunning; and if we were not careful, they would endeavor to manipulate us for their own ends. But I fear my warning shot misfired, and all the dauphin heard was a controlling Austrian wife. I clenched my fists in frustration until my fingernails imprinted tiny crescents into my palms.

Every time I took a step forward, I fell back two paces. The following evening, as we lay abed, failing once again to fulfill our conjugal duty, the dauphin blurted, "You need not trouble yourself with such matters as taxes. As dauphine it is none of your concern, and when you become queen you will be merely my consort."

I felt as if I had been struck. This was not the Louis Auguste I knew, or at least the youth who had apologized for wounding me the day before. "You told the duc about our conversation!" I exclaimed, aghast.

"I did not, I assure you." In the dark he reached for my hand, but I pulled away in anger. "That much I promise you."

After the *grand couvert* the next afternoon, I insisted on pursuing the discussion. Sunlight streamed through the tall windows, creating geometric patterns of light on the carpet. As we conversed, I toyed with one of my diamond bracelets, trying to catch and refract a sunbeam with its facets.

"If you do not relay the substance of our private conversations to your tutor, then he must be spying on us. And he fills your mind with his rancid opinions. For better and for worse we are man and wife. Imagine if in *our* marriage we could be like our parents were in theirs, overcoming the spite of those who wished them ill and who sought to sunder them as companions of the heart."

Louis Auguste grew thoughtful. "I do not like Monsieur de la Vauguyon any more than you do, Antoinette, but I fear him," he admitted.

"*Shh.*" I put my finger to my lips. Footsteps approached the door as if on tiptoe, to prevent the person's court heels from clicking against the hard parquet. Then there was silence. I pointed to the door and whispered, "I will bet you a hundred *écus* that the duc de la Vauguyon is listening to us even now. Shall we discuss his unpleasant complexion? Or the little red lump alongside his nose?" I said mischievously. "Or the fact that the wretched man listens at keyholes!" I pointed to a little silver bell. "Ring it," I urged. Louis Auguste did so, and a groom-of-the-chambers emerged from the adjacent room. I cocked my head toward the door and waited for the dauphin to speak.

"Good sir," whispered the dauphin, "would you oblige the dauphine by opening yonder door?"

The *valet de chambre*, who was either a fool or a very honest man, did as the dauphin bade him. And as the tall white portal swung open, there indeed was the duc de la Vauguyon, his face a mask of fright and indignation, clinging to the door as if it was a fencepost.

I gasped in amazement, for while I had suspected the duc of eavesdropping, I never would have imagined him to have done so in such an undignified manner!

Louis Auguste appeared unsure how to react. At first I thought he was going to burst out laughing, but the matter was far from amusing. Finally, the dauphin found the nerve to confront his tutor. "*Eh bien*, what do you have to say for yourself, monsieur le duc?"

The duc de la Vauguyon scrambled to right himself. He planted both heels on the floor and thrust his chin in the air, declaring with impunity, "What do you intend to do, Your Highness? You cannot dismiss me; you have not yet reached your majority!"

My husband looked to me for reassurance and guidance. I gave him a smile.

"Who said anything about dismissing you, my *esteemed* tutor?" I had never before seen the dauphin employ the irony for which French courtiers were so renowned. It fit him like a six-fingered glove; Louis Auguste was far more comfortable in his own skin, as a plain-speaker—open, honest, and unaffected. "*Non*, I shall do far worse," he told the duc. "While I may be obligated by His Majesty to retain you, you will never again have my trust or respect."

The duc de la Vauguyon endeavored to stammer a few words in his own defense, but Louis Auguste raised his large hand and said, "You are a meddler, monsieur." His tone was even and resolute, marred only slightly by the nasal timbre of his voice. "A meddler and an *intrigant*—and the king will hear of this."

"I would think twice about crying to your *grand-père*, monsieur le dauphin," the duc sniffed haughtily. "After all, I am a good friend of Madame du Barry."

My husband and I exchanged nervous glances. But then the dauphin found his courage. "Do you presume to threaten the future king of France?" he asked the duc, in a manner that left not a scintilla of room for remonstrance. The arrogant duc tried nevertheless to get a word in, but could only manage to open and shut his mouth stupidly like the carp in the royal fountains, before my husband lifted his hand and said, "Cease. There is nothing you can say to induce me to change my mind. Henceforth, I account you a scoundrel. Now leave us."

The tutor puffed out his chest and strode away in a huff, refusing to appear vanquished. The footman closed the door, and the dauphin and I dissolved into gales of laughter. "You were absolutely *magnifique*!" I cried. I glanced at my husband as my eyes filled with happy tears. I had never seen him act so decisive, so regal. And I knew that I had finally made a true friend.

But I feared that I had also solidified a dangerous enemy.

With slow and steady measure the dauphin and I were becoming partners. But I was at pains to understand why he had yet to make any effort to consummate our marriage. He knew as well as I that it was our duty to beget the Bourbons' heir. But Maman had taught me that I must permit my husband to take his pleasure as he would, and not to reach for him in the night with the sort of ardor reserved for men; for it was not only unbecoming to well-bred young ladies, but might so intimidate the diffident dauphin that it could ruin everything, postponing indefinitely the event we all hoped for.

At night, in the stifling darkness cocooned by the red and gold bed curtains, we confided in each other, as spiritually naked as two souls could be, even as we remained clad neck-to-knee in our lace-trimmed nightgowns. Yet in the light of day my direct gazes were met with averted glances.

One Sunday night as I lay abed fretting about the potential consequences of our chastity, sobs began to bubble in my throat. On the opposite side of the feather mattresses, Louis Auguste stirred. "Are you awake?" he whispered.

"Yes," came my strangled reply. I sniffled noisily and wiped my eyes with my sleeve.

"What is it?"

"What do you think?" I answered crossly. I swallowed hard. "Louis, what do you suppose will happen if I do not become *en-*

ceinte soon?" He mumbled something—too softly for me to hear. "A foreign-born princess who fails to conceive can be sent back to her homeland in disgrace." Maman would likely shut me up in a convent. No other prince would offer for my hand; the world would look upon me as damaged merchandise. But I did not voice these horrifying thoughts. Instead, I said, "Think of what that failure would mean for the Franco-Austrian alliance. It would in all probability sunder it." I rolled over and found his hand. "Already we are the subject of whispered gossip." My voice grew small and plaintive. "What is wrong with me, Louis? Do you not find me pretty? Do I smell? For I assure you I will take twice as many baths a week if you find the odor of my body repugnant. Is it my teeth? My eyes? My hair? My chin? My limbs?" He was silent. "And besides, whether or not we find one another pleasing to the eye—or the nose—we must fulfill our duty." A thought suddenly struck me, like a bolt from heaven. "Tell me," I timidly whispered, "do you not know what to do?"

The dauphin exhaled several ponderous, wheezing sighs. Finally, after what felt like an eternity, he spoke. "I am not ignorant of what happens between a man and a woman beneath the sheets," he said with a rueful chuckle. "I have not—we have not—because..." His voice trailed off.

"Because?" I asked softly.

"I wanted to wait," he replied.

"Until...?"

"My sixteenth birthday."

"Why did you never mention this before?" I did not know whether to be exasperated by his reticence or elated that we'd finally have a definite date on which we would consummate our marriage.

"On August twenty-third the court will be at Compiègne for the hunting," said the dauphin. "And there—I give you my solemn promise," he avowed, gently touching my hair for the first time, "that we will join together with all the intimacy required of our union." And with that, he rolled onto his side and immediately fell asleep.

But my husband's birthday came and went—and still *rien*.

No sooner had we arrived at Compiègne, but he caught a dreadful summer cold. The only remedies, according to the dauphin's personal physician, Monsieur Lassone, were foul-smelling compresses slathered with mustard to relieve his congestion, and plenty of bed rest. Of course, it was not the sort of bed rest Louis Auguste had promised me. With a frightfully hoarse voice he told me he felt as though the comte de Provence had been holding his head in a bucket of water, the way he had done on more than one occasion when they were boys. I offered to sit by his bed and read to him (quite a sacrifice for me!), or even to play cards with him, but Monsieur Lassone insisted that the dauphin required peace and quiet and I was not to disturb him, lest I become ill as well. The unspoken fear was that both parents of the much-longed-for heir to the throne could not be placed at risk.

At length, Louis Auguste recovered and was removed from quarantine. My hopes that he would recall his birthday promise soared and I greeted the convalescent with joyful smiles and hinted at how much I looked forward to the intimacy that would follow our *couchers*. For the remainder of our stay at Compiègne, I dressed in varying shades of blue, from robin's egg to indigo, because I knew he was fond of the color; my hair was lightly frizzled and powdered, dressed softly off my forehead, cascading in fat curls that grazed my shoulders—a style he had once admired. Now that he was well enough to go about, I had become so giddy, so foolish, as to confide in some of my ladies that the time was nigh: Any night now I would forfeit my dubious status as a virgin bride.

The dauphin resumed his customary pleasures with renewed vigor. By day he rode and hunted with an energy he displayed nowhere else, working himself into an exhausted, if exhilarated, lather. At night, his hearty appetite fully restored, he would gorge himself until he was sated, devouring meat pies, oyster loaves, and fish dishes slathered in sauces, capped off with several helpings of confections and glacés. Then, pleading indigestion, he retired to a separate bedchamber, although I awaited him in my nightgown and cap. This would not have been unusual at the French court; it would be assumed that at some point during the night he would visit me. What had everyone scandalized was that he did not leave his bed even once to exercise his conjugal obligation. Compiègne was abuzz. Had the young couple quarreled? Rumors spread like butter over warm bread: that the dauphine never bathed (utterly untrue!); that the dauphin had taken a *maîtresse*, introduced to him by none other than the comtesse du Barry (ridiculous to the point of comical). Although I gave the impression of staring straight ahead as I glided through the rooms, I could spy my detractors out of the corners of my eyes, glancing directly at my still-flat belly as they offered their reverences, the women tilting their fans away from their faces just far enough to reveal their smirks.

My expectations had been utterly dashed—and in a most public arena. My rejection turned to anger, which metamorphosed into disappointment, and finally manifested itself as a profound sadness. What made matters even worse was that "Générale Krottendorf" had not visited in the four months since my marriage. She had never been terribly punctual, and now I had even more cause for anguish. I knew the chamber servants examined the conjugal sheets for the telltale signs—the emissions that would signal my monthly courses, or the stains that heralded the loss of my virginity. But morning after morning they found nothing—*rien*—to report. What gossip must be spreading through the servants' quarters to the ministers and courtiers? *With no sign of blood, surely she must be with child—and yet she does not increase? What is going on (or not going on?) in the dauphine's bed?*

With each passing day I grew more concerned. For want of a son, would my husband become the last Bourbon king?

TWENTY-ONE

Versailles

As the weeks plodded dully along, one day very much like any other, I began to dread going to bed every night almost as much as I deplored the *couchers*. The hot months of summer were filled with *fêtes champêtres*, long walks in the impeccably manicured gardens, and lazy boat rides along the Grand Canal. But indoors, I felt trapped in an endless round of ludicrous rituals.

By then, the court etiquette irked me more than ever. The first time I'd had to endure a presentation at court I'd been as anxious as one of the debutantes, and as curious and intrigued as they by the mystery of the ritual. The preparations, which lasted for hours, contained as many rules of etiquette as the presentation itself, but the comtesse de Noailles had guided me with brisk efficiency. Yet only a few months later, the novelty of it had disappeared. For those who had been born and raised at the French court, or who had aspired all their lives to gain entrée to it, these events were the culmination of a lifetime of expectation, while I quickly found them appallingly dreary.

The late-August heat didn't help. Beginning in the early hours of the morning, perspiration would trickle from the nape of my neck to the small of my back in meandering rivulets as my ladies tightened the preposterously unforgiving *corps de baleine* about my torso. It was an unavoidable concession; the court dresses would not fit correctly without the proper stays beneath them. "*Arrêtez!* I am feeling light-headed!" I exclaimed one morning, ordering them to cease. Teetering a bit, I reached for the rounded back of a chair.

"Then it is perfect!" replied the comtesse de Passy, giving the strings a final tug.

Presentations at court required the formal *robe de cour* and the voluminous *grands paniers* tied beneath it. With the panniers about my waist I looked like I was standing between a pair of three-foot-wide end tables. Ribboned garters had been tied above my knees to hold my white silk hose in place. I lifted one foot, then the other into a pair of cherry satin slippers. My gown, sewn from several yards of apple green silk embroidered with delicate orange blossoms, was lowered over my head with the utmost care. Sieur Larsenneur had styled my hair in the traditional coiffure required for court presentations: an elaborate confection piled high off my head. Achieving the requisite altitude required the addition of numerous lengths of false hair (both human and horse) fashioned over a larger wire cage than I'd ever worn before. It was an art in itself to manage such a creation. What a picture we women made, artificially elongated with at least an extra foot or two of hair atop our heads, and falsely widened by the court panniers until we resembled a ship of state, displacing about eight feet of space as we glided across the floors. And men considered us the weaker sex! Faugh!

The first time my hair was dressed for a presentation at court, I needed to take several turns about the room with my arms out-

stretched for balance before I began to grow accustomed to wearing such a heavy coiffure. I was flooded with memories of shuffling about the Rosenzimmer while Monsieur Noverre kept time
with his lorgnette. How I despaired then of learning the Versailles Glide!

"Of course, you do realize, madame la dauphine, such a *port
de bras* is not *comme il faut*," the comtesse de Noailles had tartly
observed. "You must hold your arms as one would naturally do
on any other occasion."

"Then how will I keep from toppling onto my face?"

"Like everyone else does. With practice."

I knew the French courtiers had expected me to make an ass
of myself during my first court presentation. But I was—had
been—an archduchess of Austria—a Hapsburg, not some country lambkin, new to the ways of a royal court. And by now I had
mastered the requisite techniques; Madame Etiquette's barrage of
admonishments made me crankier than usual. The dauphin's recent rejection remained in the forefront of my mind and I was in
no mood to stand and smile benignly while silly daughters of sil-
lier noblemen were introduced by their equally noble sponsors,
who droned on about their protégées' pedigrees and coats of
arms.

"In order to be presented at court, a lady must satisfy two rules
of etiquette," the comtesse de Noailles had informed me that
spring, when I prepared to attend my first presentation. "She
must be able to prove her noble descent all the way back to the
year 1400; and she must be introduced by a woman who has herself been presented at court." I'd wondered what had happened in
France in the year 1400 that made it so crucial, yet I'd dared not
ask, for she would have been horrified at my ignorance.

The Salon des Nobles was stifling in the heat of high summer.
Although it was considered poor etiquette to flap it about furi-

ously as if one were swatting at flies, I had never felt more grateful for my fan, painted especially for me by Monsieur Boucher. Even so, today the image seemed to mock me; it depicted my wedding to the dauphin, but as I glanced at my husband out of the corner of my eye, standing on the opposite side of the king, his expression vacant, I felt nothing but resentment.

Ahh...here came the first young lady now, a homely thing trying terribly hard to conceal her squint. She made it through the first of her three reverences, the shallowest of the trio, according to court etiquette. Would she fare as well on the next two curtsies? She was followed by her chaperone, the duchesse de Gramont. I knew her well, and I liked her, although there were days when I was tempted to shun her for recommending Sieur Larsenneur and his severe coiffures.

Madame de Gramont's protégée had managed the curtsies tolerably well. The paces between them were measured and stately, and she sank to the floor with appropriate elegance, abasing herself until her forehead was a whisper above the polished parquet.

Rising from her third reverence the elegant duchesse introduced the young lady who was now all smiles at having successfully completed her three deep court curtsies. *Wait until you have to reverse the process and walk backwards out of the salon without tottering*, I thought to myself, as a smile played across my lips. It had happened—I'd seen it, and cruel as it sounds, their mishaps did provide the occasional bit of mirth in an otherwise stultifying ritual.

"Your Majesty, Your Royal Highnesses, permit me to present Émilie Eveline l'Étoile, madame la comtesse de Saint-Pol."

I enjoyed interviewing the débutantes; it gave me something to do besides stand there and contemplate my fan. Papa Roi never seemed to mind. In fact, he had made the requisite small talk for so many decades, that he seemed glad to be relieved of the burden of reciting the same litany of questions; and the dauphin was far too reticent to utter a word. It was enough that Louis Auguste didn't resort to his usual manner of shifting his weight and shuffling his feet. "And so, what qualifies you to be presented to us today, madame la comtesse?" I inquired of the young lady.

"The hithorian William of Tyre nameth my anthestor comte Hughes de Thaint-Pol ath one of the knighth who joined the Firtht Cruthade in 1068," lisped the young comtesse. She could not have been older than sixteen.

"Well, then, your coat of arms is most certainly ancient enough." I smiled encouragingly.

"And it ith very handthome, too," the comtesse replied, "with a white croth on a red shield, enthircled by a golden chain of offith, and the cretht ith a crown!"

"*Très distingué*," murmured the king distractedly. His eye was already on the next débutante, waiting her turn. She was standing in the doorway at the far end of the room, but her diamonds, which illuminated a substantial décolleté, twinkled with promise.

I decided to have some fun with the comtesse de Saint-Pol. "Tell me, why is it that you wished to be presented at court?"

"Oh, madame la dauphine, the honor ith incalculable!" The girl's gloved hand, tightly clasping the ivory handle of her closed fan, flew to her breast. "From now on, I shall be allowed into the prethenth of the royal family on every official occasion—and have the opportunity to meet the motht important courtierth in all of Franth!"

"Are you a pious girl?" I asked coyly.

"Oh, yeth—and I will appreciate the privilege of being able to worship from the gallerieth of the Royal Chapel."

"Anything else?" I couldn't resist; it was becoming like a game to test her, even if I was the only one who knew we were playing it.

"Oh, forgive me, I am tho thorry!" I hid a giggle behind my fan; I couldn't help it; her lisp made me laugh, so I wished to hear her speak even more. "Being prethented at court meanths that I may enter the queen'th bedchamber, but ath there ithn't a queen now . . ." The young comtesse colored naturally behind her circles of rouge. "One day I do hope to have the honor and the pleasure and the privilege of doing tho when you are queen of Franth."

"Prettily said," I replied, and meant it.

One might be tempted to think that my days were passed leisurely, filled with naught but gaiety and pleasure. In truth, they were crammed with ceremony—religious, gustatory, and social. In addition to the presentations at court, I hated the *cercles*—another banality of life at Versailles. Various ladies would gather in my salon, in a sort of loose social circle; as dauphine it was my honor to act as the hostess; and I was expected to speak to each one of them directly. The comtesse de Noailles never tired of shepherding me through the *cercles* as though I were one of the Lipizzaner stallions being put through his paces at the Spanish Riding School back home in Vienna. I was to avoid all generalities; instead I was expected to say something polite (and quite specific) to each of my guests, and it was an onerous task to devise so many distinctive witty pleasantries.

Oh, how I wanted to scream, "*Who cares?*" It was all I could do not to poke fun at the ceremonies, the women, and especially the haughty Madame Etiquette. Finally, I yielded to the temptation, reasoning that if I must endure such rigidity, at least I could find some entertainment in it. So prior to a *cercle*, I would torment my *dame d'honneur* with inane questions, pretending that I was preparing myself, storing up a cache of remarks individually tailored to my guests. "What is the proper protocol, madame la comtesse, for addressing a lady who has smeared her rouge so frightfully that the apples of her cheeks resemble pears?" Or, "If it is so important to find something singular to share with each of my visitors, what should I say to the duchesse de la Rochefoucauld, who always chews with her mouth open? Should I remark upon it?" It was worth the time it took to invent such ludicrous questions just to receive Madame de Noailles's horrified reply and to watch the tips of her ears grow red with consternation.

Mesdames *tantes*, those mistresses of the art of *médisance*, had taught me how to turn my wit on an unsuspecting target. Frustration with my still-virginal state was relieved by raillery, and I found comfort in laughter and mockery. My targets were none the wiser if I giggled or rolled my eyes behind the safety of my open fan.

I found the elderly ladies particularly amusing, for they tried so hard to recapture the flush of youthful radiance that was the raison d'être for the mandated court maquillage. The prominent circles on their pixilated cheeks resembled wrinkled plums; and on some of the women, whose sight was evidently not what it once had been, the false blush was so clumsily applied that these aging aristocrats resembled the impoverished marketwomen of Paris who, I was told, stained their cheeks with cheap red wine because they could not afford rouge. On occasion, when boredom got the better of me, I would hide behind my fan so that only some of my ladies could see my features, and I would mimic the tipsy sway of a drunkard (as I imagined it, for I had never seen the genuine article) and roll my eyes heavenward with ennui.

One day, I was receiving some newly minted comtesses. My ladies-in-waiting were arrayed behind me like petals on a rose, including the bookish Madame Campan, who as Mademoiselle Genet had been Mesdames *tantes'* reader, though she was but three years my senior.

Out of the corner of my eye, I noticed the comtesse de Noailles nodding her head up and down and emphatically raising and lowering her eyes as though she were following the progress of a fly. This odd motion was followed by a series of strange hand gestures. I could not decipher a bit of it. What had sent the comtesse into such a tizzy? It dawned on me that the furious movement was not a signal to me, but to someone standing behind me, so I turned ever so slightly to regard my ladies—and there was Madame Campan, with the white linen lappets of her cap still pinned to the crown of her head.

"Your lappets, Henriette!" I muttered out of the corner of my mouth.

"*Quoi?* What?" she whispered. "I can't understand what you're saying."

"Your lappets!" I repeated, a bit louder. Endeavoring to contain my laughter I added, "Don't you know that it is the etiquette when receiving that the lappets must be down by your ears, like a spaniel? Let down your lappets or the comtesse de Noailles will expire from apoplexy!"

I found another source of release in riding out to the hunt with the dauphin and the king. After the initial fun of suprising the party by clattering up in a carriage, the excitement subsided. So I ordered a horse to be saddled and caparisoned for me, that I might join them, if for no other reason than to enjoy an exhilarating gallop as I'd done on my pony when I was a little girl. Of course I could not accomplish this expedition alone; court etiquette dictated that my women accompany me. But several of them were afraid of horses in general, and not a single one had ever ridden astride, let alone attired in a man's habit of split coat, breeches, and boots, as I had taken to doing.

It irked me how the royal hunting party often rode roughshod across the fields in pursuit of their quarry, heedless of the consequences to the local farmers. Frequently I insisted that the entire cortège divert its course in order to avoid trampling the wheat fields. The compensation Papa Roi offered to these poor men for despoiling their crops was so meager that I would privately supplement it from my allowance.

The absence of charity at Versailles appalled me. Maman had taught her children to have compassion for a fellow Christian in distress, regardless of his place in society. I tried to lead by example, but the courtiers were too convinced of their own superiority to offer aid to anyone who was not born a comte or a duc. They even turned their backs on a peasant who'd been wounded by a frightened stag during a hunt near Fontainebleau. The man had been digging a ditch when the beast, pursued by dozens of galloping horses, careened into him with great force, piercing him in the belly and groin with his antlers.

Upon hearing her husband's agonized cry, the villager's wife tore out of their cottage, her hair and dress in disarray. When she saw him lying in a pool of blood, she collapsed beside him, wailing hysterically and wishing for her own death.

Papa Roi drew up his horse and paused for several moments, his face a picture of concern. Yet he did nothing to ameliorate the man's suffering. It saddened and embarrassed me that he did not even offer the family so much as a sou, let alone send someone to summon a doctor.

"Here, madame." I knelt beside the woman and cradled her head in my arms. "Your husband most needs you to be strong when he is weak. Breathe, now," I coaxed her, until she inhaled my smelling salts. How I wept to see her so distraught; I tried to imagine how she might manage, were she to lose her spouse. I dispatched several members of my retinue to Fontainebleau to fetch the royal surgeons. When the doctors arrived they placed the wounded man on a litter and carried him back to his humble cottage, where I lit a fire, put the kettle on the hob, and brewed a pot of coffee. Their hovel, with its floors of packed earth and walls made of mud and thatch, reminded me of some of the places I used to see when I accompanied Maman on her visits of charity. I gazed about the room at the contemptuous expressions on the courtiers' faces and the gratitude etched on those of the cottagers. My guards were wary; my ladies of honor thought I was foolish. But I knew that God would not forgive me if I ignored the suffering of a fellow man.

Before I departed the cottage I handed the villager's wife my purse filled with gold *écus*. Her shining eyes, appreciative not only of the coins but for my compassion, were all the thanks I needed. A few days later I sent a messenger to inquire after the cottager's health. He would mend, I was told, but the process would be a slow one and not without pain. It would be several months before he would be able to feed his family from the fruits of his own labors. I spoke with my almoner and ordered that baskets of food—fowl and bread and cheese and wine—be brought to the cottage every week until he was fully recovered.

Why, I later asked the dauphin, was such Christian charity alien to the members of the French court? But Louis Auguste could only mumble a reply about how the Bourbons did not walk among their subjects as the Hapsburgs so often did. And yet I had seen him yield to his own philanthropic impulses, and it had gladdened my heart. There was hope for France yet.

It soon became the talk of the court that the dauphine was participating in the hunts and exhibiting her enthusiasm as an equestrienne in riding habits that resembled military uniforms—conduct that was evidently not *comme il faut*. Other distaff members of the royal family rode to hounds on occasion—in fact, Madame Adélaïde was an accomplished horsewoman—but my predicament was unique. Thus, it was only a matter of time before my spirited activity was curtailed. Madame de Noailles put her silk-shod foot down, declaring that even a canter was too strenuous for the dauphine, who of course might have an announcement any day. I dared not blaspheme by retorting that such an announcement would give me much in common with the Blessed Virgin. But at the comtesse's insistence, from then on, if I persisted in my wish to join the hunters, my mount would be a donkey.

On my first such adventure, I plodded along with great docility, as bored as it was possible to be, until the beast lost his footing on a root and stumbled, throwing me off his back and onto my well-padded derrière—plop in the center of a mud puddle. My ladies gasped and dismounted from their own asses, rushing to my aid.

"Why is she laughing?" quizzed the duchesse de Ventadour, much confused. "She is covered head to toe with *la boue*."

"Oh, I don't mind the mud at all!" I told her between peals of giggles. "I think the color suits me, don't you? We shall have a silk of just this shade woven in Lyon next season and name it *'boue de la chasse'*—mud of the hunt! Duchesse," I said, beckoning the timid woman closer, "run and fetch the comtesse de Noailles and demand to know the correct etiquette if a dauphine should fall off her donkey!"

October 7, 1770

Your Imperial Majesty:

I have made sure of three persons in the service of the dauphine: one of her women and two of her menservants, who now give me full reports of what goes on. Then, from day to day I am told of the conversations she has with abbé Vermond, from whom she still hides nothing. Besides that, the marquise de Durfort, who is in their service, passes on to me everything she says to her aunts. I also have sources of information as to what goes on whenever your daughter sees the king. Added to this are my personal observations of her conduct so that there really is not an hour of the day when I lack information concerning what the dauphine may have said, or done, or heard. I have made my inquiries this extensive because I know how essential it is to Your Majesty's tranquility that you should be fully informed of even the smallest detail.

Consequently, I must dutifully report the following: Madame la dauphine is putting herself in a precarious position by heeding the advice given by Mesdames, her aunts. We must own the blame for this, having so long labored under the misapprehension that the king's three maiden daughters were an anchor in the treacherous seas of the French court. Instead, the case has proven to be quite the reverse.

All the good qualities of our charming princess are nullified by Mesdames, who, devoid of principles and reflections (not to mention any education to speak of), conduct themselves in the most contemptible manner, encouraging the dauphine in mockery and mimicry of others the way one teases a kitten with a toy mouse on a string. The cat, of course, is not aware that she is being manipulated in order to provide them with entertainment. Who can answer for such conduct? I can only postulate that, as Mesdames were the highest-ranking women at court after the death of the queen, perhaps they do not appreciate being supplanted, let alone by one so young.

Not content to influence madame la dauphine's conduct and turn her mind against others at court, Mesdames even endeavor to poison her thoughts against one another.

Madame Adélaïde and Madame Sophie are trying to make
the dauphine dislike Madame Victoire, who is without doubt
the best of the sisters, being the princess with the most character and the least malice in her. At your request I shall continue to observe madame la dauphine and to submit my
reports.

> Your humble servant,
> Mercy

TWENTY-TWO

Enemies Within

In the absence of marital intimacy, I found other projects to fill the void, chief among them the ostracism of the king's mistress, who was thick as thieves with the duc de la Vauguyon and the odious duc d'Aiguillon, Emmanuel-Armand de Richelieu. Ever since the summer, when my aunts had counseled me to snub Madame du Barry, I had taken pains to put the creature in her place. I knew she continued to mock me behind my back, and it irked me that Papa Roi appeared ignorant of her deviousness. When the du Barry was in her lover's company, no one else existed; she made sure to dazzle the king with her eyes, her smiles, her jewels, and her décolletage.

I relished opportunities for revenge, particularly proud of the way my entourage had cut her back in September, when the court visited the Château de Choisy. We were crammed into the small theater to view a command performance; several of my ladies occupied the first row of seats, their wide skirts billowing about them, dangerously grazing the cans concealing the footlight torches. The du Barry had entered the room with her little coterie after we were already seated and the chandeliers had been raised, and demanded that room be made for them. Well, that would not do for the duchesse de Gramont! The sister of His Majesty's chief minister, the duc de Choiseul, could not permit such a coarse woman to sit in our midst, whether or not she was dripping with diamonds—and the du Barry was wearing a necklace that out-shone all others in the room. But, according to Madame Adélaïde, Béatrice de Gramont would have disdained the comtesse no mat-ter what she wore or where she wished to sit, because Madame de Gramont had at one time desired the king as a lover! Alas for her, Papa Roi had no interest in tall women with broad shoulders and russet hair, and in any case, he then fell in love with Madame du Barry.

The women exchanged words and their contretemps esca-lated to such an extent that they nearly came to blows. I smiled with delight to see the king's paramour so openly humiliated.

However, my triumph was so short-lived that it took my breath away. The following day, the creature complained to the king—her bosom heaving with sobs, so I had heard—and Papa Roi banished the duchesse de Gramont to her country estate! Even if the duchesse had lost some of my esteem, an insult to her was also a slight against her noble brother, and I owed the duc de Choiseul much.

I believed that the duchesse had been wrongly dismissed, but was afraid to approach His Majesty on my own to tell him so; when it came to matters of import, the king's magnificence in-timidated me. So one morning I sought my aunts' advice on the matter after the king had breakfasted with us in their apartments.

"We supped together, Papa Roi and I, after the card game on

the nineteenth and I urged him, as sweetly as I knew how, to allow the duchesse to return to court. I poured his wine for him, I let him hold my hand, I complimented his skill at cavagnole—I don't know what more I can do."

"What did he say?" Madame Victoire inquired. She was still swathed in her *négligée*—a morning gown of striped satin embroidered all over with tiny bouquets of roses. I could have had at least two dresses made for myself from the same amount of yardage.

"Not much," I admitted. "He gave me a cordial smile—not warm, just cordial, for I am learning the distinctions when it comes to his ways—and told me that he would think about it."

Madame Sophie, whose sea green watered silk made her appear to recede apologetically into Madame Victoire's floral wall covering, fiddled nervously with her cup of chocolate. "Did he say when he might arrive at an answer?"

"Perhaps it is best to leave the matter alone for now and allow our father to see his way clear to the right thing to do," Victoire suggested.

Madame Adélaïde rose and began to pace, her footsteps silent on the colorful Aubusson carpet. She circled the room like a bird of prey, coming to roost beside my right shoulder. Leaning toward me, her large white cap a puff of taffeta meringue, she murmured in my ear, "Do not react to what I am saying; just nod your head and smile. My sisters are idiots and I despise them. Their counsel is not worth a sou.

"Then we must take the subject firmly in hand," she said loudly, straightening her posture. "Papa does not understand what is good for him—and good for France." At that moment, I recalled one of my nocturnal conversations with the dauphin. He'd said it was hardly surprising that Mesdames should be so critical of their father, and that likewise the king did not think much of them. "He treated my grandmother the queen most cruelly," Louis Auguste had remarked, "flaunting his mistresses before the court; refusing Her Majesty permission to accompany him, and she, poor lady, was so humiliated by it. Her daughters naturally took her part against their straying Papa."

Adélaïde wheeled on her sisters and exclaimed, "That woman," pointing toward the door, beyond which the royal mistress's apartments were situated, a mere three rooms separating the two grand suites. "She who came from the streets and now glides about Versailles with an entourage to rival our own—such presumptuous ostentation! As if she was one of us! I take it, madame la dauphine, that you have seen how she swans about the château—with that little blackamoor following her like a trained monkey! Surely you would not wish her to continue to feather her nest, *mes chères*; the du Barry is a viper and she must be strangled!"

I had often seen the du Barry's page, a Bengali boy named Zamor who was nearly my age and who always wore a pink velvet jacket and trousers, his head wrapped with a white turban to set off the unique color of his walnut-hued skin. He shadowed her every move, most often with a tall parasol to shield his mistress's pale complexion from the harsh glances of the sun—even indoors. It was true that none of the royal family had such an exotic train, which in and of itself was scandalous—that a common trollop should command such attention. That the former Madamoiselle Bécu should lord her triumph, and that the duchesse de Gramont, whose family had been loyal courtiers for decades, and who herself had not been well, should suffer a swift and terrible punishment that did not fit the crime, was more than I was prepared to bear. "Then what must I do next, Madame Adélaïde?"

"Use a deputy—the duc de la Vrillière, for example. He has the king's ear. If our father will not hear reason from a girl who is not quite fifteen, despite her rank, then perhaps he will heed the suggestion of one of his ministers, a man who is well respected by hundreds of courtiers. Use the duc to do your dirty work, my dear, and I suspect that it will lead to success."

Sophie and Victoire exchanged glances. Madame Victoire crooked a plump finger and beckoned me to sit before her on the low upholstered tabouret.

I sank down onto the little stool. While Madame Adélaïde was busy with the pot of chocolate her sister whispered, "*Prenez soin*—be careful—about following our elder sister's lead. For what it is worth to you, madame la dauphine, Sophie and I would not do so ourselves." She stole a glance at Adélaïde. "For the truth is"—Victoire lowered her voice even further—"that Adélaïde is a controlling and mean-spirited *chienne*! And who would know this better than her younger sisters?"

Bitch or no, I decided to follow Madame Adélaïde's advice. I received the duc de la Vrillière, Louis's longtime minister for the Department of the Maison du Roi, or king's household, at my *lever* on the morning after he had spoken to the king.

He was an older gentleman, jowly, but distinguished. A man who favored bright colors, he was attired in a suit of peacock blue velvet embroidered with silver thread.

"At your request, I told him that the duchesse de Gramont was ill," said the duc.

"And?" I raised an inquisitive eyebrow.

"And His Majesty said that someone would have to be sent out to visit the duchesse and verify the gravity of her condition."

"Well, she is ill!" I exclaimed. "I am mortified that the king would not believe a woman whose family has served him so well and for so many years. *Mon Dieu*, her brother is one of his most distinguished ministers!"

The duc de la Vrillière sucked on his teeth and shook his

head. "There is more to it than that," he added, after an awkward pause. "It falls within the purview of Madame du Barry, as... as the royal favorite...to decide whether to consent to the duchesse's return."

"And?" I asked expectantly.

"And she does not. Consent." The minister's jowls quivered with annoyance. "Madame la dauphine, I regret to have failed you on this occasion. I suggest you approach the king again on your own. Be your sweet self. Between us," he added, bending down to give Mops a scruff on the back of his neck, "your *grand-père* can deny you nothing. But you must understand, my dear, that His Majesty is a man who is governed by his passions. And at present his passions are governed by the comtesse du Barry. Moreover, he is not the sort of person to make the quick decision. Rather—and maddeningly so for his ministers—he prefers to wait until a situation sorts itself out, as they often do, thereby preventing him from undertaking the unpleasant task of having to take action." The duc's tone was so confidential that I felt as if I were becoming privy to a state secret. "It is the duc de Choiseul, as his chief minister, who is truly governing the kingdom. Without him, madame la dauphine, we would have nothing but prevaricating."

I smiled, and a hint of playfulness crept into my voice. "Without monsieur le duc, I should not *be* dauphine, monsieur le duc."

"No, *bien sûr*," the duc de la Vrillière concurred. "But Choiseul is powerless to aid you in this little contretemps, although I am certain he would do so, if he could. The du Barry despises him, and I fear that anything he might mention to the king on your behalf, or his sister's, will do more harm than good. As I said," added the minister, ostentatiously clearing his throat, "the king is ruled by his passions."

On the advice of the duc de la Vrillière, I steeled myself to approach the king after the *grand couvert*, the public supper, two days later. The spectators who were compelled to stand during the meal were exiting the Queen's Antechamber in a rustle of silks and the clicking of red-heeled shoes as the footmen removed the tabourets from the center of the room, where the duchesses had been seated. Their rank entitled them to the privilege of the low stools during formal court ceremonies.

I appealed to His Majesty as a man who was sensitive to the frailties of women—all women, for my plea was on behalf of my lady, the duchesse. But Papa Roi remained unmoved. "Madame, I thought I had told you I would give you an answer when the time came."

Yet I sensed the slightest quaver in his voice and seized upon it, determined to remain undeterred by what Mesdames *tantes* referred to as their father's obstinacy. I held my ground, yet did so with the smile that I had been assured would melt the sternest heart. "But, Papa Roi, besides motives of humanity and justice, think how upsetting it would be for me if a woman who is a part of my household were to die in your disgrace."

King Louis looked ever so slightly chastened by my rebuttal. The corners of his generous mouth softened and the fire behind his eyes diminished to a sepia glow. "*Eh bien, ma petite*, it touches our breast to know that you are so concerned with our welfare. *Et je te promets*—I promise you—that you will soon be satisfied, and we can all slumber with a clear conscience."

My eyes became moist with gratitude. I raised myself on tiptoe and kissed his cheek. He smelled of civet. "*Gramerci, Grand-père*. It is so easy to see why you are called Louis *le Bien-Aimé*—the Well-Loved!" I most assuredly kept to myself the snatches of conversation I had overheard during endless games of cavagnole—mutterings about how the people of France no longer adored him, but saw a sovereign out of touch with his subjects, a king who would tax them into starvation if it would buy another château or a new diamond necklace for Madame du Barry.

I fell asleep with a smile on my face. I had won the first round; it was now my adversary's turn to experience the underside of fortune's wheel.

Hundreds of beeswax tapers flickering merrily within the tall, freestanding candelabras in the Hall of Mirrors created innumerable false reflections that winked back at their originals from the imposing looking glasses and the windows that faced the parterres. Beyond, the conical topiaries that lined the pebbled allées in serried rows were silhouetted against the dusky October sky. Inside the overcrowded ballroom, the enthusiasm of the orchestra, particularly that of the first violinist, made it difficult to overhear clandestine conversations (or to have them), which was often one of the greatest benefits of a masquerade ball. Although everyone seemed to recognize the dauphine no matter what I chose to wear, I preferred to tie my mask about my head with a ribbon, rather than carry it on a stick. It made dancing that much easier. That night, my mask, in the Venetian style, had been fashioned from papier mâché covered in ice blue satin, and embellished with white diamonds and seed pearls. Atop my coiffure, as if Sieur Larsenneur had not frizzled and teased it high enough already, was a triple plume of white egret feathers that bobbed and swayed with even the slightest movement of my head.

I had my own little nestling to look out for, enjoying, for the first time in my life, what it felt like to have a younger sister to chaperone. I tapped the comtesse de Saint-Pol on the shoulder with my fan to draw her attention, for her undoubtedly enraptured gaze was elsewhere. "How are you enjoying your first *bal à Versailles?*" I inquired.

She squinted up at me; at least I thought she did—it was hard to tell through the eyeholes of her mask. Covered as it was with green and amber feathers, she resembled an owlet. "Itht the motht magnifithent thing I have ever theen!" she gushed. "The danthing!" She clapped a hand to her breast, prettily displaying a topaz ring. "My papa gave me thith as a gift to wear to my firtht royal ball," she said, her voice dreamy. "Do you think I might danth?" she inquired, as if such an activity were reserved for only the rarest of mortals.

"Of course you will dance," I gaily assured her. She was not a beauty, nor ever would be. But she was young, and she was game. And I knew just the gentleman who would partner her gallantly. Fortuitously, amid the crush of revelers my flirtatious brother-in-law was at this moment within arm's length. I reached out and pinched the sleeve of his coat of coral-hued moiré. The comte d'Artois turned around abruptly, breaking off an intimate conversation with a particularly alluring, and significantly older, marquise. "*Excusez-moi*, madame," I apologized, stealing away d'Artois. He looked glum. And glummer still when I added, "May I present my new protégée, la comtesse de Saint-Pol. It would do each of us the greatest honor if you would partner her in the gavotte." I gestured toward the open floor with my fan, then spied Madame du Barry amid a few of her coterie. No, a gavotte would not do. The tempo was too quick for my purposes.

With another brief apology, I borrowed an overrouged courtier's beribboned walking stick; he was merely using it as an affectation, anyway. I rhythmically thumped it on the floor until the room grew silent. Then, having obtained the attention of the orchestra, I requested an ancient and classic—and slow—court dance: a pavane.

I knew how fond the king's favorite was of dancing; she would not be able to resist. And with the ballroom in a suspended stillness for a few moments, it was all the time I required to whisper to the comtesse de Saint-Pol, "Do you see the woman in sapphire blue?" I pointed discreetly with my fan. "Ah, *oui*, the one with the ruby and emerald parure, pale blond hair, and a coiffure all too much like my own. It would make me unspeakably happy if you would listen very closely to the conversation she has with her partner on the dance floor. Remember everything you can— and later we will speak of it, in private."

The young comtesse could scarcely contain herself. "I will thpeak with you alone, jutht you and I?"

"Like sisters, *oui*." I pressed her hands. "*Bonne chance*. And for heaven's sake, enjoy yourself!"

Then I clasped the comte d'Artois's arm and murmured into his ear, "Stay as close as you can to the du Barry. She always makes such a display of herself; but while all the men will be looking at her, their partners will secretly be ogling *you*."

He was bright enough to know that I was up to something, but vain enough to accept my compliment at face value. Offering his arm to the wide-eyed ingénue, the comte d'Artois escorted madame de Saint-Pol to the very edge of the dance floor.

In a room thronged with thousands of hedonists, no one noticed two petite young women slipping out onto one of the terraces. The dauphin had long since made himself scarce. He had a propensity to flee for the shadows whenever the musicians picked up their bows. His eyesight was even poorer than the comtesse de Saint-Pol's and he could never manage a lorgnette and a mask simultaneously. Besides, he was forever counting the steps and measures under his breath, trodding upon my toes and trampling my hems.

The evening air had become more bracing; the comtesse and I folded our arms across our chests to keep warm, although the necklines of our gowns were so revealing that our efforts were largely unsuccessful. I clasped the comtesse's elbow and steered her into a corner of the terrace where the light was especially dim. "So, what did you hear?"

"She wath very angry," the girl replied, sounding somewhat astonished that a woman with so many evident assets would have anything to be angry about. "Firtht she wath danthing with a thmall man who lookth like a monkey—"

"The duc de la Vauguyon," I interrupted. "He was wearing a yellow coat, *oui*?"

She nodded. " 'Thith ith war!' she told him, and then she thaid that she didn't like to be bethted by a fourteen-year-old girl."

"She didn't like to be bested by a fourteen-year-old girl," I repeated. She must have been referring to me. And my victory in gaining the duchesse de Gramont's reprieve. The king had recalled the ailing noblewoman from her estates and welcomed her back to court.

"Then she told the duc that she had tried to be your friend at firtht—well, the friend of the fourteen-year-old she had been referring to."

"She lies!" I exclaimed. "Unless she believes that bringing me a gawdy little trinket as a wedding gift is amity. I have heard the names she calls me."

"Who ith she?" the comtesse de Saint-Pol asked.

"The king's favorite," I hissed. "His lover. And she is not content to accept the fact that because she lies beneath His Majesty, she is not above the future queen." I rubbed my hands over my arms to warm myself. "Let's step inside. I'm feeling chilled. Besides, I wish to hear more."

What a change it was from the almost eerie silence of the terrace and the crisp night air to reenter the Hall of Mirrors, reeking as it did from perfume and perspiration, with thousands of chattering voices competing to be heard above the strains of the orchestra. We managed to maneuver ourselves toward the side of the hall where the comtesse and her cluster of admirers, known as "Barryistes," had formed an impromptu court of their own. The shadows cast into the corners of the room by the candleglow altered the shades of our gowns, making me less easily recognized; and our masks, aided by the strategic placement of our fans, allowed us to plot a course that brought us unremarked to our destination.

Thus unnoticed, with our faces to the wall and our backs to the royal mistress's coterie, we were able to overhear fragments of their conversation.

Her page boy, Zamor, whose white turban barely reached the comtesse's chin, stood by her shoulder, wielding a long-handled fan constructed of egret feathers, with a slow, methodic rhythm.

"The babes are outgrowing their swaddling." It was the sardonic voice of the duc de la Vauguyon. "Why, the boy behaves as if he's been just breeched—feeling his oats!"

I took the young comtesse by the arm and drew her deeper into the shadow by the wall, angling ourselves so that we might get a better view of their faces. "Oh, thith ith like thpying!" she whispered giddily. "Tell me, *th'il vous plaît*, who ith the gentleman with the fat head, thmall mouth, beady eyth, high forehead, thinning hair, and no neck?"

I stifled a laugh behind my fan. I could not spare even a chuckle. The entire French aristocracy could recognize the dauphine by her laugh. "Ah, *oui*, you mean the man who looks just like a toad. That, *ma petite amie*, is the duc d'Aiguillon. And as slippery as the animal he so much resembles."

"Well, the dauphin is sixteen," we heard the duc d'Aiguillon purr disdainfully. "Rather long in the tooth to discover he's a man and not a tot." With his thumb and forefinger he removed a bit of fluff from the cuff of his brown velvet coat—a wayward feather that had molted from Madame du Barry's headdress.

"From what I hear, he's still not yet a man!" The royal favorite clasped her hands over her skirts in the vicinity of her nether regions and laughed uproariously. "How much longer can France wait for the dauphin's little dauphin?"

The duc de la Vauguyon guffawed. "Very clever, madame la comtesse! There is no one at court to match you, bawdy wit for wit." It took him several moments before he caught his breath. "It's *l'Autrichienne* who controls him, you know. But for her, the boy would still be in my pocket. *Our* pockets," he emended, nodding to the du Barry and the duc d'Aiguillon.

As if the hall were not hot enough already, I began to seethe, feeling my blood boil even as the bare skin on my arms and *poitrine* pebbled with anxiety.

Madame du Barry absentmindedly adjusted one of her breasts, which her laughter had partially dislodged from her tightly laced bodice. Evidently, the creature had no compunction about displaying her ample charms in public. I wondered where the king had gone off to. Even he, who managed to find the comtesse's most vulgar behavior enthralling, might not have been so delighted to see her manipulate her chest in such a manner, and on such a public stage.

"You know, many at court find *la petite rousse* attractive, but I can't see it." Madame du Barry's affected aristocratic lisp became more pronounced. "*I,* for one, see nothing attractive in red hair, thick lips, a sandy complexion, and eyes without eyelashes. Had she who is thus beautiful not sprung from the House of Austria, I assure you, such attractions never would have been the subject of admiration."

How dare the comtesse mock my looks? My jaw dropped in

shock; I had never been so insulted. I clutched the hand of my hapless acquaintance and clenched it so tightly that the poor little comtesse de Saint-Pol nearly yelped in pain.

Madame du Barry grazed her reddened lips with the tip of her open fan, a gesture that was as seductive as it was contemplative. Above it, her eyes glittered with intensity. "*Et alors*... the duc de Choiseul, in his eminent wisdom and foresight, brokered a marriage of ninnies. I ask you, gentlemen, what sort of chief minister is that? If I were the king—or had his ear... or any other sensitive part of him..." She giggled wickedly. "I should dismiss a man who made such a muddle of my legacy." Her voice dripped with bitter sarcasm. "Not only does he take every opportunity to remind me that I was once a lowly *grisette;* but there is the matter of his rude sister, the Gramont, not to mention, *mes amis,* we are talking of a minister who secretly encourages the men of the Parlement, and the commune of Paris to block the king's authority and insist upon their right to self-governance! We are talking of a minister who foolishly gave his word to the Spanish to support them in a war against England over a silly little atoll near South America. Naturally, France will be dragged into the mess as soon as the cannons begin to roar. And Louis already complains that he emptied the treasury to fight the Seven Years' War. Such a minister—if I had my way—would be sitting in his carriage facing the gates of Versailles before the year is out." She glanced out the window at an eddy of dead leaves, caught upon the breeze that swirled across the parterres. "And if I were king, I should appoint someone who truly had my interests at heart. And that person would be..." She spiraled her index finger in concentric circles and pointed it at the ambitious duc d'Aiguillon. "*You.*"

Just then, the lively gavotte ceased. I clasped the comtesse de Saint-Pol about the wrist and touched my finger to my lips. The relative silence between dances would threaten to betray our position.

"*Boutez en avant!*" the du Barry said tersely, invoking her motto. "Push forward." As she stepped out of the shadows, the magnificent emerald-and-ruby choker about her throat caught the light, distilling it into thousands of fractured sparkles. The Barryistes dispersed, leaving only Zamor to trail after the comtesse on his short legs, until he too, was swallowed into the mass of revelers.

"*Mon Dieu!*" gasped the comtesse de Saint-Pol. "I had no idea the court wath tho exthiting!" But then, even behind her mask I could tell that her expression had grown dark with concern. "Wath that *treathon?*" she whispered. "Should we tell the king?"

I shook my head. "Unfortunately, I think there will be nothing we can do about what we heard tonight. Except despair. And hope—desperately hope—that it does not come to pass. The comtesse believes she can have everything she desires because she pleases the king. But," I said, seeing, for the first time, my own power reflected in the du Barry's machinations, "her influence will not last and she knows it."

TWENTY-THREE

Rumblings and Grumblings

Less than two months after the celebration of my fifteenth birthday, Madame du Barry got her wish: After years of faithful service to the king, on New Year's Eve, December 31, 1770, the duc de Choiseul was invited to retire to Chanteloup, his château in the country. I was heartbroken; and I was angry. His political and diplomatic strategy had brought me to this place, elevated me from being the youngest archduchess of Austria to a breath away from becoming queen of France. My eyes wet with tears, I bade him farewell and thanked him for all he had done. I did not expect to meet his like again; certainly I would not find it in the ambitious and unctuous duc d'Aiguillon whom the king had appointed Choiseul's successor. I had an inexplicable feeling that it was the comtesse du Barry who was the duc d'Aiguillon's rumored clandestine lover. Basking in her triumph, she had moved into an even grander suite. Her new apartments were connected to the king's own rooms by way of a secret staircase. Memories of my father's long-standing affair with the glamorous Princess

Auersperg flooded my mind: my mother's silent tears; the grim faces; the false smiles; the lies. I could taste my disgust.

I penned a brief letter to Maman on the state of affairs, telling her that the king had replaced Choiseul with the duc d'Aiguillon and held a *lit de justice* at which he suppressed the former Parlements, or judicial bodies from the various provinces. The Parlements had possessed the authority to assert themselves independent of any royal authority, which included blocking the crown from passing any laws. Papa Roi then ordered the creation of a new Parlement; his action was so autocratic that the Princes of the Blood, his cousins Condé and Conti, and the duc d'Orléans, refused to appear, in protest of the king's overexertion of his will. For such insubordination, Louis banished them. A few ducs joined the protest as well, with the result that about a dozen of them had been exiled.

I understood nothing of politics, merely parroting what I had overheard and reporting it to my mother. My husband had a keener grasp than I, but even he was at pains to explain his grandfather's actions. All I knew was that everything had begun with the dismissal of one of my few friends and Austria's rare allies at Versailles. The loss of Choiseul made me more determined than ever to cut Madame du Barry down to size. But I vowed to do so with silence.

March 17, 1771

To Her Imperial Majesty Maria Theresa:

    Monsieur le dauphin, who until recently had seemed either unaware of or indifferent to the current intrigues (or both), suddenly evinced a tremendous disdain for his tutor, the duc de la Vauguyon, as well as absolute contempt for the comtesse du Barry. His scorn is also directed at the duc d'Aguillon, and all those who belong to their party. This was of course brought to the king's notice by the obvious source, along with hints that this change had been provoked by madame la dauphine, whom the Barryistes are convinced has the dauphin wrapped around her finger. I am informed that the king believes this propaganda and is displeased.

Consequently, madame la dauphine spoke to the king and said, with the consummate grace that comes so naturally to her, that she was sorry that her *grand-père* did not care for her enough to speak to her directly on what might please or displease him. Caught up short, the king looked extremely embarrassed, avoided all particulars, and assured madame la dauphine that he thought her charming and loved her with all his heart; he kissed her hand, hugged her, and assured her that he agreed with everything she had just said. The king's rather maddening behavior is the result of his weak character and his habit never to scold his children. He would much prefer to bear what he does not like, rather than remedy it by a direct confrontation.

Your humble servant,
Mercy

· · ·

March 31, 1771

Your Imperial Majesty:

In spite of the contents of my official dispatches, it is nearly impossible for Your Majesty to form a complete idea of the horrible confusion that reigns here in everything, particularly since the departure of the duc de Choiseul, who, owing to the king's lassitude, was the true governor of France.

The throne is submerged by the indecency and extent of

credit to the king's favorite and the wickedness of the Barry-istes. All decisions taken here depend on the caprices of the *maîtresse en titre* and the intrigues of a few ministers and courtiers. The nation exhales seditious suggestions and disseminates satirical publications in which the monarch himself is not spared. Versailles has become the center of lying, hatred, and revenge; everything is affected by intrigue and personal opinions, and it appears as if all good feeling has been abandoned.

I must, however, ask Your Majesty to do a bit of prevarication herself. The dauphine has begun to suspect the author of this dispatch as the source of Your Majesty's intelligence regarding her day to day conduct and activities. I have endeavored to disabuse her of this notion, because if she is ever to learn the truth, I will lose her trust, and the same of course is true of her relationship with the abbé. But if you assure the dauphine that I am not your eyes and ears here, we may be able to continue as we have done, and may I say, indefinitely.

In reply to my last dispatch, Your Majesty commands me to state whether the king has taken to drink. The report is unfounded, but may arise from the frequent evidences of absence of mind resembling the aftereffects of intoxication. It is certain that the king's head is becoming weaker, though it is more likely due to the natural effects of aging compounded by decades of political indecision and indolence.

> Your humble servant,
> Mercy

On the fourteenth of May, Louis Auguste's brother, the comte de Provence (just fifteen days younger than I), waddled to the altar. His bride was the seventeen-year-old Marie Joséphine

Louise of Savoy, and I do not think it would have been possible for the comte to have found a shorter, squatter, smellier wife. One might have overlooked her hairy upper lip or her beetle brows, or even her coarse, ruddy complexion; but it would have taken a brave soul to surmount his adversity to her overwhelming bodily odor. Papa Roi was so repulsed that he wrote to Marie Joséphine's family in Savoy demanding that they compel the girl to wash her neck, and for him to take such a decisive tack, her filth must have been truly repugnant! I felt sorry for her ladies-in-waiting. Had she not been assigned a bath attendant as well? But Provence was terribly glib about his prowess in the boudoir, boasting to the dauphin and me that he had been made "four times happy" on his wedding night. I tried to cheer my husband by telling him I doubted that they were even *once* happy! At least I made Louis Auguste laugh when I said that I was certain they could not have consummated their marriage because the pair of them were so rotund that they could not even have located each other's nether parts.

Luckily for them, the Provences were not subject to the same degree of etiquette that we, or the king, were. The higher the rank, the greater the number of rules governing our conduct. Although no one could punish the dauphine for failing to follow the proper etiquette of one thing or another, my transgression would become the subject of gossip; and the rumors, as they flew from mouth to mouth, might change shape, magnifying, or even transmogrifying the slightest breach into a chasm.

One chilly morning, during my *lever*, I had gotten undressed and was standing behind a folding screen, waiting for my undergarments. According to protocol, I could do nothing for myself. It was the office of my First Lady of the Bedchamber to prepare my underthings for the Mistress of the Household, who would then hand them to me, one by one, as I dressed. But these attendants would be superseded in their privilege of handing me my chemise by the appearance of a noblewoman of higher rank.

Shivering, I poked my head out from behind the screen, noticing that my Mistress of the Household had removed her glove in preparation to present my chemise. She was on the verge of handing me the undergarment when there was a scratching at the door; at Versailles, it was considered ill-mannered to knock.

My ladies paused to admit my visitor. It was the duchesse d'Orléans, the wife of a Prince of the Blood. So the duchesse began to peel off *her* glove so that *she* might have the honor of handing me my shift—when another *scritch-scritch* was heard at the door. My flesh by then was pebbled with cold, my nipples painfully erect. *Would they please hurry—the dauphine is freezing her derrière off*, I longed to cry.

My second visitor was my new sister, the comtesse de Provence, who outranked the duchesse d'Orléans. Already, I had had my fill of court etiquette for the day. "Oh, this is odious!" I exclaimed. "What a ludicrous inconvenience! Marie Joséphine, *vite, vite*! Quickly, I am about to perish from the cold!" I crossed my arms over my chest and rubbed them vigorously, hopping about to stay warm.

The comtesse de Provence, who was terribly nervous, as this was her first time attending my *lever*, hastened to remove her glove, but ran into difficulty peeling it over her plump forearm. "Here!" she cried. "I am so sorry. *Pardon!*" She grabbed my chemise and thrust it toward me, accidentally clouting me in the head and knocking off my mobcap. By that time I was so cold and so frustrated by the insanity of the entire charade that I lost my temper and scolded her for being so clumsy.

But when I came to know my new sister-in-law a bit better (for being the only young royal women at Versailles we were very much in each other's company), I felt bad for having disparaged her appearance as well as her hygiene. Marie Joséphine's northern Italian accent was charming, and she kept us in stitches the way she would mispronounce something so that it came out sounding like a different word entirely, completely changing the meaning of what she was trying to say. She didn't smell any better, but what I first mistook for a cold and embarrassed demeanor turned out to be awe. She had never seen anything nearly as grand as Versailles. In private, she was rather sweet-natured and agreeable. In one of my letters to Maman I told her that my new sister "likes me very much and has much confidence in me."

But Marie Joséphine and I would never entirely be friends. Now that the dauphin's next younger brother was married, my husband and I had found ourselves in a race to procreate. It would be our son who would inherit the throne of France—but what if we did not have one? What if Louis Auguste and I *never* had a son? If the squat and swarthy comtesse de Provence bore her new husband a boy, that child might very well become king one day.

One thing was certain. The dauphin and I would most assuredly lose the competition if we failed to consummate our marriage.

On this point, Maman had much to say. I knew she had corresponded with Papa Roi on more than one occasion to ask—no, the empress of Austria did not ask; she *demanded*—what was wrong with my husband, and that Louis had tried to assuage her fears by insisting that the dauphin was still quite young and immature when it came to certain matters. All I knew was that Louis Auguste was a strapping youth, and if the king expected him to grow any further before he reached maturity, I would have wagered a month's allowance that the direction of his growth would have been out, rather than up, for his grand passion was not me, but food.

Maman had written me a letter from Schönbrunn dated the eighth of May, although I did not receive it until after Provence's nuptials.

May 8, 1771

I have in front of me as I write the miniature portrait which represents the image of my dear daughter Antoinette, but it does not bear the youthful look she had eleven months ago. Would that the cause of such strain was a change in your condition, but from what you tell me of your relations with the dauphin, it is clearly not the case. Therefore, I hope that the wedding which is shortly to take place will bring my wishes to fruition. Surely you cannot let the comte de Provence and his bride outstrip the dauphin and dauphine!

As concerns your conjugal situation, let me counsel you never to be ill tempered about it. Do not let frustration gain the upper hand. Rather, use caresses and cajoling—but sweetly, tenderly. If you are too urgent or impatient you will spoil everything. Let sweetness and patience be your only tools. Nothing is lost yet; you are both still so young. In fact, it is better for your health that you have waited; you are on the brink of maturity now. Remember, it is natural for us old parents to wish for a speedy consummation, so that we may live to see our grandsons and great-grandsons!

This brings me to the care and protection you show for your homeland. I am both surprised and disappointed that it is not as strong as I had expected. Trust me: The French will respect you more if you display the solidity and frankness that are the hallmarks of the German character. Making people like us is one of the chief amusements of a royal personage; and it is one of the things that you do to perfection! Do not lose this skill by neglecting everything that brought you this far: You owe it neither to your beauty (which is not terribly great), nor to your artistic abilities (which you know very well you lack). You must be doubly amiable, as you have no natural talents of your own. Remember, it is your amiability as well as your kind heart and your frankness, combined with your good judgment, that make you exceptional.

My love for you is boundless, Antoinette, so please forgive me for going on so. I have only your best interests at heart.

Before I close, I must tell you that it was not Mercy who provided me with all of this information about you; however, it may surprise you to hear how much we know here of your activities. Although I correspond with no one but yourself and your *grand-père*, many others are copious letter-writers, and do glean even the smallest details about your conduct.

Your loving Maman

TWENTY-FOUR

Envy

≈ JUNE 1, 1771 ≈

The comte de Mercy affected a low bow as he entered my music room. As he rose, he realized that he was clearly outnumbered, not only by French, but by females. A *cercle* was just breaking up; and the capacious chamber, with its delicate white boiserie moldings enhancing equally creamy walls, resembled a hothouse of exotic and fragrant blooms—suffused with the scents of orange blossom and rosewater, frangipani and jasmine, lilac and lily of the valley.

I recognized the telltale signs that the ambassador wished to speak with me: the tight set of his jaw, despite a placid smile, and an expression of benign complacency in his eyes that masked the avidity to complete his errand.

I asked the comtesse de Noailles to shoo everyone from my apartments and motioned for Mercy to make himself comfortable. While we waited for the stragglers and servants to depart, the ambassador seated himself on a chair that had been abandoned by one of the ladies at the *cercle*; the ice blue satin brocade looked terribly dainty beneath his suit of tobacco-colored moiré.

"May I?" he asked me, reaching into a pocket for a small enameled box.

I nodded. "Where would you gentlemen be without your snuff?"

The comte snapped open the lid, and took a pinch of brown powder between his thumb and forefinger. "I don't suppose Your Royal Highness would care for a bit?" he teased.

We waited until the doors were closed around us. "I am always honored by your visits, monsieur le comte. *Dites-moi*, to what do I owe the pleasure today?" The ambassador frowned. "I don't like that look. It heralds bad news. I am in no humor for bad news."

"Well, then, it doesn't have to be," he said brightly, crossing one leg over the other. "Now, you tell me, madame la dauphine, what is this nonsense I have been hearing about your refusal to speak to the comtesse du Barry."

My spine stiffened. "For one thing, *monsieur l'ambassadeur*, it is far from nonsense. The duchesse de Gramont—"

"Is a seasoned courtier who can fight her own battles," the comte de Mercy interrupted. "Your mother and I applaud your loyalty to one of your ladies, particularly in light of her relation to the duc de Choiseul and his connection to our interests. But the duc is gone. And the Gramont is forgiven. And you began to snub the comtesse weeks before the Gramont affair took place. I understand that you received Madame du Barry here in your apartments."

"That was before I found out what she was," I replied stubbornly, drawing a circle in the carpet with the toe of my slipper.

"She is the king's favorite," Mercy said evenly.

"She is a whore," said I, with venom in my voice.

The comte took another pinch of snuff with what sounded like an angry inhalation. He rested both feet on the rug. "Who told you that?"

At this I could not resist a laugh. "Why, comte de Mercy, is this a catechism? I have a stable full of priests for that, not to mention our dear abbé Vermond!"

But he would not be deterred from his course. "I asked who told you this, madame la dauphine?"

"Someone who is an image of propriety. Someone Maman herself urged me to consort with as frequently as possible. Someone with impeccable morals."

The ambassador placed his hands on his knees and pitched himself toward me. The ruby he wore on his pinky finger flashed, caught in a sunbeam. "Who?"

"Why, Madame Adélaïde."

He sat back against his chair and closed his eyes for a moment. Then he rested his elbows on his knees and steepled his hands together in contemplation. After some length, during which I began to look forward to my next appointment, he spoke. "Madame la dauphine, I wish you to listen very closely to what I am about to say. Your mother was wrong. Mesdames are not the positive influence she had expected them to be. Your allegiance is, and must always be, to the king above all others. You are the king's first subject and if it pleases him for you to be pleasant to the woman he loves, then—no matter what you think of her, of her morals, or of her past—your obligation is to the king."

"Mesdames *tantes* told me we should save His Majesty from himself. When the *king* is behaving immorally by flaunting such a wanton woman before the entire court—what sort of lesson does that teach his subjects?"

The comte de Mercy shook his head dolefully. "You are still

only fifteen years old, madame la dauphine. Too young, and still too newly come to Versailles to be so proud."

"I am my mother's daughter," I said, with a touch of defiance. "And if she does not wish me to spend so much time in the company of my aunts she should be delighted to hear that since the marriage of the comte de Provence, I have been hosting the evening card parties in the dauphin's apartments owing to our new rank as the senior couple." This meant that I now spent far fewer hours in Mesdames' rooms. In truth, I was glad of it, for my aunts were more than twice my age and cared naught for anything but gossip.

The ambassador pressed his fingers to his temples. "I believe you should know, madame la dauphine, that your mother has, for the sake of—" He paused abruptly, as if he had caught himself about to say something he should not reveal, or else had changed his mind about what he intended to say in the first place. "Your mother," he repeated, "firmly believes that you should resume an acquaintance with the comtesse du Barry. You spoke to her once when she visited your rooms to bring you a wedding gift—perhaps you even said a word or two to her on another occasion over a round of cavagnole or a hand of cards. It would not be such a terrible thing to countenance the favorite again."

I narrowed my eyes, doubtful that he was telling me the truth about Maman's desires. After all, his talents lay in convincing people to do things that would not necessarily benefit them. I had already informed Maman, *It is pitiful to see the king's partiality for Madame du Barry, who is the most stupid and impertinent creature you can imagine. You can be well assured that I shall commit no fault either for her or against her.*

"It would make the king happy. It would make your mother happy."

"I cannot believe, for one thing, that Maman would give credence to the superiority of a woman of the streets, no matter whose bed she warms. For another, she raised her daughters with unparalleled propriety." The ornate gold clock on the mantel chimed the half hour. "I regret that our interview must end," I said, rising from my chair. "I am late for a visit with my new sister."

The comte de Mercy stood and bowed in farewell. As I escorted him to the door, I continued our conversation, for I wished to have the last word. "Did you know that for two months prior to my proxy wedding in Vienna, I spent every night in Maman's bedchamber so that she could lecture me on how to maintain our good German morals in the licentious French court? And to always honor the teachings of our Holy Mother Church. And now you come here this afternoon and ask me to abandon them?" It was all I could do not to stamp my foot. Instead I raised my chin and straightened my shoulders because I knew that *I* walked the higher ground, not the former Mademoiselle l'Ange from the rue de la Jussienne. And even if Mesdames were chattering old magpies, they were also chaste women, and they most assuredly cared deeply for their father and wished to see him one day enter the kingdom of Heaven. "You tell me it would make the king happy were I to speak to the comtesse, and yet he has never made that request of me directly, nor chastised me for ignoring her. Maman spent months instructing me to *avoid* the debauchery of Versailles and yet you say she would be pleased if I countenanced the du Barry—quite the opposite of what she taught me—and you cannot give me a reason for it. So my answer, monsieur le comte, is *non*. I will not speak to Madame du Barry."

The comte left my rooms defeated in his embassy, perhaps for the first time in our long acquaintance. But how could I violate everything I had been inculcated to believe—with only the flimsiest rationale to salve my conscience?

"Mon Dieu!" The bookcases that the comtesse de Provence had commissioned to be built in their apartments had been the talk of Versailles for the past few weeks. I pretended not to hear the rude comments comparing our scholarly interests, in which I emerged unfavorably—such as the jibe from the duchesse de Valentinois, another intimate of the comtesse du Barry, in which she asserted that the Provence's comprehensive library conferred her with far more "spine" than the dauphine—a dig at my lack of intellectual rigor as well as my refusal to wear a corset.

The sawdust had been swept away, and the lacquer had dried, revealing a masterpiece of décor. The giltwork alone was stunning, and the carved and routed embellishments *nonpareil*. I set my gift of a large beribboned basket of oranges in the center of the room and sought out my new sister who was superintending the unpacking of her library. Wooden crates with her initials burned into them covered nearly every square inch of the room. As the covers were pried off, an army of servants hastened to remove the straw packing.

"Stai attento! Be careful!" she shrieked in Italian, as a particularly diminutive maid struggled to lift a heavy, leatherbound volume from one of the crates. It slid out of its large velvet pouch and tumbled to the floor with an audible thump. *"Stupido!* How dare you touch my Catullus with your dirty hands?"

Marie Joséphine's double chin trembled with rage. Even the dark hairs above her upper lip stood on end, so offended was she by her servant's clumsiness. I stood agape, having never seen her like this. Where was the amiable and diffident creature who despaired of putting a foot wrong at her new court?

The comtesse looked up and caught my eye. Smoothing her hands on her saffron-satin skirts—an unfortunate hue for a sallow complexion—she cocked her head coyly, and offered a wan smile. "Forgive me, sister," she said in her lilting Savoy accent. "You are lucky that you are not a reader, because it is such a headache to organize so much." She gestured flamboyantly at the numerous crates and the multiple bookcases that lined the walls. "And everything must have its proper place or I will never be able to put my thumb—my finger, I mean—on it when I need it. There are the Greek books and the Latin ones, the history, the poetry—and I have one shelf just for Dante." Her hands flapped like the wings of a sparrow and flew to her heart. "Ah, Dante!" she exclaimed, casting her eyes heavenward. "Have you read him?" I shook my head. "I didn't think so. You are welcome to borrow a volume—if," she forced a chuckle, "your hands are clean. Do you read Italian?"

Meeting her artificial smile with one of my own, "Only French and German," I replied.

I glided back to the dauphin's apartments with uncommon speed, my thoughts fixated on a single purpose. I made a grand sweep of all of the rooms with a discerning eye toward the décor and was disappointed with the shabbiness of what I saw. The apartments had not been redecorated since the dauphin's late father was a youth. Carpets, curtains, hangings, and upholstery, once vibrant, had long since grown faded and dingy; furniture was nicked, some pieces having been scratched and gnawed for years by the claws and teeth of generations of overindulged dogs and cats. My own general inattentiveness since my arrival at Versailles had not ameliorated matters. I had been too lax; in that, Maman was right, and the advent of the comtesse de Provence threatened to usurp my place—at present, as the arbiter of interior décor, and someday, perhaps as the mother of the future king of France if things remained the same in my *lit matrimonial*.

I turned to address the comtesse de Noailles. "Madame, I should like to have a library built in these rooms. Please arrange for Monsieur Gabriel to come and see me so that we may draw up the plans."

Madame Etiquette arched an eyebrow. "Monsieur Gabriel? But he—"

"*Oui, oui*, I know that he is the *premier architecte de France*. If he can design the opera house in which the dauphin and I were wed, if he can design le Petit Trianon, then surely he can build me a room full of bookcases!"

Aware of my impatience with reading, the comtesse de Noailles looked as if she wished to humor me. I don't suppose she realized that the dauphine of France needed cabinets to rival the magnificently carved bookcases that had been made for the comtesse de Provence. No, not rival: *exceed* them.

"And I would like this mess disposed of." My broad gesture encompassed the entire suite of rooms—both the dauphin's and the dauphine's. "We shall commission miniature houses for the dogs so that each has its own place." In addition to my little Mops, the maréchale de Mirepoix, hearing of my fondness for pugs, had made me a gift of four of them. "Please see that the apartments are thoroughly aired and cleaned and the broken furniture repaired. If there are stains, the upholstery and carpets are to be replaced." The comtesse de Noailles looked astonished, her mouth and eyes widening. But I was not finished. I pointed to a pile of dirty clothes, some of which had been shredded by little canine teeth or ripped by the servants' children when they played "dress-up" in them. "Please see that those are patched and distributed among the poor. I will no longer have it said, madame la comtesse, that the dauphine glides about Versailles looking like a match girl."

"Absolutely, madame la dauphine. It shall be done *tout de suite*!" Madame Etiquette looked so elated that she was almost ready to scoop up the offending garments herself.

"One more thing," I said, as the chambermaids began to bustle about, doing my bidding. "Because such shabby gowns are not in keeping with the dignity of the first woman in France, I should like to see the royal dressmakers first thing tomorrow." The comtesse de Noailles dropped an obliging curtsy. *Well then*, I said to myself, *take* that, *Madame du Barry and Comtesse de Provence. From now on there will be no mistaking who is the future queen of France.*

When the dauphin returned to our apartments, I began to regale him with all the events of the day, but he interrupted me with news of his own. "Monsieur Gamain is teaching me how to make a new kind of lock," he said proudly, as Clery, his chief *valet de chambre*, helped him out of his coat and waistcoat. Then, grimy and exhausted from spending several hours at his forge, he flung himself onto a chaise and extended his arms expansively across the emerald-colored damask. His batiste chemise was marred with unsightly yellow rings beneath his armpits. I knelt at my husband's feet, my salmon silk skirts billowing about me like a *macaron*, and gazed into his light eyes. "I do believe that if you had not been born a Bourbon, you would much rather have been apprenticed to the royal locksmith," I opined candidly. He did not demur. "I will send the servants to fetch a basin and ewer," I said, with wifely solicitousness. "We can't possibly host your brother this evening with you looking like that."

The dauphin clapped his hand to his head. "Oh, *mon Dieu*, I'd forgotten! After a long day with Gamain, I lack the stomach to parry with Provence."

I laughed. "No matter—he has stomach enough for both of you! And so does his comtesse." I settled onto a stool beside him and told him about our little tête-à-tête that afternoon. "You should have heard her abuse her maid," I told the dauphin. "Or perhaps not; it was hardly a pleasant thing to witness. But the comtesse is quite particular about her treasures." I glanced about the room at the faded splendor of our furnishings. "When we are king and queen, considerable renovations must be done!" I declared. "In the meantime, I will not have the comtesse de Provence lord her library over me, as if to say not only are her accoutrements finer than mine, but her mind is superior as well."

The dauphin reached for my hand, entwining his fingers with mine in a rare gesture of intimacy and affection, particularly as it took place in the light of day and in the full view of his *valet de chambre*. "Envy, *ma chère*, is an ugly thing." He chuckled to himself and squeezed my hand. "And yet we cannot seem to avoid it. But all the *friseurs* and *tailleurs* and *marchands de mode* in the kingdom have not the magical arts to transform that fat, hairy, ill-tempered sow into the charming and radiant beauty who is the dauphine of France."

He raised my fingers to his lips, practically lifting me off the tabouret in the process, and gently kissed my knuckles. I felt a blush begin at the bridge of my nose and spread from my cheeks up into my hairline and down over my *poitrine*. And then I smiled more broadly than I had ever done since I arrived at Versailles. "*Merci*," I whispered. "*Tu es très gentil et doux*. Now, let us show the Provences our mettle this evening!"

But things did not quite turn out as planned.

The other young royals detested cavagnole as much as I did, so we had one of the gaming tables set for piquet. Provence and I had sat down to play, while the comtesse, her lawn green silk made bilious in the candle glow, leaned over her husband's shoulder observing his hand and whispering strategies in his ear as to which cards to discard and how many to draw from the stock at the center of the table. As it would have been unseemly to openly snipe at each other, we found common ground for our *médisance* at the royal mistress's expense, taking delight in performing the ribald songs and repeating the scathing jests that were making the rounds of the palace.

"Brother, have you heard this one about the *ci-devant* Mademoiselle l'Ange?" Provence asked the dauphin. For some reason, Louis Auguste had decided to hang back from the table. As he observed the game, he toyed with one of his riding crops, petulantly striking his brother on the arm from time to time.

The comte slid his chair a foot or two away from the gaming table and declaimed,

> *"I wonder that* it *isn't slack*
> *From all that work upon your back;*
> *And does your* other *lover wheedle,*
> *When he longs to thread his needle?"*

"*Oh*," I gasped, "you have managed to *skewer* the duc d'Aiguillon, too!" It was now commonly surmised by all but the king that Madame du Barry was also pleasuring his foreign minister, and *aiguille* was the word for "needle."

My portly brother-in-law was very clever, and far more articulate than the dauphin. It made his company refreshing, but only in modest doses; the comte could just as easily turn his sharp tongue against his purported friends.

Thwack went the riding crop against Provence's upper arm. It had to have been the seventh or eighth time my husband had struck him. I caught his eye and shook my head. "*C'est tout*," I mouthed. "Enough." I knew what could happen when the boys allowed their baser natures to get the better of them. I knew they were envious of his place in the birth order, even though it was all because their oldest brother had died. But Provence was the clever boy and Artois was the handsome one, and both believed themselves to be infinitely more accomplished—let alone ambitious about becoming king of France, a fire that admittedly did not burn in my husband's belly, regardless of his birthright.

I don't know whether it was Provence's pointed refusal to react to the first several blows that angered my husband, or whether the dauphin was jealous that his brother and I were having such fun (for Louis Auguste had never before expressed the slightest envy when I amused myself with his siblings), but evidently, he struck his younger brother one time too many for the comte to continue to consider it a game. With a sudden movement Provence grabbed the loop of the leather whip, abruptly pushed his chair back from the table, and tugged my husband toward him. The two boys faced off, fists raised against each other.

"*Arrêtez!*" I shouted, as the comtesse tried to squeeze herself into a corner. "Both of you, stop this nonsense!" I ducked under Provence's arm and snatched the whip from him. Then I flung the riding crop across the room; it landed under a chaise. Mops and my other pugs, frightened by all the commotion, began to bark. The comtesse held her ears as she released a string of oaths in her native dialect. Then she grabbed her husband by the sleeve and the pair of them waddled out of our apartments without so much as a *bonne nuit*.

Later that evening, when Louis Auguste dutifully came to my bed, I scolded him for behaving like a jealous fool. The comte de Provence was my brother and although I admired his wit, I saw nothing else of merit about him. "We are one, you and I," I assured the dauphin, "and you must never doubt my fidelity. And I'll tell you something else."

"What?" he demanded sullenly.

I tentatively touched his arm, feeling his warmth through the sleeve of his nightgown. "Although our union was not of our making, I am more and more convinced that if I had to choose a husband from the three of you—yes, Artois included—I should prefer the one Heaven has given me." True, Louis Auguste was awkward and ungainly; he was diffident to the point of exasperation; but in his own odd way I think he was finally trying to show me every possible attention and kindness, and for that I was immensely grateful. How much worse it could have been!

TWENTY-FIVE

The Battle Royal Continues

↬ JUNE 15, 1771 ↫

My mother's letter quivered in my hand, so livid had I become at her words. After months of filling my head with sermons and warnings about falling prey to the licentiousness of the French court, after endless lectures assuring me that no matter how louche, they would love me all the more for adhering to my sturdy German morals, *now* Maman was encouraging me, in no uncertain terms, to set aside all she had taught me.

But why? Had her piety been naught but platitudes? If so, then her entire life was a sham, for the world knew that the Hapsburg court, and the empress herself, were above reproach. This I would not believe. And as she was so free with her opinions and her undisguised efforts to encourage me to become an agent of Austrian interests, if there were a motive behind her insistence that I countenance the comtesse du Barry, surely she would have revealed it to me.

The only consistency I could salvage from any of this was her perpetual insistence, then and now, to make myself beloved. And yet did she really intend the dauphine of France to bow and scrape so low that she picked up the refuse from the gutter? I could only surmise that Maman did not know the full story of the du Barry's lineage, her origins as a natural daughter—of a friar, no less! How she had been passed from one nobleman to the next before she was judged ready to be dangled under the nose of the king the way a dog is teased with a tempting morsel of meat. She was coarse, and cutting, and cruel. I had even told Maman about the conversation I had overheard at the masquerade ball, about the du Barry's spiteful sobriquet for me, *l'Autrichienne*—and still, my mother urged me to set aside my pride and tread the higher ground.

How could she expect me to be cordial to the woman? Instead, she had accused me of being *hochnäsig*, or high-nosed, about the whole sordid affair.

≈ JULY I, 1771 ≈

"Why, monsieur le comte, your visits have become so frequent that madame la comtesse de Noailles is beginning to think you are now a member of my household!" Greeting. him at the threshold of my apartments I extended my hand for him to kiss and offered him a beaming smile, although I knew the nature of his business. For the past several weeks, every time the comte de Mercy had come to call, it was to deliver a lecture—of late it was to inform me that my refusal to speak to the du Barry was jeopardizing the Franco-Austrian alliance. And when he had run out of his own words, he would hand me an angry missive from Maman, chiding me for the same perceived offense, even as she continued to withhold her reasons for urging me to act in a certain way. "She treats me like a marionette on strings, a witless puppet expected to dance," I muttered to Mercy, as I led him through the first and second antechambers, my drawing room and bedchamber, into the relatively tranquil intimacy of my private study. I was aware of the murmurings within my entourage regarding the Austrian ambassador's perceived omnipresence in my rooms, so I thought it best to conduct our conversations well beyond their hearing.

"So, what is it to be today?" Unlike Maman's correspondence, my letters to Vienna never contained unpleasantries. I could not bring myself to share bad news. My heart was always with my family in Austria. I was afraid to tell them when things went wrong, and if I quarreled with them I felt that my duties here would be too heavy to bear.

Mercy began pacing about the study. "Madame la dauphine, you must believe me when I say that I have always had your best interests at heart—as an archduchess of Austria, and now, as the future queen of France." He leaned against a heavily gilded rococo chest and turned to face me, exhaling heavily. "As the ambassador from the Austrian Imperial Court to the Court of Versailles, I am privy to the thoughts of *two* distinguished sovereigns."

I rested my chin in my hands; my *engageantes* dusted the surface of the writing desk behind which I sat. "Which is far more than I. As dauphine I have no business being concerned with affairs of state, even though Maman should like me to make it my business. And yet she does no more than paint her demands in the broadest of strokes."

The comte de Mercy cleared his throat. "I see. Then I shall take a finer brush to the canvas and limn some of the details of the larger picture. I do so now only because your mother has—*finalement*—given me leave to explain some things to you, which we hope will convince you that a certain diplomatic assignment—on your part—must soon be accomplished."

I grinned at him. "I am terribly fond of you, monsieur le comte, but I do wish you would come to the point."

"Well, then!" He rubbed his hands together as if he were about to embark upon a great expedition. "Your mother has of late been placed in a difficult situation." He glanced searchingly about the room. "Tell me, have you a globe?"

"There is one in the dauphin's private study. Shall we go in there? He is not at home and no one will disturb us."

As the ambassador and I strolled back through my rooms toward the apartments of the dauphin I was aware that we were being watched. In my two antechambers, my ladies glanced up from their conversations or their games of piquet and *Écarté*, and leaned toward each other, inclining their heads to whisper behind their fans. At least this time they had something else to gossip about besides the fact that my belly was still flat.

And when the comte and I passed through the dauphin's pair of antechambers, we received the same reaction from the gentlemen of his entourage, only they lacked the discretionary benefit of a fan. Finally, we closeted ourselves within my husband's private study, where the comte de Mercy immediately made for the globe that rested inside an elaborate stand near the center of the room.

"Poland," he began, "is a commonwealth or protectorate of Russia located in central Europe." He spun the globe and located the country with his index finger. "Come." I stood beside him and regarded the great globe over his shoulder. "This is the Austrian Empire," he said, drawing a wide swath with his hand. "And these are the lands that belong to your mother's neighbors and two greatest enemies—the 'greats' themselves—Frederick the Great of Prussia and Catherine the Great of Russia."

"*Mein Gott*, that's a lot of the globe," I murmured. "It's more than we have—I mean more than Maman has."

"And Russia has grown even more vast of late; for the past

few years, during the ongoing Russo-Turkish Wars, the armies of
Catherine the Great have been able to conquer enemy territories,
so that now her borders are closer than ever to Hapsburg Austria.
Your mother became understandably quite anxious about this
and began considering a war with Russia. King Louis, being your
mother's ally, suggested, perhaps, that a peaceful solution might
be found, a redistribution of lands in central Europe so that Imperial Austria would no longer feel small or diminished when
compared to Russia." He bunched his hands over the globe to il-
lustrate the relative sizes of the empires. "Louis suggested that
Austria might be happy with Silesia, but Frederick the Great—"

"'The Devil,' Maman calls him—" I interjected, pleased to
know something at least that was germane to our discussion.

"'The Devil.' Yes, quite," the comte agreed. "Frederick was
not about to willingly part with Silesia, having so recently con-
quered it himself. The Prussian king's solution was to turn
Poland into the great roast instead. So, now we have Frederick
and Catherine conspiring to carve up Poland for their own empires—claiming territories that will benefit each of them in some
way, leaving only a small portion of Poland to the Poles."

"What does Poland have to say about all this?" I wondered
aloud.

"Nothing," the comte replied sadly. "For Poland to try to assert herself against the combined armies of Russia and Prussia
would be like a beetle expecting to win a battle against the heel of
your boot."

"But what does any of this have to do with Maman? Or me for
that matter?"

"The empress is much disturbed by this unprecedented, and
equally unprovoked, plan to invade an innocent kingdom,
madame la dauphine; but I believe you should know that your
brother, the Emperor Joseph, supports it."

I regarded the ambassador with increasing discomfort. "My mother and my brother do not always see eye to eye, as they say." The truth was, they rarely did. Joseph was very forward-thinking, while Maman was quite the reverse. "What, then, does Joseph see that Maman does not?"

"If the Austrian Empire supports the partitioning of Poland by Prussia and Russia, then Austria will *also* be able to slice off a piece of Poland to add to her empire. Consequently, your mother has been dragged into the middle of the negotiations. Here is the predicament as it now stands: If Her Imperial Majesty obeys the dictates of her conscience and *objects* to the partitioning of the innocent and unsuspecting commonwealth of Poland, the event will take place anyway and your mother will end up with none of the territory for Austria, while her enemies' empires will be expanded around her."

"Making them even greater enemies," I reasoned.

"Of course," said the comte de Mercy, nodding his head. *Partitioning.* It sounded so neat, so effortless, when it would surely be nothing of the sort. I imagined that armies would march into towns and villages, preceded by men on horseback flashing their sabers. What would they do? Draw a line at the edge of the town or the forest and tell the villagers, "You are all Prussians, now"?

The comte rapped on the globe with his knuckles. "Now we come to the next obstacle. Austria and France have signed a treaty to aid Poland, should the commonwealth be invaded. Poland *is* about to be invaded. Invaded and partitioned; with some of her lands going to Russia, some to Prussia—and some, yes, to *Austria*. Which is why Austria isn't going to do anything to stop the invasion, despite the language of the Franco-Austrian treaty. And Austria now needs France—desperately—to support her change of heart.

"And here, madame la dauphine, is where the matter directly

concerns you." Comte de Mercy had lowered his voice to a conspiratorial whisper. I stood a little straighter. "As I mentioned at
the beginning of our discussion, I am the confidant of two rulers.
Your mother's political predicament is a precarious one. Austria
needs France. But France is not just a place on a map. France is
Louis. And it pains me to admit to you, madame la dauphine, that
Louis would be very much inclined to leave your mother dangling from a political limb unless the insult to his *maîtresse en titre*
is addressed; and the comtesse du Barry's reputation, stained as it
may be, is restored."

I wasn't entirely certain I understood him. "What are you saying?" It all seemed so convoluted. "Why can't you diplomats ever
speak plainly?"

The ambassador took a deep breath. "All right then, I will be
perfectly blunt. The partition of Poland might very well lead to
war, and all because you are behaving like a spoiled little girl instead of like a princess—by refusing to speak to a whore."

He took full advantage of the shocked expression on my face
and my inability to formulate a reply, by providing me with additional details of his conversation with the king about the whole
affair. "I told you, by virtue of my embassy I am privy to the
thoughts and wishes of two distinguished rulers. I have the ear of
the king of France on the matter of your uttering a few words to
the comtesse du Barry."

"'I love my granddaughter,'" Papa Roi had told the comte de
Mercy. "'She is the epitome of charm, grace, and spirit, and a delight to behold. So here is what I would like you to do: Impress
upon her that my love and generosity will be boundless; all she
must do is speak to Madame du Barry. A few simple, innocuous
words. And the storm clouds will disappear, leaving a clear blue
sky.'"

"He really said that?"

The ambassador nodded and offered me his arm. "He was speaking of several clouds, you realize: not merely the ones that lower over the du Barry's apartments, but those that rumble over Austria and Poland. Shall we return to your rooms now?"

My heart felt so much lighter, free of the burden it had borne. The only thing that gnawed at my conscience was that the king himself had never said a word to me regarding the subject of his favorite, and he seemed quite aware that I had been deliberately snubbing her. And perhaps the little exchange between himself and the king that the ambassador had so colorfully reenacted for me had merely been the comte's invention, in order to sway my decision. After all, wasn't that what diplomacy was all about?

Yet... if a few little words might forestall, or even eliminate, any unnecessary carnage, what were a few scruples compared to the possibility that thousands of lives might be lost?

But by the time we reached my drawing room, where I bid *au revoir* to the comte, I was exhausted from being pushed in so many directions. Still, I knew what I must do, even if it pained me. "Little said, soon amended," the Countess von Brandeiss used to say to Charlotte and me when she wanted us to apologize for something. "Say it quickly and put it behind you."

I sought out my *dame d'honneur* and assigned her the task I dreaded, for I was terrified to go to the king directly. My heart beat wildly; I could only imagine how much worse it would be on the evening itself. "Madame de Noailles, kindly inform His Majesty that I will honor Madame du Barry with a word or two at the card game after supper on July the eleventh." It irked me just to utter that sentence.

She always wanted me to do the proper thing in matters of etiquette, but I knew from my first night at Versailles that she disdained the royal mistress with every fastidious fiber of her haughty being. With disappointment in her eyes, the comtesse de

Noailles pressed her lips together. "It shall be done, madame la dauphine."

I groaned and clutched my head in my hands. My heavy coiffure was giving me a headache. The incessant chattering of my ladies-in-waiting, and the vibrant red damask walls of the drawing room, "*couleur de feu*," were giving me a headache. *Everything* was giving me a headache.

Then the dauphin loped into the room, reeking of animal blood and dead flesh, and shocking the *soi-disant* delicate sensibilities of my attendants, who daintily pinched their noses as they used their fans for something other than flirtation and gossip. Heedless of the mess, he used his dusty brown tricorn to blot the sweat that had beaded on his forehead and then sent the hat sailing onto the seat of an armchair.

"Not again! It is enough! No more! I won't have it!"

The dauphin regarded me with a befuddled expression. "Won't have what? What is enough?" he asked lethargically.

I slipped my arm through his and briskly led him out of the drawing room toward our more private chambers. "My mother, the king, Mesdames, the comte de Mercy! I am beset with demands from all sides. Everyone is telling me something different. Meanwhile, you ride off to the hunt, leaving me to sort out right from wrong without your guidance." I could sense my temper beginning to get the better of me, but it was like steam escaping from a kettle and I could not call it back.

By now we had reached my private study. He tried to evade me, but my wide panniers impeded his efforts to pass. "When you are not hunting, you leave my bed while I am still a-slumber—to *go* hunting! Heaven forfend you should wake with me and we could enjoy a *petit-déjeuner*. But never once—not even on the morning after our wedding night—have we breakfasted together. When the weather is poor, you head off to your smithy.

When the weather is fine, you hunt with your brothers and the king—and *then* you go off and play with your hammer and tongs! Or you spend hours with the masons and the carpenters, exhausting yourself by heaving paving stones, lumbering about as though you were one of the laborers. And after the sun has gone down, do you come to your wife of your own volition? No—you wait until the last possible moment. When we dine, you have no conversation and I am once again left to fend for myself while you eat enough to fill a wheelbarrow! And every time I believe that you and I are finally growing closer, that we are comfortable enough with one another to—to do what we must, for the good of France, I find myself humiliated yet again."

"That's enough," the dauphin said quietly. He plodded past me toward the door at the far end of the room.

"Where are you going? I have not finished talking to you!"

"I am going to my own rooms. And you are not talking; you are scolding," he said simply.

I followed him into the next room. And the next, and the next. "And finally—when that awful *coucher* is over and everyone has left, you come to my bed looking as though you are about to face the executioner—not your wife!"

Louis Auguste bent over as if the weight of the world rested upon him. He placed his large hand on a marble tabletop to steady himself. His overburdened shoulders began to heave with sobs.

Mon Dieu, I thought, *what have I done?* I tiptoed behind my husband and very gently placed my hands on his broad back, then rested my cheek against his grimy hunting coat, smearing my rouge. "Oh, dear God, what has become of me? I am so sorry, *mon cher*, so sorry." My hot tears stained the brown velvet. "I became my mother and the comtesse de Noailles all rolled into one. Please forgive me. I did not mean to hurt you so.... I am so sorry and ... and I love you." Those three little words slipped out of my mouth, astonishing the both of us. But I would not call them back, for no one was as surprised as I was to realize that I had meant them. A secret smile crept across my face and a silent tear rolled into the crescent of my mouth.

We remained that way for several moments. The room was quiet, but for the sounds of our weeping. Finally, the dauphin turned around to face me and we slipped our arms around each other. He pressed me to his chest and shyly stroked my hair. "I am sorry, too," he whispered. I felt his warm breath on the crown of my head. "I didn't realize ... I go on as I always did before we were wed."

"Did it ever occur to you how lonely I am?" I asked him, my voice small and strained. I scrubbed away a few wayward tears with my fist.

"No," he replied quietly, truthfully. "We are surrounded by people nearly all day, so I never thought about being lonely. And when I am at my forge I revel in the solitude. In his own pasture the black sheep doesn't know he's the odd one out," he added with a chuckle.

I had not thought of it that way. Yet he had found a way to embrace his isolation, while I, more naturally sociable, was fighting it like a demon.

"But I am sorry I did not think about how it must be for you," my husband said gently. "I will try to be more sensible of it in the future. I promise." He pulled away and regarded me at arm's length. "Do you forgive me?"

My nose crinkled as I fought off more tears. "With all my heart," I whispered, and drew him toward me again.

The dauphin kept his word, although I was disappointed that his newfound consideration for me did not lead to the consummation of our marriage. But his strong, if mostly silent, presence bolstered my courage to capitulate to the pressure exerted by Mercy, Maman, and Papa Roi, and publicly acknowledge Madame du Barry with a few innocuous words. At breakfast one morning I told my aunts that I had chosen the day on which I would finally speak to the du Barry. This time they did not speak a word either for or against it. I suppose they reasoned that if they resumed their denigration of the royal favorite—aware that I had already resolved to countenance the creature—they might risk losing my goodwill as well as my society.

On Thursday, the eleventh of July, I spent the entire day in an anxious mood. Butterflies fluttered in my belly and I frequently requested a chamber pot. I could not eat a single thing at the midday *grand couvert,* and just stared at my supper, moving the food around my plate with my silver fork.

In my apartments candlelight flickered everywhere, casting an amber glow on the players and their bejeweled fingers, wrists, and throats. Being a midsummer evening, the air was still to the point of stifling; my drawing room was so crowded and the atmosphere so thick with tension that I was certain everyone was aware of, and eagerly anticipating, my *rencontre* with the du Barry. After Madame de Noailles informed the king of my intentions to publicly acknowledge his paramour this evening, Papa Roi must have shared the information with the comtesse du Barry, who I suspect had alerted her *dévots.* I doubted there was a soul within the château who had remained unaware of the import of this evening's game of cavagnole.

Knowing that I would be the center of attention, I had undergone an extensive toilette. My hair had been dressed quite *à la mode* by Sieur Larsenneur, in a teased halo about my barely powdered head; the rest of my red-gold ringlets were fashioned into thick sausage curls that grazed my shoulders. My gown was the color of moonlight, with a triple cascade of lace at the elbows, drawing attention to the gracefulness of my arms.

There was scarcely any space in which to mill about the room; in their wide panniers, many of the noblewomen were compelled to navigate the salon sideways, or, when they clustered together to gossip behind their fans, were crushed against one another like blooms in a bouquet. I spied Madame du Barry conversing with a knot of comtesses and duchesses, but I took care to be circuitous in my movement as I made my way about the room, welcoming my guests with a pleasant comment to each of them. It helped to imagine the women as stepping stones in a muddy stream.

The comte de Mercy gave me a surreptitious smile as I began to approach the royal mistress.

"Good evening, comtesse de Passy." I tilted my head in greeting to an elderly woman whose rouge circles had been irregularly (and thus comically) applied. "You are looking lovely this evening. *Très élégante*." Without her ear trumpet I doubt she heard a word I'd uttered.

One step closer to my rival.

"I hope you are well, madame," I said softly, smiling at the duchesse de Chartres, who was with child. If only she knew how I envied her condition!

Another step. My heart was racing. I hoped that what felt like the rapid rise and fall of my chest remained undetected. I became aware that all eyes were upon me and grew warm from the intensity of their gazes.

"Madame, I do hope you will permit me to peruse your library now that you have arranged all of your volumes," I told my sister-in-law, the comtesse de Provence, deliberately raising my voice so that my comment would be overheard, particularly by those who continued to depict me as empty-headed.

"But you don't like to read," she whispered.

"I do now," I replied, between my teeth.

The last step. No one stood between the king's mistress and me. She was wearing a treasury's worth of diamonds. Even the heels of her shoes, covered in diamanté pavé, glinted in the firelight. I raised my chin and fixed a smile upon my face. Lifted my foot and took a half step toward her. The room had grown completely silent. The players turned to face me as if they were one body, their hands suspended in the air holding their cards or cavagnole markers, frozen in a single moment of time.

Suddenly Madame Adélaïde swooped down like a hawk and tightly clasped my arm. I had not even noticed her in the salon before that moment. "It is time to leave!" she announced. "Come along, we will await the king in my sister Victoire's room!" Before I realized what was happening, she had me sailing out of the salon and down the passageway toward my aunts' suite, with Mesdames Sophie and Victoire falling in behind. She had caught me off-guard and then knocked me off-balance just as she noticed me wavering in the mission that had been so long in coming to fruition. I had been weak; and in that moment of indecision I had permitted myself to be humiliated not merely by Madame Adélaïde in my own drawing room but in the presence of the Barryistes, who lived to see me made the fool.

The silence we had left behind was deafening, and not until we had fully retreated from the salon did the room erupt into a roar. I could hear the comtesse du Barry's voice rising above the din as she gave the Austrian ambassador a severe tongue-lashing. From the sound of things, her fury, humiliation, and indignation were as colossal as my own.

"Well, monsieur de Mercy, you don't seem to have achieved much. Apparently *I* must come to *your* aid!"

TWENTY-SIX

Victory—but Whose?

October 13, 1771

Madame, my very dear mother:

Please allow me to justify myself by addressing the several points you made in your last letter to me. First, I am terribly sorry that you believe all of the lies that people write you from Versailles instead of taking my word (or the comte de Mercy's) for it. I suppose you believe that we want to fool you. I am perfectly convinced that the king does not wish me to speak to Madame du Barry; he has never mentioned it to me; in fact, he is even friendlier to me now that I have refused— and if you were here yourself you would understand that this woman and her clique would never be satisfied with a single word, and I would be expected again and again to recognize her. You may be certain that I need be led by no one when it comes to politeness.

I do not say that I refuse outright to address Madame du Barry, but I cannot, for a second time, agree to speak to her on a fixed date and at an appointed hour known to her in advance so that she can crow about her triumph. I suppose the entire unpleasant business would have been over and done with in July, if Madame Adélaïde had not exploded it. But if an appointed time were now to be fixed, it would look to the entire court as though I have announced that I hold the losing hand. At least allow me the element of surprise so that I may retain my dignity in the event of another fiasco *à l'Adélaïde*.

The debacle of July 11 had left a bitter taste in everyone's mouths, but most especially in mine. I saw Madame Adélaïde through new eyes, as an *intrigante* who had used me for her own sport and amusement, no better, perhaps, than the du Barry herself. It became more difficult for me to spend so many hours in the company of my aunts because the eldest of the three, and the one who was undoubtedly a strong influence on her sisters, no longer had my trust. Our conversation over coffee and needlework was now strained; my words were guarded, and Madame Adélaïde surely knew why, although Mesdames Victoire and Sophie were perhaps unaware, if they noticed at all, that I was not as effusive and ebullient as I once had been in their society.

I recalled the conversation with abbé Vermond from several months' past in which he had indiscreetly revealed that some at court had been against my marriage to the dauphin. At the time I had assumed it was the progressively minded Orléans branch of the family that had spoken against the alliance. But perhaps *Mesdames* had been the detractors. Had they posed as my confidantes and mentors purely to win the trust of a girl so naïve and eager to please that she would never comprehend their intent to undermine her until it was too late to repair the damage? The contemplation of such duplicity left me seething. My *poitrine* erupted into a rash that left my usually milky complexion damasked with splotches.

Desperately in need of cheering, I regaled my former governess, the Countess von Brandeiss, with all the distasteful details of the ongoing contretemps. We had been corresponding every month or two ever since I had left Austria. She would write to me with news of home, and share the sort of anecdotes that Maman would never dream of imparting. The countess, always a warm and open soul, provided the friendly and sympathetic ear I so deeply craved—and sorely lacked.

I also wrote to Charlotte in Naples, asking if she had any suggestions on the management of Maman, who had been barraging me with letters ever since my failure to address the comtesse. Our mother had never been a princess at a foreign court, never had to play a game by another's rules. And even though I would know that if I spoke to the creature, it was really in the service of Austria; from the perspective of the courtiers at Versailles, it would appear that the Barryistes had worn me into submission. And I could not allow people to believe that a woman who had once prowled the streets of Paris was more influential at court than I; it would thoroughly diminish the respect that it was imperative I command as dauphine.

Charlotte comprehended the delicate nature of my predicament—and precisely because she understood just how fragile it was, refused to offer me any advice on how to handle it. "It will be viewed as meddling," she wrote. "The queen of the Two Sicilies cannot be perceived as involving herself with the *petits scandales* of the French court, especially when rumors have tentacles, like the *polpi* that they eat here, slimy legs that grip and suck and reach as far as Austria, Russia, Prussia, and Poland. Were Naples perceived to weigh in as well on the '*crise du Barry*,' it might create an incident of international proportions."

So I was left to battle Maman and the comte de Mercy on my own. The months dragged on as letters flew between Vienna and Versailles, and the stalemate continued.

But finally they wore me down and I raised the white flag of surrender. The year 1771 had come and gone, if only by a few hours; and as 1772 dawned, it seemed to represent a fresh start. It was a New Year's Day custom at Versailles for the royal family to accept the congratulations of the courtiers. We stood for hours in the resplendent Hall of Mirrors while they filed past us in strict order of precedence, offering their reverences and felicitations on the New Year. It was a silvery day, although the crush of people obscured the tall mullioned windows, hiding the frosty vista from view. Along the parterres, the sculpted evergreens flanking the dry fountains resembled lonely sentinels. Snow lightly dusted the branches of the trees that lined the long allées leading away from the château.

I was clad in a gown of striped satin, pale blue on silver, with dyed ostrich plumes in my hair and a triple strand of pearls at my throat, the better to emphasize my long neck. On one side of me, in a suit of deep gray velvet, stood the dauphin, his dark hair abundantly powdered; and on my left was the king, in cloth of silver. I hoped that no one would see me shift my weight from side to side, because my feet were beginning to ache. As the ladies of the court filed past us with studied grace and maddening *longueur*, and I continued to offer innocuous remarks in reply to their congratulations, I knew what I had to do: put the whole unpleasant business—*finalement*—to rest!

Here came the fat, fabulously wizened, and ostentatiously overdressed duchesse d'Aiguillon with her piles of false red hair, the mother of the even more repugnant duc d'Aiguillon, who, precisely one year earlier, had replaced our beloved duc de Choiseul as Minister of State. As she rose from her reverence, I complimented her on the beauty of her ivory-handled fan. She nodded and simpered. Then I drew a deep breath and addressed the woman who accompanied her and who had just made her curtsy. Madame du Barry sparkled with rubies. Her court gown of rose-colored damask set off the pink flush of her cheeks.

Our eyes met. I parted my lips to speak. *"Il y a bien du monde aujourd'hui à Versailles*—there are a lot of people at Versailles today."

There! I had done it! The entire hall seemed to exhale a collective breath. Papa Roi broke into a wide grin and clasped me in his arms. Blushing with pleasure, Madame du Barry turned away and thrust her round chin into the air, but it was the triumphant look in her eyes that made me wish to decapitate her. My capitulation turned to humiliation.

After the ceremony, comte de Mercy came over to congratulate me, taking my hands in his and thanking me, on behalf of both Austria and France, for finally speaking to the du Barry. I froze my face into a cordial smile and between my teeth, assured the ambassador, "I have addressed her once, but that is as far as I will go. That woman will never hear my voice again. Happy New Year to you, monsieur le comte."

Later in the day I closeted myself in my private study, sat down at the inlaid escritoire, and informed Maman, writing:

January 1, 1772

Madame my very dear mother,

I am sure that Mercy has told you of the momentous event that transpired today, and I hope you are pleased; but there is more to it and I wish you to hear it from me directly. Rest assured that I will always be ready to sacrifice my personal prejudices, provided that I am not required to do anything that would contradict my sense of honor.

Your loving daughter,
Marie Antoinette

But Maman could not see things through my eyes, nor look with my heart. At the end of the month I received another scolding.

January 21, 1772

Antoinette, you make me laugh if you imagine that either I or Mercy would ever want (or expect) you to act contrary to your "sense of honor." Your remark makes me see just how much you have been influenced by bad advice. And when I read that you should work yourself up into a tizzy over a few words, declaring that you will never again speak to Madame du Barry, I tremble for you. I have your own best interests at heart. Once again I must remind you that no one else at court can better advise you than my minister, who knows your country better than any other and is fully aware of all the factions that must be pacified.

But my new vow of silence did not seem to matter to the king, who was kinder than ever to me, lavishing me with gifts and honoring me with his presence in my rooms at breakfast. He even brought his own coffee maker, a silver urn of which he was tremendously proud—and which I found frightfully amusing, for he had thousands of servants who could have brewed it for him. Yet the most powerful man in the kingdom took great pleasure in doing this one small thing for himself. Sometimes I thought of mentioning that the pride he took was perhaps akin, in some small way, to the happiness the dauphin derived from his lock making or his cabinetry, but I was afraid of saying the wrong thing, and incurring His Majesty's displeasure, so I kept my own counsel.

France agreed to turn a blind eye to Austria's support of the tripartite partition of Poland and the agreement was signed in Vienna on the nineteenth of February, 1772, less than two months after I had publicly spoken to the comtesse. But the royal mistress was much mistaken if she took my single civil sentence as an offer of friendship. She wrote several letters to me, seeking some sort of rapport between us, but they went unanswered. For me to have responded would have implied, even tacitly, that we were social equals. But Madame du Barry was undeterred by my silence. In fact, she raised her stakes. When she realized that I was maintaining my intention to ignore her, she employed an unnamed intermediary (though I was sure it was the king) to purchase a pair of diamond earrings from Herr Böhmer, the court jeweler, which she then offered me as a gift, knowing my fondness for fine jewelry. I dared not consider the loveliness of the setting or the quality of the gems, because *au fond*, when all was said and done, the offer was highly inappropriate. After all that had transpired, how could the dauphine of France be seen accepting a present from a trollop?

Consequently, I employed a liaison of my own, the princesse de Lamballe, to inform the du Barry that I already owned plenty of diamonds and had no need of her gift. The princesse was no mere attendant; and she had not been assigned to my household. Rather, she was the first woman I had met in the twenty months I'd spent at Versailles with whom I immediately felt *sympathique*, and she quickly became my only true friend and my sole confidante.

Although the princesse de Lamballe had been presented at court and attended nearly every ceremonial event, I did not become truly acquainted with her until one of our sleighing parties during the early months of 1772. I had not gone a-sleighing in years, and the jingle of the bells as the runners glided over the snow, the horses' heads bobbing in time to the motion, and their snorting in the brisk air, the sharp tingle of snowflakes on my cheeks and the chill on my tongue as I tried to catch them—what memories they conjured! How I missed my family! I recalled how my dear sister Charlotte and I would descend from the sleighs and build snow forts from which we pelted our brothers with snowballs, usually ending up the worse for the battle ourselves. The Countess von Brandeiss had been our captain.

But I had not heard from my former governess in several months. Maman had forbidden it. Because the countess was always so open and unguarded, my mother feared that she would be too indiscreet in her correspondence. Charlotte, too, had been prohibited from writing to me anymore because our mother did not trust the Neapolitans; she was certain that my sister's letters would be opened by spies and their content disseminated among those who would seek to damage the Hapsburgs.

My recollections were tinged with such sadness that wintry day that perhaps I recognized in the princesse de Lamballe a kindred spirit. When she pushed back her ermine trimmed hood, and gazed at the cold gray sky, with her halo of palest blond curls and her sweet, doleful expression, she resembled a melancholy angel.

I wished to know everything about her. Side by side we sat in my rooms with our embroidery silks; I was still working on the vest for Papa Roi that I had begun upon my arrival in France.

I knew she was a Savoyard by birth, a cousin to the garden-loving prince de Condé as well as the comtesse de Provence, though the princesse was as lovely as Madame de Provence was homely. "You know, I think I was predisposed to like you because you have the same names as my mother—Maria Theresa," I said to the princesse. "So, your father is the duc de Penthièvre? He is a very kind and generous man. There are not many of those at

Versailles." As I chuckled, I wondered if I had said anything to upset her. Her eyes were so sad that one might have been tempted to think that her dog had just died.

As if he'd read my thoughts, Mops peered at us from his new abode, a blue velvet doghouse studded with golden nails.

"*Non*, madame la dauphine, the duc de Penthièvre is my father-in-*law*. But you are right about his kindness. He took me in as if I were his own daughter after the Prince de Lamballe passed on."

I had heard the rumors: Her late husband, Louis Alexandre de Bourbon, was a grandson of the comte de Toulouse, one of the Sun King's natural children who had then been legitimized. Monsieur de Lamballe had been fabulously wealthy and just as wild—a dissolute, a gambler, and an adulterer with a penchant for the most disreputable women imaginable, all of which had hastened him to a premature grave.

"Alexandre died in my arms," said the Princesse de Lamballe. "I was only nineteen. And everyone in France knew about his... his behavior," she said diplomatically. "There were all the women. And he gave them so much money." She swallowed hard. "I am sure you heard that he sold my diamonds to pay the debts he incurred keeping an opera dancer. Everyone else did." I wondered if she had loved him despite his debauchery, for her deep brown eyes were wet with tears.

"Are you crying for your husband or your diamonds?" I asked, trying to make a little joke to cheer her. I reached into my bosom and withdrew one of my monogrammed handkerchiefs. "Here," I said, pressing it into her hands. "You are quite courageous to hold your head so high in the face of such adversity. I have heard nothing but praise for your character. As soiled as the prince's reputation was, yours, madame la princesse, is spotless."

Even though she was about five years older than I, I saw my-

self in her. A little bit lonely, a little bit frightened, highly princi-
pled, and very much in need of a friend. In the absence of my siblings, whom I thought of every day and still missed terribly, I saw
the princesse de Lamballe almost as a sister.

At my request, the princesse was the only one keeping me
company in my music room one afternoon in late February when
my harp lesson was interrupted by an insistent knock at the door.
I lowered the instrument to the floor so that it rested fully on its
pedestal and looked up. "Please see who it is," I told Madame de
Lamballe. She rose to her feet and crossed the room with studied
grace, her ice blue train forming an elegant wake.

An agitated comte de Mercy was ushered into the salon
clutching a letter, his face a mask of fear. Even from across the
room I recognized the seal immediately. My brother Joseph's. "I
have news of your mother, madame la dauphine." The music
master bowed and made a discreet exit.

Mercy offered a brief reverence to the princesse de Lamballe.
"Madame la princesse, I suggest that you help the dauphine to a
chaise longue."

With the calm manner and swift efficiency of a good nurse,
she immediately saw that I was comfortable, removing my brocaded slippers and easing a cushion behind my back.

"What is it, monsieur le comte?" I reached my hand toward
the princesse and she knelt beside me, clasping it tightly in her
own. My flesh had suddenly grown quite cold.

"The empress is gravely ill," said Mercy solemnly. "She has
twice been bled and her fever has not abated in four days." His
lips pressed together grimly.

My complexion turned as pale as parchment. "*Heilege Gott!*" I
breathed, making the sign of the cross on my breast. I couldn't
breathe. The princesse de Lamballe began to untie my bodice,
deftly working her fingers through the laces at my back. "Send

for the dauphin!" I gasped. A footman set off down the corridor,
fleet as a greyhound. I turned my frightened gaze to the ambassador. "Will she... is the empress expected to live?" The thought
that Maman might not recover, that there would never be the
possibility of seeing her alive again under any circumstances, was
too terrible to contemplate.

Comte de Mercy's expression was grave. "At this point, no one
knows what will happen. She recovered from the pox in the past,
and has survived several other illnesses, besides the birth of sixteen children. But she is nearly fifty-five years old."

It was almost an hour before the dauphin arrived. Wheezing
and breathless, Louis Auguste fairly slid into the room, wig
askew, and dripping with sweat. "It's Maman," I told him. "They
don't know what's wrong." He gently stroked my cheek and I
clasped his hand; I noticed there was dirt under his nails from
working at his forge.

As I couldn't think of what else to do, I asked him to pray
with me. My eyes were moist, beseeching. The princesse de Lamballe fetched the little chaplet of beads that Maman had given me
on the day I left Austria. I clasped them in my hands and knelt
beside the dauphin. We closed our eyes and murmured the paternoster and a couple of psalms before offering orisons of our own,
both voiced and silent.

I stole a glance at my husband, looking so earnest, so devout,
so concerned, and my heart flooded with love. I knew he was not
enamored of Austria, and was not much fonder of Austrians. He
had never met Maman, and assuredly was not terribly enamored
of *her*, if only because of the dreadful epistolary scoldings I received with such alarming regularity. But he had seen his own
beloved mother, Marie Josèphe of Saxony, waste away from con-
sumption; he recognized and understood the terror and sadness
in my eyes.

That evening, he came to my bed. "I thought you might want company tonight," he offered shyly.

I burrowed against him, as if his back were a bulwark, sheltering me from unpleasantness and pain. "You know, if Maman"—I could scarcely say the words for weeping, even as I tried to see my own life with my mother's unsentimental vision. "If Maman . . . does not recover, it would mean the world to me to know that she went to her reward in Heaven with the knowledge that we . . . that we . . ." In the darkness, I groped for his hand. I felt his entire arm stiffen with fear.

"I . . . I am . . . no, not tonight," he whispered hoarsely. His breath was ragged with apprehension. "Please forgive me. I am so sorry, Antoinette."

For yet another night I swallowed my pride. "What a husband you are," I said with forced gaiety. "Do you know that I could have married young Herr Mozart instead?"

Relieved from his conjugal obligation, the dauphin's tone brightened. "No! Really?"

"Yes!" I told him about the command performance Mozart and his older sister Nannerl gave for the imperial family at Schönbrunn in 1762. "Wolfgang was all of six years old, and I was only seven. And after the concert, he was making his way across the drawing room to where Maman was seated so he could offer her a reverence, when he slipped and fell on the highly polished floor. Down he went on his little bottom in his blue satin breeches. You can imagine the collective hush. But then the entire court began to laugh at him and he grew red in the face. I felt so dreadful for him; he had played so magnificently and we all thought he was so remarkable; we had never seen such talent, and in a child no higher than your waist, and then—plop—he was just for one moment a clumsy little boy. My heart went out to him, so I scampered to the center of the room and helped him to his feet and gave him a little kiss on the cheek. 'You are so kind,' he said to me, 'I would like to marry you!' 'Whatever for?' I asked him. I'm sure I was blushing. 'Why, out of gratitude,' he replied. And then he finally made his way over to Maman and she lifted him onto her lap and gave him a sweet to eat. She gave him a proper present as well, to thank him for his performance." My mood darkened as I grew thoughtful. "Do you know that she never did as much for any of us? Her own children, I mean? No laps and petting and soft words and sweets."

"But just think, Frau Mozart, what your life might have been like if you had married him!" The dauphin playfully poked me in the ribs.

"Ouch! You don't know your own strength sometimes. You are a big boy and I am just a little slip of a girl," I chirped.

"Not so little anymore," Louis Auguste retorted. "You have grown quite a lot since you first came to Versailles."

"*Up*, mostly," I agreed. I placed my hands over my bosom. "Not so much *out*. Not yet, anyway." I sought to change our subject of discourse from my underdeveloped *poitrine*, as it would only double back to the conversation regarding our nonexistent marital relations. "Mozart has me thinking," I began. "One day I should like to bring an Austrian composer to Versailles; perhaps Herr Gluck, my former music master." I sighed. "I should like to commission an opera. That will show her," I murmured.

"Show who what?" the dauphin said sleepily.

It amazed me how he could appear so wide awake in one instant, and in the next be resting comfortably in the arms of Morpheus. "The du Barry. Please stay awake a bit longer," I urged him. "She thinks that Neapolitan composer—Niccolò Piccini—is such a talent. But the Italians are nothing compared to the German composers."

My husband chuckled. "Now you sound like your mother."

"You don't know what she sounds like! However, I used to be able to imitate her very well." But then, as I heard her voice in my head and was about to mimic it, my throat caught. "I can't," I murmured sadly. "Not tonight. Just imagine a euphonium. With a tempo *con brio*."

I rolled over onto my side and smoothed my nightgown beneath me. "Besides, I'm certain that she wouldn't approve of my real reason for inviting Herr Gluck to France. Of course it would be for his brilliant opera—but it would also prove my superiority over Madame du Barry. Didn't you hear that Papa Roi is trying to arrange a divorce from her husband? If the king weds her and they have a son—he would be dauphin. And we would be—"

A massive shudder reverberated through the dauphin's body. "Superfluous," he said, his voice as hollow as a reed.

TWENTY-SEVEN

The Dauphin's Little Problem

Madame du Barry organized a grand fête to celebrate the king's gift to her of le Petit Trianon, the little jewel box of a villa on the grounds of Versailles that he had originally commissioned for her predecessor in his bed, Madame de Pompadour. The centerpiece of the event was a stage spectacle featuring one hundred singers and dancers and elaborate moving sets that parted to reveal a Cupid—the triumph of true love. But to the du Barry's immense embarrassment, her royal paramour did not even make an appearance at the festivities, nor did most of the courtiers, although hundreds were invited. Instead, a meager complement of thirty souls attended, and few of them held any position of great rank.

I wished to revel in Madame du Barry's humiliation, but I hadn't the stomach to gloat. My frustration with my still-virginal state after nearly two years of marriage was now my chief occupation.

To my immense delight, Maman was recovering from the sudden illness that had befallen her. The princesse de Lamballe had been as dear to me as any of my sisters during those dark days and wept as much as I did when we feared the worst. Louis Auguste was patient and kind; and Papa Roi remained quite solicitous during those anxious weeks while we waited for news. Naturally, he rejoiced when the comte de Mercy informed us, with palpable relief etched into his face, that all would be well.

Convalescing comfortably, with no additional crises on her hands, my mother resumed her favorite litany. Her letters grew increasingly inquisitive. She could not comprehend (nor could I, of course), "*la conduite si étrange*"—the odd behavior—of the dauphin when it came to the consummation of our union; why did he continue to shy like a horse at a stile? I assured her that the rumors of my husband's impotence were just that, but of course I had no evidence, such as a swollen belly, to prove the gossips wrong.

One night I dared to place the dauphin's palm against my breast, but he snatched his hand away as though he had accidentally stuck it in the fire. A week later, he tentatively returned to that location of his own volition, but did not remain there for more than a moment. Another week went by; the same frustrating exercise with the same maddening results. Finally I gently placed my hand over the dauphin's and left it there so he could feel the stirrings in my flesh. But that seemed to agitate him all the more.

During the summer months, things progressed a bit further. One night in July he slid his hand under my nightgown and gently pressed it against my thigh. His fingers trembled so much that silent tears coursed down my face; what wife can be happy when she believes that it causes her husband such consternation to touch her bare flesh? Was I so repugnant to him?

On the night of the twenty-third of August, the dauphin's eighteenth birthday, I pushed aside my timidity and my fear that I physically disgusted him and mustered every ounce of courage. My heart pounded as my arm inched toward his body. Smoothing my palm over his nightgown, my hand found his belly, and tentatively crept downward until it rested on his manhood.

"Ah!" Louis Auguste nearly jumped out of his skin. "What are you doing?"

He had startled me as well. "What do you think I am doing?" I tried to touch him again, but my husband pushed my hand away.

"Don't," he said. His voice sounded pained.

"Louis . . . you don't have to love me," I whispered, barely able to speak the words for what it was costing me emotionally. In the darkness, with the bed hangings pulled around us, he could not see my tears and I was determined that he not hear them in my voice. "We just have to *make* love." His breathing was ragged and heavy. "We both know what is expected of us." Silence. "It is our duty." More silence. My voice was small and plaintive. "People are talking."

"Let them," he groaned.

"You know we can't do that."

My husband ignored me and soon fell asleep. But I lay awake, my unseeing eyes fixed on the bed hangings and the underside of the canopy as the steady rumble and wheeze of his snoring filled the room, reverberating within our silk cocoon.

Finally, as a seventeenth birthday gift to me on November 2, 1772, when the dauphin visited my bed, he set about the business, if clumsily, of making me his true wife. In his furtive effort to climb on top of me, he knelt upon the fabric of my nightgown so that I could scarcely stir; and when I whispered that we might be better off if I could move my limbs, he stammered a profuse apology and rearranged his legs about me, pressing his knees into the soft feather mattresses. I trembled with fear and the skin on my exposed legs and downy nether regions began to pebble as he pushed my nightshirt northward toward my chest.

He raised his own gown, adjusting himself so that our private parts were touching. Our heavy breathing owed a greater debt to dread than to passion. Of course I had never felt a man against me, had not a notion of what to expect. My premarital conversations with Maman had scarcely prepared me for the real thing. Against *die Schiede—mon vagin*—he felt the way a stick of wood enveloped in velvet might, were it to be pressed against a sensitive spot. I was too afraid to touch him with my hands, to guide him where I knew he needed to go. That much, Maman had taught me. We were not ignorant, the dauphin and I: We were terrified.

"Oh, non!" My husband had scarcely found me with the tip of *son pénis* when he cried out and rolled away. I turned over and snuggled beside him. *Caresses, cajoleries*, Maman had reminded me. I gently stroked his broad back. *"Shh,"* I soothed, "it's all right."

"No, it's not," my husband muttered angrily, before drifting off to sleep.

It would be several more months before the attempt would be repeated.

⇜ MARCH 1773 ⇝

The dauphin and I arrived at the King's Chamber separately, in order to avoid any unnecessary gossip, although the hour was so late that no one was about but a few Swiss Guards. Even the most avid of gamblers had dropped off to sleep, dozing and drooling, and dreaming of better luck the following evening. The rainy night belonged to shadows: those that scampered, like the occasional mouse racing blindly along the moldings; those that slinked, like the unattended cats that silently prowled the tiled floors of the galleries, their glowing eyes caught momentarily in the torchlight; or those that hovered, like the busts and statues of cold marble that seemed even more imposing than when the halls were thronged with living souls.

The layout of the state apartments in the château de Versailles reminded me of a topiary maze. Along the perimeter were the salons in which the public was welcome. They were perennially noisy, crowded with humanity—courtiers, foreign dignitaries and their entourages garbed in the most colorful and exotic costumes I had ever seen, and even common travelers who had come all the way to see where and how the king of France and his family lived.

Just inside the outermost row of salons lay a second, more irregularly arranged set of rooms, which were primarily audience and presence chambers. There, I thought of the royal family as actors upon a stage, offering an opulent performance of our daily activities for select members of the public. We ate; we received visitors; we entertained.

Yet this inner series of rooms concealed innumerable secrets. A gentle touch upon a certain spot on a damask-covered wall would reveal a door instead, a cunningly concealed portal that was often so low that a taller gentleman, and, *certainement*, a lady with a towering coiffure, would have to stoop to pass through it. Beyond the doorways, depending on where you entered, you might find a staircase, unprepossessing in itself, that led to a rabbit's warren of rooms, modest in size but opulent in décor. Or the door might open to a corridor that led directly to a set of apartments that could be reached only through these clandestine means. Even the state apartments themselves, where the monarch resided and reposed, could be accessed from a secret, labyrinthine passage.

I knew that the dauphin had been dreading this audience with his *grand-père* for weeks. The king's legendary appetite, not for the gustatory pleasures in which my husband derived such satisfaction, but for the amatory delights he found in the arms of his mistresses, only heightened the dauphin's humiliation. Papa Roi was still a vigorous lover at the age of sixty-three, while my eighteen-year-old husband, after nearly three years of marriage, remained as chaste as the day of his birth.

"Please come with me tonight," Louis Auguste had whispered, just before our respective *couchers*. We had undressed in our separate bedchambers and waited, abed, until our clocks struck the hour of half past three. Then, with the aid of a single, trusted attendant to dress us—the princesse de Lamballe for me; and Monsieur Clery, the dauphin's young *valet de chambre* who was so much wiser than his years—we crept out of our rooms and independently began the lengthy walk to the king's apartments.

My husband had arrived before I did. He was seated on the edge of the enormous bed of state that dominated the room in which Louis XV officially slept and held court. I had never before seen it at night. By day the bed conveyed such majesty; from the white plumes above the golden fringe on the tester to the bedskirt of woven brocade, it represented the potency of the sovereign, the patriarch and father of his subjects. But by night the crackling warmth of the fire and the softness of light conferred upon it other qualities entirely: a frightening, almost thrilling melding of sensuality, power, and magic.

I regarded the dauphin, too terrified to firmly plant his derrière on the coverlet of red and gold brocade, too timid to own the bed in which he would one day sleep as king of France. Even in the gentle, amber candle glow, I could tell that the armholes of his suit of pale blue satin were dark with nervous sweat. Clery had not tamed his snarled mass of thick brown hair. My heart was breaking for him. I sat beside him on the vast bed and took his hand in mine, but Louis Auguste seemed too absorbed in his own terror to notice. Instead, his head was bent like a penitent as he picked at the embroidery on his waistcoat.

The king was conferring softly with another gentleman, the bespectacled Dr. Joseph Maria Francis de Lassone, the dauphin's physician.

"Well?" demanded Louis anxiously. "I am heartily sick of the volley of letters I have been receiving from the empress of Austria. Please tell me something that will set her mind—and mine—to rest. We are of the same vintage, you and I, Monsieur Lassone. Surely you understand the imperative of ensuring one's legacy. Without an heir to follow Louis Auguste, France could descend into chaos. Factions will form, if they have not done so already, in favor of one or the other of his brothers. And *they* may produce sons, although Provence and his wife seem to be as slow off the mark as the dauphin and dauphine. The comte d'Artois will be married in November—" The king began ticking off the months on his fingers. "That's eight months from now, and he's very much in my own mold—nothing like his elder brothers—so add nine months to eight and we still have more than a year and a half before there's even a chance for a little duc d'Angoulême—" Papa Roi threw his hands into the air in disgust. "And if I worry about whether the duc d'Orléans will try to claim the throne in the absence of an heir, you will be treating me for apoplexy."

I wasn't so certain that the comte d'Artois could be depended upon to become the first of the Bourbon grandsons to become a father. He was to be yoked in matrimony to his own sister-in-law,

Marie Thérèse, the younger, and even uglier, sister of the comtesse de Provence. Papa Roi had granted the comtesse du Barry the honor of arranging all the wedding festivities, as she had done for the comte de Provence; and it rankled every fiber of my being that she should be given a role that the queen would ordinarily assume.

I wondered if the smirk would disappear from Artois's too-handsome countenance when he found himself in the dark with a girl who had been described as having a thin, vulpine face, an ugly tip on the end of her long nose, crossed eyes, and a large mouth! And if her hygiene was as nonexistent as her sister's...

The king and the dauphin's physician approached the bed. Monsieur Lassone was a dignified-looking man who dressed in black and white from head to toe, and was obviously fastidious about his toilette—a reassuring quality in a medical man. "Why is madame la dauphine present?" he inquired. "It is most irregular."

"Because I asked her to be here," the dauphin mumbled.

Papa Roi shrugged. "Perhaps the dauphine would prefer to wait behind the screen," the doctor said. He gestured to a six-paneled gilt-edged screen embellished with floral motifs.

"Will the physician insist on examining me without my clothes?" Louis Auguste asked. His voice was high and frightened. He squeezed his eyes shut and clenched his fists until Monsieur Lassone assured him that he could remain fully dressed, although he maintained that he could not observe the dauphin's heartbeat unless His Royal Highness relaxed his hands.

"Then if I am not to disrobe, my wife may remain." The dauphin patted my hand. His palms were damp and cold.

Monsieur Lassone raised his lorgnette and peered at him. Then he felt his pulse. Louis Auguste held his breath. I watched while the doctor assessed my husband's height and measured his girth. He pitched forward on his toes to *relevé* and examined the dauphin's eyes. "Myopic, but not rheumy," he informed the king. "Well, at least we know he can *see* madame la dauphine!"

The men discussed the dauphin's customary activities as well as his prodigious appetite. I listened with avidity, for Maman would expect a full report. I would tell her that my husband's physician had declared that the dauphin's constitution was lethargic from overexerting himself during the hunt and at the forge, and from devouring too much rich food and confections. "As such he lacks the fire in his belly to do his duty," were Monsieur Lassone's words.

"I wish I were dead," the dauphin whispered in my ear. I had never heard him sound so glum. His eyes were moist and he swallowed hard, as if he were trying to fight back the tears forming in his throat. "They have no idea what it feels like to be me. To be discussed as though I were not in the room, or worse—am present, yet have no feelings."

The king pulled the dauphin to his feet. "So, my boy, Monsieur Lassone's diagnosis seems to me to be well reasoned. What do you have to say for yourself?"

"I like to eat," the dauphin muttered defensively.

"Speak louder," the king commanded. "This is a serious matter." He began to grow agitated. "The fate of France hangs in the balance like the sword of Damocles. Close your eyes and imagine people cheering *Vive le roi Stanislas Xavier, le ci-devant comte de Provence*. And if he is carried away by disease, imagine the cries of *Vive le roi Charles Philippe, le ci-devant comte d'Artois!* And if your brothers both die young, are you going to let one of those ugly Savoyard sisters married to them bear the next Bourbon heir? Or will the princes of the blood fight it out? Will your successor be an Orléans? The son of the pretty little duchesse de Chartres?"

"I like to *eat*," Louis Auguste repeated emphatically. "And I like to ride. And hunt. And to build my cabinets and forge my locks under the tutelage of Monsieur Gamain."

"That's all very well and good," replied the king. "But if they interfere with your ability to do the one thing that is required of you at this stage in your life, such activities will have to be curtailed."

The dauphin was horrified. "For how long?"

Louis Quinze glanced at me. "I would say, until madame la dauphine is increasing." He turned to the physician. "Would that be a reasonable assessment, Monsieur Lassone?" The doctor nodded his assent. "I am certain Her Imperial Majesty Maria Theresa would approve as well," the king added, meeting my gaze.

I said nothing. Whenever I was in Papa Roi's presence, I felt more like a child than a woman. Seated on the bed of state, whose inescapable symbolism seemed to mock my own conjugal inadequacy, I was cowed all the more. The only thing that could have made it worse would have been the presence of the king's most powerful minister, the duc d'Aiguillon, lording his triumph over my misfortune. I could just imagine the creature of the comtesse du Barry's advancement, standing beside the bed and urging the king to send the inadequate *Autrichienne* back across the border, for surely there could be nothing wrong with His Majesty's grandson.

Louis Auguste shuffled his feet and stared glumly at his diamond shoe buckles. "It's not the food," he mumbled. "Nor the riding, neither."

"Oho!" The king's eyes widened with mock horror. "So you know better than your physician now."

A log exploded with a loud pop and shifted precariously on the andirons. The candles hissed and guttered. The dauphin looked like an old dog that had been kicked for stealing table scraps. After several moments of silence, he found his voice. "It is not from exhaustion that I am unable to...to do my duty. I find my wife charming, Papa Roi. I love her, but I still need a little time to overcome my timidity." Was it the warmth from the fire, or his embarrassment that caused his face to blush?

I began to tremble, not from fear, but with amazement. Adjusting myself on the great bed of state, my eyes wet with happiness, I pressed my lips to his warm and rosy cheek.

He *loved* me? Why had he never said so before?

TWENTY-EIGHT

The *Joyeuse Entrée*

⁓ JUNE 1773 ⁓

Ever since I'd come to Versailles, I had been begging Papa Roi to arrange a formal, official visit to Paris, but the answer was always a resounding *non*! I had even tried to wheedle Mesdames *tantes* into pleading with him on my behalf, and had spoken to the comte de Mercy as well. "Do you think my *grand-père* is afraid that the dauphin and I will be received there with too much enthusiasm?" I jested. But as time wore on, I had overheard, from vendors in the courtyard and corridors, from hopeful petitioners, and from backbiting courtiers, that Louis Quinze was no longer considered "*le Bien-Aimé*," by the Parisians.

In the three years since my arrival in France, the scales had fallen from my eyes. At first I had revered Papa Roi with appreciation and awe; he was tall and handsome, with a noble profile—in short, everything a king should appear to be to an unschooled girl of fourteen. But I was seventeen now, and had absorbed enough of the jaded ambience of the French court to adopt a certain cynicism. My fervently held beliefs as a good Catholic, and the prolonged contretemps over my refusal to acknowledge Madame du Barry had taught me much; I had come to see the king for what he was: a vain and selfish man with alarmingly fluid morals.

But finally (and more than likely because Papa Roi felt the cold breath of his own mortality on the back of his neck), as it was the custom for the king's heir to present himself to the people of Paris before the reigning sovereign died, Louis relented and set the date of June 8, 1773, for the "*joyeuse entrée*," the joyous entry that would mark the first formal visit of the dauphin and dauphine to the capital. Even Louis Auguste grew excited at the prospect, so much so that he was willing (along with his brothers) to become a party to a scheme I was concocting. I was certain the *joyeuse entrée* would be a grand and glorious event, but would it not be just as exhilarating, if not more so, to first visit the capital incognito? To see the areas of the city beyond the narrow scope of our previous excursions to the Palais Royal and the adjacent opera house! After the eighth of June we would never be able to do so with such surety because by then everyone would know what we looked like.

The comte d'Artois, who of all his brothers possessed a playfulness of character most similar to mine, elected to undertake the planning of the adventure; and thus it was on the night of June 1, 1773, two hours past sundown, that the five of us—the dauphin and I, the comte and comtesse de Provence, and the comte d'Artois, cloaked ourselves to the point of anonymity in voluminous black dominoes, their capacious *calèche* hoods tugged over our heads. The comtesse and I feared for our highly piled coiffures at first, but the wicked pleasure we derived by flouting court etiquette in sneaking into the capital unattended far outweighed our vanity. A burgundy-colored carriage, unmarked, conveyed us the ten miles from Versailles into Paris, rumbling along the rutted King's Road, the coachman having been bribed with the promise of a bottle of Imperial Tokay at the conclusion of the illicit excursion.

Upon our arrival at the city gates, four footmen alit from the carriage, and acting as runners or linkboys carried torches to illumine the capital's dark and labyrinthine streets. I parted the curtains and peered out of the window. I had expected broad, cobblestone *allées,* lined with grand and imposing facades, like our streets in Vienna. Instead, the narrow houses leaned against one another like a string of drunken sailors intent on holding themselves upright as they faced their admiral's inspection. The coach almost immediately became stuck in the mud, muck evidently being an omnipresent symptom of the unpaved *rues.*

By another comparison, the city's stench made the dank, urine-permeated corridors of Versailles as fragrant as lilacs in May. "Are you sure this is Paris?" I breathed, tempted to hold my nose and unsure what to make of it, as fascinated as I was repelled.

Although they were none too pleased about such a filthy and onerous task, the footmen managed to disengage our coach with a minimal amount of difficulty and we were able to continue our adventure. At length the carriage clattered over a narrow bridge onto the Ile de la Cité, arriving in the public square outside Notre-Dame de Paris. There in the looming shadow of the cathedral, even after nightfall, and just like the Cour Royale of Versailles, were every sort of vendor imaginable, from ribbon sellers to pamphleteers. University students perused the bookstalls, and sharp-eyed marketwomen surveyed the cheap pottery. Live chickens scrabbled and squawked in their crates. A young woman trudged past our coach, her slender figure nearly doubled over by the weight of a large wicker basket on her back.

"Oysters, fresh oysters," she cried, her clear voice rising above the hubbub.

"Oysters?" exclaimed the dauphin. He rapped on the roof of the carriage with the golden pommel of his walking stick. "Halt!"

Our coachman drew up his teams. In a trice, the doors to the carriage were opened and the traveling steps lowered. The comtesse and I were handed out first, descending straight into a mud puddle. I burst into a fit of giggles. "However shall I explain *this* to Madame Etiquette? Five gold louis to whoever comes up with the best story!"

The comte d'Artois clapped me heartily on the back. "I accept your challenge, madame!"

"You accept *any* challenge where there is wagering to be had," the dauphin retorted prudishly. "And one day you will ruin yourself by it."

"Papa Roi will pay my debts," Artois replied cockily.

"When Papa Roi is dead I won't pay them—you can be sure of that," my husband retorted.

"The dauphin is far too earnest," the comte de Provence teased. "Did he ever tell you about the day—this was many years ago—when he told off his equerry during a riding instruction?" Without waiting for a reply, the comte continued his anecdote. "The dauphin here was not performing terribly well; his horsemanship was an embarrassment to everyone. So the equerry scolded him. 'Monsieur le dauphin, don't you know that a prince who is destined to become a great king must know how to ride?' And my brother, his face all serious, pushes his hat further down upon his big head, as if it would help him to assert himself, and says to the equerry, 'No, sir, I was not aware of it. I only know that a great king should be just and make his people happy.' The equerry and I laughed so hard at that!"

"It's not funny," the dauphin insisted. "In fact, it's true. And, besides, no one could accuse me *now* of being a laggard on horseback," he added sullenly.

"Oh, come, come, *mon cher*! Don't be such a"—I discovered that my blue satin slipper had become entirely trapped in the muck—"a stick in the mud." His brothers began to laugh heartily at his expense. The comtesse de Provence clasped her husband's arm and tittered behind her ebony-handled fan.

"Ho, there!" my husband called to the oyster seller. "How much for two dozen?" From a hidden pocket in his domino he withdrew a velvet purse with his initials worked in silver thread. I stifled a gasp, for his insatiable hunger threatened to give us all away. Mercifully, the oyster girl, her eyes as round as the golden coins counted into her palm by my husband, showed not the slightest glimmer of recognition. Of course, how could she? It was not our profiles that graced the currency, and one well-fed nobleman in a large hooded cloak with a fat purse probably looked the same to her as any other.

With nothing in which to carry his precious cargo, the dauphin enlisted the aid of his brothers; there would be some additional explaining to do at the palace when the crowns of the comtes' tricorns smelled of oysters and brine. This my husband found utterly hilarious. His braying laugh, so unmistakeable to the rest of us, echoed off the stone façade of the cathedral, and we found much amusement in the fact that Louis Auguste's gaping maw was a mirror image of the grinning gargoyles overhead.

We took a stroll about the square, stopping to admire the organ grinder and his monkey, who was dressed in a little silk suit, complete with embroidered waistcoat and frothy cravat. "Don't you think he looks exactly like the duc de la Vauguyon?" I exclaimed as the creature leapt onto my shoulder. "Although I daresay this little stinker is much more clever!" A few yards away a stiltwalker whose face was made up to resemble a Pierrot strode through the crowd, high enough above it to become the perfect lookout for his confederate, a scrawny pickpocket who could not have been above the age of eleven or twelve. Vagrants, some shoeless and clad in rags, huddled in the gloomy recesses of the cathedral's façade. I had seen their like before, on occasion. Beggars who had parleyed the coin they solicited into the proper accoutrements rented from vendors at the gates sometimes wandered the corridors of Versailles, making themselves at home by dozing off in various remote corners of the château, but were invariably detected by the royal bodyguards with their spaniels.

We sidestepped a puddle and moved on. Twin sisters displayed their magic lanterns, which were no more than cunning little candlelit boxes that illumined painted slides of pastoral scenery or exotic oriental landscapes. "A peek for a sou!" they cried.

The comtesse de Provence and I opened our purses and paid the price of admission. The magic lanterns were nothing terribly special—certainly not compared to the pyrotechnics one might see in the theater or the opera, but we were caught up in the strange and colorful atmosphere, as foreign to us as Versailles might have seemed to any of them. By then our skirts were utterly spattered with mud; we would have the devil of a time explaining ourselves to our respective *dames d'honneur*.

The cathedral bells tolled the hour of eleven. People began to disperse. I noticed the little pickpocket circling our party like a dog in search of a place to do his business or a hungry bird of prey. My husband, by far the most cautious among us, tugged at my cloak. "Perhaps we had better return," he murmured.

We clambered into our carriage, the comtesse and I cocooned in the voluminous poufs of our filthy skirts as the boys struggled to pry open the oyster shells with their pocket knives. Imbued with the odors of Paris we returned to the château amid gales of laughter, swearing each other to secrecy.

Yet for all my bravado, I was afraid of receiving a scolding from Madame Etiquette regarding the myriad transgressions of protocol and my ruined garments, and thanked heaven that she had retired for the night by the time we reached the palace. With the aid of the sympathetic princesse de Lamballe I removed every stitch of clothing I had worn and concealed it in various places about the apartments. One by one I intended to surreptitiously dispose of them.

Adventurous as it was, our clandestine night in the capital did not begin to prepare us for the spectacle of the *joyeuse entrée*.

On the morning of June eighth, precisely at eleven o'clock, our arrival was heralded by the sound of the great guns booming from the prison fortress known as the Bastille as well as those in front of the Hôtel de Ville, the City Hall, where the governor of Paris, the duc de Brissac, presided. Our state coach drove up to the steps of the Hôtel de Ville, where the duc awaited us, presenting the dauphin and me with the keys to the city.

Glorious sunshine! A sky of purest blue. The air smelled sweet and clean and was filled with music and the sound of joyous voices raised in song. The streets had been swept and tamped down to eliminate any traces of dust or mud. Breathless with excitement as I surveyed the multitude that had come out to welcome us, I turned to the dauphin and exclaimed, "*Mon Dieu*, how many of them there are!" There was nary a vagrant or beggar in sight. Instead, the citizens were decked out in their finest attire, as though it were a festival day. The aprons of the marketwomen were blindingly white; the balconies of the narrow houses were garlanded with flowers and ribbons and wreaths of welcome. Cheek by jowl the people were crushed together, turning out in the thousands to see us. Several must have awakened before dawn in order to secure a choice vantage, but at least they were not compelled to forfeit their breakfast: Enterprising women shouldering tin vessels steaming with aromatic café au lait did a brisk trade selling a cup of coffee for two sous.

"*Vive le dauphin!*" they shouted. "*Vive la dauphine!*" We heard no cries of "*Vive le roi.*" The total absence of a cheer for him voiced his subjects' discontent louder than any shout of derision.

University students doffed their caps in greeting; children pelted us with flowers. It seemed as though every hospital, every convent, every shop and dwelling, had disgorged its residents into the crowded streets. Laborers mingled with tradesmen, the nobility with the bourgeois, apprentices with their masters.

"Madame la dauphine!" I turned toward the shout, to see a frantically waving sister, wimple askew. I recognized her as the prioress from the Hôtel Dieu, the hospital that had recently been devastated by fire, resulting in a sorrowful loss of life. As I urged our bodyguard to let her pass, the nun pressed her way through the crowd. I reached for her hands and clasped them in mine. "May the Almighty bless and keep you forever!" she exclaimed, dropping into a deep curtsy amid the noisy crush of humanity all about us. I raised her to her feet; and as I kissed her on both cheeks, she whispered, "Do you know, madame, that you are the only one of the royal family to have opened your privy purse and sent us a donation?"

"How could I have done otherwise?" I replied, privately appalled that none of my Bourbon relations, including the dauphin, had thought to do the same.

The archbishop stood in front of Notre-Dame, his arms outstretched in welcome. I stole a secret smile, in recollection of my nocturnal adventure there the previous week. I had heard that the archbishop was a good man, a true man of God. I could not fail to be reminded of the last time a prince of the church had greeted me outside a cathedral. My thoughts drifted to my arrival in Strasbourg, my earliest footsteps in France and the memories of the Coadjutor Bishop, my distant relation the unctuous Prince de Rohan. A particular favorite of Madame du Barry, and at her instigation, he had been named by Papa Roi as his ambassador to Austria, recalling the marquis de Durfort. Maman remained appalled by the appointment, for the prince had nothing good to say about the Hapsburgs and was particularly insulting to her. In the presence of the *maîtresse en titre*, the prince de Rohan repeated a jest Frederick of Prussia had made at Maman's expense after the partition of Poland was finally affected in August of 1772. "The Devil" had said that in one hand my mother held a handkerchief and wept for the poor innocent Poles, while in her other, she wielded a sword against them.

I was jolted back to the present as the archbishop welcomed us into the cathedral where we attended Mass. And what a revelation awaited me! Viennese architecture was quite different from the soaring High Gothic church—lace in stone. Sunlight refracted off the vibrant stained-glass windows, scattering bits of colored light all around us like ephemeral gems.

We emerged from the cathedral to discover that an even greater crowd had gathered. My eyes shone with delight. As the dauphin and I squeezed through the throng, I heard people exclaim, "Look, how beautiful she is." I had never felt so much love. Remarking upon my husband's countenance came the assessment, "He looks so kind." I glanced at the dauphin; he, too, was beaming. And when he addressed the people, he was both commanding and humble. Louis Auguste spoke with grace and nobility and promised that when the time came he would make a worthy and judicious steward of France.

Even the comte de Mercy seemed moved by all the adulation we engendered. Noticing that his jaded eyes were moist, and knowing how important our reception was to the people of Austria as well as to the Bourbons, I clasped his arm and drew him toward me, vowing, "I shall make as few mistakes as I can. And when I do make any, I shall always admit it."

Luncheon had been arranged at the Tuileries palace. Like the *grands couverts* of Versailles, the meal was a sport for spectators, except that the privilege was not reserved for those of noble rank alone. Fifty women from the Paris market, fishwives and cheesemongers among them, had been invited to dine with us. Afterwards, the dauphin and I shook their hands and thanked them for sharing our meal. How fascinated they were by my jewels and my gown, reaching out to touch the silk, rubbing it between their fingers like cloth merchants, and ogling the grandeur of my coiffure.

No sooner did we return to Versailles, flushed with the headiness of our ebullient reception, than I sat down at my escritoire and scribbled an exultant letter to Maman.

I shall never forget it as long as I live. As we were driving to the Tuileries in the royal coach, the crush was so great that the carriage was stopped at a total standstill for upwards of three-quarters of an hour! And just before we began to make our way back home, we waited for a half hour on the open terrace, waving to the throngs of people who dared not let us depart. How happy we are to be able to gain the affection of a whole nation with so little trouble! Their broad smiles touched me to the core. As for honors, we received every tribute that one could imagine—yet all of those encomiums were not what pleased me most. What bestirred my heart more than proclamations and ribbons and speeches was the fondness and eagerness of the poor people who lavished their adulation upon us despite the taxes that burden them. Truly, they were swept away with joy at the sight of us!

TWENTY-NINE

Very Much a Woman... Yet Still Not a Wife

≈ OCTOBER 1773 ≈

"Wait—no. There." The dauphin and I fumbled beneath the crisp linen sheets. I wriggled my hips under his so that our anatomies settled into the optimal position. I felt him poking against me.

"Ouch!" He tried to roll away, but I gently placed my hands on his shoulders, pressing his bulk against my breast, holding him in an awkward embrace. "I didn't even touch you down there."

"I know, but..." He sighed heavily. "It hurts. I can't explain it."

"*Mon cher*, I am so sorry," I soothed, shocked nearly to tears that something purportedly enjoyable should cause him any discomfort. "Am *I* hurting you?" I asked softly.

"No, it's not you—it's me, somehow. I don't know why. I mean—I *want* to," he added with an anguished moan.

"Want to or *have* to?" I murmured, afraid to hear the answer.

"No—I want to. You are beautiful, Toinette."

"Really?" My eyes welled with tears and I held him even closer, although his weight was nearly crushing me. Gaining courage from his words I took a breath and asked the most painful question that ever came to my lips. "Remember when Monsieur Lassone examined you...and you told Papa Roi that you loved me? Did you really mean it?"

My husband became so silent I could hear the rapid beating of our hearts as they pressed together. Finally, he replied, almost incredulously, "Do you doubt it?" I didn't know what to say—because in truth my answer would have been, *Perhaps*. "I love you sincerely, Antoinette. And," he added, our faces nearly touching, "I respect you even more." He stroked my cheek so tenderly that I nearly bathed his hand with tears.

My heart became so full that it took my breath away. My thoughts jumbled together. I had not thought it possible, and felt ashamed for believing all this time that he was incapable of love. He was not by nature sentimental. When he'd told the king he loved me I had been immeasurably touched; but after his confession that evening, which was more of an explanation than anything else, there had been no tangible proof of it.

My rank entitled me to *deference*. Men bowed and doffed their hats, and women curtsied as I passed. But *respect* was another thing altogether. It was a rare achievement. Think, I told myself, of all of the people who no longer respect the king. No one else had ever told me they respected me. Maman loved me, but I knew she did not respect me; I had always known that. So perhaps it was an even greater gift than love that the dauphin was giving me.

"I didn't know you thought that, Louis," I murmured. "I mean—you never said it. That you respect me, I mean."

"Just because I—ow!—never said it doesn't mean I don't think it. *Ooh!*"

"What is it this time?" I asked, holding him closer still.

"Don't—ooh—*dooo* that. It only makes it worse."

"Hugging you? Louis!"

He winced, his mouth widening into a grimace of pain, and rolled over onto his back. Tears welled in the corners of his eyes as he cupped his hands protectively over his *pénis*. I had never felt more humiliated—or hurt—not only for myself, but for my husband. Between my thighs, on the fabric of my nightgown, and on the bedlinens beneath my derrière was a warm, sticky liquid. I edged away so that I would not have to fall asleep in the puddle. The maids would notice it in the morning and report the stains to whoever was crossing their palms with coins in exchange for our connubial news. Moments later, my husband's snores, the telltale sign of deep slumber. The room was filled with noise, while I remained empty inside.

On November 2, 1773, I celebrated my eighteenth birthday. Appraising myself in a looking glass I noticed that the coltishness that had distinguished my figure upon my arrival in France was all but gone, replaced—finally, *Gott sei dank*!—with a rounded bosom and the gentle curve of a pair of woman's hips, a chrysalis on the verge of emerging. And with this new silhouette came stirrings within me I had not previously known. I found myself the object of adoring gazes and suddenly noticed that they were worn by handsome faces. Flirting, not merely *de rigueur* at the court of Versailles, but raised to an art form here, had never had an effect on me. Now, I would find myself blushing to the roots of my hair.

My new sister-in-law, Marie Thérèse, the comtesse d'Artois, who wed the dauphin's youngest brother the same month, immodestly remarked (in company, no less) that I had no need of rouge when certain well-made courtiers came to my *cercles*. She, ugly little thing, insinuated that I should take a lover to palliate the stirrings in my loins that my husband could not satisfy. It was easy for her to be smug: Her spouse was handsome and charming and had managed to overcome his aversion to her ugliness on their wedding night.

I almost slapped her for her impertinence. Such dishonesty embodied everything I detested; it would have made me no better than Madame du Barry. And besides, even if my nature were so inclined (and it was not!), until I bore the dauphin a son, there could be no thoughts of other men. It would never do for the paternity of my heir to be in any way questionable. And if I did not remain pure, I could be sent back to Austria, destroying the delicate alliance between my homeland and France with a single heedless act. As it was, my *chastity* threatened to damn me, not only in the eyes of my native and adopted lands, but in those of the Catholic Church. Barrenness was as great a sin as promiscuity.

THIRTY

New Passions

⪻ JANUARY 1774 ⪼

For the past half year I had been enjoying a love affair—though of course the dauphin knew all about it. Having tasted the adulation of the people of Paris during our *joyeuse entrée*, it became an elixir I could no longer live without, ambrosia that sweetened the pain of my husband's connubial neglect. I yearned to forget, if only for a few hours, how little he wished to touch my body. Instead, several nights a week I allowed the Parisians to touch my soul, losing myself in the soaring strains of operatic arias and the delicious anonymity of myriad masquerade balls.

Literally terrified of being bored, I had thrown myself headlong into every form of entertainment that could be devised. At Versailles, I played lansquenet into the wee hours of the morning, fortified by orangeade; by day I immersed myself in our amateur theatricals. We—meaning the dauphin's brothers, their wives, and I, with Louis Auguste as our only audience member—performed in an entresol room in his apartments, on a cunning stage that folded out and then disappeared into the wall—a tremendous advantage because no one, including Papa Roi, knew what we were up to! The comte de Provence was quite a talented actor. It came as no surprise to me that he made an excellent Tartuffe, as he was merely playing himself—fat, witty, and balding (for he had a skin ailment that for some reason caused him to lose much of his hair at the age of sixteen). Still, he possessed a sharp eye for the right clothes and accoutrements, so the business of costuming our clandestine little troupe fell to him. The comte d'Artois was quite skilled as well; he made a wonderful lovesick swain and excelled in any role that called for dancing. I enjoyed playing the myriad maids and shepherdesses, grateful for the opportunity to wear lighter clothing. It was all grand fun, and it tickled me to pretend I was someone else, if only for a while. But I needed a wider audience than the dauphin.

The masquerade balls in Paris provided the perfect stage. My husband had little use for them; he believed quite heartily in the adage about being early to bed and early to rise, and by the time the clock struck ten he would be yawning ostentatiously. So I would ride off to the capital with my ladies. With our enormous skirts, three or four of us managed quite well, if not entirely comfortably, in my elegant glass coach.

On Sunday, January 30, 1774, I attended an opera ball, yet another masquerade, following the Parisian premiere of Sacchini's *Armida*. My gown was silver and pink and I wore white plumes and diamonds in my coiffure. I carried my mask on a stick, like an elaborate lorgnette, the better to emphasize the cascade of Chantilly lace at my elbow. With such a disguise it took great discipline to conceal my identity, as my hands were known to flutter during excited conversation. My ladies and I promenaded about the crowded salon as best as we could, offering a nod of the head here and there. Because of my rank I curtsied to no one, but there was such a crush of people that not a soul seemed to take notice of it. The high windows remained shut to ward off the wintry chill, rendering the room even more stifling.

"Madame, change with me," the princesse de Lamballe whispered in my ear. "There are so many people here that the room has grown warm. You will want a glass of lemonade and it will be too difficult to manage at once the stick and the goblet."

She was right, of course. "*Vous avez raison*," I agreed, and we found a quiet corner where, obscured by a gilded column, we exchanged disguises.

We reentered the ballroom. A lively tune was being played and I longed to be invited to dance. Men and women swirled about us in eddies of silk and perfume as our nostrils were assailed by the pungent aromas of hair pomade and perspiration. A deep voice at my elbow said, "You looked thirsty, Madame."

I turned, startled by the interruption. A tall man, perhaps the dauphin's height, though with a finer, more slender figure, was offering me a glass of wine. "I-I—*pardon,* monsieur," I stammered. "I do not drink. Spirits."

"Lemonade then?" He smiled warmly and with his other hand proffered another crystal goblet filled with the only other liquid refreshment on offer. I accepted it gratefully. The stranger watched as I brought my lips to the glass, draining half its contents.

"*Merci*, monsieur." I smiled and downed the remaining lemonade. "I was indeed quite parched. And you are my Samaritan."

He clicked his heels together like a soldier. "It is always a privilege to oblige a woman in distress."

I began to laugh. "Are you always so serious?"

The gentleman chuckled, following my lead. "We Swedes are not known for our humor. Forgive me, please, madame. The

French are very good at flirting; it is their national pastime, but I have not their native skill—not being a native," he added, leaning against the pillar.

"Nor I," I replied. His proximity unnerved me. I found myself staring at his smile, for I could scarcely make out his eyes, impressed by his gallant manner, and intrigued by the way his jaw tensed when he was about to say something in earnest. "I am not a flirt. Nor am I French," I admitted. "But perhaps you know too much about me already." I glanced anxiously at the princesse de Lamballe. "I should go."

The Swede raised his hand, as if to stop me. "No, madame; please do not leave. Not yet, anyway." He offered me his upturned palm. "Would you care to dance with me?" His smile was warm: safe and yet inviting. I gazed up at him. Light brown hair, barely powdered. Strong jaw. Elegant carriage. His eyes—I could not discern their color because of his mask, but even so, they appeared intense, with perhaps a hint of melancholy when one peered more deeply.

My cheeks grew warm. "I-I dare not," I replied. "Dance, I mean. I should be heading home."

"And where is home, may I ask?" His voice sounded like the sweet, low music of a cello.

"You may not ask," I replied gaily, "for then you might discover who I am. And what would be the purpose, then, of a masquerade?"

The stranger paused to consider his reply. Then he leaned over to whisper softly in my ear, "I already know who you are."

"You cannot. How . . . ?"

"Your secret is locked in my bosom, madame la dauphine," the gentleman murmured. "I am Count Axel von Fersen and I was presented to you barely a month ago at your New Year's Eve ball."

I gasped. "How—how did you know it was me tonight?"

"Because, madame," replied Fersen, offering a courtly bow, "you are by far the most graceful woman in the room. From the way you carry your head to the way you move your wrist. You wear your birthright and your nobility like a diamond necklace, for all to admire. Your laugh is easy and unmistakeable. And your accent, while you are an excellent mimic, still bears traces of the Austrian about it. Take it from another who was not born speaking French. And it is charming."

My cheeks felt warm. "Forgive me, monsieur le comte, for not recognizing you. There were so many people that night—and I tried to speak to everyone."

Fersen smiled. Behind the mask his eyes were shining. I endeavored once again to divine their color. Not blue; not green; somewhere in between. Perhaps even brown. "But you did speak to me," the count said. "And I shall never forget it."

I wished I could recall the subject of our discourse that night; and I was far too discommoded by his presence to ask if he might refresh my memory. As if he saw what was inside my mind with his powers of "*magnétisme animal*," like my childhood penmanship teacher Herr Mesmer, Fersen said, "You asked me whether it was much colder in Sweden on New Year's Eve than it is in France."

My hand flew to my mouth in embarrassment. "What a silly question!" I exclaimed.

"I did not think so at the time, madame," said the count chivalrously. "After all, it was like a *grand cercle* and you were expected to speak of something personal, yet brief, to everyone in the room."

My *poitrine* flushed with color, a telltale signal of my discomfiture. My bosom was now a damasked pink and white, a state of affairs that I knew would not abate until I had regained my equanimity. "Specific? Why, monsieur le comte, I spoke to you of the *weather*!"

"The weather in *Sweden*," he emended. "Which, to my mind at the time was quite specific enough."

I felt a hand placed gently on my arm, a delicate hint from the princesse de Lamballe. "I must go," I said, though there was something in Count von Fersen's manner that made me long to linger. "My husband will worry for me . . . out so late, and so far abroad."

"Your husband is a fine man," Fersen agreed without the slightest hint of irony or envy. "You are fortunate in each other." He bent over my hand and gently kissed the back of my fingers. His lips were soft and warm. I nodded my acknowledgment and turned to leave. The princesse helped me don my velvet cloak and adjusted the voluminous *calèche* hood so that my face was all but obscured. As I began to walk away I felt Count von Fersen's gaze upon me, but I would not turn around. He had been presented at court, which meant that he was always welcome there, would have such rights and privileges as riding in the king's carriage and attending *levers* and *couchers*. I would see him again.

As I climbed into my gala carriage and settled back against the lush upholstery, I realized that my belly was as full of trepidation as it was of elation.

THIRTY-ONE

The Beginning of the End

February 14, 1774

Your Imperial Majesty:

We are nearing the accomplishment of the destiny of the dauphine. The king ages; he constantly repeats himself. He is isolated, without comfort from his children, without zeal, attachment, or fidelity on the part of the bizarre assemblage that composes his surroundings. He has no resources in his old age but those he finds in your daughter.

But there is one point that I must stress and which merits all of Your Majesty's attention: the dauphine understands business with extreme facility, yet fears it to excess. She never allows herself to suppose that she may one day possess both authority and power, with the unfortunate result that her character has acquired too dependent and passive a nature, displaying itself in timidity on the least occasion. She fears to speak to the king; she fears to speak to the ministers—even the persons who are her closest attendants appear to intimidate her.

In addition, the dauphin, with good sense and excellent ingredients in his character, will probably never have the strength or willpower to permit him to reign by himself. If the dauphine does not govern him, he will end up being ruled by others.

As their ascendance is inevitable, I believe that at this stage it would be judicious for us to remind the dauphine of her innumerable strengths, rather than continue to illuminate her deficiencies. With your permission I will endeavor to school her (with all due discretion) in the issues, both foreign and domestic, that it will be imperative for her to comprehend.

Your humble servant,
Mercy

～ APRIL 28, 1774 ～

The court was reeling from the news. The previous day the king was suddenly taken ill during a hunting party at the Grand Trianon. The royal physician, *le premier médecin*, Monsieur Lemonnier, at first suspected it was nothing worse than a fall from his horse, which may have been why we had not been informed of the incident right away. But it soon became evident that His Majesty's condition was more alarming than anyone had surmised. He had floated in and out of consciousness, confusing the hour, recalling that he had just been on his feet pointing toward a leaping stag—or was it a hare? Or a fox? Or had he been on horseback? And in the next instant he found himself being lifted onto a litter. Or had he been abed the whole time? The comtesse du Barry had been by his side from the beginning, holding his hand and hovering above him, her décolletage doubtless resembling a pair of constellations to the delirious sovereign.

Finally, the king's first surgeon, Monsieur La Martinière, was summoned to the Trianon to assess the situation, and was shocked to discover that for two days the king had been growing steadily worse, yet had been attended by no one but his valet and his mistress. After conferring with the *premier médecin*, Monsieur La Martinière determined that the king's illness was grave enough to convey him to the seat of the monarchy. With a somber countenance the royal surgeon told the king, *"C'est à Versailles, Sire, qu'il faut être malade*—you must be ill at Versailles, Your Majesty."

Papa Roi had insisted. "I can ride—my mount...."

But his fever had risen so high that he struggled to remember his hunter's name. He was lifted into one of the royal coaches like one might nestle an egg into a bed of straw. The most docile teams of horses bore him to the château. The ailing king was smuggled up the back staircase to his bedchamber, the same path so ignominiously taken by countless courtesans, and was gently lowered onto the imposing bed of state, where once he had lain with them.

But nothing in the French court remained a secret for very long. By the time the cluster of medical experts—a half dozen physicians, a quintet of surgeons, and a trio of apothecaries— began to bustle about efficiently, checking the royal pulse every ten minutes without fail, the news had spread to every corridor and closet, up the wide marble staircases and down the labyrinthine warrens of secret, narrow backstairs passages.

A page boy had come running to the dauphin's apartments, breathless with the news. I had been locked inside my private study with the comte de Mercy and the abbé Vermond. Twice a week, so as not to arouse suspicion, the Austrian ambassador had arrived at the hour appointed for my lecture with the abbé; but the discussion was of a different nature entirely than Vermond's reading to me from *The Life of Saint Anthony*, the current subject of our four o'clock tête-à-têtes. Mercy was attempting to school me in the intricacies of the French government and the king's policies. On that awful April day he had been explaining that the Contrôleur-Général des Finances, the elderly abbé Terray, was facing opposition over his restriction of the free trade of grain. Was it naïve of me to ask whether the chancellor, the equally ancient and equally sly duc de Maupeou, had anything to do with the matter?

As soon as the page arrived with the dreadful news, my first impulse was to see the king. I unbolted the doors of my study and gathered my skirts, clutching fistfuls of olive-colored silk as I glided faster than I had ever moved before through my suite of rooms. I raced through the dauphin's apartments—where was he?—and up the grand marble staircase. My heart was pounding so hard, I could scarcely breathe. Then I ran, quite inelegantly, through the seven-salon enfilade or parade apartment that led to the Oeil de Boeuf, and from there to the King's Chamber, dodging countless knots of anxious, whey-faced courtiers. Guards were everywhere. I tried to circumvent them to reach the secret staircase, but they blocked my way. The closest I could get was the Oeil de Boeuf, where I encountered a crowd: nobles, ministers, and priests; ambassadors; and finally, the people I sought most—Mesdames and the dauphin.

I embraced my husband. His face was pale, but whenever he became anxious, his forehead and chin would develop unsightly little blemishes. "I wish to see my grandfather," he insisted, endeavoring to press past the sentry, but the physicians, as well as court protocol, demanded that the dauphin and dauphine keep away from the ailing monarch.

Madame Adélaïde clasped me by both elbows. "Do you have any messages for the king?" she asked me. "My sisters and I intend to remain by our father's side day and night."

"Tell Papa Roi that both the dauphin and I pray for his swift recovery and wish to have been able to attend him. Tell him that we are praying for him."

The dauphin's aunt laughed. "Well, he should be amused by that last part."

"I am sincere in my prayers, even if he is not," I murmured, casting my eyes toward the floor.

Mesdames *tantes* were admitted to His Majesty's bedchamber. As they were not in the line of succession, whether they became ill was not a matter of national concern. The dauphin and I returned to our apartments where we ordered a cold supper, although even my husband could not touch a morsel. We sat in silence on opposite ends of his drawing room, not knowing what to say, our thoughts in a state of suspension, for no one yet knew what was the matter with the king.

That evening, a servant accidentally raised a torch, illuminating the musty darkness to which the king had been consigned by the medical men. His Majesty heard the collective, horrified gasp, the cries of "*Mon Dieu*—the pox!" and the scuffle of retreating footsteps that sounded like the thunder of hooves during the hunt. With the exception of the doctors and a handful of gallant courtiers and even braver servants, only his daughters—disagreeable and disapproving as they so often had been—and the comtesse du Barry, intent on martyring herself, remained to give comfort to the king during his final days.

But he would have to send her away so that he could die in a state of grace. No matter how much the *maîtresse en titre* meant to him, she was noble only through his making. Jeanne Bécu had been a whore, and her trumped-up coat of arms was as false as her patches and paint. As false even as the hair she took great pains to lighten, so I had heard, turning its naturally mahogany hue into spun gold.

Papa Roi was an old man of sixty-four. A dying man. One who had sat on the throne of France for nearly six decades. I had thought the sun rose and set in him when I first arrived at Versailles. Now I pitied him almost as much as I loved him.

Dread raced through the palace, spreading the terror of infection as well as the fear of the future regime. Would the dauphin keep the same ministers when he became king? Who would be retained and who would find themselves replaced or disgraced? And how much influence would the dauphine wield? they wondered. Would I persuade him to send the duc d'Aiguillon off to his country estate, and bring back the duc de Choiseul as chief minister? The Barryistes were particularly nervous, especially the duc de la Vauguyon and the young princesses' governess Madame de Marsan, loyalists to Louis Quinze, and loyaler still to his lover.

Meanwhile, a fretful and restless crowd gathered in the Oeil de Boeuf on the other side of the door to the King's Chamber, waiting for news, prepared to abide there indefinitely. They slumped against the walls and slumbered on the floor, forgoing all the niceties of their toilettes, strangers for a while to tooth powder and combs, to clean linen and scent, while in the royal bedchamber, the stench grew appalling, as day by day the old king's body began to bloat and turn black with decay.

Two days later, in the bright sunshine of my library, I faced Monsieur de Clichy, who had assumed the prerogatives of first physician, elbowing Monsieur Lemonnier into the shadows. "They tell us he has remained conscious the entire time—that he is still alert. Why will you not let me go to him?"

"Madame la dauphine, your body will bear the future king of France; you cannot—the kingdom cannot—risk your exposure to the pox. It is a fatal disease," he added condescendingly. How I wished to tear off his wig and toss it to the squirrels on the parterre!

I steeled my resolve and confronted the doctor. "*Monsieur le médecin*, with all due respect, I happen to know that you are wrong. Although I have lost several of my most beloved relations to the pox, I myself survived it, and have been inoculated against the disease. My mother the empress of Austria, who herself overcame it, is very forward-thinking when it comes to one's health. It is my understanding that Mesdames *tantes* have not been inoculated because the French court does not believe in it. When the unhappy event arrives that places some of these decisions within my small and untried hands, I assure you that the royal family, every one of them, will receive an inoculation. It is only common sense."

"They will not listen to me," I later fretted to the dauphin. "And when they listen, they will not hear." My husband and I had scarcely slept since Papa Roi had taken ill. We cleaved to each other, avoiding all but our nearest relations. The comtesses de Provence and d'Artois had already tried what remained of my nerves, sparing me no sympathy as they clucked about my pallid complexion, and the unattractive state of my eyes, swollen and red rimmed from frequent tears, and half encircled with dark *demilunes* of fatigue.

Louis Auguste and I spent the better part of every day in his apartments on our knees in prayer, or side by side on a settee, clutching each other's hands as if each of us could somehow, through that intimate gesture, transmit from one to the other what little strength we harbored. The days passed with agonizing *longueur*.

There was nothing to do but wait.

On the fourth of May, Louis's confessor counseled him to purify his soul. It had come: the moment the king most feared. It was not death he dreaded so much as bidding farewell to

Madame du Barry, Madame Victoire told me later. "Do I really stink that badly?" he whispered to the comtesse, a frightened little boy again after so many years a king. He could tell that she was holding her breath. His mistress had laughed through her tears and pressed his hands to her ample breast. "Yes, you do, *mon amour*," she assured him. "And once I have quit the palace, it means you will be dead, and then it will be Saint Peter's problem!"

Louis had kissed her hands. "I thank you for your levity. I thank you for many things, you know," he added, too weak to enumerate them. His chief minister, the duc d'Aiguillon, gave him the eye; it was time to dismiss his *maîtresse en titre* so that he could be shriven—a moment that had been prolonged for as long as possible. Madame Adélaïde had most emphatically believed that as soon as her father heard any discussion of the Blessed Sacrament, he would know that his final hours were at hand and he would lose all will to recover. At the king's behest, the duc had placed his château at nearby Rueil at the du Barry's disposal. In time, perhaps, Louis hoped she might be able to return to Louveciennes, the château that had been his gift to her. Madame Victoire grew quite sentimental when she told me that her father had expressed the wish that the new king would not rescind the largesse, although it lay within his power to do so.

I had heard stories about Louveciennes. I supposed the comtesse's heart would heal in time, if she had truly loved the king, and not merely the perquisites and influence their liaison had brought her. It would take some time for me to find it in my own heart to forgive the du Barry's cruelty to me; and therefore, I could not spare my tears for her when I had many still to shed. Evidently, her château was a palace in miniature, where scores of servants in their crimson and pale yellow livery would wait on her and her houseguests hand and foot in the huge white dining room where the boiserie moldings were painted with pure gold leaf. Although exiled from our court, she would remain surrounded by the luxuries befitting a royal mistress—an extravagant décor, lavishly appointed, with enormous crystal chandeliers, sumptuous carpets, handsome furniture, and innumerable priceless items of bronze, glass, and china.

I heard that Madame du Barry was weeping when she departed Versailles. I wondered if she looked back as the duc d'Aiguillon's carriage rumbled through Mansart's majestic gateway for the last time, or if she embodied her motto, *Boutez en avant*, and continued to push forward.

On May the seventh the king discovered that he was nearly bereft of speech. And yet he had to make his final—and as court etiquette required, public—confession. He had not done so in nearly forty years; yet now he literally *could* not utter words he *would* not speak for so many decades.

Monseigneur de la Roche-Aymon, the Grand Almoner of France, made his way from the chapel to the king's bedchamber amid a candlelit procession of clerics and courtiers, past a phalanx of Swiss Guards and Household Cavalry that lined the grand staircase, through the parade apartment and the Hall of Mirrors. Until now, the dauphin and I had not been permitted to approach the king's apartments. My husband's brothers, along with their wives, had joined the solemn procession as well, although we were stopped at the threshold of the King's Chamber, forbidden entry for fear of contagion.

The doors of the king's chamber were open. Morbidly curious onlookers jostled their neighbors and craned their necks in the expectation of a final glimpse of what was left of Louis Quinze. I was sickened by their callous incivility. The king had been taken from the bed of state and placed on a camp cot. On either side, holding his communicant's napkin, knelt two of the princes of the blood, Conti and Condé.

The king's head had swollen to twice its normal size. The black scabs that stippled his decaying flesh offended the flock of priests who were waiting to witness his confession. Even the physicians seemed surprised by the extent of the mortification. But I had seen it before. Two Josephas had departed this world for a better one, their souls, pure and white in Heaven, even if their blackened bodies rotted further in the Kaisergruft.

His Majesty was nearly mute now; certainly inarticulate. So the Grand Almoner spoke the words of his confession for him. "Gentlemen: The king instructs me to say that he begs God's pardon for his transgression and for the scandalous example he set for his people. Should the Almighty see fit to restore him to health, he vows that for the remainder of his days on earth he will devote himself to repenting his offenses and to the welfare of his subjects."

My husband feared that his tears would be thought unmanly. We stood outside the King's Chamber, each with a lighted candle, keeping vigil while Papa Roi's last confession was pronounced by the cardinal. I stole a glance at the dauphin's brothers. Their eyes and cheeks were dry, not because they were stronger, but because I knew they didn't love the king the way my husband did. Our *grand-père* had not always been kind to the dauphin; I knew he did not think much of my husband; and sometimes I imagined that he would have preferred to see either of Louis Auguste's brothers assume the throne instead. I had once overheard him say that if the dauphin ever ascended the throne, his brothers would starve. But Papa Roi was—I dared to think it at this moment when he might breathe his last in any instant—wrong. He would make a better king than either Provence or Artois, for Louis Auguste had two endearing qualities that they both lacked: honesty and compassion. Would either of the comtes have sent two hundred thousand francs from their privy purses to distribute to the impoverished people of Paris, as the dauphin did when we returned to his apartments after the king's confession?

I, too, had made a contribution to the poor by electing to forgo a silly outmoded custom that had been in place since the Middle Ages: the *Droit de Ceinture*, or right of the belt, a tax that was levied on the people at the start of a new reign. It harkened back to an era long since gone, when queens wore golden girdles about their waists. "Belts are no longer fashionable," I jested. But the truth was that I already had much, while many of our future subjects had so little. There would be no tax for the Queen's Belt once I became the consort.

At the onset of the king's illness, a candle had been placed in each of the windows of the royal bedchamber. For thirteen days, overwhelmed by the increasing stench of their father's decay, Mesdames had maintained their unpleasant vigil, joined on occasion, as if it burdened them to do so, by the princes of the blood. The morning of May the tenth broke like any other perfect spring day in France. Larks sang above the trees that lined the pebbled alleés beyond the château of Versailles and big-bellied white clouds, pregnant with abundance, floated serenely across a cerulean sky.

At ten minutes after three that afternoon, the king's bedchamber was thrown into shadow, as if the Almighty Himself intended to capture the attention of the devoted onlookers. His Majesty's breath had been labored and ragged since dawn; his eyes, which had remained closed since the day before, still fluttered almost imperceptibly beneath his lids. And then, King Louis heaved a tremendous sigh, a single exhalation as if to expel the last bit of life remaining to him; and in a fraction of an instant, he was gone. With great solemnity the duc d'Orléans strode over to one of the windows and pinched the candle flame between his thumb and forefinger, quickly snuffing it out.

THIRTY-TWO

The End of the Beginning

◈ MAY 10, 1774 ◈

The dauphin and I had been sitting in one of my rooms for hours holding hands, scarcely daring to breathe. Two days earlier, I had donned black mourning and refused to rouge my cheeks. It seemed disrespectful to be concerned with one's appearance in such a time of sorrow. No one had brought us news of Papa Roi since sunrise. The clock struck once to indicate the quarter hour. I glanced at its face. Three-fifteen. We heard a sudden commotion, and from a distance, growing louder and nearer with each step, it sounded like a hundred people were fleeing for their lives and headed straight for our apartments.

As they drew closer their shouts and cries grew more distinct, their words discernable.

"The king is dead! Long live the king!"

I gasped hysterically, and sank into a deep curtsy, gulping out the words between inevitable sobs. Louis *le Bien-Aimé*—the

Well-Loved—was no more. "Your Majesty. You are king of France now!"

My husband cried out and fell to his knees in prayer, clasping my hand to pull me down beside him. "I am the most unhappy man in the world," he murmured. He looked utterly shattered, a young man broken on the wheel of fortune even as it rose to its zenith.

The door burst open. The comtesse de Noailles, breathless, was at the apex of the stampede; she approached us and sank into a deep curtsy. "God save Your Majesties."

Our hands were still clasped in prayer. "God save us indeed," I whispered.

Louis Auguste's sisters, the princesses Clothilde and Élisabeth, were among the first to offer their reverences, but my husband raised them to their feet and I embraced each of them with all the love of a sister. "What will happen to us?" Élisabeth murmured, clinging to her older brother.

"We will not part," he assured them with tears in his eyes. "I will be all things to you."

His youngest sister kissed his hands. "Then I will never leave you, brother."

Madame Etiquette—did she sense that her days of service were numbered now that I was queen?—ushered us into the Long Gallery. There, introduced by the *ta-ra ta-ra* of snare drums, we passed under the crossed swords of the Household Cavalry and for the next forty-five minutes received felicitations from a stream of ministers and courtiers. As eager as they were to ingratiate themselves with us as their new sovereigns, we could tell that they would rather be elsewhere—in haste to depart the contagion of Versailles for their own estates. For that reason, none of them was permitted to kiss our hands. Mesdames *tantes*, themselves infected with the pox, remained away. Within the hour they were bundled into one of the sixteen state coaches that had been standing at the ready since morning, embarking on the five-mile journey to the Château de Choisy along the banks of the meandering Seine. The palace of Versailles would have to be thoroughly cleansed of disease before the royal family and our vast households could safely return.

My husband and I would join his aunts at Choisy, along with his sisters, his brothers, and their wives, although Mesdames would remain in a secluded wing until they had fully convalesced. Nonetheless, Madame Adélaïde, already exerting her influence over her nephew, sent word that my husband should recall the comte de Maurepas, a former chief minister of the late king's, who had been in exile for twenty-five years for purportedly disseminating defamatory epigrams about Madame de Pompadour.

I heard shouts outside for "The queen's horses!" Trunks had been packed for days, ours among them, in anticipation of this hour, although no one dared to leave in advance of the old king's demise. There had been other casualties, too, we learned. Seventeen brave men and women who had attended Papa Roi in his extremity had perished as well, and the king and I now prayed for their immortal souls.

"What will happen to our *grand-père*?" I asked the comtesse de Noailles.

"Contagion remains a concern," she said quietly, feeding the words between her teeth. "The coffin was constructed with a double layer of lead and was filled with spirits." I shivered as the memories returned regarding the death of my beloved sister Josepha just days before she was to depart for her royal wedding in Naples.

"Those who attended the late king's bedside have already received the last rites," the comtesse continued. "To avoid risking more lives to infection, His Majesty's corpse will be conveyed with all due speed to the royal crypt in the cathedral of Saint-Denis where it will be immediately interred."

Louis Quinze had been king of France for nearly sixty years. Endowed by the divine right of kings he was worshipped and adored for decades. How sad that he would arrive at his final resting place with so little fanfare, quickly put out of mind, better shunned than mourned. And then I had another thought: The king's apartments, all those rooms of state already draped in black and purple mourning, would be ours upon our eventual return. Yet everyone, including the servants, was departing in droves, like hundreds of rats fleeing a sinking ship. Who would scrub them free of contamination?

By four o'clock, scarcely three-quarters of an hour after Papa Roi had breathed his last, the royal coaches were prepared to depart. Mesdames Clothilde and Élisabeth, accompanied by their governess, the odious Madame de Marsan, who had been a Barryiste, clambered into one of them. The outriders dug their spurs into the flanks of their mounts as their team of eight horses was given the command to walk on.

I turned to my husband and placed my hands in his. Nerves fluttered in my belly. "Well, King Louis Auguste, I suppose it is time for us to start out as well."

"Louis," he corrected. "Louis Seize. Merely Louis the Sixteenth. There is nothing 'Auguste' about me," he added with a rueful chuckle.

"Then long live Louis the Sixteenth!" I said, bringing his knuckles to my lips.

We stepped outside into the sunlight, the amber glow casting late-afternoon shadows on the cobbled yard of the Cour Royale. Mops was tucked under my arm; the other dogs traveled with our relations. The comtes de Provence and d'Artois and their wives waited for Louis and me, as their new sovereigns, to ascend first, taking our places in the capacious royal coach. Persons of higher rank faced forward. My husband sat to my right; on his other side was the comtesse de Provence, nervously fidgeting with her fan. Opposite us, her younger sister, squeezed in between her slender husband and the portly Provence, tried to wriggle closer to the comte d'Artois and rested her dark head upon his shoulder. Before we had passed the gilded gates of Versailles, the comtesse d'Artois had fallen asleep, lulled by the gentle rocking of the carriage.

The glass coach bearing the coffin of Louis Quinze, draped with a silver pall that was embroidered with golden fleurs-de-lis, had left the courtyard just moments before us. It clattered northward along the King's Road that led toward Paris and Saint-Denis with what appeared to me unseemly speed, as if the burden resting within it was an embarrassment; it was all the outriders could do to keep pace. More shocking still was the reception it received along the route. The roadside was crowded with people eager to bid the old king farewell in the most disrespectful manner. They shouted *"Taillaut!"* just as Papa Roi used to do when he spurred his horse beneath him as they raced to hounds. The excited waving of their hands and handkerchiefs were gestures of farewell and good riddance. *"Adieu, le 'Bien-Aimé'!"* they hollered derisively. I shuddered to wonder what they might cry as our carriage passed.

But my worries were for naught. With joy we beheld their happy, hopeful faces. *"Louis le Désiré,"* they called to us. Peasants hoisted young children above their heads, so their shining eyes might glimpse their new king and queen as the horses pranced by. Louis and I waved to them through the glass, and I repaid their giddy grins with broad smiles of my own.

"'Louis the Desired'!" I exclaimed, squeezing my husband's

right hand, as with my left I acknowledged our subjects standing by the road. "Imagine! See how much they look forward to your reign?" But my husband's complexion was green. "Tell me, *mon cher*, is it the motion of the carriage?" I asked solicitously.

"No," he murmured. "It is the responsibility."

I glanced at Artois and Provence, the forced cheer in their faces an effort to mask their envy. They had shed no tears for the late king, unlike my husband, who cupped his large hand over his eyes in an attempt to conceal another onslaught of sobs. "They mock him now, where once they loved him," he said quietly, pointing toward the carriage ahead of us. "I loved him, too."

"Oh, come, he hated *you*," Provence said peevishly.

I glared at him and stroked Louis's hand with my thumb. "*Shh*. Pay him no mind. I am sure he is grieving for Papa Roi too—in his own way." Maman would have been proud of my diplomacy.

"No, I'm not," the comte insisted.

"He didn't hate me," my husband mumbled, looking at his feet so that his brothers would not see his cheeks quivering with strangled emotion. "He just didn't understand me."

The comtesse de Provence reached across the coach and rapped her husband's knees with her fan. "Stanislas—now is not the time to be a bully." She gestured toward the road, the golden light falling on the fields, the sky above still bright and blue.

"Marie Joséphine is right. Let us talk of something else," I suggested.

"Absolutely," said the comtesse de Provence. "Does anyone else detect that foul smell?" She sniffed the air and the rest of us followed suit.

"Ugh, what *is* that?" inquired the comte d'Artois. He held his nose with one hand and searched for a handkerchief with the other. I offered him mine.

"They are too long in the hot sun," said the comtesse d'Artois, waking up with a start. Her command of French was still on shaky ground, just as her older sister's had been at first, although the pair of them shared the tendency to mispronounce things, utterly mangling their meaning.

"Do you smell something?" her sister asked, ignoring Marie Thérèse's apparent non sequitur.

"What is too long in the hot sun?" said Louis.

"*Vos cheveux*, *Votre Majesté*. *Faugh*, what a dreadful odor!"

Everyone grew completely silent. None of us could believe that she had just insulted the person of the king.

"What? What did I say?" asked the comtesse d'Artois naively. Her face was a picture of confusion as her dark eyes darted nervously from one of us to the other.

"You—you've just told the king that his hair smells bad!" I said.

Marie Thérèse's tiny hand flew to her breast. Her cheeks grew as red as the silk upholstery she sat upon. "*Non, non*, that is not what I meant to say at all." She tried to adjust her position, swiveling herself about to face forward, but her husband and brother-in-law were seated on her skirts, making the situation even more comical. In any event, she would only have smashed her long nose against the front wall of the carriage, had she succeeded. "The horses. Ah, it is the team of horses that stinks so!"

I began to laugh. "Oh, *mon Dieu*. You meant to say '*vos chevaux*'—your *horses*! 'Che*vaux*' is the word for 'horses.' 'Che*veux*' means 'hair.'"

Riding on the crest of my laughter, the comte d'Artois pointed at his older brother and joined in the mirth. "How your hair—I mean your horses—smell, Your Majesty." He held his nose ostentatiously.

His wife pursed her lips into a little moue and elbowed him in the ribs. "Don't make fun of me! It is not polite."

"But you are funny!" the comte d'Artois insisted.

It took him a bit longer than the rest of us, but my husband finally smiled. Then he chuckled. And finally he laughed. "That is the last time I will permit myself to be insulted!" Louis proclaimed. "And by my own family!"

"Better your own family than *them*," I teased, indicating the joyful throng gathered alongside the road. All of us erupted into gales of laughter, glad, if only for a few moments, to be shaking off the yokes of mourning and etiquette. From now on the world was going to be ours—filled with dancing and music, with young people enjoying life to the fullest. The days of doddering old men and fussy old women were past. Ahead lay the fragrant gardens of Choisy; and beyond that, for years and years, a kingdom that was ours, Louis's and mine, to fashion in our own mold.

"All France is at our feet today," I observed, my belly full of impatient butterflies. I touched my fingers to my lips and blew kisses at the crowd. "And just imagine what we shall make of it!"

Bibliography

Although it is not customary to provide a bibliography for a work of fiction, my research for the Marie Antoinette trilogy has been so extensive that I wished to share my sources with my readers. I am indebted to the following fine scholars and historians.

Abbott, John S. C. *History of Maria Antoinette*. New York: Harper & Brothers, 1849.

Administration of Schönbrunn Palace. *Schönbrunn*. Vienna: Verlag der Österreichischen Staatsdruckerei, 1971.

Asquith, Annunziata. *Marie Antoinette*. New York: Taplinger, 1976.

Bernier, Olivier. *Secrets of Marie Antoinette: A Collection of Letters*. New York: Fromm, 1986.

Boyer, Marie-France, and François Halard. *The Private Realm of Marie Antoinette*. New York: Thames & Hudson, 1996.

Cadbury, Deborah. *The Lost King of France: How DNA Solved the Mystery of the Murdered Son of Louis XVI and Marie Antoinette*. New York: St. Martin's Griffin, 2002.

Cronin, Vincent. *Louis and Antoinette*. New York: William Morrow, 1974.

Erickson, Carolly. *To the Scaffold: The Life of Marie Antoinette*. New York: St. Martin's Griffin, 1991.

Fraser, Antonia. *Marie Antoinette: The Journey*. New York: Anchor Books, 2002.

Haslip, Joan. *Marie Antoinette*. New York: Weidenfeld & Nicholson, 1987.

Hearsey, John. *Marie Antoinette*. New York: E. P. Dutton, 1973.

Hibbert, Christopher, and the editors of the Newsweek Book Division. *Versailles*. New York: Newsweek Book Division, 1972.

Lady Younghusband. *Marie-Antoinette: Her Early Youth*. London: Macmillan, 1912.

Lever, Evelyne. *Marie Antoinette: The Last Queen of France*. New York: Farrar, Straus & Giroux, 2000.

Pick, Robert. *Empress Maria Theresa: The Earlier Years, 1717–1757*. New York: Harper & Row, 1966.

Thomas, Chantal. *The Wicked Queen: The Origins of the Myth of Marie-Antoinette*. New York: Zone Books, 2001.

Weber, Caroline. *Queen of Fashion: What Marie Antoinette Wore to the Revolution*. New York: Picador, 2006.

Zweig, Stefan. *Marie Antoinette: The Portrait of an Average Woman*. Translated by Eden and Cedar Paul. New York: Grove Press, 1984. Originally published in the United States by Viking Press in 1933.

Acknowledgments

Tremendous thanks to my agent, Irene Goodman, and to my editor, Caitlin Alexander, for seeing the story of Marie Antoinette in the same way I do and for their passion and support for my vision; to Maria Zannieri who taught me how to perform the Versailles Glide; to Christine Trent for her expertise on eighteenth-century fashion dolls, and for being a sounding board as well as an encouraging presence throughout the process of writing this novel; to all who chimed in regarding my (now moot, but nonetheless arcane) opera questions on Facebook—your enthusiasm, passion, and knowledge overwhelm me; to Elena Maria Vidal for her generosity in sharing her own wealth of expertise and research. Finally, the words "thank you" could never be nearly enough to express my love, gratitude, and appreciation to Scott, my husband and biggest fan, who thought nothing of hopping on a plane with me to visit Paris and Versailles.

BECOMING
Marie Antoinette

JULIET GREY

A READER'S GUIDE

Juliet Grey on Writing
Becoming Marie Antoinette

I fell in love with Marie Antoinette (and with Louis Auguste) while I was researching a nonfiction project. Before I began, I knew very little about her life and had more or less imbibed the popular narrative served up by European history courses that painted Marie Antoinette as a bubbleheaded spendthrift. And when I discovered that she was *not* the flaxen blonde she is so often depicted as in novels and films (she was, in fact, a strawberry blonde—*la petite rousse,* "the little redhead," as Madame du Barry famously insults her), a whole unexplored side of her character opened up.

The more I read about Marie Antoinette and the dauphin, the more I understood that they began their life together as a pair of quite lovable and sympathetic teenagers who were in over their heads politically—so naïve and sheltered that they were completely unaware of the social changes taking place in cities and towns all around them thanks to the writings of men such as Voltaire and Rousseau, whose ideas were being discussed in salons across Europe. These privileged, pampered royals were both so eager to please their elders that they ended up surrounded by people who took advantage of them. Neither was stupid, but having been raised to believe in the divine right of kings, they were stubborn when it came to any ability to bend with the times. And neither Marie Antoinette nor Louis was particularly well educated—not when compared with the princes of the Renaissance, for example. In fact, because her academic education was so minimal, Marie Antoinette really did have to undergo an intellectual (as well as a physical) "makeover" before the French deemed her adequately prepared to become the dauphine.

While *Becoming Marie Antoinette* is a work of fiction, the events of the novel are entirely based on facts. Every one of the characters involved in Marie Antoinette's makeover is the actual historical figure responsible for that aspect of her transformation. Once I discovered how extensive and exhaustive her makeover was, I became passionate about tracking down the identities of all the players. The envoys and ambassadors in the novel are the actual historical figures as well.

Most of the letters I use in the novel are based on the genuine correspondence between the parties. The empress Maria Theresa was quite a formidable figure and such a canny politician that I enjoyed letting her speak for herself; I also wanted to show how much was going on behind the scenes, unbeknownst to Marie Antoinette. She did have an inkling that she was being spied on, but she had no idea of the extent of the manipulation or that her own mother was the puppeteer—or that the very people in whom she was assured she could place her trust were in fact betraying her.

There are a few instances where I used a novelist's license. The events surrounding the *remise* happen on the days they actually took place. There was a barrage of correspondence between the comte de Mercy and Maria Theresa at the last minute, but I estimated the dates because I couldn't find any factual information on when exactly the letters were sent. To keep them within the necessary two-day time frame, I envisioned chains of couriers riding hell-for-leather from Kehl to Vienna and back.

The family dinner on the night before the wedding, when Marie Antoinette first sees Madame du Barry from a distance and naïvely inquires as to her role at court, actually took place at the pretty Château de la Muette, a royal hunting lodge located on the edge of the Bois de Boulogne. But since it was the event itself that was of import and not its location, in the novel it seemed simpler to have the dinner take place at Versailles so that there was a minimal amount of shuttling the reader back and forth to locations that would not be germane to the story. Shifting the location of the dinner also gave me the opportunity to place the reader in Marie Antoinette's shoes, enabling the comtesse de Noailles to enlighten her from the start on some of the protocol of Versailles and the reasons behind it.

Another fictional modification was making the comtesse de Provence, Marie Joséphine of Savoy, more Italian than French. Savoy, or Savoie, was a territory that changed hands several times over the centuries; and it is a fact that the comtesse and her younger sister, Marie Thérèse, the comtesse d'Artois, were notorious for mispronouncing French words, with unintentionally comical results—a detail I make use of in the final scene of the novel. More than likely, the comtesse de Provence would have grown up speaking French but with a regional accent. However, I decided it might be more fun to write her as a native Italian speaker, given some of the other elements of her personality.

One of the reasons I became so eager to tell the story of Marie Antoinette's early years and of the first few years of her marriage was because I have never found a satisfactory explanation or rationale for Louis's infamous dread of physical contact with Marie Antoinette. Historians and biographers concur on Louis's initial reaction upon seeing his new bride for the first time: He winced. And he purportedly had the same physical response time and time again upon seeing her.

Never, in any of the several biographies I read, was this reaction analyzed. Louis Auguste's personal physician, Dr. Lassone, after first suggesting that the dauphin was merely overeating and overexercising, subsequently posited that he suffered from a medical condition, and biographers generally agree. But it was also assumed by many scholars that Louis was simply indifferent to Marie Antoinette, that he wasn't interested in sex, that he was plodding and dull.

Gentle readers, may I submit to you that this is utter poppycock! The dauphin's affliction will be revealed in the sequel to *Becoming Marie Antoinette,* but the more I read about him, the more I wanted simply to reach out and hug him. No wonder he couldn't bring himself to consummate their marriage, despite being fully aware of his dynastic responsibility. Add to this the dauphin's natural diffidence, his nearsightedness, his podginess, and an adolescent's gawkiness.... Despite his entitlement and birthright, I envision him as all too human, and very much a figure deserving of sympathy.

And of course I find Marie Antoinette to be tremendously sympathetic, as well as far more complex than she is often given credit for being. Marie Antoinette was only fourteen years old when she arrived at Versailles, expected to bear an heir to the Bourbon throne sooner rather than later, and not merely to seamlessly fit in at a foreign court with famously rigid and arcane etiquette but to dominate its social sphere. She was desperate to please but was sent mixed messages by her mother. Marie Antoinette admitted that the empress filled her with awe; she feared her more than she loved her. Unfortunately, two of Marie Antoinette's major missteps at court were the result of trying to please her mother by slavishly following her advice.

William Werner, my favorite high school English teacher, used to say, "I can never read *Hamlet* without hoping he doesn't die in the end." As I wrote *Becoming Marie Antoinette,* especially the final scene, in which she and Louis, still only teenagers, are now the sovereigns of France, their hearts filled as much with joy and hope as with trepidation, I wanted so desperately to believe in as bright a future as they did driving along the road toward the Château de Choisy, enjoying the adulation of their subjects who cheered for "*Louis le Désiré.*" The irony of their eventual fate filled me with sadness.

I hope you enjoyed *Becoming Marie Antoinette,* and that it piques your desire to continue her story. The second part of her dramatic life will be told in *Days of Splendor, Days of Sorrow,* to be published in summer 2012, followed by the third novel in the Marie Antoinette trilogy in 2013.

Questions and Topics
for Discussion

1. Why does the author choose to open the story with the dead butterfly? What does it come to represent, and at what other moments throughout the novel does the butterfly become significant? Discuss its significance.

2. "Hadn't Maman taught us that there was no such thing as ghosts or goblins or demons? There was no room for superstitious silliness among the Hapsburgs; we were not dwellers in the Dark Ages, but children of the eighteenth century—the Age of Reason." Given Antonia's observation, what explanation would you give for Josepha's strong premonition that she is going to die? In what ways does this early event shape Antonia's character?

3. Monsieur Ducreux says that he never paints empty dresses, and Antonia mocks him by declaring that she is an empty dress. How much truth is there in that joke? Give specific ex-

amples from the rest of the story in which Antonia either fits or flouts your definition of an "empty dress." Do you place more value on academic skills or on other talents?

4. Discuss the appeal of fashion in the novel. What is suggested by the fact that many of the styles that are de rigueur at Versailles are considered outmoded by the Austrian court? Would you enjoy dressing every day in those enormous gowns and huge hairstyles?

5. What, to you, was the most surprising detail of Antonia's makeover? Do you think her transformation was ultimately beneficial? In what ways do you imagine Antonia would have been a different dauphine if she hadn't had those experiences?

6. Juliet Grey makes the court etiquette described in the novel lively and colorful, although Antonia finds it burdensome and tedious. If you were being groomed to become the dauphine of France, would you handily sail through the hours of lessons and preparations that it took to memorize all the rules, and perhaps even enjoy abiding by them?

7. Before Antonia departs for Versailles, she spends a week with her mother at the convent at Marizell. Why is Maria Theresa so insistent on this trip? Discuss the role of religion in both the Austrian and the French courts. In what ways does Antonia embrace or ignore her Catholic upbringing, particularly as it relates to the controversy over Madame du Barry?

8. Consider the Hapsburg family motto that serves as the epigraph to the novel: "Others wage wars; you, happy Austria,

marry." At what other moments in the story is the motto recalled by one of the characters? Why is this significant? What
do you think the French see as the primary benefit of the alliance? How effective is Antonia at handling the tremendous
political pressures of her role, and what, if anything, would
you have done differently? Can you think of a modern equivalent to this sort of political marriage?

9. Why does Marie Antoinette envy Madame du Barry at
   first—before she realizes who (and what) she is? Which
   woman do you admire more?

10. In Maria Theresa's first letter to Antonia, she writes, "Avoid
    consorting with those who are underlings, for their trust may
    be both fleeting and fickle; and grant no requests unless the
    abbé, Comte de Mercy, the duc de Choiseul, or the king him-
    self has sanctioned your ability to hear them." How does this
    advice become particularly important? In what ways does it
    become a hindrance? Discuss, too, the repercussions of the
    correspondence between Maria Theresa and the abbé Ver-
    mond, comte de Mercy, and the king that takes place without
    Antonia's knowledge.

11. Louis Auguste and Antonia first bond over the terrible fate of
    the citizens who were killed in the trenches outside the Palais
    Royal. What does this say about their characters? Given what
    you know about history, does this incident surprise you?
    What prevents them from building on this initial bond until
    much later?

12. Antonia's shining moment as dauphine is arguably her pre-
    sentation at the Tuileries, described vividly in a letter to her

mother. Why is she so well received by the people of Paris, despite their feelings about the king? Contrast Antonia's stumbles throughout the novel with her successes: What are the common denominators that determine whether or not she will triumph?

13. All of Europe seems to be speculating on Antonia's marriage, but nothing can make Louis Auguste consummate the relationship. Read the author's essay in the reader's guide on writing *Becoming Marie Antoinette*. Do you find Juliet Grey's portrayal of Louis Auguste to be sympathetic? While you were reading the novel, what did you speculate was Louis's problem? How do you think he really felt about his wife?

14. Do you think Antonia truly comes to love Louis, despite her reservations? How, if at all, would their relationship have been different if they had chosen each other?

15. When Papa Roi dies, Louis Auguste tells his wife, "I am the most unhappy man in the world." What does he mean by that? Compare Louis Auguste's relationship with his grandfather to Antonia's relationship with her mother. In what ways have these relationships defined the dauphin and dauphine? Is there a decisive moment in the story in which each steps out from the shadow of his/her elder? If not, do you think there will come a time when it's possible for them to do so?

16. In the final lines of the book, Antonia observes, "All France is at our feet today. And just imagine what we shall make of it!" Why does the author choose to end the book with this line?

Given what you know of subsequent events, in what ways is this comment prophetic?

17. If you could spend an afternoon in the company of one of the characters from *Becoming Marie Antoinette*, who would it be? What's the first question you would ask him or her? Which of the locales in the novel would you most want to visit?

Would I view Versailles through new eyes, now that I was no longer someone waiting—now that I had become?

Marie Antoinette's enthralling story continues in

DAYS OF SPLENDOR, DAYS OF SORROW

A novel of Marie Antoinette by Juliet Grey

On sale in Summer 2012

READ ON FOR AN EXCLUSIVE SNEAK PEEK

ONE

Queen of France

TO: Comte de Mercy-Argenteau, Ambassador to the Court of Versailles

May 8, 1774

My dear Comte de Mercy,

I understand that the death of my sovereign brother is imminent. The news fills me with both sorrow and trepidation. For as much as I account the marriage of Antoinette to the dauphin of France among the triumphs of my reign, I cannot deny a sense of foreboding at my daughter's fate, which cannot fail to be either wholly splendid or extremely unfortunate. There is nothing to calm my apprehensions; she is so young and has never had any powers of diligence, nor ever will have—unless with great difficulty. I fancy her good days are past.

Maria Theresa

❧ La Muette, May 21, 1774 ❧

"My condolences on the passing of His Majesty, Your Majesty."

"Your Majesty, my condolences on the death of His Majesty."

"Permit me, Your Majesty, to tender my deepest condolences on the expiration of His Majesty Louis Quinze."

One by one they filed past, the elderly ladies of the court in their mandated mourning garb, a murder of broad black crows in panniered gowns, their painted faces greeting each of us in turn—my husband, the new king Louis Seize, and me. We had been the sovereigns of France for two weeks, but under such circumstances elation cannot come without sorrow.

Louis truly grieved for the old king, his late *grand-père.* As for the others, the straitlaced prudes—*collets montés,* as I dubbed them—who so tediously offered their respects that afternoon in the black-and-white-tiled hall at the hunting lodge of La Muette, I found their sympathy, as well as their expressions of felicitations on our accession to the throne, as false as the blush on their cheeks. They had not loved their former sovereign for many decades, if at all. Moreover, they had little confidence in my husband's ability to rule, and even less respect for him.

"*Permettez-moi de vous offrir mes condoléances. J'en suis désolée,*" I giggled behind my fan to my devoted friend and attendant the princesse de Lamballe, mimicking the warble of the interminable parade of ancient crones. "Honestly, when one has passed thirty, I cannot understand how one dares appear at court."

I found these old women ridiculous, but there was another cause for my laughter—one that I lacked the courage to admit to anyone, even to my husband. In sober truth, not until today, when we received the customary condolences of the nobility, had the reality of Papa Roi's death settled upon my breast. The magnitude of what lay before us, Louis and me, was overwhelming. I was overcome with nerves, and raillery was my release.

The duchesse d'Archambault approached. Sixty years of rouge had settled into her hollowed cheekbones, and I could not help myself. I bit my lip, but a smile matured into a grin, and before I knew it a chuckle had burbled its way out of my mouth. When she descended into her reverence I heard her knees creak and felt certain she would not be able to rise without assistance.

"Allow me, Your Majesty, to condole you on the death of the king-that-was." The duchesse lapsed into a reverie. "*Il était si noble, si gentil....*"

"*Vous l'avez détesté!*" I muttered, then whispered to the princesse, "I know for a fact she despised the king because he refused her idiot son a military promotion." When the duchesse was just out of earshot, I trilled, "*So noble, so kind.*"

"Your Majesty, it does not become you to mock your elders, especially when they are your inferiors."

I did not need to peer over my fan to know the voice: the comtesse de Noailles, my *dame d'honneur*, the superintendent of my household while I was dauphine, and my de facto guardian. As the youngest daughter of Empress Maria Theresa of Austria, I had come to Versailles at fourteen to wed the dauphin, and had been not merely educated but physically transformed in order to merit such an august union. Yet there had still been much to learn and little time in which to master it. The comtesse had been appointed my mentor, to school me in the rigid rituals of the French court. For this I had immediately nicknamed her Madame Etiquette, and in the past four years not a day had gone by that I had not received from her some rebuke over a transgression of protocol. Just behind my right shoulder the princesse de Lamballe stood amid my other ladies. Our wide skirts discreetly concealed another of my attendants, the marquise de Clermont-Tonnerre, who had sunk to her knees from exhaustion. I heard a giggle. The marquise was known to pull faces from time to time and kept all of us in stitches with her ability to turn her eyelids inside out and then flutter them flirtatiously.

"Who are you hiding?" quizzed Madame de Noailles. My ladies' eyes darted from one to another, none daring to reply.

"*La marquise de Clermont-Tonnerre est tellement fatiguée,*" I replied succinctly.

"That is of no consequence. It is not *comme il faut.* Everyone must stand during the reception."

I stepped aside. "Madame la marquise, would you kindly rise," I commanded gently. With the aid of a woman at either elbow she stood, and the vast swell of her belly, straining against her stays, was as evident as the sheen on her brow. "I believe you know the comtesse de Noailles," I said, making certain Madame Etiquette could see that the marquise was *enceinte.* "I am not yet a mother, mesdames, although I very much pray for that day. I can only hope that when it comes, common sense will take precedence over protocol. And as queen, I will take measures to ensure it." I offered the marquise my lace-edged handkerchief to blot her forehead. "As there is nowhere to sit, you may resume your former position, madame, and my ladies will continue to provide you with a screen from disapproving eyes."

I glanced down the hall to see the line of courtiers stopped in front of Louis, a few feet away. I returned my attention to the comtesse de Noailles. We were nose to nose now, and I was no longer an unruly child in her custody. One mother who scolded me at the slightest provocation was sufficient; I had no need of a surrogate. "You and your husband have served France long and faithfully," I began coolly, "and you have devoted yourselves tirelessly without respite. The time has come, therefore, for you to take your *congé*. My husband and I will expect you to retire to your estate of Mouchy before the week is out."

Her pinched face turned as pale as a peeled almond. But there was nothing she could say in reply. One did not remonstrate with the queen of France.

"The princesse de Lamballe will be my new *dame d'honneur*," I added, noting the expression of surprise in my attendant's eyes and the modest blush that suffused her cheeks. I had caught her completely unaware, but what better time to reward her loyalty?

The comtesse lowered her gaze and dropped into a deep reverence. "It has been an honor to have served Your Majesty." The only fissure in her customary hauteur was betrayed by the tremolo in her voice. For an instant I regretted my decision. Yet I had long dreamed of this moment. From now on, I would be the one to choose, at least within my own household, what was *comme il faut*. As the comtesse rose and made her way along the hall to offer her condolences to the king, I felt as though a storm cloud that had followed me about from palace to palace— Versailles, Compiègne, Fontainebleau—had finally lifted, leaving a vibrant blue sky.

At the hour of our ascension to the throne, after the requisite obsequies from the courtiers, we had fled the scene of Louis Quinze's death nearly as fast as our coach could bear us, spending the first nine days of our reign at the Château de Choisy on the banks of the Seine while the innumerable rooms of Versailles were scrubbed free of the smallpox contagion. Yet I was bursting to return, to begin making my mark. No one alive could recall when a queen of France had been much more than a dynastic cipher. Maria Theresa of Spain, the infanta who wed the Sun King, was almost insignificant at court. She spent much of her time closeted in her rooms drinking chocolate and playing cards with

her ladies and her dwarves and had so little rapport with her subjects that when they were starving for bread she suggested they
eat cake instead—this much I had learned from my dear abbé
Vermond, who had instructed me in the history of the queens of
France when I was preparing to marry the dauphin. The abbé
had journeyed to Versailles as my reader, to offer me spiritual
guidance, and he remained one of my few confidants.

In any case, Maria Theresa of Spain had died nearly a hundred years ago. And her absence from public life had afforded
Louis Quatorze plenty of opportunities to seek companionship in
the arms of others. They, not his dull queen, became the arbiters
of taste at court.

My immediate predecessor, Marie Leszczyńska, the pious
consort of Louis Quinze who died two years before I arrived at
Versailles, had been the daughter of a disgraced Polish king
forced to live in exile. She bore Louis many useless daughters but
only one dauphin to inherit the throne—the father of my husband—and he died while his papa still wore the crown. Like the
queen before her, she endured a shadowy existence, maintaining
her spotless propriety while my husband's *grand-père* flaunted his
latest *maîtresse en titre*. No one noticed what Marie wore or how
she dressed her hair. Instead, it was Madame la marquise de
Pompadour who had defined the fashion in all things for a gen-
eration. And then Madame du Barry, Louis XV's last mistress, set
the tone, but there was no queen to rival her—only me. And I
had failed miserably, never sure of myself, always endeavoring to
find my footing, desperate to fascinate a timid husband who
could not bring himself to consummate our marriage. I had
wasted precious time by allowing the comtesse du Barry to exert
her influence not only over the court but over Papa Roi, much to
the consternation of my mother.

But I was determined to no longer be a disappointment. Not

to Maman. Not to France. In the aftermath of Louis Quinze's demise, the du Barry was now consigned to a convent. Her faithful followers at court, the "Barryistes," would simply have to accustom themselves to the absence of her bawdy wit and gaudy gowns. I was queen; morality and good taste would prevail from now on—though not at the expense of gaiety, glamour, and fun.

The condolences of the nobility at La Muette marked the end of the period of mourning. When the last of the courtiers had risen, the king and I made our way outside to the courtyard, where the royal coach awaited us. I dared not voice my thoughts to Louis but I felt as though we had spent the past ten days in Purgatory and now, as the gilded carriage clattered over the gravel and out onto the open road toward Versailles, where we would formally begin our reign, we were finally on our way to Heaven.

I had first entered the seat of France's court through the back route in every way—as a young bride traveling in a special *berline* commissioned by Louis Quinze to transport me from my homeland. How eager he had been to show me Versailles, from the Grand Trianon with its pink marble porticoes, to the pebbled *allées* that led past the canals and fountains, all the way to the grand staircases and the imposing château that his great-*grand-père* the Sun King had transformed from a modest hunting *boîte* into an edifice that would rival all other palaces in Europe. And oh, how disappointed I had been on that dreary afternoon: The fountains were dry, the canals cluttered with debris, and the hallways and chambers of the fairyland château reeked of stale urine.

How different now the aspect before me as we approached the palace from the front via the Ministers' Courtyard. The imposing gateway designed by Mansart loomed before us, its gilded spikes glinting in the soft afternoon sunlight. At such an hour less than two weeks earlier we had fled the contagion. I rolled open the window of the carriage and peered out. Then turning back to my husband, giddy with anticipation, I exclaimed, "Tell me the air smells sweeter, *mon cher*!"

"Sweeter than what?" He looked as if he had a bellyache, or a stitch in his side from a surfeit of brisk exertion. As neither could have been the case, "What pains you, sire?" I asked. I rested my gloved hand in his. He made no reply but the pallor on his face was the same greenish hue that I recalled from our wedding day some four years earlier. He was terrified of what awaited him, fearful of the awful responsibility that now rested entirely upon his broad shoulders. And as much as I desired to be a helpmeet in the governance of the realm, I was no more than his consort. Queens of France were made for one thing only. And *that* responsibility, I was painfully aware, I had thus far failed to fulfill.

I pressed Louis's hand in a gesture of reassurance. Just at that moment, the doors of the carriage were sprung open and the traveling steps unfolded by a team of efficient footmen. "*Sois courageux*," I murmured. "And remember—there is no one to scold you anymore. The crown is yours."

I was astonished to see that the Ministers' Courtyard and the Cour Royale just inside the great gates were once again pulsing with people. The vendors had returned to their customary locations and were already doing a brisk business renting hats and swords to the men who wished to visit Versailles but were unaware of the etiquette required. The various merchants of ribbons and fans and *parfums* had set up their stalls as well. I wondered briefly where they had been during the past two weeks. How had they put bread on their tables while the court was away?

My husband adjusted the glittering Order of the Holy Spirit that he wore pinned to a sash across his chest. But for the enormous diamond star, his attire was so unprepossessing—his black mourning suit of ottoman striped silk was devoid of gilt embroidery, and his silver shoe buckles were unadorned—that he could have easily been mistaken for a wealthy merchant. As we were handed out of the carriage into the bright afternoon, at the sight of my husband a great cheer went up. "*Vive le roi Louis Seize!*" How the French had hated their old king—and how they loved their new sovereign. *Louis le Désiré* they called my husband.

Louis reddened. I would have to remind him that kings did not blush, even if they were only nineteen. "*Et mon peuple*—my good people—*vive la reine Marie Antoinette!*" he exclaimed, leading me forth as if we were stepping out onto a parquet dance floor instead of the vast gravel courtyard.

They did not shout quite as loudly for me. I suppose I had expected they would, and managed to mask my disappointment behind a gracious smile. When I departed Vienna in the spring of 1770 my mother had not so much exhorted as *instructed* me to make the people of France love me. I dared not tell her that they weren't fond of foreigners, and that even at court there were those who employed a spiteful little nickname for me— *l'Autrichienne*—a play on words, crossing my nationality with the word for a female dog. Did Maman realize that the French had been Austria's enemy for *nine hundred years* before they signed a peace treaty with the Hapsburgs in 1756? Make the French love me? It was my fondest hope, but I had so many centuries of hatred to reverse.

The courtyards teemed with the excitement of a festival day. Citizens, noisy, curious, and jubilant, swarmed about us as we made our way toward the palace. A flower seller offered me a bouquet of pink roses, but I insisted on choosing only a single perfect stem and paying for it out of my own pocket. Sinking to her knees in gratitude, she told me I was "three times beautiful." I thanked her for the unusual compliment and tried to press on through the crowd. After several minutes of jostling and much waving and smiling and doffing of hats, we finally reached the flat pavement of the Marble Courtyard and the entrance to the State Apartments. For days I had imagined how it would feel to enter Versailles for the first time as queen of France. I rushed up the grand marble staircase clutching my inky-hued skirts, anxious to see *my* home, as I thought of it—*my* palace. Would I view it through new eyes, now that I was no longer someone waiting— now that I had *become*?